FOUND

THE CONDUIT CHRONICLES

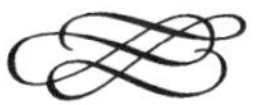

ASHLEY HOHENSTEIN

Linda,
It has been such a pleasure getting to know you. Thank you so much for your support & friendship.
In Gratitude,
Ash

Copyrights
This is a work of fiction. All names, characters, places and incidents are either from the authors imagination or are used fictionally; any resemblance to people living or dead as well as places or incidents are unintentional and coincidental.

Copyright 2018 Ashley Hohenstein

All rights reserved.
No parts of this book may be reproduced in whole or in part, scanned, photocopied or stored in a retrieval system, nor transmitted electronically, digitally or by means of any other electronic, audio or mechanical distribution without the permission of the author.

This book is dedicated to my husband Erik. His unwavering support of my dreams and aspirations made all of this possible. Without his ongoing encouragement and consistent belief in me, I would not be the woman I am today.

PART I

ELIAS

My plane landed shortly after 6 am. I looked down at my watch, we were twenty minutes ahead of schedule. *I preferred being early.* The flight attendant secured the door and gave me another sultry glance as I pulled my carry-on luggage from the overhead compartment. Her name badge read Elaine. She was pretty — petite yet curvy. Her long blonde hair was pulled up into a tussled bun on top of her head. She had full lips that she painted pink and they framed an uncharacteristically large mouth, almost too large. Her eyes were a warm brown and she knew how to communicate with her stare. She had been flirting with me the entire flight from Ontario. The poor woman must have been bored. There were no other passengers in the first-class compartment below the age of sixty. I waited for the other two passengers to meander down the short aisle in front of us and out of the plane. Elaine had still not taken her eyes off me. As I passed her and the pilots she took my hand aggressively.

"It was a pleasure serving you Mr. Kraus, I hope to see you very soon." I nodded and as I pulled away I found a small folded note in the palm of my hand. It was her phone number, she had hinted she would be staying the majority of the day in Chicago before she picked up her next shift on a flight to Cancun. I threw the slip of paper in the closest bin as I exited the gate.

Under different circumstances I may have taken her up on her proposal, but I did not have time for such tomfooleries during this particular errand. I needed to be swift and remain undetected.

I traversed the airport terminal cautiously as I made my way to the taxi queue. I could not be too careful, I had taken extensive precautions making my arrangements to Chicago. But the truth was, you could never be certain you evaded an enemy you could not see.

The cab line was short and I popped in a car with little to no wait. "Take me to West Town please."

"You got an address man?" The driver asked.

"Sorry sir I do not. Any street corner will have to suffice." I stared out the window as the Chicago skyline loomed near. I took a deep breath and rubbed my eyes. The driver was watching me in the rearview mirror.

"Long flight man?"

"Long year." I rested my head against the seat and closed my eyes. I was so close to answers, I could feel it. The vacuous task of finding the appropriate location for the summit was coming to a close. I wondered, had my father realized how all-consuming and downright treacherous the assignment was, would he have still imparted it to me? I had felt nothing but the weight of this mission since my parent's murders. Every moment of every day was spent hunting down leads and covering my tracks. *I resented it. I often found myself resenting them.* I immediately chastised myself for the thought. I loved my parents. I simply detested the responsibility they bestowed upon me and me alone. Their deaths made it abundantly clear that no one could be trusted, so it left me in utter seclusion. If the Kraus family could be betrayed, no one was safe. My parents were honorable pillars of our community, always welcoming, always kind and in hindsight too trusting. It made me hyper vigilant, I would not succumb to the same demise due to credulousness.

The driver honked the horn violently and in rapid succession. "Move out of the way asshole!"

My eyes shot open. Four car lengths ahead stood a man pacing in the middle of the street while cars were honking and slowly maneuvering around him.

"This dick won't move, probably a crazy homeless guy." The driver ranted.

But I knew better. "Here is the fare and a generous tip for your time." I slipped him a hundred-dollar bill and slid out of the back seat then hit a full sprint ducking through the oncoming traffic. *How had they found me?*

I heard the traffic behind me begin to let up. He was in short pursuit and unless there was a miraculous intervention I would be dead shortly. I bolted off the main drag onto the quieter avenues. I had no idea where I was or where to go to evade this inevitable blood bath. I heard a trash bin tumble behind me, not more than ten feet back. If he was that close, it was time to face him and fight. I skidded to a stop and turned to see the face of my would be attacker. *Relief.* It was not Yanni, it was one of his henchmen. He was a formidable opponent, but not impenetrable.

He was nearly six feet tall with long unkempt black hair and a mangy looking beard. *No wonder the cabby thought he was homeless,* I thought. He was wearing a brown tunic that went to his knees, it was nearly the same color as his skin. His white pants were disheveled and dirty. He was barefoot. I assessed his body and found my way to his face and in the tangles of that wild hair and olive skin were two dark coal eyes.

"Salzar. I did not anticipate seeing you acting as errand boy to Yanni." He looked alarmed that I had stopped running, I suspected he had foreseen a longer chase.

"Elias." He hissed. "Errand boy I am not, for that is beneath me."

I raised a brow. "It was your intention to stalk me, by your own accord?"

"It was a gift from Chitchakor himself." He cocked his head sideways. "I was honored to get the privilege to kill you myself."

"Very well. If it was desired by Chitchakor I am prepared to succumb to my finis." Salzar still stood unmoved. I would not go down without a proper affray. I beckoned with my hand for him to proceed. He growled a fierce guttural roar and flung himself in the air. I threw my satchel to the left of me between two parked automobiles, simultaneously withdrawing a dirk from a sheath cloaked in magic under my pant leg.

Salzar could not see the blade but he was acutely aware that I was now armed. He took noticeable pause as he filled the rest of the gap between our two bodies. We collided and I shoved him forcefully off me. I simply had to keep him away from my neck—that was where he would inflict the most damage.

"What trinket do you hold?" He asked.

"Are you afraid?" I taunted.

"Salzar –afraid?" He scoffed. "I just wish to know what I will be collecting after you are dead."

"Come closer my friend and I will better acquaint you with my trinket." He roared back at me and kicked off of his left leg, at the same time scissoring his right leg and projecting a massive blow to my chest. I dodged just out of his reach. The wretched sound of crushing metal erupted in the air as he landed on a red BMW. *I hoped they had good insurance.* I noticed the small crowd pooling at the end of the street. I did not want any casualties because they were in the wrong place at the wrong time. So, I gave Salzar a mocking smile and started sprinting off in the opposite direction of the onlookers. He was cackling, hissing and snarling as he raced after me.

I would not be able to maintain this pace for much longer without losing all reserves to actually engage in battle. I scaled the backyard fence to the closest house and hoped the residents were not home.

I landed on my left knee and felt a twinge of pain shoot down to my ankle. I definitely jarred something. No time to assess the damage I had mere seconds before Salzar would be over the fence. As I thought the words, he propelled himself over and landed on my back —my face was now sandwiched between concrete and his rough hands.

"Viraclay tsk tsk tsk. You should have known better than to turn your back on Salzar." His fingers started to elongate and work their way to my neck. I had managed not to stab myself with the dirk as he landed on me, but now his right leg had my arm pinned. It would appear that he had forgotten I was armed or perhaps he was just that confident he had me bested. Either way when he shifted his body to get a better grip on my neck I was able to ratchet my arm forward and apply enough bend in my elbow to gore his calf.

He wailed in shock then thrust his weight harder onto my forearm trying to prevent any further injuries. He still could not see my weapon—he growled in frustration. "What did you spear me with? It must be as tiny as your prick because I cannot see it."

I had released my grip on the handle, and it was resting in close proximity to my hand in the event I got a second chance to pierce him. His lengthened fingers had paused around my neck as he searched for my weapon and situated himself more securely over my arms and torso. I only needed seconds for the poison of the knife to set in. I could only hope he would take his time strangling me. I felt his fingers grow in length again and become rope-like as they encircled my neck for a second time. They felt like eight snakes slithering in opposite directions rhythmically moving and playing with their prey.

Before I could not speak due to the pressure around my throat. I coughed out. "Even if you succeed in killing me on this day, you will bemoan that you underestimated yourself against my tiny prick of a weapon." He laughed mockingly at me and it was apparent that play time was over as he began to tighten the noose of his vine like fingers he had strategically placed around my neck. My eye lids got heavy and the deep dark heaviness of unconsciousness started to wash over me from the lack of oxygen to my brain.

Then I felt him jerk. I demanded that my mind stay present for just a few more moments. He jerked again—more violently this time. His grip loosened and I gasped. His foot shifted on my arm and I took command of the blade again. He stumbled, still unsure what was happening. I scrambled backwards on the pavement and got to my knees while violently gasping for air and assessing the damage to my throat.

Salzar still had not made a noise, although he was clearly distressed. As I took in deeper and slower breaths I was able to make clarity of the situation. I had never used the Dirk of Inverness before, so I was uncertain what its effects would be, only that it could incapacitate those it wounded.

Salzar was now standing about six feet away from me, pure terror smeared across his treacherous little face. I could tell by his expression that he could not speak, although he was attempting to, but to no avail. He appeared frozen in place, only his eyes reflecting the true fear he was feeling. No visible wounds, not even the one I inflicted on his calf. I circled him cautiously. His eyes followed me, his mouth contorted into a silent unending scream. After a few more rounds and still no change, I touched him. His skin felt normal, unscathed, but hard as a rock. I could not simply leave him in the middle of this poor family's back yard frozen. Eventually they would happen upon him and what on earth would they think? I chuckled to myself as I imagined the headlines, *MAN FOUND FROZEN in Chicago Suburb*!! No, that would not do at all.

"What do I do with you Salzar?" I tossed the still invisible blade into my other hand. "Truth be told, I had no idea what the Dirk of Inverness would do. It would appear it stupefies its victim. But what do I do with such a hideous statue? Furthermore, how long can we expect you to maintain this kindly disposition? Someone should really construct an instruction manual for the remaining Rittles, do you not agree?" The Rittles were several weapons wielded by one man who enchanted each object with its own unique poison. There used to be thousands, now there were only a few left in existence and no one knew who brandished them. Salzar's eyes continued to follow me. It was rather disturbing the way his body stood unmoved, yet his eyes watched every gesture.

I nudged him to see how heavy he was. I estimated two hundred pounds. The weight would not be the issue, however, the awkwardness of maneuvering his strangely postured body would be cumbersome at best. I could hear that it was beginning to get busier on the neighboring streets. It had to be nearly 8 am by now which meant the people in this suburban neighborhood would be heading to work or taking their kids to school shortly. I peeked out the gate of the yard and saw an apartment building three blocks down on the right; they would most certainly have a dumpster to dispose of him in. Time was not on my side. This would be a temporary solution until I could formulate a proper plan of action.

I stowed the dirk in a bush near the sidewalk just outside the backyard fence, then hoisted him awkwardly over my shoulder. I did my best to lock up behind us, but I would need to sweep by and secure the gate later. I lumbered down the street just in time for the morning bustle to begin. Mothers quickly ushered their children into their cars as I passed by. I could not blame them. Not only was I a stranger in their community but I was carrying around a huge life size statue with frighteningly long fingers and a gruesome facial expression. One woman actually shrieked when she saw Salzar's face. I laughed and mumbled "See Salzar. I told you, you were repulsive."

I reached the apartment complex and to my dismay it had a full dumpster. Not all was lost, because this probably meant it was trash pick-up today and that could be very fortuitous for me. I threw back the garbage bin lids and tossed the body in. I purposefully stationed him face down, but his arm would not quite fit, so it could be seen it projecting from under the lip. I sourly dug in the trash to find something suitable to cover it with. An old sweater would have to suffice. After I decided he was suitably camouflaged I jogged back to the shrub I hid the dirk in, secured the gate and then ran several blocks back to where I had flung my satchel with my laptop and several other important items. I re-sheathed the Dirk of Inverness and kissed the sheath when it was secure. Thank Malarin for his good graces and my mother who had the sense to bequeath the dirk to me in the first place.

While I had been collecting my things I was devising a plan for Salzar. I sprinted back to the dumpster just in time to see the contents of the bin being flung into a dump truck and then slowly compressed. I let out a sigh. It would not kill him, but he would be detained for some time. I smelled my hands. I was ready for a shower.

I pulled out my phone, "Siri, where is the closest hotel?" After a moment, her familiar voice suggested a Best Western only a mile and a half away. I started south as the directions suggested. Now that the immediate danger had subsided I had time to realize the larger threat. Someone in my confidences had to be colluding with the enemy. It was the only explanation for Salzar finding me in Chicago.

All signs for months had been heralding this obvious truth, but I could not fathom anyone in my coterie choosing treachery. They had all lost so much during this war. What on earth would elicit them to band with their trespassers? I suppose it did not matter. All that mattered was that whatever trust I had frugally shared must now be rescinded. My shoulders tightened around my neck and my hands clenched into fists.

There was no dancing around the actuality of my situation. My father bestowed upon me a seemingly impossible charge. Unite our people and save them from complete annihilation. He and my mother died pursuing this cause. Now here I was in solitude, undertaking the painstaking task of balancing running from those who intended to kill me while, leaving no stone left unturned in the pursuit of saving our kind.

I would live out my remaining years on this glorious planet completely alone, until I died or eradicated the threat to our world.

OPHELIA

I looked around the restaurant, and finally down at the chip in the laminate on the tabletop. I didn't mind eating alone. I actually appreciated the silence.

I loved this place, Pho Le, a quaint spot with wonderful soups in the heart of the Richmond district of San Francisco.

I was ready for the check. I scanned the room for my waitress and then it hit me like a ton of bricks—the emotional climate of the room shifted drastically, and suddenly I felt intense grief.

I glanced around to see where it was coming from—the far-left corner of the restaurant. I couldn't see the tears, but I could feel the pain and thick sobs building in the soft chest of the individual across the room. I felt such deep sadness. I found I couldn't differentiate between the stranger's anguish and my own. Memories swiftly flooded my mind, memories of my distorted childhood. When waves of sadness danced on the shores of my consciousness, they always referred back to my childhood. I guess that is because it was the most obvious wound to open. My eyes welled up with tears.

My upper lip trembled, and just before I thought I would crack, the stranger in the corner bellowed a horrific cry. The room began to buzz with curiosity, and then just as quickly, the swell of sadness subsided in the room and curiosity mixed with bewilderment took its place. I caught my breath and was able to repress the memories from my youth that had seeped to the surface.

The waitress made her way to my table. “Can I get the check?” I blurted out. As soon as she handed it to me, I threw a twenty on the table and scurried out the door. The poor waitress looked at me like I was nuts. I wanted to say—*I just might be.*

I regained my composure as I found my stride on the sidewalk; silently chiding myself: *Get it together Ophelia.* I caught a single tear with my finger as it cascaded down my face. When I stuck the salty drop in my mouth, I halfway thought it would taste like it came from someone else—the person in the corner. *OK, now you are losing it!*

I've always been bombarded by these intense emotional fluctuations, for seemingly no reason. The emotions just came and went as they pleased, oftentimes vanishing before I had a moment to dissect the cause. I had never been one to put much thought into the possibility of my own mental illness, although my entire family had been consumed by it.

My mother was born in an insane asylum while my grandmother was receiving electroshock therapy and other experimental remedies for schizophrenia. *Maybe it was time to rethink the possibility of crazy in my own makeup?*

Just then my phone buzzed in my pocket. I looked at the name on the screen, wondering, *How did she do it?* It was Eleanor, my mother. She had impeccable timing.

“Hey mom.” I tried to sound normal.

“Olly?” She asked. “Ophelia?”

“Yeah, mom. You called me, right?” I hated when she played this game.

“I just don't even recognize your voice. It's been so long since I have heard from you—at least three months.” That couldn't be more of an exaggeration.

“I think we spoke last week when I finalized my flight to Chicago,” I casually corrected. My mother was what I called an energy vampire, but what the doctors called severe borderline personality disorder.

The woman could suck the energy out of everyone around her when she entered a room. After five minutes, you were exhausted.

"I don't think so, it's been much longer than that." I sighed, remembering yet again that it was futile to argue with her. "Anyway, I was calling to make sure you're still coming tomorrow, because I have to work all day and will be bushed. I don't want to stay up for you after a day like that and find out you're not coming, or that you will be late. Couldn't you have been more considerate and booked a flight that got in at a normal hour? Really child, it isn't all about you."

I didn't really know what to say to all of that. Eleanor had insisted I come in on Friday night instead of Saturday morning, even though I tried to tell her that a morning flight would be more convenient for everyone. "I'm sorry for the inconvenience. I know you'll be exhausted. Rest assured, mom, I am still all set to go. If the flight's delayed I'll let you know immediately."

As she continued to rattle off how problematic all of this was for her, my mind drifted back to the restaurant. Yes, I'd always suffered from severe mood shifts, but recently I felt like the inception of each of those feelings was coming from an outside source. Like tonight, the onset was triggered by the stranger across the room, whose feelings were so overwhelming that they saturated the air. I couldn't help but inhale the toxic mood. In all these cases, I realized, I'd become consumed with thoughts of my own sadness, anger or happiness, which began to boil over until I exploded, or by some grace of god, was saved by a sudden shift in the room's emotional atmosphere. *Wow, I've reached a whole new level of crazy.*

"Olly? Olly are you even listening to me?" Eleanor had caught on that I wasn't giving her my undivided attention. "For Christ's sake child, do you have any respect? I am your mother!"

In reality, I'd virtually raised myself, but that didn't change the fact that Eleanor was my only parent—and that I loved her despite her flaws. "Sorry mom, I'm walking home," I replied. "Can we cut this short? I am nearly home and want to get a good nights sleep."

"Oh dear, were you on a date? Is that what you are walking home from?" She sighed and didn't wait for a response. "No of course not, you are just my old spinster daughter. Very well, get home to your apartment and tuck yourself into bed." Then she hung up.

With that I put my phone in my purse and buttoned my last button on my jacket, it was a typical cool evening in the bay.

Eleanor was something special alright. I took a couple cleansing breaths.

ELIAS

After the run in with Salzar I had to take extra measures to ensure I did not have another tail. It took a few days of meaningless errands and walkabouts of the city to be certain. I felt as good as I could about the security of my situation. Running in circles trying to detour any trackers had already taken too much time—time was the one thing I had very little to spare right now.

I scanned my surroundings as I walked. This part of Chicago seemed quaint. If I ever wanted to live in this city I would choose the West town neighborhood. It was mostly inhabited by families, but close enough to downtown that you could most certainly walk.

It was late and these streets were very quiet. I could, however, still hear the faint hum of the nightlife coming from a few blocks over.

As I strode, I noticed that one of the single-family homes had their drapes open just enough to see a large classic portrait of a nude female above the mantle. I paused. I had seen that painting before. I leaned against the brick wall of the neighboring home behind me, suddenly finding myself strolling down memory lane, seventeen years earlier and in a very different place.

"Mother, what are they yelling about?" I asked. My mother was sitting across from me, reading some large art history book. I did not understand her fascination with the lives of artists—the paintings were nice, I supposed. I looked around the room where hundreds of pictures littered the walls. "Mother, is that father yelling? Who is he yelling at?" I asked again, hearing the voices from down the hall getting louder.

"Come sit by me," She said as she patted the couch beside her. She pointed at an abstract piece on the page. "Do you know who painted this?"

"Whistler."

"Very good my son, you are so brilliant." She leaned over and kissed my cheek.

I fought the urge to wipe her kiss off—after all I was ten, not two anymore. But that would have been rude and my mother did not deserve that. "Mother? Are you going to answer my questions? Is father going to be alright?"

"Oh of course, he is passionate about these things. You are not ready to know what the men of this house are disputing. You have the rest of your life to be a grown up," She pushed back my hair from my forehead, "But for now you are still my young son who needs a nice cool lemonade, what do you say?"

I smiled at her. Lemonade sounded good. As she left for the kitchen, I decided that I would not be sidetracked so easily. I did not have much time to spy, my mother moved with lightning speed. I crept past the sunroom and kitchen, moving fast and tight against the wall. The voices were coming from the dining room, and were getting louder, but I still could not make out what they were saying. The door was shut, so I would have to be just outside of it to truly hear the conversation.

But even with my ear against the door, I still could not catch it all. I turned the knob ever so softly until I heard the latch click, and then gently nudged the door open, just a crack. I dare not open it any further, afraid someone would spot me. I could not see everyone in the room, but I could see my father, standing at the head of the table. He was angry, I could see his chest rising and falling rapidly with aggravation.

"You are not hearing me, my friends. People are dying, there are lives at stake!" He threw his fist onto the table. I felt like my ears were trembling from the blow. I had never seen him cross. He was menacing.

"We hear you," someone replied, "but how many lives are at stake if we decide to go to war again?" I did not recognize the man's voice.

"We are already in the middle of a war," my father said. "The other side is claiming casualties mercilessly. We are just not fighting back." I saw his eyes shift around the table. "Think about our children, our brothers and sisters, our entire people. We are losing it all, and mark my words they will die—as will we. Hunted down one by one and slaughtered."

Suddenly the door swung open in front of me. I pinched my eyes closed. My mother put her hand on my shoulder and I nearly jumped out of my skin. I held back a squeal.

"You knew your son was listening," She said. It was not a question.

My father did not look at her or anyone else in the room—only me. "This decision today will frame how you fight this war tomorrow, Elias. I will do my best to abet you." He knelt in front of me, his tenacious eyes promising me something I did not yet understand. "I love you."

My mother then turned me around and shut the door behind us.

A man walking his dog jostled me back to the present and the quaint neighborhood in the Chicago suburbs. I nodded at him and casually began walking in the other direction toward an outlet between two houses.

I had been circling the fifteen-block radius for nearly eight hours, ensuring that if someone was following me I would have noticed them. Something would have given them away: a familiar face, a cough, a smell—but I had seen nothing that would indicate I was still being tracked. My window of opportunity was small. I knew it would be only a matter of time before someone caught up with me again.

I felt I was walking a tightrope. Conditions had to be perfect to ensure that I did not get myself or anyone else killed. My fate was truly in the hands of Chitchakor's strokes. I loomed in the alley across from the townhouse I had been staking out. It was now or never. I took a deep breath and headed toward the front door.

~

ALISTAIR SAT ACROSS FROM ME. *Finally,* I thought, *here was the man I had been searching for, for nearly two years. His gift of mapping could change everything, and turn the tide in this war.* The trouble with a man who has a knack for finding obscure places, however, is exactly that—he is a master of evasion. Until now. His dear friend Emerson was finally able to help me nail down his whereabouts.

I cut to the chase. "I need to find a venue Alistair. I came here exclusively to get your input. Can you help me or not?" His nearly lifeless pale blue eyes just stared blankly beyond me. "I do not have time for this!" I shouted, hating to raise my voice, but I was exasperated by his seeming apathy. He knew the stakes.

"I know my friend, please give me a moment," he finally responded. I had asked around for months and this is where it led me. Sitting on a stale couch in downtown Chicago, across from a man I did not know, asking questions he seemed little invested in answering. The inside of my mouth was raw from chewing on it and my leg was impatiently shaking.

I stared intently at him, but his face was unchanging. "I need twenty-four hours to give you a thorough analysis and answer." He was not asking, he was telling me.

"That is too long. I have to keep moving, I need an answer within ten." We were in negotiations.

"You ask too much, my friend." He now looked at me, keenly. I could sense a demeanor change. "For the answers you seek I need to dig deep, this is no trifle of a task and it puts me in danger. You have given me the criteria. I need time to be as efficient and as thorough as possible. You are speaking about an event that will put many lives at risk. In good conscience, I must guide you to the very best of my ability."

I could not argue with that logic, I too wanted the safest possible scenario. But there was something off, something that I could not quite put my finger on. The longer we drew this out, the dodgier it got. The greater the chance there was that we would be caught or that information would leak.

"Can you do it in twelve hours?" I pleaded with him.

He stared coolly back and I thought it was a lost cause. I watched as he gently moved his left hand repeatedly over an odd tattoo that lay between his thumb and forefinger on his right hand. Then he nodded. "Now leave me." He waved toward the door. "Be back here in twelve hours."

I did not say a word as I left. I could only hope to return to answers.

OPHELIA

I loved that moment in the morning when the new day was starting fresh and untarnished. I twisted and rolled around in my bed.

The morning routine had begun, with a little twist, because I needed to be packed and ready to go before I left for work. I wasn't excited about gearing up for another long day—I was booked solid with patients, and I knew I wouldn't get much sleep on the red-eye I was taking to Chicago that night.

I resembled a zombie as I prepared coffee and breakfast. Headlines over coffee made me want to crawl back in bed and hide, so instead I started my day with some soothing Norah Jones tunes. Half a cup of java down and I was ready to pop in the shower.

I trudged into the bathroom to begin my morning procedure. Half an hour later I was as presentable as I was going to get—teeth brushed, curly mass of red hair combed back into a messy bun, a little blush to cover my freckles, a touch of mascara and *voilà!* I did the once-over as I adjusted my blouse. If anything didn't look right, I didn't look close enough to notice.

As I grabbed my bag I had a sudden urge to lock the apartment door and stay inside. I sensed someone was waiting on the other side of the doorway to ambush me. *Too late now to cancel my appointments,* I thought, *here we go.* I smiled as I opened the door; I always believed even the most painful situations were better when approached with a smile.

There she was, all five foot two of her. Sure, I could out run her, but she would just be here when I returned. "Hello Mrs. Mueller."

"Oh hello Ophelia, I am so glad to see you this morning." *I bet you are,* I thought.

"Can I help you with something?" I offered. Mrs. Mueller was a classic "dump truck" as I called them. Not only did I have the uncanny ability to empathize with the emotional climate of a complete stranger from across the room, but I also seemed to have a sign on my forehead that said, *"Come Share Your Baggage With Me!" No wonder I was single,* I thought.

"No, but thank you dear. I couldn't sleep a wink last night."

Here we go, I thought, anxiety filling my chest.

"My daughter called me yesterday evening with the most disturbing news. She's leaving her husband."

"Mrs. Mueller, don't you think this is a conversation better suited for a close friend or family member? I don't think Lizzie would appreciate me knowing the intimate details of her marriage." But I already knew far too much about her daughter Lizzie, her-son-in law Thomas and their three foster children. I knew it all, because Mrs. Mueller felt it necessary to share every innermost detail of her life with me. At least once a week, she'd unload all her emotional havoc into my lap then continue on her merry way pleased as punch. Meanwhile I'd feel like I got hit by a freight train.

"But Ophelia, we are friends, and I always feel so much better after I vent to you about these things." She smiled. Her angst was already subsiding while mine was growing, deep in the pit of my stomach. *A perfectly good day, off to a tumultuous start,* I silently fumed. *Thank you Mrs. Mueller.* As she followed me down the stairs, rambling about an affair her daughter was having with her piano teacher who liked bondage. I did my best to suffocate the emotional fire burning in my core. I tried to focus on the next part of my day, a long drive with

Miles Davis. As we approached my car, I did my best to politely end the conversation.

"Well Mrs. Mueller, it sounds to me like Lizzie has some important decisions ahead of her and she's lucky to have you to talk to and support her. I hope it all works out for you and your family. Have a fantastic day." I conjured up the biggest smile I could and ducked into the driver's seat. I was pretty sure she was still talking as I pulled out of the parking garage.

I turned up the music and buckled my belt. I couldn't blame Mrs. Mueller. I had several "dump trucks" in my life—people who loved to share their emotional garbage. It wasn't always their toxic waste—some people shared their happiness as well—but it was all the same to me. A lot of information that I didn't always, or most times, need to know.

I cherished my alone time and the unassuming splendor of silence. I loved to help people, I just wish people understood I could only handle so much.

As I drove, my mind drifted back to one of my least favorite memories from nineteen years earlier.

Sandra was the only friend I was able to make after my mom uprooted us again and brought us to a tiny town in Wyoming. My hands were covered in mud. Sandra and I had been digging and rolling around in the dirt for hours. Her parents had just arrived home from work. I was so jealous of Sandra. She had two parents and two brothers and she'd lived her whole life in one town, in the same house.

"Girls come inside for dinner," her father hollered from the front porch. They owned the small convenience store in town. Sandra's brothers were older, and they would watch her in the afternoons while her parents worked. I'd grown accustomed to spending my afternoons here with her family, it was a safe haven compared to what I had at home. My mother's current husband, Harvey, was a gambler and a drunk.

We both ran straight to the bathroom to clean up. It was the first time I'd been invited to stay and have dinner with them. I was so excited. I couldn't remember the last time Eleanor had cooked. I could smell the mashed potatoes on the stove and the roast in the Crockpot.

"Maybe you can sleep over tonight," Sandra chirped as we dried our hands and headed for the kitchen table. We all sat down and said grace. Sandra's brothers talked about football practice and her dad discussed who had come into the store that day. It was exactly how I had pictured a family could be. Everyone asked me about how my day had been and how I liked their town. Everyone but Sandra's mother—she kept looking at me with a weird uncertainty in her face. She would open her mouth, then close it, as if to say something and then change her mind.

After dessert Sandra asked if I could stay the night, and her father insisted that I call my mom to get permission. I knew Eleanor wouldn't care, she was probably already at the casino keeping an eye on Harvey. But I called and pretended to talk to her, when it was really only the answering machine. When I hung up I noticed that Sandra's mom was standing behind me. I panicked for a moment, thinking she was onto my ruse and knew that I hadn't really talked to my mother.

Instead she knelt down next to me and asked if I had a second to talk. I nodded, but something was telling me this was not good. She took my hand and stared into my eyes. My stomach knotted up, like someone was wringing it out like a towel.

"How old are you Ophelia?"

"Nine," I muttered.

"You don't seem that young." I'd heard those words before. I pulled my hand away, terrified of what was coming next. "I have a secret to tell you, because I must tell someone and my heart tells me I can tell you."

"Please." I pleaded. "I don't want to know any secrets."

"I'm having an affair." It was too late, she had said the words. "With your stepfather Harvey. It's foolish I know; he's a worthless man, gambles way too much. But something moves inside me when he touches me. Something that hasn't moved with my husband in years."

I shook my head in disbelief. I'd felt this brewing at the dinner table. "Please don't say anymore."

Sandra's father stormed into the room. He'd obviously been within earshot of the confession. "Get out of here, Ophelia!" He yelled. "Go home and don't ever come back!"

I grabbed my things and ran out the door. I didn't even get to say goodbye to Sandra. I cried the whole way home as I ran back in the dark. I knew I'd lost the only friend I had. Sandra never spoke to me again. She'd avoid me at school, and even started rumors that I had lice. I didn't blame her. I knew she was told she couldn't speak to me again and this was her way of coping with the loss of our friendship.

I hated that memory. Anytime someone regurgitated too much information on me, it was the first place my mind went. Now here I was, a 28-year-old professional on my way to my office to sift through more people's problems—but at least they paid me for my services.

I considered how I'd created my thriving psychology practice. I finished my undergrad in abnormal psychology and I headed to the West Coast to attend grad school. I was accepted into the developmental psychology grad program in San Francisco at SFSU. Since I graduated, my success with dissolving client challenges has been incredible.

I know I have an ability that enables people to share things with me freely, and unlike the outside world, which takes advantage of my magnetism, my patients are grateful and the compensation helps.

I took a deep breath. It was nice to remember how much I loved what I did.

As I pulled into my designated parking spot behind my office, I glanced over my schedule. It looked like it was going to be another busy day.

ELIAS

I paced up and down the block adjacent to Alistair's townhouse as I waited for the eleventh hour to conclude. I looked at my watch again, he had one minute. I started in the direction of his home.

I paused when I smelled the smoke. I could not see it yet, but I could detect the charred particulates wafting in the evening air. I knew that stench well—and it suddenly brought back the horrific memories of my parents' murder, and immediately put me on edge. I looked behind me, no one was there. The memories soon flooded my brain with a frenzy of terror and pain, the two emotions combining to leave me momentarily catatonic. Then I heard sirens in the distance and they hurtled me back to the present. Alistair.

I ran up his steps, the smell stifling my nose, although I still could not see flames. I pounded on the door several times, to no avail. I glanced around, there was no one on the street. It gave me a moment to pick the lock without any witnesses. The sirens were getting closer. Clearly someone else had caught a whiff of the smoke as well. I had only moments to spare if it truly was Alistair's dwelling in flames. When the door opened it confirmed that it was indeed coming from within.

"Alistair!?" I shouted as loud as I could. "Are you in here?" Perhaps he had managed to escape, this was just coincidence and he was somewhere safe and would get in touch with me later. I ran down the hall, the smoke getting thicker and burning my eyes and throat. "Alistair!" Still no answer. "In the name of Malarin and the river Tins, answer me!"

Squinting through the smokescreen, I glimpsed an orange glow dancing on the walls in front of me. I turned the corner to find a heap of body parts fully engrossed in flames. I leaned closer to make out any distinguishing features that might confirm an identity. The smoke made it difficult to see anything, but as I examined the victim's right hand, on it were the strange markings I had seen Alistair massaging only hours before. I stood there for what seemed like an eternity, but was merely seconds. The sirens were undoubtedly nearly upon us. I had no time to gather my thoughts or formulate a plan. I ran to the study adjacent the hall, a brief respite from the sooty air. My lungs were burning and my eyes were watering fiercely, but I spied a backpack beside a chair and began filling it with everything I could find—a box, papers, journals, three small bags and Alistair's laptop. I zipped it up as I heard the firefighters enter the apartment.

I opened the closest window and leapt out, then scaled the fence and took the back alley to the closest arterial. I must have looked like hell. I needed to find somewhere to clean up before a passersby became curious and called the police. I pulled out my phone, thinking *What did people do before smartphones?*

"Siri, direct me to the nearest hotel." My voice was hoarse.

"Due East," my phone replied. "Continue up three blocks. Ambassador Boutique Hotel will be on your left-hand side."

I put the phone back in my pocket. Not wanting to draw attention to myself, I smoothed my clothing. I maneuvered the bag I took from Alistair's and my own satchel in a less awkward position and attempted a casual stroll. I sighted the hotel sign a few minutes later. The revolving door spat me out in front of a nice young woman behind the counter. She smiled brightly as I walked toward her. I must not have looked too disheveled.

"How can I help you sir?" Her gaze did not leave my face.

"I would like a room." I pulled out my wallet and placed it on the counter.

"Certainly sir, do you have a reservation with us?"

"No, I was walking by and this establishment appeared to be an agreeable place to rest one's head." I laid into my English accent. I knew that for some reason American women loved a little foreign charm. I was raised in many places around the world but spent most of my youth in the English countryside, so I found it quite easy to thicken my accent as needed.

"Of course sir. Let me see what we have available." Her cheeks blushed slightly as her fingers busily worked the keyboard. "Will it just be you this evening sir?"

"Yes, just me." I looked behind me to make sure I was in fact alone.

"I'm sorry sir, all we have available is the executive suite. It's very large for a single occupant. I can direct you towards our sister hotel just a few miles away—I can see here that they have more vacancies."

"That will not be necessary, I will take it."

"Are you sure, sir? It's our priciest room." Now she was looking at me oddly.

"I am certain." I did not have time for this. I needed to sit down, clear my head, take a shower and regroup.

"Do you want to know how much it is first, sir?" She was obviously not going to drop this.

"Most certainly." I tried not to sound impatient.

"For one night?"

I nodded.

"$1,800 plus a $1,000 holding deposit on your credit card." She was clearly waiting for me to recoil.

"Very well, let us proceed. I will be paying in cash, including the deposit. Is that acceptable?"

OPHELIA

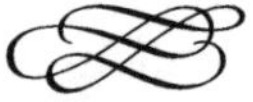

Eleanor's here, and wow doesn't she look excited I thought as I spied my mom. *I feel exhausted already.*

The baggage claim was full of people pushing and shoving, attempting to navigate with their oversized bags past hordes of other inpatient travelers through the narrow corridors between baggage carousels. *Oh the joys of travel.*

"Ophelia, Ophelia! Olly!"

We had already made eye contact, she knows I saw her. This was the start of the first act. I knew this one well. The whole drive home would be statements dripping with guilt as she poured on the shallow gratitude. I could already hear it in my head: *"Oh how I have missed my only child, I just don't see you enough, you just don't have the time for me, I'm so happy you finally made time for your family, blah blah blah blah."*

My nightmare reverie was broken up by the real thing standing beside me. "Hi mom, it's good to see you." I said, reaching around and patting her shoulder with my free arm. She grabbed my torso and awkwardly drew me in closer. I gently pulled away.

"It was a long flight. Shall we get my luggage and get out of here?" I started towards the carousel, my mother in tow.

ELIAS

I quickly wrapped the towel around my waist as I heard the third knock on the door. I peeked through the small peep-hole. Room service. The shower had felt so good that I had forgotten I ordered dinner. The attendant looked legitimate. I cracked the door slightly, the man smiled.

"Did you order room service sir?"

"Yes, I did. Forgive me. I was in the shower." I was stalling, making sure my instincts did not scream *trap!* He appeared harmless enough, but I thought I would test his patience. "What did you bring up? I forgot my order." Indeed, I had not, but I figured that should almost surely weed out someone just trying to gain entry to my room.

"Oh of course sir." He lifted the plate cover and the food made my mouth water. "You ordered the grilled salmon and mixed seasonal vegetable."

"Indeed." I stepped aside. "Please come in."

He gently rolled the cart to a dining nook, with a small table and chairs. The suite was huge, more space than any one person could ever utilize.

"Are you finding everything to your satisfaction sir?" He looked around, as though he had never been up here before. I had a moment of panic. "This is the first time I've served this suite," he added.

"Yes, everything is quite satisfactory. I look forward to enjoying my meal. Thank you for your service." I slipped him a twenty dollar bill and walked him to the door. He was still examining the room as I opened it, and looked embarrassed when he realized I had to usher him out.

"Of course sir, please enjoy your evening." He looked in his palm. "Thank you so much."

I was not trying to be rude, but I did not like having my door open or a stranger in my quarters. "You are welcome," I said, then shut the door briskly behind him, locked every lock, and pulled an armchair against it. It would not be much of a deterrent for an intruder, but it might give me more forewarning, should someone enter without my admission.

The food smelled delectable. I was acutely aware of my hunger pangs. I threw on a shirt and some shorts and sat down. The salmon was cooked perfectly, moist and delicious. As I finished up, my mind was pulsing. The shower and meal were enough to distract me momentarily. It was time to examine the artifacts I had salvaged from poor Alistair's home.

I laid the contents of the backpack on the bed—the box, papers, journals, three small bags and his laptop. I would need to find a charger for the laptop as I did not think to grab his in the chaos. I pressed the power button and the screen lit up blue, but then immediately powered down. I would find a cord first thing in the morning. I picked up the box. It looked old. I was no historian, but I would say it had early twelfth-century craftsmanship. The medium size rectangle container was most likely made of oak with iron strappings adorning both sides. Its clasp moved with little effort. Inside were maps—many maps. Most were ancient and tattered. I gingerly unfolded each of them, shuffled through my personal satchel and found some tape. I hung them on the wall and sat back down on the bed. I did not recognize any of these places. I knew the language they were written in, but the names were completely foreign to me. I drummed my fingers on my lap. "Where in Chitchokor strokes might these lands be?"

I took photos of each one with my phone, and then emailed them to myself. I would have to do some serious research to uncover their origins. I sifted through the little pile of paperwork I had salvaged—from what I could tell they were notes about specific buildings, albeit once more I was baffled about the whereabouts. The last four pages were written in what I had to assume was Alistair's personal code. I would need a substantial amount of time to decipher the pattern. *Certainly not a task to be undertaken on this particular evening.* I organized the papers as best I could, took more photos and emailed them as well, then put them in a folder that the hotel literature was previously in.

There were three journals, and each looked older than the next. The first was a notebook, the second was a hardbound black book, and the third was leather-bound and weathered. To my dismay, they were each written in not just one code but in a rotation of three codes per journal.

I sat back on the bed. "Dear Alistair," I said aloud with a sigh, "you were nothing if not vigilant about your security measures." I did not expect his ideas to be out there for the world to see, but I had hoped for a simpler undertaking. I guess there was a reason why the man was so renowned for his skill. I closed my eyes and the image of his burning body engulfed the back of my eye lids. "Poor man."

Who had killed him and why? Could it have been my pursuer? Was it due to our meeting? Did Alistair tell him anything before he was killed? If he did, there were far worse things to come.

I rolled over and the three small leather bags toppled onto each other. I picked one up. The contents felt solid. I untied the string and let the sack flop open. Out came three large crystals, almost identical in size and shape. The next bag felt soft so I did not untie it completely, so as not to spill the contents. I peeked inside—it held a rich black sand, very fine and odd-smelling, alike to sulfur and prunes. The last satchel had some kind of scentless herb in it, dark green and dry.

"Perfect I nicked your spices," I said, rolling back over. I assessed my situation. I was certain I could find something on the laptop, and eventually I would get to the bottom of the code and the maps. I gently took down the maps and put them back, then placed the three small leather pouches in the box. Everything went into my satchel and I threw the back pack in the foyer trash bin.

I pulled out my own laptop and looked up the closest electronics store, where I might find a replacement for Alastair's cord. Then I looked up flights to Europe. I was not positive that was my next move, but it would be good to know my options.

As I closed down the computer I heard the doorknob rattling. Someone was trying to get in the room.

OPHELIA

By the time we reached the house, it was two a.m. and I was beat. Eleanor had talked the whole way home, filling me in on Simon, her current husband. They'd been married for less than two years, and I considered the man a saint. He was passive and stable —exactly what Eleanor needed. Of all her suitors, I felt like this one might actually last a while.

I stood in the entryway trying to remember which way the guest bedroom was. The one and only time I'd stayed here before had been a year earlier.

As if on cue, Eleanor interjected. "Down this way Olly, don't you remember? Oh wait that's right, you've only been here one time in what like, three years?"

"Mom you've only lived here for two years."

She paused. "You're right, it just seems like it's been three years . . . I see you so infrequently." She turned around and smiled as she attempted to inject her venom again. "Here we are, you have your own bathroom, and I put fresh towels on the sink. Can I get you anything else, honey? Do you want a glass of wine? Water? I'm so worn-out from working at the hospital and then having to pick you up on such a late flight. But you know me, I'm just so happy to see my long-lost daughter." She gave me another quick smile.

"Thanks mom, I'll be fine. Get some sleep." I escorted her towards the doorway, blew her a kiss and steered her the rest of the way out of the room, gently closing and locking the door behind her.

I was out before my head hit the pillow.

ELIAS

"What the hell are you doing here?!" My heart was racing. "You scared the piss out of me."

"I wanted to check on your progress with Alistair, maybe lean on him a little or call in an old favor in case he was giving you a hard time." Alistair's friend Emerson, looked startled himself, his speech onerous and eyes wide. I realized I still had him pinned, so I slowly pulled the dirk away from his throat. "Thank you," he said curtly, as he rubbed his neck.

I straightened up and glared at him. He was a rail of a man with thin lips and even thinner short brown hair, his sharp black eyes darted back and forth. I observed as he assessed me, we could not be more different looking men. I am about a foot taller with blonde hair and light eyes.

"How did you find me? And why did you not simply knock?" I had appreciated Emerson's help in finding Alistair in the first place, but was currently feeling quite uneasy considering that he had managed to track my whereabouts to this hotel suite. *How long had he been following me and how come I did not detect it?* I wondered.

"I saw you pick the lock on the front door just as I turned onto his block. I couldn't follow you in, because the firefighters were right behind you. So I went around back and saw you get out the rear window. I followed you here."

I looked down at my watch. "That was nearly two hours ago." This did not sound right at all.

"I wanted to call out to you, but I didn't want to make a scene. Then I paced for some time outside the hotel, trying to decide how to approach you. I couldn't just knock on the door, I knew you'd be on edge. Besides, only you and room service can take the elevator up to this floor. I had to find a way to get up here." He was squirming in his skin and I could not tell if it was because he was scared of me—or something else.

"Why are you in Chicago?" I asked. "Was it not just last week that we spoke in Ontario?" My voice was noticeably agitated.

"I told you, I was worried that Alistair would give you grief." Emerson made eye contact. Then he asked, "What happened to him? Is he alright? Was he in the house?"

I shook my head. He knew exactly what I meant. He threw his face into his hands and I instantly felt the rest of my misgivings about him subside. I put my hand on his shoulder, but he did not raise his face. "I am sorry—I know he was a dear friend." I hoped he heard the sincerity in my voice because I *was* sorry. For a million reasons, I was devastated.

I heard gentle sobs leaving his chest, and piloted him to sit. "Who was it? Why?" he whispered.

I walked to the minibar and grabbed him a glass of wine. He did not object. "I think we both know who was capable of getting to him so quickly. I am so sorry, I thought I was truly careful. If I had suspected I was being followed I would have returned at another time, no matter how urgent the situation."

"This isn't your fault, we are all aware of the time we live in—Alistair was so cautious. But for all we know, he may have led them straight to you."

I caught and held his gaze. "What are you suggesting?" I demanded.

"Forgive me, my friend," he replied. "I understand how that may have sounded. I'm sure Alistair didn't conspire against you, I meant that someone may have known you were looking for a person of his talents and assumed you'd eventually make your way here." Emerson suggested, but I was not entirely convinced. He was, after all, the only one who knew I was here.

I sat there for a while, wavering but saying nothing. I wanted—needed—his help. I knew he was Alistair's oldest confidant. And he was the one who had finally told me where to find the mapping virtuoso. But his unexpected presence meant that Emerson could also have been an informant. I sighed. Or perhaps he truly had come here to ensure my success. Either way I was confident he could give me some insight into what I had found at the apartment, but I had to deliberate. Was it worth the risk of possibly tipping off my enemy as well? If he was a defector, he would certainly share my findings with his comrades. If my findings were of no consequence, then it would not matter much. But if they were of some significance, the results would be disastrous.

All considered, I did not know the first thing about Alistair except rumors, which meant unraveling his code would be extremely difficult and time-consuming. I also would not know where to start with his laptop. I could only assume that the information on it would be just as cryptic as his handwritten notes. I could call my technical analyst, but the less involved, the better. I did not want to put more lives in jeopardy than were necessary, and time was of the essence.

Emerson broke me out of my rumination. "What? You're looking through me. You can trust me."

"How well were you acquainted with Alistair, honestly?" I looked at him sideways, so he understood a lot rode on his answer, and I was not going to be easily deceived.

"He has been my closest friend for ages. We travelled the world together for nearly twenty five years before parting ways in Algiers. Times are hard these days and Alistair was a paranoid man, if he could trust me, you must." He nodded at me assuredly. "It's true he wasn't an overtly social man, but he confided in me above all others."

I had to risk it. I would not show him everything I salvaged, but perhaps a small portion could give me a lead. I needed somewhere to start. I was at a loss. More importantly, I simply did not have time to wander around in the dark for days.

"Wait here," I told him. I was convinced at this point that if he was one of the traitors, his mission tonight was to see what information I had, and determine my next move. If he was here to kill me he would have tried already. I shut the bedroom door and, after a moment, decided to rip one of the single-coded pieces of paper in half lengthwise.

When I walked back into the living space he had not moved.

"I was not able to pilfer much, and unfortunately what I took from his study was in code. Have you seen this before?" I showed him the piece of paper, careful to keep it so I could study his expression for any signs of recognition. He instinctively reached for it and I pulled it away. "You did not answer me, have you seen this writing before?"

"I'm not sure—I have to look closer." He rubbed his face. "There are many strange scripts in this world, and I have not seen them all."

He appeared eager to help, I reluctantly handed it to him.

"You found this is Alistair's home?"

"Yes, in his study."

"Where is the other half?"

"I tore it when I was scrambling to get out before the firefighters saw me" I fibbed.

"They were on your tail." He peered at it, bewildered. That or he was masking his knowledge exceptionally well. "Hmm, I think this is in fact Alistair's pen, he said. "He had impeccable penmanship. There are certain characteristics I recognize, even in this odd language."

He set it down on the table. "You see here?" He pointed at a squiggly symbol that looked like a *K*. "That has the same uplifting accent that Alistair used in his writing. And again here with this shape, that is also a familiar accent." He placed his hands on his hips, clearly proud that he had identified the author. I needed a lot more than that.

"Have you ever seen this before, this language or code?"

"No, not this one." He paused. "But I have seen something similar."

"Similar—how so?"

"Alistair loved to spend time with aboriginal people around the world. He said it felt like home. I guess that made sense considering his upbringing, the way his father traipsed the family around from one small village to the next."

Emerson could see me anxiously waiting for a purpose to this story.

"Here I'll show you." He pulled out his phone and hurriedly moved his fingers across the screen. "He sent me this last summer."

The text was small and almost indistinguishable on the tiny screen of the phone, a picture of a small wood totem and there was no mistake some of the characters looked almost identical. I took a deep breath, this could be a huge break.

"Where is this writing from?" I was pacing. "I mean where was he when he took this photo, which tribe?"

"I understood the question. I'm trying to think." Emerson's brow was furrowed and he looked pained trying to come up with the answer. "He travelled to five different tribes last year. I don't know which one this is from exactly. He had his favorites, many of the same ones we had travelled to years ago."

"Can you tell me what five?" I pressed. "I can narrow it down from there." In fact five was better because it gave me more leads for the rest of the cryptography.

"Sure, the Boruca of Costa Rica and the Bhils in India. I love the Bhil people." He said fondly. "The Khakas of northern Asia and the Rapa Nui of Easter Island. There was one more, give me a second, oh yes, the Tukano of Colombia." He looked at me skeptically. "I don't think you'll just find a copy of their texts online."

"I am confident you are correct, I will just have to track them down personally."

"I don't think all of these tribes will simply allow you into their villages." he continued. "Alistair had a special rapport with them because of his father."

"You are very perceptive Emerson—I do not doubt your acuteness. But I must get answers and this is the only clue I have to follow—so do not doubt me when I say I will pursue it mercilessly until they answer my questions—if only simply to get rid of me." I was already devising an itinerary.

"Where will you start?" He asked seemingly helpful, but I was not going to share that information with anyone.

"I am not sure," I replied, that was a lie—I already knew I would start with Easter Island—I could work my way North and East from there. "If it is not too much to ask, I have appreciated your help but I would like to have the rest of the evening to organize my thoughts."

He nodded sheepishly.

"Do you have somewhere safe to go?" I asked. We had already lost one man tonight. I hesitated as I gestured towards the door. This place was clearly large enough to house both of us, and if he was a true friend and I sent him to the slaughter I would never forgive myself. I thought about what my father would have done in the wake of the nights events, he would have offered a safe refuge. But it was his mislead trust that beguiled my family and resulted in their deaths. I would not let that be my fate, but I wrestled with what was polite and what was wise.

"Yes, I think I do." He moved slowly toward the door, and I could sense his anxiety.

"By all means stay here," I relented. "There is another room across the hall." I hoped my altruistic heart had not just betrayed me as my father's did him. He appeared relieved and nodded excitedly. I pointed to the door of the adjacent room and entered my own bedroom.

I began pulling extra pillows off the bed when I heard an almost inaudible twist of the doorknob. I quickly moved to the bedroom doorway and glared at Emerson. "What is this about?" His head jerked toward the door as well.

He shrugged and we both waited to see if we could hear anything else on the other side. Silence. Not a good sign. I motioned toward the balcony. Emerson scuffled in that direction.

"Excuse me, sir," A voice said from the corridor. The unwanted guest knocked this time. I could hear his breathing hasten. "Sir, I just wanted to make sure you're okay. Someone reported seeing a stranger in the elevator and they thought he was attempting to get to this floor."

I glared at Emerson, uneasy. Was this a trap?

"Just one moment," I called to the stranger on the other side of the door.

As I inched toward it, I could hear his feet shuffling.

"Pardon me if I am acting peculiar," I started, peeking through the peephole, "but can I ask who you are? You do not look like the bellboy or the room service attendant I saw earlier." My heart was pumping in an unhealthy rhythm. He was tall, easily over six feet, he had well-manicured brown hair. He could be in his early 30's, hard to tell because he looked like he was in great shape under the beige long sleeve button down shirt and forest green tie. I read his tag: *Henry Witt, Manager.*

"Of course sir, I understand. I show up at this late hour, talking about strange men on your floor. My name is Henry Witt. I'm the manager on duty here at the hotel." Henry's voice said shakily, his eyes narrowing in on something to his left. There was something or someone else in the corridor with him.

I stepped away from the peep hole. "Give me a moment I was in bed and I am indisposed." There was no way I was opening that door. I motioned for Emerson to continue onto the balcony. I heard some more shuffling on the other side of the door as I slipped on my shoes and grabbed everything from the hotel suite. Best to leave no clues behind.

"Sir, it will only take a moment to verify your safety. Please open the door." Henry's voice was now shrill, full of panic.

Emerson was clumsily maneuvering his way over the balcony railing, *I hope he had better skills than that,* I thought. I pointed down to indicate we needed to make our way to the ground as swiftly as possible. Then I heard a loud crack as a body hit the door, presumably Henry's but not on his own accord. There was a growl and then most of the noise was drowned out by the fire alarm I set off as I swiftly found my way beside Emerson. I made sure my satchel with all of

Alistair's clues along with my belongings was secure before I flung myself over the railing.

I landed safely on the adjacent buildings ledge two stories down. "Emerson you better act hastily my friend. Whoever was on the other side of the door is now in the suit." I still could not make out who it was, but they were tossing the room like a two year old in a tantrum. "Now." I insisted.

Emerson hurled himself off the ledge and ineffectually caught a hold of the window sill a level above me. "Drop down." I asserted. "You will be fine." He glanced over his shoulder uncertain of my assessment. I could hear the hotel occupants filing out the front doors of the establishment. My attention, however, was redirected back to my hotel suite balcony where I heard a guttural growl erupt that shook the windows through the entire alley.

It was Salzar. "Emerson you have to jump now!" I could not wait to see if he did because I knew Salzar could make easy prey of the both of us at this proximity. I leapt off the terrace I was on and took a hold of the drainage pipe three feet away. I awkwardly slid down the remaining three stories of the building. My hands were burning and bleeding from the tears that the protruding errant metal gashed open as I fell. I heard a noise above my head. I did not look up. I might have a fighting chance if I hit the ground before Salzar, but I would be dead if I let him bridge any more of the distance.

I looked up only when my feet hit the ground. Salzar had not moved. But his elongating fingers afforded him that grace. They had projected beyond the expanse of the two buildings and now one hand was laced around Emerson's torso, constricting and drawing him back to Salzar. The other hand was diving toward me. I did not know the enormity of his reach and I did not intend to stay there to find out. I turned on my heel and ran. All the while ignoring the terrible knot in my stomach as I replayed the image of Emerson's limp body in those monstrous tendrils.

OPHELIA

"Olly! Olly!" I tried to ignore the rapping at the door, but the yelling as Eleanor drifted from one end of the hallway to the other was too antagonizing to tune out. I rolled over and stared at the clock: 7:07 am.

"Ooollllllyyy…." With that I threw the musty, dilapidated comforter off me. I staggered out of bed, feeling the grimace smeared across my face as I tramped toward the door. I reached for the doorknob, glancing back towards the bed, desperately wanting to crawl back under the covers instead of facing the daunting task ahead, breakfast with my mother. I glanced around the room one more time noting that in fact the room itself was small and dark. Only one petite window offered any natural light, and you could tell from the space's smell it had not been opened in a while. The wobbly brass bed likely had belonged to one of Simon's daughters when she was a teenager, and the mattress was probably just as old—or at least that was the signal my lower back was giving me as I hesitated at the door.

I took a deep breath and turned the knob. There she was, standing not two feet away.

"Oh you're up early," Eleanor chimed as she smiled at me. I swallowed hard.

"Yeah, just couldn't sleep I guess." I muttered and tried my hardest to conjure a smile. "We must have a busy agenda for you to be up and preparing breakfast so early."

"Oh don't be silly dear, I didn't make breakfast! You know I hate cleaning up those messes in the kitchen. But I thought maybe you would like to make something. You know Simon loves your cooking, and we never see you. I mean, he has two daughters and we see them all the time, but not you. He's always talking about how wonderful your eggs Benedict is—of course it is the only thing you know how to make. I try to tell him that."

It never ceased to amaze me how my mother could simultaneously pay me a compliment, send me on a guilt trip, and somehow cap it with an insult. It really is quite the talent. "Anyway," she carried on, "Simon's been up since six, he's probably starving now. It's either you cook breakfast or I just give him a cereal bar." Eleanor glanced toward the kitchen.

"Of course, I'll make breakfast for Simon. I wouldn't dream of disappointing him." I tried to sound sincere. Eleanor smiled over her shoulder as she paraded into the living room.

So, she woke me up to make breakfast, I deduced. I can't say I was surprised. I needed coffee fast before my morning fogginess wore off and I strangled her. Toddling around the kitchen, I wondered if matricide would be more common if all mothers were like Eleanor. I had to remember that she herself was orphaned at a very young age, left to circuit from one foster home to another until she was finally adopted at age ten. Her story was sad, but it didn't fully explain Eleanor's emotional misfiring.

I stared at my hollandaise sauce as I stirred it gently. Had my grandmother been the same as Eleanor, and had she realized it? Is that why she'd killed herself?

Eleanor was only six months old when Lilith strangled herself in the confines of Connecticut's Silver Hill Mental Hospital. Was it a mercy or was it a life sentence?

Her sharp tongue awoke me from my contemplation. "Ophelia, you burnt the English muffins! What are you doing, child?" Eleanor scowled as she threw the scorched muffins in the trash and manipulated the twisty tie on the packaging of those remaining. "I guess you won't be getting any." She huffed as she placed two of the fresh halves into the toaster and stomped out of the kitchen. To someone else this may have seemed ridiculous. I just stared after her and thought: *Thank goodness she left the room. I didn't really need the extra carbs anyway.*

I turned back to the delicate hollandaise sauce before I destroyed that too.

I sighed and took solace in the fact that she usually started letting up on me after twenty-four hours—or at least her assaults became less frequent. *I bet she thinks I forgot her birthday,* I thought. Just as well, I wanted to surprise her with a gift anyway. If I could survive the abuse for another eight hours, I realized I might just be able to pull one over on her.

ELIAS

My head was swarming with questions. How did Salzar find me? Why did he not follow me? Was Emerson a target or a casualty? Is Emerson alive? Whose side was Emerson on? I cannot fathom him betraying Alistair, but I could not trust anyone at the moment, least of all a man who materialized from seemingly nowhere, followed by a would-be assassin that I put in a very foul mood a few days earlier.

I knew one thing: it was time to leave Chicago. I needed to find a charging cord for Alistair's laptop, and then I would be able to head off to whatever far corner of the world my next mission led me to. I did not know how long I would be wandering the globe looking for clues to the script that Alistair had coded in his journals. I was certain that the answers I was seeking would unfold on those pages.

OPHELIA

Eleanor had only one photograph of her with her mother, when she was an infant. Lilith had finished labor only hours before the image was taken. She was sitting in an armchair facing a barred window, staring out at a world that seemed far from her reach. Her long, wavy, pale locks fell on either side of her face, framing her strong cheekbones and full lips perfectly. She was a classically beautiful woman. Eleanor was in her arms, although Lilith's expression implied she'd just as soon be holding a doll rather than her own child.

I always found my grandmother's expression saddening, as if she knew something happened that should never have come to pass. Nevertheless, Eleanor adored the small four-by-six-inch photo, the only relic that seemed to attest to her own mother's very existence. As a child, I would stare at the print, admiring Lilith's beauty, wondering what she was thinking. My mother used to keep it on the mantel in our first home, but as we moved around and she remarried the photo got misplaced in one of the storage boxes.

I was sure Eleanor thought she'd lost it. So, when I stumbled upon it in an old chest full of my elementary school mementos, I couldn't wait to frame it and return it to her. Eleanor was not typically the sentimental type. While other mothers hung their children's artwork,

I was lucky if my mom kept it at all. Gifts she received usually ended up in a box buried in the basement or attic. But I knew this gift would be different.

I'd already researched the finest framers and photograph restorers in the area, and I had an appointment that afternoon at a place downtown called Ivan's Love for Photos. I was trying to calculate how I would evade my mother's company. I knew she'd give me a hard time about leaving her during such a short visit. I chuckled as I thought, *let's be honest, she's going to hassle me all day no matter what I do.* Maybe I could use the excuse of needing to catch up with my friend Cathy over a quick lunch.

"Olly!" I jumped as I heard her voice. I hadn't even realized she'd re-entered the kitchen. "I am having this issue with my bathroom sink, do you think you could have that friend of yours check it out while you are here— what's his name? Larry? No, Terry? I don't have the money for a plumber right now." Bingo! She'd solved the problem for me. *Thank you, God,* I thought.

"Of course, I can," I chirped. "I will arrange for him to come by right after breakfast. I am sure Tim will give me a great rate and of course I will cover it mom."

My mother was pleased as punch. She was determined to get a birthday present one way or another.

After breakfast, I called Tim and he was kind enough to come by on a Saturday and see what he could do. I showered while Tim spent an hour under the master bathroom sink. Sure enough, it wasn't going to be easy. He was writing a supply list when I grabbed my bag and said goodbye. I caught Eleanor in the hallway on my way out. "Hey, I'm going to grab coffee with Cathy. Do you want me to pick up anything else while I'm out? And when he's done I can treat you and Simon to dinner." I smiled and left before she could argue with me.

The door shut behind me and I took a deep breath, I needed these intermissions during the time spent with her. It was like running a marathon—and these breaks were like a refueling stop. I walked down eight blocks to the L, getting there just in time to hop on the train heading towards downtown Chicago.

ELIAS

I had a list of electronic stores. I figured one of them had to have the correct cord for the archaic laptop I was lugging around. I had hoped to catch a flight to Chile, South America, by evening. I had two options, a 7:15 p.m., or the red-eye at 11:45 p.m. I needed to be on one of those two planes.

The clothes I had worn to Alistair's apartment smelled like smoke. I decided to dispose of them—I was travelling light anyway. As I emptied the pants pockets to make sure I did not leave any crucial pieces of information behind, I smelled another scent clinging to the garments, and I immediately thought I was going to be sick.

It was faint, but there was no doubt about what it was, the wretched smell of burning flesh. I had encountered the odor only once before, the night my parents were murdered, four years earlier. Again, I found myself deep in thought as I recalled that fateful moment.

"I told you I was exhausted and that you had an unfair advantage on the court tonight," I jabbed at Rand as he dodged my blow. Rand was basically family. My father considered him a brother and I in turn thought of him as an uncle.

"Too slow, young chap," he jeered as we approached the north side of my parents' estate in South Africa.

"I will show you too slow," I challenged as I chased him halfheartedly through the back courtyard. I was truly exhausted. My father had kept me up all night researching a new location for the summit he had just discovered in Greenland. My eyes were heavy and my last ounce of energy had been exerted in the match.

Rand suddenly stopped thirty feet ahead of me and turned ghostly white. He had caught wind of something that had not tickled my senses yet. I instinctively stopped to listen, but I heard nothing. I glanced around—nothing seemed to be lurking in the shadows of the slowly setting sun. When I looked back to Rand he was gone, and it was then that I caught wind of the smell that had alarmed him. Even though I could not identify it, I knew it signaled something inauspicious.

My adrenaline skyrocketed as I sprinted toward the back door. Just as I got there I heard my mother scream and a terrible ripping noise reverberated off the walls. I concluded the noise came from upstairs, so I took the steps two at a time. When I reached the top, the first traces of smoke stung my eyes and they welled with tears. I could see, however, that down the hall my parents' bedroom door was ajar and there was an orange glow emanating from within.

"Mother? Father?" I whispered shakily. I heard nothing. I did not want to alarm an attacker, but I also knew whoever was in the house likely already knew I was here. I stepped slowly down the hall, crouched low, ready to strike. The floorboards creaked under my feet. *Where the hell was Rand?*

When I reached the bedroom door a second wave of smells accosted my nose like nothing I had ever smelled before. A rancid, foul, putrid stench filled my lungs and I felt sick. I peeked around the corner and into the room. Flames were engulfing my parents' mangled, broken bodies, which were in heaps on the floor. I gasped, but before I could make my way to their defiled forms someone came careening out of the room and knocked me to the floor. We wrestled on the ground and I kicked, clawed, and punched every wicked appendage I could grasp. The shadows of dusk had reached the house and I could not make out distinct features of the murderer. The orange glow was growing wilder and the smoke was now thick in the hall.

The assailant threw me down the staircase and I hurtled to the bottom. He or she—I am not sure which it was—landed gently just above my head and crouched down near my face. My eyes were on fire and my head was throbbing. I was seeing stars from the fall.

I accepted that I was going to die. I would be in the same state as my poor parents in a matter of minutes and in that instant, I welcomed the relief. Then I heard a noise to my left and Rand's voice ringing in my ears. "Get up! Run! Now!"

Rand was hunched on top of the assailant and latching onto his or her worthless neck. "Run!" he yelled again, looking at me with a ferocity I have not forgotten. Again, the walls reverberated with a terrible ripping noise.

I ran and did not look back. I sprinted for miles until I found my way to the small town just east of my family's home. There I hot-wired a truck and drove for hours ... and hours ... and hours.

The sounds, the smells and the anger all flooded back to me. I threw my clothes, with Alistair's acrid scent, in the garbage and quickly left the hotel. I had to get the hell out of here, away from all of this.

First on the list, though, was Best Buy.

OPHELIA

The train car was pretty empty except for a young couple in the corner clearly blissfully in love. I didn't know if it was them or the excitement of this gift for my mother, but I was on cloud nine. I stared out the window at the passing cityscape, I loved the L.

The L is called the L because it's an elevated train that surfs above the city streets. I liked watching the buildings speed by. I remember the excitement when I was a teenager as we approached downtown—you could see the gigantic buildings looming ahead, beckoning your arrival. There's no other city with a skyline like Chicago—after all it was the birthplace of the first skyscraper over a hundred years ago.

The Sears Tower impressively soared above the other remarkable architectural masterpieces as my train approached it. I sighed, thinking *I miss this city.* I stood up, my stop was next. As the train came to a halt I glanced once more at the rapturous couple. I was slightly envious. They looked euphoric in each other's arms. I don't know if I'd ever experienced such wild love, but I knew it existed—I saw it in them. I didn't know if I could really handle that kind of intensity. The way I seemed to absorb the feelings around me, I might explode if my partner and I were so jubilant. But I might be willing to try.

The doors parted and I stepped onto the platform. *Alright time to find my bearings and locate this shop,* I thought as I scuttled down the stairway onto the bustling street. Downtown was always clamoring with noise—people talking, cabs honking and the ever-constant rumble of the train above. I turned right and found myself on the buzzy State St, a few blocks north and I should see the shop. As I walked I took some deep breaths. I could smell coffee being roasted in the cafes as I passed. Sometimes a sweet pastry smell would follow, the delicatessens contributed to the symphony of aromas.

Of course, there was the dirty smell of the streets, too—didn't all major cities share that trait? An underlying odor of fuel, alcohol and stale food from the trash cans—or from the drunks walking home the night before and leaving yesterday's dinner on the cement. As I came up on the fifth block I saw the sign, Ivan's Love for Photos. Perfect, I was early. I liked being early.

I strode into the shop, rifling through my purse for the folder that contained the photo. The man at the desk was a plump Middle Eastern man with a welcoming smile and a name badge that read Ivan.

"You must be Miss Banner?" he asked and smiled even bigger. "Early, I appreciate punctuality."

I liked Ivan already. I felt comfortable handing over my only family heirloom to him. "Here it is," I began. "I trust your expertise in the framing and any restoring you see fit. How long do you expect the project to take?"

Ivan didn't respond. He was gazing at the photo, entranced by Lilith's beauty. I'd seen that look many times before.

"Ivan? How long do you expect the process to take?" I repeated.

"Oh, I am sorry Miss Banner, the woman in the photo is stunning." I smiled and nodded. "You look like her," he added.

I found that hard to believe, but tried to be gracious. "Thank you."

"It will be about two hours." He was still staring at the image. "Barnes & Noble is just down the street, if you like bookstores." He waved in that direction and started to head into the back of the shop, so I took the hint and saw myself out.

"Be back in a couple hours."

ELIAS

It had been a frustrating day, to say the least. I had frequented five different electronic stores to no avail. Each one sent me to the next. However, I called ahead and the customer service person assured me he had the correct cord for this clearly outdated PC. I got off the L at Adams. The streets were busy this morning.

I glanced at the piece of paper with the store's address, thinking I wanted to head west from the platform. I looked east just to be sure—and saw a flicker of a familiar face. He had found me, Yanni had found me. He must have decided two failed attempts of my capture was inadequate and he would just do it himself. I crouched slightly so that my six-foot frame fit in with the rest of the crowd. I considered jumping back on the train. *Piss—too late,* the doors were closing.

I darted down the stairs, swung a sharp left and sprinted across the lanes of traffic. I wanted to turn around to see if he was following me, but I knew he would be there and I need not squander energy on panic. I was digging my heels into the asphalt. He could undoubtedly outrun me. I was going to need some luck to get out of this alive.

I made the next right. The street was packed. This could either help my cause or simply cause a scene. I was in a major intersection and I required refuge. A café? No, too small—he would just create a spectacle.

The Art Institute? Perfect—multiple rooms to hide in and a mass of people. I darted into the street again. I heard his laugh behind me, faint but definite. I squeezed between two strangers in the lobby entrance, then turned around and saw that he was still standing on the other side of the street, staring with a grin that froze my soul.

Why was he not coming in after me? I wondered. There was no time to sort that out. If nothing else, he preferred to play with his prey. I casually turned around and headed toward the exhibits. Realizing I had not purchased an admission, I saw two emergency exits on the ground floor. I was not concerned with whether or not my exit sounded an alarm, that could be a welcomed distraction.

The alarm did not sound and I slipped out unnoticed. I took off running and found myself on West Jackson Blvd. another busy avenue. I ducked through clusters of people and when I still did not sense him behind me I spotted a small inlet behind a large building, a place to seek refuge or at least catch my breath. I knelt down for a few moments, my chest heaving and my heart racing.

When my chest stopped burning it was time to get out of here. I would find what I needed elsewhere. I turned right and began sprinting down the narrow alley toward the noise of the street and the crowds. I stepped forward into the mainstream of pedestrian traffic, just as a young woman hurled herself into my path. As we collided, I felt an electric shock wave surge through me, down to my toes. *Did she just try and taser me?* I wondered. *No, it could not be, she was still sitting on her bum on the sidewalk about to be trampled.* I reached down to help her to her feet.

"Oh, I am so sorry—piss! I did not see you. Are you OK? Hurry get up before you get trampled."

She looked up at me as if she had never fallen down before and did not know what to do. This was no time to dilly-dally. I reached for her wrist, and the electrical impulse once again surged up my arm. I let go immediately. But it was too late, it was already done.

OPHELIA

As I entered Barnes & Noble I saw a young man to the left of the door sitting on the cement. He didn't look homeless, he looked lost. I paused for a moment, and as he saw my hesitation, he jumped to his feet.

"Hmmmm, aren't you a pretty one," he said. "Do you know who you are?" The question caught me off guard. Did I know who I was? I don't know—did I? As I took a step back, he stepped forward. "Well do you know who you are? I know who you are." He smiled. I don't think he was trying to scare me, he seemed genuine, that was the scary part. I turned to the entrance of the bookstore and fumbled to get inside. I studied him as I stood there in the middle of the entryway, foot traffic clearing on either side of me. He just continued to stare, surveying me like I was the lost one, and didn't know it.

I turned around and made a beeline for the escalator. I didn't know where I was going, I just knew I was getting out of there. He continued to look after me as I elevated up to the second story. Chills ran down my spine and I shook my hands as if to shake the disturbed feelings right out of me. For the first time ever, I was relieved when I reached the second story and a child was throwing an all-out temper tantrum. The mother was so embarrassed that I could feel her humiliation wash over me and I was able to distract myself from my own jumbled thoughts.

I stepped around the terrible toddler and into the café. I needed something to drink, anything. I ordered an ice tea and sat down until my knees stopped trembling. A few deep breaths and I almost felt normal. *What was that about?* I wondered. Of course, I knew who I was —how could *he* know better than me? He was a stranger, a vagabond. I'd never seen him before. I don't know what really jarred me, what he said or how he looked at me. I felt violated, like he could see things I didn't even know were there.

I felt my knees get wobbly again. I had to get it together. I took a couple sips of my tea.

Was I crazy? What had just happened and why had it sent me into such a tailspin? I stared up at the room's crown molding, I felt sick.

I couldn't remember ever feeling so shaken in my life, and it seemed so silly. I pulled out my cell phone and looked at the time. I had about an hour before I needed to head back to the framing shop. I finished my drink and was feeling much better, so I moseyed over to the fiction section. I had some favorite authors that I could always count on for a good quick read. I found two novels I thought would do the trick. One about a female detective I loved and the other about a female bounty hunter. I was excited to have a good book to occupy me at the airport and on the flight back the next day. I genuinely hated to fly. It didn't seem natural to me. If god had wanted us to fly he would have given us wings.

Then there was the other aspect of flying I hated. It was bad enough half the time I didn't understand my own feelings, but put me with hundreds of people cramped into a cylinder and there was nowhere to hide from their tornado of emotions. There were those who were afraid of flying, those excited about their new destination, those who were sad about departing the previous location, screaming children—you name it. All the chaos of an emotional typhoon trapped in an inexplicable flying metal tube. If my love for travel didn't drastically outweigh my fear of flying I would be content to live the rest of my life with my two feet on the ground.

As I grabbed my purchase and ambled towards the exit I got more anxious. Would that guy be waiting for me outside the door? I swallowed hard. There was only one way to find out. I looked around and didn't see him so I dashed for the door and took a sharp left. I was walking at a fast clip, dodging and weaving through the steady stream of pedestrians.

When I arrived back at the frame shop, Ivan wasn't at the counter, so I just stood there awkwardly in the middle of the store. I shook my hands again, once more attempting to dislodge the uneasiness in the pit of my stomach.

Then suddenly he appeared. "Miss Banner. Early again and just in time." He looked very proud of his work as he paraded the framed photograph over to me. It looked fantastic. Ivan had picked the perfect matting and frame. The color of the beige matting lightened the photo while the chocolate frame warmed the image.

"Thank you, Ivan, that's perfect." I beamed back at him. My anxious encounter with the young man completely dissolved as I thought, *I hope Eleanor likes it*. I paid Ivan and was eager to get back to Simon's house before it got too late. I waved goodbye as I closed the door to the shop.

I looked to my left, trying to remember the fastest way to the train station. I looked to my right and there he was—the young man from the bookstore, standing three feet away and staring at me with that same disturbed look on his face. I froze. How did he find me? Had he followed me while I wasn't looking, or was it a horrible coincidence that he happened upon this street? Then I quickly turned on my heels and strode away. I could hear footsteps close behind me, but didn't want to look and see if it was him. I just walked faster, narrowly avoiding collisions with other pedestrians.

I turned left onto a busy street, and only then did I turn around to see if I'd lost him. I thought I saw his head bobbing about ten people back, so I ran the stretch of the whole next block. I didn't even know why I was running—I only knew I was afraid of what he might say, of what he might have seen in me. I could hardly catch my breath by the time I made it through the next intersection. I put my hands on my knees and tried to remember how to inhale.

The rush of people around me was making me sick. I felt like I was swimming in my own head, no, not swimming—drowning. I pressed my back against the wall of the closest building. My feet were still in the way, though, and a woman flipped me off as she stumbled over my right foot.

I saw a way out. A narrow lane between the buildings a few yards ahead of me: *a refuge,* I thought, as I stumbled through the crowd. Just as I attempted to retreat into the passage, someone came hurtling out of the alley and knocked me on my ass. I felt a shock pulse through my body.

"Oh, I am so sorry—piss! I did not see you. Are you OK? Hurry get up before you get trampled."

His voice sounded so familiar. I was still trying to regain my composure and get to my feet when his arm reached down and clasped my wrist. Whoa there it was again—a pulsating sensation coming from his hand. This time he felt it too, and he let go of my arm immediately.

I looked up and into his eyes. They were a rich hazel with mesmerizing, caramel-gold centers. For a brief, but intense, instant it felt like they penetrated my soul at a depth I'd never experienced before. He looked terrified, amazed and bewildered all at once, and with that he backed up into the narrow corridor as I fumbled around to find my footing.

I finally managed to climb to my feet, but when I looked down the alley, he was gone. The image of his eyes was still burning in my mind. I stepped further into the passage and could smell a faint sweet woodsy scent. Was that his aroma? It was intoxicating. I closed my eyes to better consume the fragrance. Again, his eyes flashed across the backside of my eyelids. I felt lightheaded. *What the hell had just happened?* I leaned against the brick wall for so long I lost track of time and place.

~

My phone buzzed in my pants pocket, jarring me back to the present. Shit! It was my mother. I pressed the ignore button on the phone and tried to gather my thoughts, but a couple minutes later it buzzed again. I pressed ignore again. I started in the direction of home.

Eleanor called me again. She never liked being ignored. I finally answered it when I was close enough to give an estimated time of arrival.

"Hey Mom, sorry I'm running late. I'll be home in less than thirty minutes and explain everything." She didn't even acknowledge what I said, instead telling me I needed to clean up the mess Tim left in her bathroom and that she noticed I was getting chubby and I should watch it, if I ever wanted anyone to love me. Then she hung up. Yep that was Eleanor.

I gritted my teeth and sifted through the evening's plans. It was still early enough to be on time for the reservation I'd made at her favorite restaurant. Tomorrow was her birthday, but tonight was my last night in town. She was upset of course, I'd have to explain my extended absence. I detested lying, but all would be revealed at dinner and I hoped my gift would be enough to quiet Eleanor and her nonstop assaults on me.

I spent the train ride trying to imagine a wonderful night with my mother—a rarity—but every time I closed my eyes I again saw those compelling caramel-gold irises encompassed by hazel rings. Not even the jam-packed train car, the sick woman to my left, or thinking about the other man—the one that had seemed to follow me—could fully distract me from mulling over those eyes, the woodsy scent and the jolt the mysterious stranger had given me with his touch.

I knew I had to get it together soon, though, or Eleanor would know I wasn't focusing on her. As I walked the eight blocks to Simon's house I took several deep, cleansing breaths.

ELIAS

I almost missed the stop. She gave no indication that this was where she was getting off. I followed a distance behind, afraid she would spot me. She was lost in thought, I could tell.

I studied the way she walked, her posture. I had known since I was a child that she was out there. That when we met my whole world would change—the prophecy was clear. But I had no idea I would feel this way, like I had been struck by lightning. Now nothing else mattered. My life's mission was to keep her safe.

She turned onto an average suburban street. Was this where she lived? I stayed at the corner and hid behind a neighbor's large oleander bush. She paused at the door of the fourth house down. She looked leery. *Maybe I should get closer,* I wondered, *perhaps she was entering a dangerous situation*. She rolled her shoulders back and braced herself for an unknown battle, determination on her face.

Then she entered the residence and was gone from my sight. I decided I would wait. Wait to see where she went next and how I could get closer to her—and to formulate my succeeding move. This was terrible timing. I was being hunted in Chicago, I needed to get away from here. But I could not just leave her. I had no idea how I lost Yanni this afternoon. I should have been dead. Something else must have caught his attention, or he was sent to run another, more important, errand.

Whatever the reason I lucked out, but I would not be so lucky a second time—and neither would she if anyone else found her.

I will sit and wait until I know more, I told myself. *Until I can be sure she is safe.*

OPHELIA

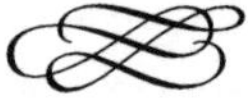

I opened the front door. There they were, sitting in the living room, staring at me like I had just breached curfew and was about to get a good talking to. So, I did what any adult would do—I walked right past them and ignored that there was any problem at all.

"Tim fixed the sink?" I asked as I moseyed down the hall. My mother said nothing and stayed put. *Uh oh,* I thought, *this could be worse than I thought.*

I turned into the bedroom deciding on a plan of action. I looked at the clock, the reservation I made for dinner was in just over an hour. I needed to get her moving.

I was sure Eleanor was out there preparing her assault rifle. Time to take my chastisement.

I stepped into the living room. She didn't move.

"Sorry I was so late," I said. "But I made reservations at that Italian place you love. Dinner is at 6:30." Nothing, she gave me nothing.

"That sounds great Olly," Simon jumped in, nodding in approval. It was a tough crowd but at least I'd got a little acknowledgement. I decided to let it be. As soon as I did the woman came to life.

"What was so important, Ophelia, that you had to spend the whole day with Cathy? Did someone die? You come here once a year. The least you could do is spend the entire time with your only parent. I mean really is that too much to ask? You are so busy with your life on the West Coast that you can't tear yourself away from your work and friends. Then when you come here you are too busy to spend time with your aging mother as well?" The aging comment meant she *did* think I forgot her birthday. I tried not to smile.

"Mom, I am sorry. Time got away from me," I said. "I will make it a point to get out here more often." I knew I'd broke through a little because she swiveled around in her chair. Her expression was still stern. I took a second to admire my mother, she was turning 45 tomorrow and I had to admit she looked good. Five foot one but a presence that demanded attention none the less. She had porcelain skin, smooth and freckled like mine. Her auburn hair was long, thick and straight as a board. Despite the fact that the woman never stepped foot in a gym, a single day in her life, she was fit. She was curvy in all the right places and somehow maintained tone like a world class gymnast. Right now, her frigid brown eyes were throwing daggers at me.

"I don't know how I raised such a selfish child. But apparently some people aren't bothered by it, you seem to have friends. Cathy obviously still likes you after all these years. Some of my good sense must have found its way in there somewhere." There were all kinds of insults in that statement. But I just smiled and put my hand on her shoulder. There really was no use in arguing with her.

"I'll make a better effort to come stay more next year." I assured her again. I wanted to mean what I was saying, but I was sure my visits wouldn't increase in frequency. I generally detested lies and saw no good reason to, except to diffuse my mother.

Eleanor, however, manipulated the truth in any way necessary to optimize the effect of guilt on her victim. It wasn't until I was a teenager that I started to really decipher the difference between my mother's reality and everyone else's in the world.

"I suppose I could come to San Francisco more often too," Eleanor relented. "After all I do love their summers." I relaxed. Mission accomplished, with very little bloodshed on my part.

I moved on to dinner plans. "I am going to jump in the shower and start getting ready. We'll need to leave in a little over an hour."

"Don't forget to clean up the mess Tim made in my bathroom," Eleanor reminded me.

I quickly did so then skipped into the hallway and into my room. I rummaged through my luggage looking for something to wear. I felt good, all things considered, so I decided to put on my favorite dress. It was a 50's vintage high wasted burgundy number, from one of the thrift stores on Haight and Ashbury. It scooped down in the back and billowed slightly at the bottom. The dress hung just past my knees, in my opinion the perfect amount of leg. I would wear my pearls and my nice black pumps. A special outfit for a special occasion.

I sped through my shower, shaving my legs as quickly as a lady could, and chose not to wash my hair but dampened it in the hopes the wild locks would be tamable.

I stepped onto the bath mat and I examined my skin in the mirror. I wasn't a muss and fuss kind of girl—my typical makeup included a little mascara, eyeliner if it was necessary, and some lip gloss. My cheeks were naturally rosy and my myriad of freckles gave my skin a warm tone, despite my porcelain shade. My strawberry blonde hair—emphasis on the strawberry—was always unruly, with a chaotic curl that cascaded down past my shoulders in more of an avalanche than a wave. If I was lucky I would be able to get it to look more curly than frizzy.

I walked out of the bathroom and I felt pretty good about my work.

I entered the living room and Simon was in his La-Z-Boy, if he wasn't wearing something different I wouldn't have even known he had moved. Simon was tall, lanky and had strong cheek bones. He wasn't particularly attractive, but he wasn't ugly by any means. He was nearly bald which made his round face look rounder. "Your mother is getting ready," he said plainly. I looked at the clock above the fireplace. There were thirty-five minutes until our reservation and it would take fifteen minutes to get there.

I watched as Simon went back to zoning out in front of the television. He was a simple man. I wondered how happy Eleanor was in her marriage. I liked Simon, but I often worried about how Eleanor was doing. I wasn't one to talk, I couldn't carry a relationship to save my life. It wasn't that I didn't want one, I just could never find anyone that didn't share their deepest darkest skeletons in their closet on the first date. *But what if there was something different out there?* Without warning the strangers golden hazel eyes immediately clouded my thoughts and my knees got weak. My thoughts were interrupted by Eleanor entering the room.

"Olly, how do I look?" Eleanor did a twirl. "Simon never compliments me, so I have to hear it from someone." She gave him a hard look, and he said nothing.

"You look ravishing mother," I beamed at her. I knew that's what she wanted to hear, because that's what I would have wanted to hear. She beamed back. "Are you ready to go?"

"*I am,* but do you think Simon could bear to part with his precious television?" Simon turned off the TV and rose to his feet. Eleanor was already out the door. I think she realized I hadn't forgotten her birthday after all and that this dinner was a celebration of *her*.

Simon drove at a snail's pace. Luckily, we arrived at the restaurant in time to keep our table. The air was filled with the herbaceous scent of Italian seasonings. My mouth began to water.

Eleanor's exultation was infectious, and I welcomed it. "I simply love the ravioli here!" she exclaimed. "What are you going to get, Simon?" My mother could hardly contain herself.

"I'm going to get the prime rib," Simon mumbled.

"Simon, it's an Italian restaurant, you never get any Italiano," she huffed. "You are such a stubborn man."

"I think I'm going to try the alfredo. Have you had that here before, Mom?" I chimed in.

"No, but I'm sure it is fantastic." She sang. "Olly, what is the occasion tonight?" She knew the celebration was for her, but she wanted to hear it. I smiled and pulled my bag onto my lap.

"Well Eleanor—Mother —tonight is in celebration of you and your birthday tomorrow. You didn't think I had forgotten, did you?" She just shook her head, so I went on. "I stumbled across something recently in my storage boxes that I imagine you've been missing, so it seemed wildly appropriate to shine it up like a new penny and hand it back to its rightful owner." I pulled the parcel from its hiding place and slid it across the table.

Eleanor looked puzzled, unsure of what to make of the small gift. I could only imagine what was flying through her head. She was probably mad I re-gifted her something. But her curiosity was clearly getting the best of her. She silently unwrapped it, and when she realized what it was, she looked as if she was going to faint. I had never seen my mother so happy about anything. Her face lit up like New York City at night. She just stared at the photograph, her eyes filling with tears. She began swallowing hard to hold back the waterworks. Simon looked terrified. The prospect of an emotional tidal wave had him looking for higher ground. I was ready for it, I wanted to see it, I was wading in the waters.

She looked up at me and that did it. The tears began streaming down her face.

"Where did you…? I have been looking all over for this damn thing."

"It was in my old cedar chest, the one you sent with me to San Francisco two years ago. I stumbled across it wrapped up in some old newspaper at the bottom of my kindergarten mementos. I had it framed and restored here this afternoon. That's why I was so late to get home."

Eleanor continued staring at the picture. She looked a little more whole than I'd seen her in a long time—like she'd found a piece of herself that she thought she'd lost. I tried to burn it into my mind as the one and only time I had seen Eleanor speechless. The air thickened with sentiment like a batch of homemade pea soup and I reveled in it.

The server approached cautiously, unsure of whether to interrupt. "Are you all ready to order?" I was sad to see her disturb the moment, but I saw the relief on Simon's face and I couldn't help but chuckle.

"I think we are, Miss," Simon answered, grateful.

She turned to me, ladies first. "For you?"

"Well I think I would like to order a bottle of champagne to celebrate." I pointed to the second one on the wine list. "Then I would like the fettuccini alfredo please, with a salad to start." She continued around the table collecting orders. She was quick to get the bubbly to us, and I was so pleased to see how perfect the evening was turning out.

"I would like to propose a toast, to Eleanor," I said, happily. We all raised our glasses in unison. "Wishing her a very happy birthday." The mood of the table was in harmony, lighthearted and fun. We were drunk on the ambiance and our mutual desire for cheer—and of course the champagne helped.

ELIAS

I took pause one more time. *Was this the best thing for her or was I leading Yanni straight to her doorstep?* I reasoned, on one hand my presence here only put her in more danger, but on the other I could not protect her if I did not know anything about her. I decided to proceed.

I felt terribly intrusive as I cracked the window, slowly, unsure if they had a dog or a security system. *This is what needs to happen to ensure her safety,* I told myself. I just kept repeating those words over and over in my head, ignoring the anxious knot in my stomach.

Over the years I had done my fair share of breaking and entering. Sometimes my life took a very creative turn, but someday I would have to explain myself to her, and this just felt wrong.

This is what needs to happen to ensure her safety. No alarms sounded and I had yet to smell, hear or see a menacing Rottweiler. So, I drew my leg over the windowsill and entered the living room. The furniture was dated and worn, but it looked homey. I scanned the room for photographs, but I did not see her beautiful face anywhere. She either must not live here, or maybe she felt as though she was not photogenic?

The single-story house had a distinctively musty smell—the smell that unmoved furniture takes on after years of use and disrepair. I skirted through the kitchen and then down the hall, stopping a couple doors down. I smelled her. Her fragrance was emanating out of this room, it was far more intoxicating than the rest of the house.

The door was slightly ajar. I gently nudged it open and stepped into the cramped space. It was empty of people, but there was a suitcase laid out on the floor and clothes neatly laid out on the bed were female. I was careful not to move a thing, but if it was as it appeared—that she was only visiting— then I needed to find her next destination.

The bathroom left no further clues, only a pungent medley of smells. *If this was not where she lived, where was she from? What was she doing here in Chicago?* I opened a small drawer in the nightstand.

Aha! A small day planner. *People still use these things?* I thought. *Then what is your smartphone for?* The page easily opened to the current date, and out flopped a plane ticket to San Francisco, the flight was leaving in the morning and the name on the ticket read— Ophelia Banner. I made a note of the flight number and read the itinerary on the pages of the planner.

~~Visiting Eleanor~~
~~Picture restoration Ivan's~~
~~Patient confirmations~~
Pack for morning flight

The list went on and on, meticulously checked, all appointments accounted for and I can only assume when completed, crossed off. She had a system, that was for sure. I could see that whatever her occupation it required appointments with patients. I was certain the book would ultimately tell me almost everything I needed to know about her, but I was ready to get out of the house before someone came home.

To be honest, I really wanted to learn everything I needed to know about her—from her. I closed the planner, placed it back in the drawer, then slid back out the living room window. My thoughts were flooded with questions.

Ophelia Banner, where are you from? Who is Eleanor? Why are you here in Chicago? Ophelia ...Ophelia...Ophelia...

OPHELIA

After a phenomenal tiramisu, we began to wind down. I was sad to see the night end, yearning to ride the emotional high for a few more hours, minutes, even seconds. Simon had begun to hush, but I was still eager to let the buzz linger.

"Well, thank you Olly for a nice evening. I am very grateful for my gift," Eleanor said as I smiled. "Although you could have told me you had been holding onto it all this time, so I wasn't frantically looking for it. It was really selfish of you to not let me know, simply to get a little rise out of your mother." That was it. The buzzer had sounded and the night was officially over. Eleanor was back to her charming self. "After all," she continued, "you know this is the only picture I have of my mother. How would you feel if someone had kept the only family heirloom you had hidden, just to get a reaction?"

I took a deep breath. I would ignore her hectoring. There was nothing I could say to assuage the situation anyway. "Well happy birthday Mother. Shall we head out to the car?" I grabbed my purse from behind my chair. Simon was nowhere to be found. After I settled the bill, I meandered toward the parking lot. I was grasping at straws trying to replay the night and linger in the victory.

As soon as I shut my door and the car pulled away, my thoughts drifted. The mood inside was a somber one. I'd need to be up by five to pack, brew the coffee and get breakfast ready before I left.

I was going over my mental checklist when I began feeling extremely restless. Something in me was stirring.

We pulled into the garage and I fumbled for the door handle. I walked into the bathroom, my head filled with an assortment of ideas. I don't think anyone else noticed, but I felt something shifting inside me. My mind was consumed with possibilities, and I was intensely aware of a gaping hole in my life.

I didn't remember turning on the shower but I was soon under a steaming stream of water. It gently pounded my scalp in a rhythmic motion that was softly tapping on new thoughts and washing away old fears. I realized I had been settling for something less than ordinary—all to avoid the potential catastrophic pain of something failing that was extraordinary. For the first time in my life I was no longer afraid that there wasn't someone out there for me. I knew with absolute certainty that what I yearned for—what I needed and deserved—was without a doubt waiting for me to step out there and take it.

What was stirring this? I wondered.

ELIAS

I was unable to get any closer. I also could not let her out of my sight. I needed to be near her. But it was too dangerous to just walk up to her and say hello. Our encounter yesterday may have already put her life in jeopardy. It was only a blip on the radar, but if anyone was listening they may have picked up the signal. I had to ensure her safety.

I sat three rows back. Thank goodness Southwest had open seating —I could choose my vantage point. Her soft curls were tangled into a wild bun on top of her head. I could see she was in a hurry to leave when she got ready this morning, although unnecessarily so, because her flight was postponed due to weather until late afternoon. She spent a long day at the airport alone, drifting from one overpriced shop to the next.

Her sweater was worn and discolored, like it had been washed one too many times. I studied the gentle curve of the back of her neck and made note of every freckle. I could not have been more than five feet away but it felt like continents. At the same time, I gnawed the inside of my cheek fearing that my proximity would be like leading a trail of bread crumbs straight to her. I had done my best to ensure I was not followed. I dotted my I's and crossed my T's and utilized every evasion tactic I knew to leave no trace of my whereabouts after Chicago. She gripped the armrest as the plane took off. *Was she afraid of flying?* I wondered.

I glanced around the plane, no one looked menacing. *That is what makes our kind so diabolically dangerous though,* I thought. *We blend in with everyone.* I took a deep breath. *Get it together man,* I told myself. *You have to be stronger than ever now. You knew this day would come.* As if giving myself a pep talk right now was going to help abate this welter of thoughts and emotions.

As the stewardess passed her seat she lurched forward to grab her attention. I struggled to listen to what she was saying, but I could barely make out the words. The flight attendant hurried back with water and then carried on with her busy work.

I watched as she hastily took a sip and threw back her head, popping a small pill in her mouth. Yes, she must be afraid of flying. I wanted to hold her hand, to mollify her fears. She suddenly looked around, furiously attempting to make eye contact with those in view. She was looking for someone, or something. Her head shifted in my direction and I ducked behind the chair in front of me, inconveniencing the women beside me with my abrupt movements. I needed to stay out of view.

When we touched ground in the Bay area four hours later it was dark outside and much cooler. I again maneuvered my way out of her sight, watched as she gathered her luggage and ambled to the shuttle bus. I managed to situate myself just close enough to overhear her telling the driver her address. I flew to the taxi terminal and ushered a cab. I would have to chance that she would be safe from the airport to her home. I blurted out the address to my driver and quickly dialed the numbers to the only person I thought could help me in this desperate situation.

"Hello." I said. There was silence on the other end of the phone. "I need your help," I began. "I need you to protect someone very special." I waited a moment, then practically begged. "Please come to San Francisco as soon as you can."

I heard a deep sigh, then the phone went dead. He would be here soon. I tried to relax for the thirty-minute drive into the city, focusing on my breathing as I replayed the images I'd memorized of the contours of her neck. Her wavy, coppery hair blazed bright in my imagination as I fantasized about every twist and turn the strands gnarled into. I envisioned her fair, slightly dewy skin, speckled with faint freckles that made her undeniably cute, yet unbelievably sexy at the same time.

I arrived at the address before the shuttle bus. I studied the neighborhood. I did not know the Richmond district of San Francisco well, but it looked like a congregation of apartment buildings and small businesses varying from yoga studios to mom and pop restaurants. The streets were well lit and quiet this time of night.

I moved to the south side of her building, out of sight but still within view of the apartment's front door. Then I saw her shuttle coming up the street and my heart skipped a beat. I knelt beside the wall and held my breath in anticipation, unable to slow my quickening heartbeat at the prospect of being near her again.

She stumbled out of the van, smiled at the other passengers, and politely shut the door. Her bags were already on the sidewalk and the driver stood for a moment waiting for a tip, I presumed. She graciously handed him a small bundle of cash and walked to her front door. She let out a huge sigh as she gazed up at the building.

She went in, and soon a light flicked on two stories up on the right. I imagined what her apartment might look like. The shades were soon shut tighter, she was unwinding and going to bed. It was late and I needed to figure out where I was going to stay, preferably somewhere nearby so I could make sure she was safe until my more qualified contact arrived to assist. I walked two blocks down to California Street, but there were no hotels, since this was a more residential area of San Francisco.

I noticed a For Rent sign three apartment buildings down and across the street from her place, so I decided to investigate. If it was indeed vacant I could stay there for the night, and the next day find more suitable accommodations for the long term.

I picked the lock of the foyer door easily. The old Victorian building had simple hardware. I examined the mailboxes in the entryway. Everyone had a name except for 3b. Assuming that meant the third floor, I took the steps up two by two. Not being able to see the door to her building was making me extremely anxious. Someone could have already found her. I quietly knocked on the door to 3b, just in case it was occupied and the manager had just simply forgotten to put the new resident's name on the corresponding mailbox. After a few moments, I figured it must be empty.

I had to fiddle with that lock a little longer, as it was a new doorknob. Eventually, the door swung open and confirmed that the apartment was indeed vacant and consequently extremely stuffy. The carpet had clearly not been cleaned yet and the fridge was moldy. No matter. I hurried to the east-facing window in the kitchen. It was not the most convenient window, but it was the perfect vantage point for watching her apartment building.

OPHELIA

I stood staring out the window of my apartment. It was a gorgeous day in the city.

I had not slept well the night before, I had weird dreams about hazel eyes and oddly enough earthquakes.

I knew why the eyes were haunting me, I had hardly thought of anything else since I had gotten home, but it was bigger than that. Something had moved inside me and it felt permanent. It was as if my soul had shifted, realigning my being into a closer version of myself, a more real me, if that was possible.

For a moment, I felt a sense of completeness that I never imagined existed. That feeling was resonating, hanging out on the periphery of my world. I could see it, just out of reach but attainable. I felt hope.

I pulled my comfy armchair up to the window and sat down with my coffee.

My body tingled as I recalled the electrical impulse from the stranger I ran into on the street. *Could it be that my entire life shifted in that moment with one touch from a stranger?* I mused. I would never see that man again, I would never touch him again. If he was the reason for my soul shift then I was in trouble.

What a silly thought, I brushed it off. I would tailor my skin to fit my soul perfectly on my own. Then maybe the right person could come into my life. But first thing was first—I picked up the letter from the kitchen counter. I had gotten a notice for a significant increase in rent while I was in Chicago. What an excellent welcome home.

I couldn't afford this place anymore on my own. I needed to post an ad for a roommate, I sighed. I wasn't going to let just anyone live with me, and finding the right fit could take time. I had a busy day ahead. I needed to clear out the spare bedroom so my new roommate could see the potential.

It was a new chapter in my life and it was going to be the best one yet. I took one more big sip of my coffee and a good long look out my window, admiring the blue skies like an umbrella over my beloved Richmond district, bordered by both Golden Gate Park and the Presidio. Then I rolled my sleeves up, braced my shoulders for the hefty work ahead and marched into the spare bedroom to begin my chores.

PART II

OPHELIA

A YEAR AND A HALF LATER

Lucas is very handsome in a rugged kind a way, I thought as I considered his attributes. His dark eyes were warm, yet brooding, and melted perfectly into his olive skin. And his wavy brown locks framed his face in such a way that most people took the time to stop and stare at him, as if observing a unique piece of art. His smile was huge—it engulfed an entire room in a moment. His teeth were not quite perfect, but in a perfectly characteristic and appealing way. His body was, for lack of a better word, *delicious.*

I felt so calm when I was around him, it was an aura he gave off. He never gushed all over me with his innermost secrets the way most people did. He just seemed content and sheltering.

I admired him so much for that, and I was astounded how reliant I had become on him, the one person I knew would never falter, never waiver. I often wondered if I loved him. Sometimes I felt like I did. I wondered if he loved me. We had been living together for over a year and I frequently caught him looking at me when he thought I didn't see him. Sometimes I'd catch a look of admiration, and from time to time I thought I saw yearning flash across his face. I woke up many nights feeling like he had been watching me while I slept, making sure not even my dreams were able to hurt me. He was very protective—but I couldn't tell if it was in the big brother way or something more.

I stared at the photo of the two of us above our fireplace. I honestly couldn't imagine my life without him in it. He had become a fixture, permanently stationed in my reality. No one I had ever known before him could put my mind at such ease. I never questioned his motives or intentions quite simply because he never did anything to hurt me.

Since the day we met for coffee to discuss the available room in my apartment, I'd felt completely safe with him. It was an odd sensation for me because I had never felt completely safe with anyone. His presence in my life was clearly invaluable. He enriched every experience we had together with his sly smile and sharp humor.

I heard keys in the door. He was home from work a little early. I turned to greet him.

"Hey there mister, you're home early."

He slipped off his shoes, "Yeah I have to take an emergency trip down to Bakersfield—one of our distributors screwed up an order big time and I have to go save their ass." He kissed me on the cheek as he passed me on the way to his room.

"Oh, what a bummer! I'm making your favorite tonight, lasagna." I smiled impishly. It was supposed to be a surprise. He paused for a moment in the hall and took a good whiff of the air, as the ground turkey and tomato sauce aroma danced faintly across the room.

"Well shit, I wish I could stay, I love your lasagna." His voice was muffled as he paraded around his room packing an overnight bag. I was disappointed. I leaned against the doorjamb with a pouty lip.

"When will you be home?"

"Early Sunday morning." *Two days, that sucked.* We usually went to the park on Saturdays and rode our bikes, or hiked in the Muir Woods across the bay. I had looked forward to hanging out with him that weekend.

"OK, well I'll save you some leftovers," I said, my voice forlorn. He peeked out from his closet and looked at my pouty lip. A shit eating-grin spread across his face.

"Olly, I'll be home before you know it." He walked over and kissed my forehead. "I'll miss our Saturday ride too. We'll make it an extra-long one next weekend." He zipped up his bag. I slowly retreated down the hall.

I guess I could call Gil then, I thought dejectedly. *I made enough dinner to feed a football team. Someone else ought to enjoy it with me.* I could rent a movie and we could drink wine and talk girl talk. That wasn't always easy with Lucas hanging around the house. I'd call her as soon as he left. Though she probably had plans—most normal people did on a Friday night.

The water turned off in the bathroom and I heard Lucas's footsteps coming down the hall. I was still sulking and knew that it would do no good for either of us, but I persisted.

"Stop frowning!" he teased. "Didn't Eleanor ever tell you that your face could get stuck that way?" I straightened up right away the moment I realized I was acting just like her.

His work had never gotten in the way of our routine in the past. The control freak in me was flipping out. Lucas was like a well-oiled machine, never late, never early, always right on time.

Our schedules paralleled each other's so we were usually home at the same time every night, and left at the same time every morning. I was a creature of habit, so I adored the consistency.

"Really Olly," he continued. "Is this that big of a deal? I'll be right back. I promise."

"No, you're right, it isn't. I just realized it's the first business trip you've ever taken."

"Oh, I see your inner control freak is perturbed." He laughed. I retaliated with a solid slug to his shoulder. He knew me so well. "I agree it's inconvenient. It'll never happen again. Cross my heart." He motioned a cross over his chest. I didn't see how he could make such a ridiculous promise when situations with work were out of his control, but I felt a little better anyway.

He grabbed his lunch pail and his overnight bag and headed for the door. I stood in the kitchen trying to remember where I'd put my phone to call Gil.

"See you on Sunday, stay out of trouble." With that, he closed the door behind him. I heard the top lock click. I rifled through my purse for my phone, and called Gil. It went straight to voicemail. I didn't leave a message, there was no point. Pajamas, wine, and a TV movie would have to suffice.

I looked at the thermostat, 65 degrees. I rummaged through my drawers looking for another sweater to put on as I tried to remember what I did with myself before Lucas and I had become friends and housemates.

I'd posted the ad on Craigslist on a Tuesday, two days after I'd arrived home from Chicago, and by that Friday evening Lucas was moved in. He had just left a relationship and needed a place ASAP. We hit it off so well, our lives blended naturally almost immediately.

Sometimes I wondered if I was as good a friend to him as he was to me, though. He was never very ardent about sharing details of his life. I didn't even know the name of his ex-girlfriend. Lucas was always quick to let things go and move on, so I let him. He never vented or dwelled on anything—it was effortless to be around him. I liked, and needed that.

We had so much fun together, we laughed constantly. I guess I took him for granted, because I didn't even consider what I would do if he ever left or met someone new and wanted to spend time with them instead of me. I was surprised how upset I was with him leaving for Bakersfield. *I need to spend more time with my other friends,* I told myself, *so I won't be devastated when he finally moves on.*

My stomach grew queasy just thinking about it. *Lucas leaving me would be horrible,* I assessed. I didn't know what to make of these feelings. *I must be in love with him,* I decided. *Why else would I be so anxious by his absence?* It seemed obvious yet elusive. *What had kept us from ever pursuing anything beyond friendship? What we had was great. Were both of us afraid of messing that up?* I cleaned up the kitchen and seriously mulled over what being in a romantic relationship with Lucas would be like. I was missing an important piece of the puzzle—I'd been distracted and haunted by the glimpse of another man for the last year and a half. Lucas knew this—I had told him about my frequent dreams, all highly focused on the man with the golden-hazel eyes.

I'd dreamt of this stranger every night since I ran into him in Chicago. The dreams were always different, but he was the same. I could see nothing but his eyes. The ring of his familiar voice was as comfortable to me as the thunderous pounding of the ocean I could sometimes hear in the distance outside my window. I tried to dream of other things. I would meditate before sleep, focusing my thoughts on anything else. But when I closed my eyes there he was, staring into my soul, beckoning me to fantasize about his whereabouts, his life, his dreams, and his name.

Lucas repeatedly told me to forget about the stranger, to let him go. I tried, but there was an invisible cord that bound me tightly to him. I'd gotten good at redirecting my waking thoughts whenever he wandered into them. But when I was unconscious he danced around my head like a Broadway musical performer, stirring my imagination and enticing sensual fantasies.

I wonder if that's why Lucas never perused anything with me. He thought I was crazy to be obsessing over a stranger. If I could do that with a man I didn't know, maybe he was afraid I would become a real psycho with a man just down the hall. I'll admit it would be a precarious situation if a relationship with Lucas went badly, but how could it? We never fought or even annoyed each other. The idea that a man as handsome and successful as Lucas would be jealous of a complete stranger I would never see again was ridiculous too. Any woman would fall all over herself to be with him. I'd seen it happen more than once; others were intoxicated by him.

All of this reflection was making me hungry, so I threw the lasagna in the oven and jumped on the sofa. Nothing looked good on TV, so I opted to read while I waited. My mind, however, kept wandering back to either Lucas or the stranger. I focused as much as I could on my novel, reading every word purposefully. The kitchen timer went off and I about jumped out of my skin. As I devoured a piece of cheesy heaven, I poured a healthy glass of red wine and sat back down on the couch. Time to put in a movie. I chose a classic, *Dirty Dancing*. Few things were better than wine and a good chick flick.

The lasagna cooled and I wrapped it up and put it in the fridge, thinking of Lucas. I was three glasses into a bottle and feeling pretty warm and fuzzy. I had an urge to call him and check in. As I dialed his number I got excited. I missed his voice already. He answered on the second ring.

"Hey you, what's up? Bored already?" He sounded like he was smiling on the other end.

"A little...you missed the best lasagna I've ever made, hands down. Feel free to be jealous," I chided.

He laughed. "Oh really? Well good thing it gets better with time—I'm looking forward to having some when I get home."

"Good thing."

"I'm going to try and come home earlier. But in the meantime, I have bad news. I forgot my charger, of all things, and my phone is about to die. I'll probably lose you before the end of this conver..." There it was, mid-sentence. The phone went silent and I put it down on the back of the couch. *Well, that sucks.*

I took a deep breath. Hopefully he'd get home soon. I decided we needed to sit down and talk. I wanted to finally throw it all out there and see how we felt about each other. Our friendship was strong enough to be honest. If we both wanted to give an intimate relationship a chance we'd need to set up parameters, of course. I wasn't sure if I loved Lucas, but I knew that discussing it with him would help me get to the bottom of my feelings. I poured another glass of wine and snuggled under a blanket.

As the credits rolled I put my glass in the sink and chucked the empty wine bottle in the recycling bin. *I'll be able to fall right asleep tonight,* I promised myself. My cold bed did nothing to deter me from falling directly into a peaceful slumber.

~

MY HEAD FELT FOGGY, but my eyes shot open. *There was someone in my house*. I paused for a moment and tried my hardest to trace the intense animosity I could sense to a more comprehensible figure and location. *They were not in my house, yet,* but close. The invader's intent was suffocating. I quickly scanned my room. *Where was the nearest exit*? My mind was misty. I'd never felt such pointed fury—it felt like daggers being thrusted into my skin repeatedly. I had to concentrate. *What was I going to do*? I couldn't call Lucas, even if he wasn't hundreds of miles away, his phone was dead.

My heart was racing. I cast the blankets over my head, an instinct from childhood, I suppose—but completely useless in the face of danger. Suddenly the blanket was ripped off me. I fought to scream, but all I could manage were heavy terrified gasps. The intruder put his hand over my mouth and stared into my panicked face. It was him. The eyes looking back at me were the very ones that had prowled my dreams and my waking thoughts.

I wasn't afraid of him. I knew he was there to protect me. As he grabbed my arm a shock pulsated through my body. It was warm and familiar, like the day we'd run into each other. He lifted me out of bed and maneuvered me toward the fire escape. I was petrified of heights, and considered darting back into bed, willing to face my stalker rather than scale this building. The stranger saw my hesitation and grasped my arm harder, as another jolt of energy travelled up my arm. I slipped into my house shoes and crawled out the window.

Gently he lowered the ladder. My knees were trembling. He took the steps two by two, while I tried my hardest to just keep my knees from giving out completely. I wasn't moving fast enough—I could tell by his angst. He didn't look inpatient, just on guard, bracing himself for an attack. He grabbed me at my waist and my stomach turned as I felt vibrations warm my abdomen. He'd already lowered the next ladder and gracefully progressed down to the street, but I was far too short to get to the sidewalk from the end of the escape. I had an impulse to climb back up, but then I looked up at my window, there was a shadow inside. The golden-eyed man had no interest in me making other plans. He grabbed my legs and tenderly placed me on the ground. The strange pulses were now radiating from almost every part of my being. I was finding it hard to concentrate. *Was he feeling it too?*

The shadow was on the move. The stranger grabbed my hand and darted for the alleyway just past my building. He was fast—too fast for me to keep up. It was as if he was gliding on top of the pavement and not actually touching the ground. We turned down the alley and he quickened his pace as I stumbled. He paused only for a moment to throw me over his shoulder, knocking the wind out of me. His pace quickened yet again.

I heard the dumpster we'd just passed slam against the wall. There was something in this dark alley with us. I felt my breathing pick back up and thought I could hear footsteps—although it sounded more like barely audible fluttering wings. I was flopping around like a rag doll on my rescuer's shoulder, my body pulsating from the currents coming off his skin.

A car abruptly squealed to a stop immediately in front of us. The door flew open and I was tossed into the back seat. My head was throbbing with confusion. *Was I being abducted? Wait. Stop and think, Ophelia. You're with the stranger, the one from Chicago.* The car fishtailed as we took off, and profanity flew out of the driver's mouth at such a speed I wasn't sure that it was even in English, but it certainly was cursing. *Wait!* I thought. *I know that voice, that's Lucas' voice.* But it wasn't Lucas' car.

"Lucas? What the hell is going on?!" I tried not to sound panicked.

"Yanni is right behind us, speed up for Christ's sake!" The stranger yelled.

I turned around and saw the small figure of a man, doing what I could only describe as leaping after the car. *Oh my God, there is a man on foot chasing us,* I thought. *Why, or better yet, how?* The car whipped right and flung me across the seat.

"Put on your seatbelt Ophelia." Lucas' voice was calm but stern. I quickly gathered the first bundle of seatbelt I could find and slung it across my lap. *Click*. All of a sudden, the back end of the car sagged. It seemed to be dragging on the asphalt. The back window shattered and before I could look up to see what caused the collision the stranger was over my body, covering my head and screaming at Lucas in a language I'd never heard before. The car whipped around and was now facing the opposite direction, from what I could tell. Suddenly the rear of the car was back to its normal position and we were peeling out again.

I heard a voice and thought, *Is that me laughing? I'm dreaming, I must be dreaming.* The car shifted left and my head whipped right. *Shit this doesn't feel like a dream,* I thought as my laugh grew more guttural.

"Ophelia are you okay?" The stranger asked me and then snapped back at Lucas. "Where the hell were you? Is she okay? Don't drive so erratic, you're going to make her sick."

"I'm trying to save our lives. She'll be fine. She's stronger than you think. She laughs when she's scared. I think it's kind of cute." I could see Lucas' smirk in the rearview mirror.

I looked back again, hysteria in my voice. "He's still back there, that man chasing us, on foot." Again, the giggles overwhelmed me, floating out of the bellows of my stomach. "How can a man be chasing a car on foot?" I leaned over the driver's seat and saw that we were going about 135 mph down California St. I turned around again, "I think he's gaining on us." As soon as I said it, I felt ridiculous. A man was gaining on us going 135 mph. My laugh grew boisterously loud and my head began to swim and pound.

"I think she is going to pass out," our mysterious passenger announced, and as soon as the words fell from his lips I could feel darkness sweeping over my eyes like a heavy, rich curtain being drawn in a play. It made its way across my eyelids, and everything went dark.

ELIAS

When we were absolutely certain we had lost Yanni, I was able to digest how intensely furious I was. I glared at Lucas.

"Where were you?" I repeated. My voice mirrored my anger.

"Just back off. I wasn't far, obviously. I was just trying to make my quote-unquote job a little more believable. I thought she might be getting a little suspicious about how little time I spent actually working." Lucas did not make eye contact with me as he spoke. He just stared out the windshield.

I looked back at Ophelia's unconscious body in the back seat. I did not believe that pretext. There was something else amiss. I thought it might have been a ruse to encourage Ophelia to miss him. He was clearly smitten. But there was some other subterfuge occurring. He had never left her unattended before. I would need to put more thought into that at a later date. For the time being we needed to execute our safe house plan as quickly as possible.

"I suspect you had ulterior motives, Lucas," I began. "That being said, we need to work together, and that entails keeping the peace. She will be going through enough without us contending one another." He did not take his eyes off of the road as I spoke.

"Of course, I would do anything to make this all easier for her. Don't doubt that." He sounded insulted. I did not care, it was crucial that I make the parameters clear.

We pulled up to the hangar and I opened my door just as the car came to a stop, feet from the jet. I went to pluck Ophelia from the back seat but Lucas positioned himself between me and the door.

"It's still best if you keep your distance right now." He was not going to be dissuaded.

"Very well, carry her into the jet and then proceed with the plan. I expect you back here in two hours or we will depart without you." I turned around and waved at the attendants looking out the window. "Hello ladies, tell the captain that we ascend in two hours."

"Yes, Mr. Kraus," replied the blonde attendant as she headed toward the cockpit.

"Is she okay?" The other stewardess asked as Lucas placed Ophelia on the bed in the main aircraft chamber.

"Yes, she will be," I said. "She's just a little befuddled. It has been an eventful evening." I looked around for Lucas, but he was already in the car and driving down the tarmac. "I have to attend to a couple of errands before we depart San Francisco. I trust that you can chaperone Miss Banner for me?"

The stewardess nodded reassuringly.

"No one is expected back here except for Lucas and myself—do you understand? If you see anyone approach this runway other than the two of us, you follow emergency takeoff protocol, without hesitation. Am I making myself clear?"

"Yes Mr. Kraus." She looked nervous. I wished I could ease her fears, but I wanted her to be on edge. I would rather her be quick to act than fainéant.

"Very good." The other woman entered the room just as I was exiting the plane. "Please be vigilant, ladies."

I casually walked to the first hangar, unlocked the door and removed the cover from the car I had stowed there. As I slid the key in the ignition I made a mental list of what I needed to do to erase my habitation here in the city, as well as any clues to the research I had been doing.

I looked at the clock. I had a little over an hour and a half to put it all into motion. Plenty of time. I made the arrangements months ago. I put my foot on the gas and headed back to San Francisco.

OPHELIA

My head— no my neck—was aching, in that unpleasant way associated with lying in an awkward position for too long. *I must have had bad dreams last night,* I thought. Then it all came flooding back. I wasn't ready to open my eyes, but I knew I wasn't in my bed. *Where was I? What was the last thing I remembered?* I was in a car, it whipped to the right...well that explains part of the neck ache. A man was chasing us on foot... there was a stranger, no not *a* stranger, *the* stranger. I remembered Lucas, then darkness.

But this isn't a car, someone is carrying me. *Is it Lucas?* I was too afraid to open my eyes and they felt so heavy. I inhaled slowly, it was Lucas— it was his scent. He started talking to someone. He was communicating in words I didn't recognize, a strange language, soft but thick and full of syllables. He sounded mad. *Does this mean I should open my eyes?* No, I'd better wait. I heard another man's voice in the odd language. It didn't sound like anything I'd ever heard before. Suddenly I felt like I was being watched.

Now should I open my eyes?

"Ophelia." Shit, I'd been made.

I opened my eyes. "Hi Lucas." I tried to clear my throat, but it was scratchy and my voice was groggy—perhaps from the hysterical laughter, if I was remembering correctly. "Where am I?" I refocused by blinking a few times. We were on a tarmac, Lucas was cradling me in his arms, it was cold and I had no shoes on. I looked over Lucas' shoulder and saw a sleek black jet, it was dark and difficult to see the aircraft. Then I looked in the direction Lucas was carrying me and saw a black Mercedes. To my right was the stranger. "And who is he?" I was staring directly into the eyes of the man I had been fantasizing about. It was scary yet comforting at the same time, my soul seemed to shift ever so slightly in my skin, like the day we had collided into each other in Chicago. He didn't even blink. His gaze was just as fixed as mine. Lucas squeezed me tighter.

"Ophelia how do you feel?" Lucas said as he placed me in the back seat of the oversized sedan.

"I'd feel better if you would give me some answers." This time I looked directly at Lucas, giving him an "I mean business" look. The best I could muster while feeling so bleary. He slid in next to me and the stranger got in on the other side.

"Right now it's best if you rest."

My head felt really foggy, the sedated kind of foggy. "Did you guys drug me?"

"We needed to sedate you while we were flying across the Atlantic, we didn't want you to wake up on the jet and be anxious." Lucas was rubbing my left shoulder as he spoke.

I was trying to decide if this was upsetting to me or an act of kindness. The drugs had clearly not worn off yet and the effects were making it hard for me to think lucidly. I rolled my head to the other side as the car began to drive off the landing strip. There were *those eyes*, not more than three inches from my face. I felt a surge of tingles dance across my scalp. I lifted my heavy arm and pointed clumsily at the stranger and asked again. "Who are you? Are you rude or just evasive?" The words slurred together slightly.

"I am Elias Kraus and it is a pleasure to finally meet you Ophelia." I caught an English accent. I loved accents.

Lucas gently drew my face back to his. My lids were getting heavier and heavier, whatever they used it was potent stuff. He cupped my cheek in his hand and kissed my forehead. "Just let yourself rest a little longer, we have a long drive ahead."

"But...." Then my thoughts trailed off. I was back to sleep.

~

THE HUGE STRUCTURE loomed over us in the dark. I saw two figures at the top of some stone pillars scurry to lift the massive gate. As soon as Elias shut the door the Humvee was gone, barreling over the landscape like a blundering wildebeest.

I apparently slept through another vehicle change and my neck was the worse for wear because of it. I scrambled to put on the shoes Lucas had handed me and stood in amazement assessing the massiveness of the bastion. I had woken up about ten minutes earlier, finally out of the fog of the sedative and now I had questions, a lot of them.

Before I walked into a fortress I might never escape from—because let's face it in the last twenty-four hours I had been chased by a superhuman man, abducted and drugged. I was going to demand some information. I darted in front of Lucas, and shouted "Stop!"

"Look, Lucas, I need some answers before I go in there. Please don't make me threaten to leave, because I really don't want to be ambling around God only knows where in the middle of the night. But I will do it if you two don't at least tell me what kind of situation I'm about to embark on once we get in there." I wearily looked up at the castle again.

They both moved so quickly I didn't even have a chance to flinch. Lucas threw me over his shoulder as Elias bounded into the castle one step ahead, lowering the heavy wooden door as we traipsed across the entry. Lucas swung me around to cradle me in his arms like a newly wedded couple crossing the threshold. This wasn't a fortress at all, it was a prison—my prison. Tears welled up in my eyes, I was so angry. I started to squirm away from him. As I did I felt his lips part only centimeters from my ear.

"I will explain this all to you very soon, Olly. Trust me." With that he put me down. I was furious, but in his face I could see he was telling me the truth. I looked down at my feet, I was pretty sure they still worked, but the way I was being taxied around I was starting to doubt they served a purpose anymore.

I didn't know what time zone we were in, and to be honest I didn't even know how many days had passed since we had been chased by Superman. I needed to get back to my own life and handle business, literally my business. I needed to at least call patients and cancel appointments until further notice. I was booked three months out. I didn't even know where to start, and I didn't have a cell phone or my calendar. The life I'd built for myself seemed of no consequence to them.

"Lucas, I need a phone. I have appointments I need to cancel." I heard a giggle behind me, but there was no time to turn around and see who it was. "I can't just leave my business unattended." He turned around as he prepared to climb a massive medieval-looking staircase.

"I've already taken care of it. No one is expecting you back in the office."

"What? When did you 'take care' of it?!" My voice rose with each word.

"While you were sleeping on the plane."

"You what? What gives you the right?!" He wasn't listening. He was climbing the stairs rapidly.

"I'll be right back, Olly," Lucas called down, now at the third story of a great courtyard.

The giggling behind me had persisted so I turned to face my cackler and take some of my frustration out on them. It was a young girl, no older than fifteen. She was gorgeous, with long golden hair down to her waist. She had caramel-colored skin that looked almost luminescent and as smooth as silk. Her eyes mimicked the color of her locks, her lips were a soft pink and her cheeks looked sun-kissed. She was wearing a violet gown that fell just above her ankles and it fit her seamlessly, accenting every important curve, discreetly and sensually at the same time. Her beauty mesmerized me for a moment and I couldn't concentrate. I was enchanted.

"Di, enough. Can't you see the poor girl is dealing with enough already," a tall man said as he stepped out from behind an adjacent pillar. The young woman ran off chortling. I shook my head, my thoughts still tethered to the image of such a perfect girl. As my eyes shifted to the man, I saw that he was beautiful as well, with strong features, long dark hair and pale radiant skin. He smiled at me.

"Pay no heed to Di, she is having a little fun at your expense. I am Aremis. It is nice to meet you Miss Ophelia." He took my hand into his. I would have usually pulled away from such an intimate gesture by a complete stranger, but I couldn't.

"How did you know my name?" My thoughts were finally starting to articulate into full sentences again.

"Aremis, we will save introductions for a later date," Elias interrupted, reaching for my arm, when out of nowhere Lucas was between us.

His voice rang in my ears "Don't touch her—I'm having a hard-enough time as it is camouflaging her!"

Elias calmly stepped back. His stare could have bore a hole right through Lucas' face. "Of Course." Although the words were of compliance, the tone was sarcastic.

"Watch it, Viraclay." Lucas scoffed. The words that followed were in that odd language, but even I was getting the message. I turned around to see that Aremis was patiently waiting on the other side of the room. Perhaps sizing both men up, considering which one he'd be able to thwart if the altercation progressed. I also noticed at least four other sets of eyes in the shadows of the castle. I wasn't frightened by the fact that their eyes all seemed to glow. I was alarmed that I had no idea how many people were really among us. After a long stare down, both men drew their glare away from each other and looked back to me. Elias began to walk away. I was confused. *What did I miss?*

Lucas took my hand in his and steered me towards a corridor.

"What just happened there?" I asked. "Why did you call him Viraclay? I thought his name was Elias? And what language is that?" I also wanted to ramble on about who was watching us with glowing eyes, where had he come from when I just saw him walk three flights of stairs, and for Christ sake, where the hell am I? But instead I waited for his response.

"There are some precautions that need to be taken for your safety."

I interrupted him. "What does that mean?" He stopped and looked at me.

"This means that certain security measures must be followed, so as not to set off any alarms." He turned back around and continued walking. *What was I missing here, was I booby trapped?* I lifted up my arms to look at my sleeves and make sure. I didn't want one of those things going off accidentally on me. *Why was I being protected, and from what?*

"I called him Viraclay because it's his nickname. The language is called Asagi."

What the hell was Asagi? Should I push my luck and ask more questions? I wondered. I usually read people so well, but I never could read Lucas. He wasn't like anyone else. I decided it was best to sort through the questions first.

The passageway got darker and colder as we walked. Finally, he stopped in front of a huge metal door. It had a lock on the outside, which made me nervous. I knew we were entering my prison cell. He opened the door and we stepped inside. The room was gorgeous and warm. A huge fireplace consumed half of the far wall. There was an enormous bed with four ornate gold posts, and purple lace avalanched from the ceiling and down along either side. The room was not enclosed with the cold cement blocks that appeared to line the rest of the castle, but instead a rustic wood.

The chamber was lit with over a hundred small lavender-scented candles. It looked like something from a fairy tale. I couldn't have dreamt up a more romantic setting if I tried. Under different circumstances I may have tried to fantasize a similar scenario with the exact man I was currently in the presence of, but at this moment I knew this apartment served a very different purpose and I was pretty sure this ambiance was a ploy in order to keep me compliant. There were two stunning oversized chairs near the fireplace and a bar just to the right of that, fully stocked from what I could see. *I could really use a glass of wine.*

Lucas walked to a door in the furthest corner and stepped through it. I followed. It was a luxurious bathroom with a Jacuzzi tub and a shower with five showerheads—and enough space to fit a soccer team. I would have thought I'd died and gone to heaven if I didn't have such a creeping feeling crawling up from the pit of my stomach. Neither room had a single window.

"I hope this will keep you comfortable for a while," Lucas said. He sounded earnest. "I had your favorite wine delivered and your favorite author's work compiled and organized on the bookshelves." He began to walk towards the door, and then added, "I also arranged for some clothes that should fit you." He gestured towards the only other door in the room. "I know you've been through a lot and you have a great deal of questions that deserve answers." He paused. "Be patient and know that I would never do anything to intentionally hurt you." With that he walked out of the room. I heard an almost inaudible clicking noise. I knew this was the lock fastening the door shut.

LUCAS

I hate this fucking place, I fumed as I walked solemnly up the stairs. It reminded me of Yessica. Every brick, every corridor—every damn thing about it. She'd loved it here. We spent summers within these walls. Long before Elias was even born, we had already lived lifetimes in this countryside.

It wasn't that I didn't think about her always, because I did. It was more that I felt this strange conflict being here with Olly. Up until now the lifetime I spent with Yessica didn't overlap with the time I have spent with Ophelia. Now I felt like I was betraying Yessica's memory by sharing this place with another woman that I loved.

Of course, Olly and I weren't in the same room, and it definitely was not the same purpose for our stay. Yessica was never sequestered while we resided here. I didn't know how long Ophelia was going to let me get away with that either. Olly hated not having control of her situation.

I stood at the door for a moment, I was afraid. Afraid of what ghosts lie in wait on the other side of it. This was our room, our home away from home. Neither Yessica nor I were ever much for planting roots, but if we had the urge to slow down, this is where we would find refuge. In this space, with the camaraderie of our dear friends Cane and Sorcey.

"Stop whining Lucas." I said the words out loud and turned the knob.

The room looked the same. Why would it have changed? We were the only guests that ever insisted on staying on the third floor. Now more than ever I valued the privacy. I wasn't in the company of my dear friends anymore, I was in some ridiculous love triangle with Ophelia and Elias.

I opened the window to let the breeze cleanse the room of the musty smell that accompanies a place that hasn't been used in years. I sat on the bed and looked at the large mirror on the vanity. Memories flooded my mind's eye. I'd spent hours brushing Yessica's long black hair at that vanity. One of her favorite things in life was the sensation of someone else playing with her hair. She had an abundance of it too —thick black Mongolian hair that fell to her knees.

I threw myself onto the bed. This was going to be a real challenge. Protecting Olly, trying not to kill Elias, and drowning in memories of Yessica. What the hell had I signed up for? I must learn to think these things through better, be less impulsive. As I thought the words I heard them spoken by Yessica as she had done thousands of time. Then she would laugh and say, "Who the hell am I kidding? I know who I married."

I sat up again. Ophelia wasn't the only one locked into a situation without any control. I was lost on memory lane and would be stuck here indefinitely. I reached for the closest thing I could throw, a book on the night stand, one of our favorites. It hit the wall and the binding split, I didn't feel the slightest bit of relief.

OPHELIA

After a long bath and a half a bottle of Cabernet I was feeling much better. Lucas had returned and asked if I felt like eating but I really didn't have an appetite. I sat in one of the oversized chairs near the spirited fire that licked the top of the hearth. It was warm and my body was peaceful, while my mind was tormented with uncertainty. I'd hoped the wine would quiet my anxiety, but it didn't. I stared at the mantel.

As I poured myself another glass of wine my thoughts turned to the mysterious man I had lived with for the past year and a half. *Who was he really? Could I even say I loved him? I obviously didn't know him. Would I ever know him?* I felt so betrayed, still for some reason I wasn't angry. An eerie serenity washed over me, an acceptance that I didn't know this man, friend and confidant but I was sure whatever the reason for this dishonesty, it was in my best interest. It was an odd paradox of emotions. It felt like it had been years since I'd wanted to discuss an intimate relationship with Lucas, not a matter of days.

I couldn't see having that discussion now. I couldn't possibly be in love with Lucas since I knew nothing about him except the façade he'd so cunningly kept up day in and day out. I looked around the room. *I may not know him,* I thought, *but he knew me. Everything about this prison cell screamed Ophelia.*

He had been taking detailed notes of my likes and dislikes, from the books to the closet full of clothes that were indisputably my style. Half the items had polka dots. I loved polka dots. The shoes were practical and cute. I don't know if I could have picked out a wardrobe for Lucas that would have been as fitting.

I wondered if it was a collaborated effort. Did Elias scrutinize me that closely as well? It was apparent that he had been watching me for quite some time too. The thought of Elias sent a shock down into my abdomen. I felt my lower belly tingle with anticipation for our next exchange. It was still so surreal. I never thought I would see the man with the golden eyes again. He'd plagued my thoughts for so long, and now here we were under the same roof.

I closed my eyes and took a deep breath. I needed to demand answers. I hoped Lucas was sincere. I had to find a way to feel in control of something in my life, before I went crazy.

My right side was stiff and my eyes were heavy with the kind of drowsiness that follows excessive hours in bed. I hadn't seen any reason to get up. I didn't know if I was going to see anyone else today. I rolled around, stretching and contorting my body, trying to revive myself gently. When I finally sat up I saw that I was not alone in my room.

I grabbed the blanket and drew it around my body. I felt exposed, although I was in pajama pants and a T-shirt. At the other end of my bed stood a petite young man. He looked no older than 16. His skin shimmered in the still-raging fire, and he held in his hand a tray of food: eggs, bacon, sausage, toast, a fruit bowl—just about anything a person could want for breakfast. It wasn't until I looked down at the tray that the savory scents of the meal tickled my nose.

I didn't know if I should say anything. We both just stared at one another while the smell of the food started to make me salivate. I hadn't eaten for hours, perhaps days, I couldn't be sure. I became intensely aware of my hunger and almost leapt over the bed and tackled him for a slice of bacon.

He smiled at me. His teeth were perfectly straight and dazzling, and his skin was very fair in contrast to his black hair. His eyes were a deep chocolate brown that expressed a depth to his soul. I sensed that even though he looked like a young teenager, he was in fact much older.

Finally, he spoke. "My name is Winston, it is a pleasure to meet you Miss Ophelia." He walked towards the side of my bed I lay closest to. "I have the pleasure of serving you breakfast. And if you will have me, I would like to keep you company while you eat." Another brilliant smile flashed across his face.

"Okay," I said, coolly. It seemed rude not to let him join me after he'd delivered me breakfast in bed.

Winston handed me the tray and he took his seat at the end of my bed, all the while staring at me with intense curiosity. I placed my napkin on my lap. The bacon was cooked perfectly, and was just the right temperature.

"Have you been here long Winston?"

"Only a few hours."

How the hell was the food still warm then? I wondered. Not to mention I was creeped out that I hadn't stirred while an unfamiliar person stared at me as I slept for hours. I shook off the unsettling vibe and resumed a conversation because it was far better than him just watching me while I ate. I don't know where Winston was from, but in my experience company usually meant some type of communication, not just a set of eyes ogling your every move.

"The food is still very warm for you having waited so long," I stated. "Thank you for your patience."

"I kept it warm for you." Winston continued to beam at me.

"Well then in that case thank you again." I considered asking how he did that but thought the better of it.

"Is it all satisfactory Miss Ophelia?"

"Yes." I could barely spit out the word as I shoved a piece of fruit in my mouth.

"Did you sleep well? You seemed to be in a deep motionless slumber, probably very restful."

Okay, I thought, *now you're going too far—it's one thing to watch a lady sleep another thing entirely to discuss it with her.*

"I slept well." I decided to keep it short. Winston nodded in approval, happy that his conjectures were spot on.

"Do you like your accommodations?" His hand gestured to the room.

"They're nice for being a prisoner." I didn't hide my aggravation.

"Oh no Miss Ophelia, you are not a captive, you are here for your own protection." He looked very pleased with his response.

"I don't know what I am being protected from. Do you Winston?"

Winston began to open his mouth, but before a syllable could leave his lips the metal door opened and Lucas stepped inside. Winston stood up and slowly walked towards the door.

"It was so nice to meet you Miss Ophelia, I will see you very soon." He disappeared behind Lucas.

"How is your breakfast Olly?"

"Your timing is impeccable." I sneered at him.

"Winston would not have shared anything that he was not directed to."

Yeah right, if that was true you wouldn't have been waiting by the door, I fumed silently.

"My breakfast is fine." I was curt. "When might I get some answers?"

"I was just coming in to suggest that you jump in the shower after your meal and when you've finished getting ready I thought we could sit down for a nice chat." My heart skipped two beats. I would have just left the food on the plate if I wasn't so starving. Lucas saw my haste and casually walked towards the door. He had gotten the hint.

I practically dove into the shower. I didn't bother with wetting my hair, I'd just throw it up into a bun anyways. I was still wet as I threw a sensible green dress over my head and squeezed my arms through the appropriate holes. I gently applied some mascara that was left for me, and did a once-over in the mirror. Not my best work but it would have to do.

As I approached the door I realized there wasn't even a knob on the inside. I stopped and stared, wondering, *Should I knock to get out?* At that moment the door opened and I hustled to escape. Lucas was there of course, standing at attention. I speculated if that was all he did, stand at my guard.

He took my arm and led me down a narrow passage. It was dark and there were no windows, so I didn't know if it was night or day. It was discombobulating to have no sense of time.

The castle smells became more fetid, like old dirt mixed with urine. It wasn't unbearable, but it wasn't pleasant. We reached a wall and stopped. After a few seconds the bricks began to fold inward and the wall opened into a longer corridor. The smell was horrid down there and I plugged my nose with my free hand.

Only a few feet in, we turned to our right and there in front of us was a cavernous room with baroque fixtures and thousands of lit candles hanging from opulent chandeliers. We stepped in and the door immediately closed behind us. Once we were locked in, the smell from the dank hallway dissipated.

Elias sat in a chair across the room. Opposite him was a couch. As we walked in his direction I glanced around the chamber. It was full of countless historical treasures, things that dated back hundreds of years or further still. The lighting made the ambiance warm and inviting, although the majority of the art pieces were cold, if not violent.

A huge tapestry hung above the oversized fireplace. The colors were vibrant and the detail exquisite. It depicted a battle scene, between the Greek gods and goddesses. The characters were dressed in garb that I associated with the romanticized stories I'd read as a teenager about Europe and the Roman Empire just before Christ. I had always been intrigued by mythology. I must have looked astounded because Elias spoke up.

"The antiquities room is impressive." He stated and I nodded in agreement as we walked.

Lucas ushered me to the sofa. It was stiff and uncomfortable. I situated myself as best I could to be able to look at both men. I liked to look in a person's eyes when I spoke with them. It must be the therapist in me.

Lucas was the first to speak. "Olly I need you to keep an open mind. Elias and I are going to attempt to summarize thousands of years of history and explain your part in all of this."

I nodded for him to proceed.

Lucas cleared his throat in that uncomfortable way. I had never seen him afflicted before, it was unnerving. "Okay here goes nothing." Immediately I felt the emotional climate of the room swarm me. There was a flurry of emotions. I gasped because it had been over a year since I had sensed a twitch of the emotional atmosphere around me. Both men lurched forward to comfort me, but I put my hand up. I just needed a moment. I closed my eyes and swallowed hard. I had been so relieved it was gone I had not noticed the symptoms of my curse had subsided.

I opened my eyes and Lucas was leaning in. I looked at him and noticed his skin was glowing just the same as the young girl Di's had and as Winston's had been this morning. I was sure it had never done that before. I could also sense his feelings and I knew without a shadow of a doubt I had never gotten even the slightest read on Lucas. But he was making up for it now, emanating love, worry and something else I couldn't put my finger on. I turned to Elias, he was not glowing. But he was radiating a whole lot of love, compassion and admiration. Then it was gone. I turned to Lucas again, he was back to his muted self.

No one said anything for a long deafeningly silent moment.

"What was that?" Was all I could manage. Lucas grabbed my hand and I pulled it away. I was not sure how I was feeling. I was connecting the dots in my head. Lucas had been sheltering me, somehow smothering my curse. I had appreciated the peace, but I felt manipulated.

"I am a conduit Olly—so are you." Lucas was trying to meet my gaze, but I was lost in thought. I was replaying memories of our time together in San Francisco. *What was real? What was genuine? Why had I not connected the dots earlier?* How could I be so stupid? I just let him infiltrate my home. I wanted to feel betrayed but somehow deep down I knew his actions stemmed from a place that had my best interest in mind so I couldn't be angry. I snapped back to the present. I wasn't done with my questions so this medley of emotion would have to be digested later.

"What are conduits?"

Elias spoke up. "Conduits were created before all other living things on this earth. We are energy vessels that express extraordinary abilities. Our creator also called the Painter, or sometimes Chitchakor, created us in pairs, an imposer and a receiver. Generally, an imposer can impress their will upon an object or living thing while a receiver tends to accumulate or absorb energy from something else. When the proper pair find each other and consummate their union, their super powers begin to blossom and grow. Do you recall that odd language you have heard Lucas and I speaking?" I nodded. I vaguely remember what Lucas called it. "It is the language of our people, it is called Asagi. We call our other half our Atoa and a pair of consummated conduits is called a Soahcoit. A consummated conduit, will not only have special gifts but can live forever, we become immortal."

"We are getting ahead of ourselves. And I definitely don't think it's time to travel down the fucking creation myth trail with all the Painter bullshit right now." Lucas gave Elias a stern look then continued. "I just showed you my gifts Olly. You must have noticed something strange about the other inhabitants of the castle you have met so far."

"What are your gifts exactly? Smothering?" As soon as the words left my mouth I regretted them, I was just frustrated with the facade and feeling out of control. I saw the recoil on Lucas' face, but my pride wasn't going to let me apologize just yet.

"No, I am an imposer and my gift is camouflage. I can disguise people, places, powers and my own abnormalities. It is why you couldn't see how my skin glowed, it is also how I shielded the onslaught of emotions from those around you—your curse. I was asked to hide you from a particular threat and that is what I did."

"What about when I was at work? Who were you hiding me from? That man who chased the car? Who sent you?" I asked.

"I followed you to work. I protected you." I was about to lose it a bit, he followed me to work? He didn't even have a job? Then Elias spoke up.

"I sent him. Do you recollect the day we collided into one another in Chicago?" I nodded and tried to stay focused as butterflies fluttered around in my stomach just thinking about it. "That happenstance changed everything."

Lucas took my hand and carried on the conversation. I was struggling to take my eyes off of Elias, but I reluctantly brought my attention back to Lucas and when he was sure I was paying attention he repeated himself. "I was asked to hide you from a particular threat and yes it was that man and his name is Yanni. Yanni and his Atoa Esther are leaders of the Nebas, a faction of conduits that are power hungry assholes. They want to dictate conduits and humans and will kill anyone who they perceive as a threat or anyone who tells them to fuck off."

"Okay so why me? I hate to break it to both of you, but I don't glow and I am not ancient or immortal. I am twenty eight and counting, I am a pale shade of white and I got sick several times last year." Lucas and Elias both chuckled. I didn't find it funny at all.

"You already have some gifts, your curse is something special—even if you hate it." Lucas conceded. "You won't know your true capabilities until the right time comes. But the point is, can you accept that there are things you have seen in the last few days that might suggest what we are saying is true?"

"I suppose." I was still considering the fact that my "gift" was being a human landfill for toxic emotional garbage –that really sucked!

"Then you have to understand how this whole thing started. Conduits were pretty damn peaceful until the Greeks. It was a simple system, find a pantheon and play a part. Polytheistic religions were the primary belief systems during those times and there was plenty of power to be had. It made life easy, find a civilization you could hang with and station yourself as a god or goddess by showing off a little bit. But something changed during Greek development—shit maybe it was all the wine." Lucas shrugged.

"Lucas is referring to an influx of Swali. These are half human half conduit progenies. Swali possess their own gifts, charisma, intelligence and influence. They are nothing compared to a Consu, a consummated conduit or even Unconcu, an unconsummated conduit but they can captivate an audience and they did. Apollo despised the Swali and campaigned to have them annihilated. His grievances fell on deaf ears." Elias said.

"The truth is the guy didn't like diluting his power, "demi gods" were a thing and it gave less supremacy to the Olympians. When genocide was frowned upon by the other conduits Apollo decided to try a new tactic." Lucas began speaking faster. "He went to what is now Poland and abducted a prophetic conduit named Aurora. He killed her Atoa and imprisoned her as the Oracle of Delphi. This made him the most influential god for hundreds of years, since even kings bent their ear to the Oracle."

Elias picked up the conversation. "The other pantheons colluded to free Aurora. It was not about the power, it was about the injustice. It was about the murder and imprisonment of one of our own. The Pai Ona faction organized several rescue operations. The Pai Ona were all the remaining conduits who refused to side with the Nebas. You see Aurora was not Apollo's only weapon, his daughter Esther is a puppet master who can impose her will on any being with a single touch and her Atoa Yanni is a detector. He can detect the whereabouts of the Unconsu, Consu and especially a Soahcoit bond. So all of the Pai Ona's efforts were thwarted until Di commanded a discreet band of Pai Ona and after seven hundred years of captivity they were able to emancipate Aurora."

"Hold up." I put my hand up. "You mean the twelve year old in the purple dress?"

Lucas laughed. "Yeah, but don't let her hear you talk about her that way. She is the goddess of love and older and more badass than almost anyone I know."

My mouth was agape and I didn't care, I was shocked. *The goddess of love?*

"Are you still with me Olly, we got two thousand more years to go." I nodded and Lucas began again. "They released Aurora—she disappeared and they exiled Apollo, Esther and Yanni to a secure location. After the whole Apollo debacle, the old timers decided it was time to dismantle polytheistic religion and hoped the power struggle would dissolve with it. In came Jesus Christ and away went any major polytheistic cultures. Well fast forward a hundred years and strange shit started happening, starting with the planned escape of Apollo and his family from seclusion. This meant there were secret Nebas hiding in the Pai Ona communities. Still most conduits believed the three fugitives would lay low and just avoid recapture."

"Five hundred years after Aurora's liberation the first disappearances were observed and the peace was over." Elias interjected.

"It took a couple hundred years to realize what was going on, because everyone had become nomadic. But what's worse is that it took another two hundred years to hunt those cowards down and administer payback." Lucas growled. "After nearly four hundred years of systematically picking us off one by one the first open war kicked off. It lasted almost a hundred years and stretched across the globe. By the time we caught and executed Apollo there were so many Poginuli it was hard to find a Soahcoit pair still intact." He paused, I didn't know what he was thinking about and I had so much to consider that I waited patiently.

Elias explained. "The Poginuli are the broken, a Soahcoit where one of the Atoas has been murdered."

"I thought conduits were immortal." It had just dawned on me that they kept saying that people had been murdered.

Both men looked at each other and back at me.

"What?! You can't tell me there are immortals out there and that one of them is the boogie man, who happens to be chasing me and not tell me how to kill him."

"You can kill us with fire, lots of fire. First you would need to dismember us, to slow us down. But a team of assassins could easily make that happen." Lucas was looking past me.

"Why fire?"

"Because we are energy vessels and energy doesn't disappear it only changes form. When you burn our flesh you dissolve our vessel. Nothing else is strong enough or efficient enough to stop us from repairing ourselves." I squeezed his hand this time, because Lucas looked so forlorn. He quickly shifted gears after seeing my concern. "So that is how we executed Apollo. But Esther and Yanni got away."

"It was apparent after the escape of Apollo and the battle that ensued that the Nebas had more allies than envisaged, so few could be trusted and the Pai Ona disbanded into smaller divisions to be less detectable. This would prove to make it more difficult to determine when the slayings began again. The Poginuli led the last open battle three hundred years ago. The Pai Ona found themselves outnumbered and defeated. After the last battle those who survived went into hiding and…" Elias' words drifted.

"And now we are being assassinated one by one." Lucas concluded. It got silent again. I was trying to process all the information and it occurred to me. "You didn't glow." I stated. Both men looked surprised and a bit confused so I continued. "When Lucas removed his camouflage you didn't glow." I guess that wasn't what they expected me to inquire about. "You said the three of us were conduits, but he was glowing like the rest of them," I pointed at Lucas, "and you were dull like me."

"That is because we have not consummated yet." Elias said.

Lucas snarled. "He means you are both still mortal."

Elias pressed on. "That is what I said."

A flurry of questions filled my head and a wave of realizations. Elias was my Atoa, he was my totality. My breathing quickened. "How do you consummate?"

Rage flashed across Lucas' face while Elias sat calmly. I had no idea what either of them was thinking. Lucas' palm began to sweat.

Suddenly the door flew open, but before I could see who had

entered or exited the figure was gone. Only a faint smell wafted behind them, an odd mix of nickel and sweet plums.

Elias stood up. "There has been a perimeter breach."

Lucas picked me up. I squirmed. "Wait, does this mean I'm done asking questions?" I know it seemed trivial, but now I had a whole new set of queries.

"For now, Olly." Lucas' voice was stern and his face was rigid. I knew better than to try and dissuade him.

"Quickly, take her behind the tapestry to the lower chamber, Elias ordered. "Lock the door and keep quiet." Then he was gone and Lucas and I were flying down a dark passage. I closed my eyes. I couldn't see anything anyway. I could only feel Lucas' arms encasing me.

We stopped, and the air was cold and decayed. Lucas whispered so quietly I didn't catch all of the words. "Lay down. There's a blanket to bundle with and I'll hold you until this threat passes. I won't let anyone hurt you, I promise."

I wiggled under a thick velvet cover. It was heavy and felt good on my skin. Lucas shimmied behind me and I realized the room must have been no bigger than a large walk in closet. My legs were stretched but I could feel the moisture coming off the brick wall both at my head and my feet. I tried to listen for any impending intruder, but I heard nothing. Every once in a while, I felt Lucas' body shift and become more alert. But I still heard nothing. I listened to the cadence of his breath for what felt like hours until sleep washed over me. It was a very deep sleep, the kind that sweeps you away when it's been an unbelievable day.

ELIAS

I was quiet as I opened the door, so as not to wake Ophelia or startle Lucas. They had been in the small chamber for nearly six hours.

"It's safe, we defused the threat," I whispered in a tone only audible to a conduit.

"Do you know who it was? Did you kill them?" Lucas' eyes were piercing, even in the dark.

"No. Whoever it was managed to evade us. They are fast. The good news is, it would appear there was only one."

"How can so many of you be so incompetent?" Lucas was disappointed by our failure, as was I. It was hard to imagine that we could not apprehend the intruder. He or she must have had an insight into our defenses. And as long as they stayed unfettered, Ophelia was still in imminent danger. I still did not know how they had found the castle to begin with. I was certain we had not been followed from the tarmac and the wards around this land are lethal if you have not been invited. I decided we would be safer in numbers in the event that Yanni tracked us down with his small lethal Nebas army. I was having second thoughts about my decision. I felt more on edge than ever, because this confirmed that someone in the confines of this castle was a defector and had invited an intruder.

Lucas shook his head again, as if to further express his dissatisfaction, then declared, "I need to get her into her chamber."

I took the opportunity to address an obvious issue that was going to persist as long as we were working together. "She knows, Lucas. I understand that we need to keep our bond from getting stronger for the time being, for *her* protection. But you cannot avoid explaining what consummating is and who I am to her." I could see the displeasure on his face. He was not trying to hide it from me. He loathed me and he hated the fact that Ophelia and I were destined to be together. He would rather murder me than explain to her that she was fated to be with another man. But even he could not deny the look on her face today. She was piecing things together, whether we told her or not.

"You don't know that. We just dumped a lot of complex shit on her all at once. She's a smart woman, but that would be hard for anyone to process." He picked her up and we glared at each other. I wished it was me carrying her to her bed. As much as I wanted to be that man I had to keep her from being any more detectable. With every touch our connection got stronger and more visible to Yanni.

Rand moved out of the corridor's shadows and into the light. "We all know who she will end up with. Your preposterous claim on her, Lucas, is only making you look foolish."

"Mind your own business Rand." Lucas was seething.

"It's painful to watch my friend, just painful." Rand was circling us and shaking his head, taking pleasure in Lucas' squirming.

"I'm going to suggest one last time old man," Lucas hissed, "that you keep your opinions to yourself."

Rand snickered. Lucas was correct in stating that he was old, about eleven hundred years, to be exact —albeit he was still spry as a jackrabbit, for he was only 27 in human years. He was not a traditionally handsome man, but he was well built, with brawny, intimidating shoulders. His long, curly chocolate-brown hair fell between his shoulder blades. On another man his locks may have looked feminine, but on Rand they added to his daunting presence, hinting that he was from another time and well versed in battle. His neutral-toned skin made his Middle Eastern lineage not quite perceptible, while his features were just ambiguous enough that he could fit into any crowd. I think his most distinct features were his flamboyant mannerisms, he was eccentric. He had been a close friend of my father's. But I didn't know what his given name was, he had always simply gone by the name Rand for as long as I could remember.

"Rand as much as I enjoy watching someone else drive Lucas mad," I said, "I do not wish to see Ophelia get hurt if Lucas should lose his temper." I smiled at my comrade. I truly did enjoy watching Lucas get heated.

"I understand your concern Elias. We never quite know when our friend Lucas here will snap, do we? Rest assured that he would rather die than hurt our lovely Ophelia." Rand stood inches away from Lucas, sniffing at the air and wafting his hands towards his nose. "Indeed, he would rather be burned alive than see her hurt by his own hand."

Lucas was holding onto Ophelia almost like a shield. But we all knew he was exposed. As much as he tried, his protective powers could not mask his strongest feelings from a conduit as powerful as Rand. Rand literally tasted emotions like a fine wine, sorting through the various flavors and deciphering what each meant. The nature of his gift made it so it was impossible to hide anything from him completely. Lucas could mask pieces, but he could not conceal everything.

For no one knew how to remove their emotions from a situation. They are as wild as they are spontaneous, so even in conduits they cannot be controlled. And although I did not share Rand's gift, even I picked up on the emotional vibrations trembling off of Lucas. He was coveting a possession. He loved Ophelia very much.

"I'd like to get her back to her room. Step aside, Rand." Lucas demanded the last statement with enough assertion that he moved.

I followed quietly behind, giving Rand an affirming nod as I passed. I hoped he would always be in my corner. He and my father were brothers, not by blood but by bond. Even now when I wanted so desperately to be sure of an ally I found myself hesitant to completely confide in him. If it was only my safety that I was worried about I might divulge everything, about the portentousness of the prophecy, the impending summit and the incessant pressure mounting on me but it was Ophelia that I had to protect above all else. We turned into her room and Lucas set her on the bed.

"We should wake her," I suggested, "let her know she is safe."

"Of course we should." Lucas was still riled, but he gently stroked her cheek. His tenderness was driving me insane. I wanted to be the one touching her and tending to her well-being. I took a deep breath and forced the air out of my lungs slowly.

Her mouth opened ever so slightly, and her tongue gently lined her bottom lip. She was brilliant, in her beauty and her strength. Lesser women would have been terrified in her position but she did her best to cope with the situation as gracefully as possible. Mostly she was just impatient to know more. She would, in time.

Her hand rubbed her eyes as she tried to get her bearings. She looked up at Lucas. "Does this mean the conversation is over?" I laughed and she shot a serious glance at me. I felt like a schoolboy caught in the girls' locker room.

"No, the conversation is not over," I said as sincerely as I could, "but it is a lot to take in. We can divulge information as needed. It will all come out in due time." She looked skeptical.

"Ophelia, we will answer your questions, if we can, from here on out." Lucas said. "You know all the basics right now."

I did not believe this was entirely true but I also was not going to upset her further with more facts. Lucas was being very selective about what he wanted her to know about our world, taking care to avoid explaining a Soahcoit and how these pairs were consummated. I knew he felt if he did not share this information that it would postpone the development of my bond with her—and at this point in time for my own reasons I too did not want to strengthen our connection. I would never let him know this, but right now we shared a common cause, protecting Ophelia and preventing her consummation.

OPHELIA

I felt like an enormous weight had been lifted, the weight of obscurity. I didn't know all there was to know about my situation. I was sure I'd only grazed the surface. But Lucas and Elias had left me with enough to ruminate on—for now.

It all still felt so surreal. And because reality had not completely set in, I came to the conclusion I would just ignore the possibility that I was in the company of my other half. I couldn't even entertain the thought. That conversation would have to come later.

I stood up to stretch my legs and simultaneously the door opened. It was Winston, and behind him was Elias. Just seeing him made my heart rate spontaneously pick up. I felt ridiculous.

I tried to play it cool. "Good day gentlemen."

"Good morning Miss Ophelia." Winston chipped. "Did you sleep well?"

"I feel like that's all I've been doing here, sleeping. So yes, I guess I slept just fine." My days were really disorientating. I slept most of the day before, after my stay in the dark closet. I vaguely remember Winston dropping off dinner the prior night. After that I'd actually barely slept, I read, a lot. "How about you Winston, how did you sleep?"

Elias still hadn't said a word. He stood back cautiously by the door while I was served my breakfast.

"That is an odd question. I do not sleep." Winston set the tray on my lap. "I hope you like your eggs over easy. Lucas said you like scrambled, but Eggs Benedict is best prepared with over easy eggs."

"Oh yes of course and I love eggs Benedict! Excuse my silliness, but you don't sleep EVER?" I was bewildered.

"No. I do not sleep ever, neither do any of the other conduits. It is wasteful to sleep. Besides we do not need to rejuvenate the way humans do. We are always at our best." He turned on his heels and headed toward the door.

My jaw must have been on the floor because Elias laughed.

"This must be so peculiar for you." Elias looked at me sympathetically. He patted Winston on the shoulder as he left. "You have to forgive Winston's abruptness, he has not been mortal for many, many lifetimes. He has no idea what this might be like."

I was trying to imagine a life without sleep. I loved sleeping.

"Do you sleep?" I asked hesitantly. Again he laughed.

"Yes, I am still just as mortal as you are, Ophelia." He sat in the adjacent chair.

I thought back to that night in my apartment when we ran from Yanni. I found it hard to believe he was mortal just like me. He ran faster than anyone I'd ever met.

"I imagine you're more than a simple mortal man, Elias. I've seen you run." I looked down at my plate and carved out a nice bite that included a little bit of everything. If I kept eating like this I'd need to ask Lucas for a treadmill in order to still fit into the wardrobe he'd so carefully chosen.

Elias looked at his hands, then back at me. "How are you doing? Honestly?"

"I'm doing good, all things considered. I just wish I could stretch my legs and maybe see the sun again someday." I looked at him intently to see his response.

"I think that can be arrange." He halfheartedly smiled. I wasn't sure how sincere he was but I had no reason to distrust him, yet. "Are you pleased with your quarters?"

"Yes, it's very nice."

He leaned forward. "This will get easier, and the more you learn about our brethren the better you will feel."

I could smell his woodsy scent again, it was intoxicating but I tried to ignore it, grasping at straws to take my mind off how irresistible he was to me. So of course, my mother popped into my thoughts.

"Elias do you know if someone got in touch with Eleanor? I don't know what you would tell her, but she can't just think I disappeared." I had thought about her several times over the last few hours. It was so weird to think she also had no idea what we were. I wondered how much all of this played into her mental state. *Was that her gift?* I wondered. Oh, poor Eleanor.

"Lucas contacted her."

"And…" I felt uneasy now. I hadn't put any realistic thought into what they would tell her. Now I was scared of what that might be. I never did find out how Lucas had gotten me out of all my appointments.

"You should discuss this with him," Elias said, looking down at his hands again. That was not a good sign.

"What did he tell her?" I asked more sternly this time. "I know you know." I was on the verge of panicking.

"I do know the crux of what he said, but he made the decision as how to handle the situation. I cannot elucidate why he made the choices he did—only he can. I will say that it was a conclusion made under distressing circumstances and I agreed with him that it appeared to be the best option."

"All of that is fluff. You're just avoiding my question, and if you won't answer it then go get Lucas, now!" I was yelling, terrified of the answer. That was a lot of explaining for a question he didn't wish to actually respond to. Elias left immediately, off to fetch Lucas.

Before I could formulate how I was going to approach Lucas he was kneeling in front of me. I didn't like the position he was in, it suggested he was already asking for my forgiveness.

ELIAS

Ophelia was irate. I could not blame her, but I also thought it was his place to tell her what his plan had been should we have to disappear from San Francisco hastily. I had left the decision up to him, he knew her better than me, he knew what she could live with—and who she could live without. I thought it was a severe resolution, but then again, I did not understand her family dynamic as he did.

A part of me hoped she hated him after this, but I knew better than that. She could get upset, but in her soul, she was too kind to hate him, perhaps anyone. She would understand why he did what he did and forgive him. I was so lost in thought that I did not notice the door to my room was ajar until I was reaching for the door knob. The lights were off, but that meant nothing in this house. Everyone in this establishment could see just as well in the dark as they could with lights on.

The question was who could get past my security measures, and who would want to? I cautiously opened the door the rest of the way. I was not exactly prepared to brawl with an intruder, but I would if necessary.

My head was barraged with possible scenarios. It must be the traitor—that was the only logical explanation. I had made it clear that no one need be in this wing without my bidding. I stepped into the room and stood there, silently. I heard nothing. I went to switch on the light and in that instant saw a shadow move toward the door.

"Elias dear boy, I hope I didn't scare you," Rand chimed as he flicked on the light. A giant grin on his face and his hands holstered on his hips.

I stood there for a moment, unable to speak.

"What are you doing in here?" I attempted to mask my angst, but I knew he was aware of every bit of it.

"Don't be alarmed. I was on my way to see you and when I arrived at your quarters I saw that the door was ajar, so I simply let myself in. I thought I would wait for you, and here you are." He clasped his hands together. Of course, Rand would know how to get past my defenses, he was a close family friend. This section of the castle had extreme magical wards, casted long ago by my parents.

"My door was already ajar when you arrived?" *Could he be the defector?* I sincerely hoped that was not the case.

"Of course, that is what I am saying. I thought it would be better if I stayed in here in case someone else stumbled upon the opportunity to rifle through your things. I know how much is at stake, and although you won't let me assist you, I had to do my best to protect all your hard work." I began questioning everything he said. It would be a brilliant happenstance that someone else was able to get through my security and that Rand perhaps managed to scare them off—otherwise why else would they leave the room open? I was skeptical.

"Did you see anyone in the corridor upon your approach?"

"No, not a soul." He was so nonchalant. Was this not the man that my father trusted above all others? Could I really be questioning him now?

"Then certainly you will comb the castle and see if you can give me any insight as to who might be acting suspiciously?" He nodded. "Report back to me immediately with your findings."

"Of course, Elias. I am always here to assist." Rand bowed ever so slightly in my direction and then was gone.

I needed to take an immediate inventory. If something was missing or moved I had to prepare for the consequences of that information being leaked.

I opened my closet and saw Alistair's laptop still on the top shelf. I pulled it down and inspected the keyboard, it was still covered in dust, it had been unmoved. The box with the maps, sheets of paper and journals also appeared unmoved. Dust encased the outside without a single fingerprint. When I opened it, all the papers seemed to be the way I had left them. I double-checked by sifting through. All accounted for.

That was all I had in the closet aside from my clothes, so the intruder did not make it to the closet before they were disturbed. I shifted to my desk—surely this would be the first place they would look. My own laptop was sleeping, but I noticed it had been adjusted. I opened the top drawer and saw my lockbox was still intact. I opened it to be confident that nothing had been taken. It was all there, seemingly unaltered.

The second drawer held the three small sacks that I had taken from Alistair's study. They were only out of the lockbox because I had been mulling over their contents the other day.

"Piss!" I stared at the contents of the drawer. All three were there, but they had indeed been tampered with—I was certain. I pulled each satchel out and weighed it. According to my notes they were unchanged, but it was clear that someone in the castle now knew I was in possession of them. I was not exactly sure of what that meant, since I myself was still hard-pressed to find out exactly what the uses of each were.

I immediately locked them up along with everything else of Alistair's, in the wall safe behind my bed. It was not much more secure than their previous stations, but it would be a bit more of a deterrent. I should have kept them in the safe all along. I would set up a different security system tomorrow.

I lay on my bed, hoping everything I had been working towards over the last two and half years was not completely devastated.

OPHELIA

"What the hell did you tell Eleanor?" I spat at the kneeling Lucas. "Don't you dare bullshit me like Elias!" I thought I saw a smirk flash across his face for a split second.

"I won't bullshit you, I know how much you hate that. But please calm down. I need you to know that I did what I did to protect you, and to prevent Eleanor from further worry. I just ripped the band aid off all at once."

"Okay enough precursor. You didn't kill her, did you?" My mind went to the worst possible scenario.

Lucas looked like he was going to choke. "No, no of course not. But I guess if that is the worst-case scenario, this is the second." He took my hands. "She thinks you died in a car accident."

I was stunned. I just stared past him. *Eleanor thinks I'm dead. Eleanor thinks I'm dead?* I just kept repeating it over and over in my head. Lucas continued to hold my hands in my lap. I don't know how long I sat there silently, but it was long enough to scare him a little.

"Olly, say something. Anything. Slap me. Tell me to explain myself. Something, dammit!"

I heard the anxiety in his voice, but I wasn't ready to hear any more about it. I had to grasp the severity of the situation, examine the consequences of his actions.

"Leave me." I pulled my hands away and pointed toward the doorway. "Get out. Now."

He was silent as he walked slowly to the exit.

"I'll knock on the door when I'm ready for some answers. I assume you will be reachable." I couldn't look at him. I was beside myself. And I wanted to be clear that I wasn't asking him to be available—I was telling him to wait until I was ready to see him again.

He nodded and shut the door. I sat down in front of the fire. I felt chilled to the bone as a billion questions surfed through my head. *Who told her? How was she taking it? How did they make it believable? Whose body did they use? Was there a funeral? Did she get my life insurance policy and my other assets? Why did she have to think I was dead? Why couldn't I be sick or busy, we rarely saw each other anyway. Why did no one ask me if this was okay with me before they assumed this was our only solution? Was she in danger?* Then my world stood still as I thought: *I will never see Eleanor again.*

I sat there for a long time, so long that my legs hurt when I finally moved. I was ready for answers. I hadn't cried yet, but I knew tears were lingering just below the surface. I felt as if I was standing on a precipice, waiting for the earth to crumble beneath my feet. I was utterly out of control of my life and there seemed to be nothing I could do about it. Huge decisions were being made and executed for me without my consent. The gravity of the situation was crushing me. There was no doubt that I would never be returning to my life as I knew it.

I knocked on the door then sat back on my bed and bundled up with a throw blanket—I still felt icy in my core. He joined me at the foot of the bed, cautiously gauging my mood before he spoke.

"Can I explain myself?" he asked gently. I nodded.

"Wait! Is she okay?" I blurted. "Have you spoken to her, or did you die with me?" I said the last bit snarkily.

"She's distraught, but Simon has really stepped it up and has been very supportive. I think this has brought them a lot closer." A huge sigh escaped my lips, then the tears came. Lucas leaned forward to console me, but I put my hand up. I wasn't ready for that. It would only make it harder to pull myself together.

"Continue," I mumbled.

"She was in danger. The truth was the likelihood of us ever returning to our lives as they were the moment you were found, was dismal. There may come a time when our lives can return to some state of normalcy—but even then, we will be in a different city with different names. I had to make a terrifying decision in a split second and I chose to cut ties with anyone who could be harmed in this war, I didn't want your mother to become an unnecessary casualty because someone was looking for you." His eyes were pleading with me.

Of course, Lucas would know that protecting Eleanor is ultimately what I would want. But I wasn't willing to forgive and forget just yet.

Lucas continued. "I couldn't risk someone baiting you out with Eleanor. So, I staged a very public accident. Your car was found literally incinerated because the gas tank caught fire. The papers said you were on a particularly treacherous part of the road leading to Stinson Beach. It had already been repaired twice this year due to rockslides. You were just in the wrong place at the wrong time."

"How could you possibly have staged something like that?" I was retracing our steps, or as much as I could remember of them. "When did you have time?"

"I move very fast Olly. Faster than you can possibly imagine. Money also helps to get things moving." I waited for more. "While you were passed out in the jet. Elias kept an eye on you at the same time, I made arrangements."

"Whose body?" I wasn't sure I really wanted to know the answer to that question.

"A freshly buried Jane Doe from the cemetery in Burlingame. I have kept an ongoing eye out for opportunities such as this, in case a situation arose where we needed to leave very quickly. That was what I was hired to do—to keep you safe at all costs. I always knew that could have entailed faking your death."

"What about my assets? My savings, the life insurance policy I had for Eleanor? My things at the apartment?"

"Everything of any value, including your savings, your retirement and the large nest egg that you had been setting aside in a CD since you were seventeen—has made it safely into the hands of your mother. I have been monitoring it very closely. She also just deposited the large amounts of cash that she found stowed away in our apartment. All in all, before the insurance policy pays her out, Eleanor has accumulated almost two million dollars from your estate. That should be enough to see her through retirement. In fact, I hope she sets the five hundred thousand dollars from the insurance aside for a rainy day."

"Lucas, I never kept money in the house. I also never invested in a CD. Is this your money? I don't understand."

"I knew you would be concerned about her well-being. I set up the accounts and left a good chunk of money strewn around the apartment. She's taken care of financially, and as I said this tragedy seems to be bringing her and Simon closer." Then he leaned in a little more. "Eleanor went through the apartment and donated almost everything. I managed to collect some stuff I knew was important to you and had it sent to a storage I have in Buenos Aires along with my things. I'll get them to you as soon as I can."

I wondered what he decided was worth saving. I was struggling to register all the information. I nodded, so Lucas continued.

"She held a beautiful ceremony for you in Chicago, Olly. You touched many people's lives and they showed up in swarms to pay their respects. You were loved. People flew out to Chicago from the Bay Area, even some friends from your time in Europe showed up. I saved the clippings on the accident and a video your mother sent me from the funeral."

"How did you explain your absence to Eleanor? She must have found that odd."

"I explained that I was still on an extended work trip, which is why I wasn't there to begin with. I told her that I couldn't handle a funeral, that I was distraught and needed to grieve in my own way. I had my things moved out of the apartment before she arrived, and I left her a note saying that to try and cope I was going to head to South America for a long vacation, and that I would contact her when I was ready to deal with my grief. She surprisingly handled it all very well. I think she was still in shock." Lucas was starting to ease into the conversation. His shoulders had relaxed and he seemed sure I'd understand his reasoning.

I did understand it. I still didn't quite get how he so thoroughly erased me from the planet in a matter of hours, but I supposed it was as he said, he was prepared to do this at any given moment.

"So, I'll never see Eleanor again?" As tumultuous as our relationship was, I did love her. She was, after all, my mom—my only family. I hated that I didn't get to say goodbye, and I would always wonder if she was safe or how she was doing with Simon.

"No, and I am sorry for that. But I know what I did was the right thing, and given the opportunity I would do it the same way all over again. I hope you can forgive me and understand that I did what was best for everyone involved. Including Eleanor."

I looked down at my hands. I was happy to have my last memories with Eleanor be such pleasant ones. Celebrating her birthday and giving her Lilith's picture was cemented into my mind as one of the best nights we'd ever shared together. I felt more tears starting, and Lucas moved closer on the bed. Again, I put my hands up.

He got the hint and started towards the door. "Lucas," I called and he turned. "I understand why, and I forgive you. But I'm still heartbroken, and need time to mourn."

Then he left and I was alone with my tears.

LUCAS

"You really think that's a good idea?" I was fuming.

"She is not going to tolerate this captivity much longer. She had a terrible day yesterday. We can give her this." Elias wasn't going to back off.

"How do you intend to keep her safe?" I looked around the room at the congregation of conduits.

"Di will be her escort, and the rest of us will be on perimeter detail." He sounded annoyed at this point.

"Like that means much when someone has already been breaching our borders," I scoffed. "Why should Di be her escort? If you're going to insist on putting her in further danger, at least let me be her chaperone."

"Di is the oldest and most skilled of all of us." No one else spoke. Their silence said it all. They sided with Viraclay. But they had nothing to lose, whereas I could lose everything.

"I will escort her," I insisted. I wouldn't let it be any other way, unless someone could convince me she'd be in safer hands.

I heard the growl before I felt her on my back. Suddenly her small hands were clenched around my neck. I could feel she was poised to break it with a simple nod from Elias. I'd be dismembered and out of commission for a while. He didn't signal her, though, so she jumped off and with a bow challenged me to combat.

I realized I might have mistakenly insulted a very old acquaintance.

"Shit, really Di?" I bowed in return and she stood there playfully shuffling her feet, toying with her prey—me. I circled right and the crowd of conduits backed up to avoid being dragged into the match. "I'm just saying, I'm the one with something at stake. How do we know you'll take the job seriously?"

I probably shouldn't have provoked her further. She smiled devilishly and I knew she wasn't going to be as gentle this time. I stepped left and she flew at me. I just evaded her forceful blow, but the wall was not nearly as fortunate—several stones fell to the floor as dust.

"Can we talk about this?" I entreated. "I'm not accusing you of being incompetent." I leapt up and landed inches from where she had been only milliseconds before. Before I could reorient myself, she was applying a bone-crunching blow to my right calf. I yelped in pain, then jumped up and turned around, lifting my broken leg and planting a kick on the left side of her perfect little face.

She just giggled, lunged at me, and took me out at my knees—then danced victoriously on my chest.

I went to grab her ankle but she flew up, her aqua-blue dress gracefully flowing behind her. She quickly did a vertical flip and landed on the cobble stones less than a centimeter from my face.

"Okay Di, I was wrong. There's no one else better for the job. I'll fall back to perimeter duty." With that, she backed off, helped me up and bowed. I hobbled out of the room only slightly humiliated. I'd been in far worse fights that ended with far more damage. Di just wanted to prove her point, and I got the message loud and clear. The old broad still had it in her, I had to give her that. I shook my head as I limped up the stairs. *That was stupid of me.*

I reached my room and lay down on the bed. What a ridiculous day. Thank goodness Ophelia seemed to be recovering from the news about her mother. I took off my jeans and looked at the severity of Di's handiwork. As I suspected, she had shattered my tibia.

I sat up, grabbed a bottle of wine from the nightstand, opened it and polished it off, "Merciful bitch, she could have done much worse."

It was already nearly healed, but the itching was terribly irritating. Nothing another bottle of wine couldn't help soothe. I popped another one open and propped myself up. I raised the bottle for a toast to the ether. "Here is to keeping your friends close and your enemies' closer." I knew the closest friend I had was in my hand, so I gulped a bit more, then sat there in the dark until the itching completely subsided.

OPHELIA

Yesterday was awful. I didn't eat despite Lucas' insistence and I didn't sleep well at all.

I stretched my legs and twisted my torso. I had no idea what time it was, but my body was squawking that it was morning. I missed the sun so much, especially at the waking hour. I sat up, and as I did there was a rap on the door. It opened ever so gently and Di stepped into the room. She looked ravishing. She just seemed to have a deeper glow than the others I had seen—a rapturous glow. I was enthralled. She giggled.

I tore my eyes away and cleared my throat. "Hello."

"Hello." She curtsied. "My name is Di."

"My name is Ophelia." This was silly, since I knew her name already, and I know she knew mine. But formality was apparently essential.

She whisked herself to my bedside, her long blond hair chasing after her. "I am going to accompany you outside today Miss Ophelia." She sang the words, and her voice tickled my ears like someone nibbling your earlobes.

Di giggled and beamed up at me. Then she sashayed towards the door.

"I will return after Winston has served you breakfast."

As she shut the door I flew off the bed and into the bathroom. I was so excited! I was going to feel the sun on my face! I wanted to clean up quickly and be ready before Winston showed up. I yanked at my hair, attempting to weave conditioner through its twisted vines in the shower. There was no way that Winston could serve me my meal quicker than I'd just gotten ready. But sure enough when I stepped into the room, there he was standing next to the armchair by the fire, tray of food in his hand. He was good, too good. I took the tray and Winston left quietly. I inhaled it all, just in time.

The door opened, and Di traipsed in again, settling on the arm of my chair. Her long hair grazed my cheek and I blushed. *If she had this impact on me, what did she do to men?* I wondered. She smelled like a sweet mix of lilacs and maple.

"I'm ready, Di!"

She smiled, and before I could smile back she was across the room and in the hall, beckoning me to join her.

Di skipped and I walked quickly behind. As she pushed off each foot, she fluidly bounced into the air, higher than a normal skip would propel you. Her movement looked like a dance. I stumbled to keep up, and my steps were noisy and rushed. Her luminescent skin shimmered brilliantly in the candlelit passage. I couldn't wait to see her in the sun.

We entered the large courtyard in the center of the castle. I had only seen it the day that we arrived, and today it looked larger and more menacing. The enormous walls loomed over the open area in the center, while huge pillars braced the massive domed ceiling.

I heard the creaking of the gate lifting and the sun peeked inside the dark structure, illuminating the room. The air smelled fresh and warm. My eyes hurt from the fierceness of the sun's rays, but I welcomed the pain. It was familiar—like when I'd wake up in the morning in my Richmond district apartment and the sun would be peering in through my window at just the right angle.

I walked under the sturdy gate and outside the castle walls, Di had already bounded in front of me. My eyes were adjusting slowly, though I could see three figures a few yards ahead. I got close and saw that Di had been joined by Elias and Lucas.

"It's a beautiful day for a walk outside, Olly." Lucas sounded optimistic.

"We are going to do a perimeter check, we will not be far. If you need anything simply call and one of us will be there in a matter of moments," Elias said.

"Okay, but Di will be with me," I said, mooning over my escort and the outdoors. "I'm sure she can enchant any impending attackers, right Di?" She just giggled.

"Anyone sneaking up on you and seeing Di would know to be far more afraid of some of her other talents," Lucas warned. "She can do far worse than making you fall in love with her." Di shook with laughter, I felt like I was missing something.

What other weapons might Di possess? "Like what?"

"Let's hope she doesn't have to use them, shall we." Lucas winked. "Have fun girls."

We walked in the only direction where the ground was fairly flat. The castle was on top of a steep mountain. The three walls I could see hovered over the sharp descending sides of the landscape and I can only assume the fourth wall overlooked the valley below as well. The terrain was rocky with sparse trees and green shrubbery. Di wasn't much of a talker, but that was perfectly fine with me. I was embracing every sensation the natural world could offer. I listened to the breeze through the trees and bushes. I heard every bird chirp. I took deep slow breaths trying to taste the scents in the air. I noticed every stone and leaf below my feet.

I never wanted the walk to end, but at one point I could tell that we'd shifted directions and were heading back towards the castle.

"Di, could we do this again?"

"Yes. I will go with you a few more times, to help you get orientated, before Elias may let you explore on your own. He would rather I be enforcing the perimeter most days." I was giddy. A sudden strong wave of satisfaction also washed over me. Then I realized that it wasn't coming from me. Di was satisfied. It must have been a strong enough feeling that it evaded Lucas' shield over me. I wondered, *What brought her such satisfaction about our exchange?*

She swiftly stepped out in front of me. "I am happy to see you smile so genuinely."

I hadn't even realized I was displaying such a huge goofy grin. Di was exuding satisfaction because she'd said something to make me happy. I was touched by her concern for my well-being. She nodded in acknowledgement, then continued walking. It was near dusk when we reached the castle. The men were waiting just as we had left them. I must have still been smiling because both their faces lit up when they saw me.

"Back safe and sound, Viraclay," noted Di. "I will head back out to the perimeter in an hour." Then she was gone.

"How was your walk?" Lucas looked eager.

"It was very nice and Di says I'll get to do it again. Is this going to become a daily thing?" I asked hopefully.

"I think we can arrange that, if the weather permits it." Lucas wrapped his arm around my shoulder. "Right now, let's get you something to eat."

"Is Winston going to be waiting in my room again?" I furrowed my eyebrows as I said it. Lucas roared with laughter.

"What, you don't like him serving you?"

"No, he's nice," I let my voice get quieter. "But he's an odd one."

Lucas laughed even harder. I looked over my shoulder, as I heard Elias chuckle. He found humor in my observation too, but he looked more withdrawn. I had an urge to run over and hold his hand. Instead I held back— there was still so much to be sorted through in my heart.

As expected, Winston was in my room, replete with a tray of tantalizing food. Lucas directed me to the armchair and sat down in the one opposite of me, as Elias drifted out of the room with Winston.

"I'm glad you had a nice day today. You look a lot more content," Lucas observed.

"I needed the exercise and the sun. You know how I love the sun." Saying those words reminded me again of how different our lives were only days before. I had a twinge of longing, *I wish life was still that simple*. Lucas must have felt it too, because he grabbed my hand and scooted his seat closer.

It felt like the perfect time to ask the question I'd been thinking about all day. I set aside my food tray and looked Lucas in the eyes. "What kind of powers do conduits have?"

There was no hesitation on his part, that was reassuring. "As you know, we've already discussed some of them. Mine is camouflage. Di is the goddess of love and as you may have picked up, she can do just that—formulate bonds of love. She can make you love her—or someone else. The one fact is—that although some conduits' gifts may be similar, they are all unique to the individual."

"You said today that Di has other talents. What might those be?"

"Well, Di is very old, she's been around for centuries. Our powers get stronger the longer we live and often we develop other gifts with time. Di is very strong. She is also very fast, another amplified skill. Most importantly, Di is very lethal. She can numb your senses with huge waves of lust or love. That saying, 'love is blind' is kind of a sick joke, but it's no laughing matter. You know that feeling of incapacitation that you feel when you're in love? It's that feeling, but augmented intensely. First, she stupefies you, then she attacks."

Chills flew down my spine. "What are some others' gifts? What's Winston's gift?" *Besides being supremely creepy.* I thought

"We call Winston a calentar. He heats things from the inside out, like a microwave. When he says he's preparing your food, he's *literally the oven that's preparing your food.* He only needs to look at something and it'll begin to boil, or warm up. His gift may seem trivial, but imagine him making your blood boil. On a lighter note, Winston is a fantastic cook." Lucas tried to make me laugh. He could see the fear in my face.

He pointed at my plate. "Your food is getting cold. And unless you want me to send Winston back in here, you'd better eat." I noticeably shivered at the thought. Lucas laughed. "You'd better not let him see you look cold—he might try and warm you up!"

I laughed nervously. "Okay, okay I'll eat."

Lucas stood up to leave. Unexpectedly he leaned down and gently pressed his lips to mine. My insides went crazy, with tingles that reached the depths of my belly. The hair on my arms stood on end as his tongue smoothly parted my lips and tenderly explored my mouth. I felt lightheaded. The kiss seemed to last forever, but was also over far too quickly. He slowly pulled away and I stayed in the same position, my eyes closed. He then leaned down and brushed a lock of hair behind my ear.

"I love you Ophelia," He whispered, his breath whisking across my earlobe. "Remember that above all else, that no matter what I do, it is because I love you."

My breath quickened and my heart raced. When I opened my eyes, he was gone. I hadn't even heard the door open or close.

There was no doubt, I loved Lucas.

LUCAS

"*Tsk Tsk Tsk.*" Rand was leaning against the adjacent wall as I left Ophelia's room. "Pity the way you are fluttering about her, attempting to distract her from her true fate, her true love." Rand's hands flitted about his head like a bird, crazy old coot.

I kept walking. I wasn't in the mood for any sparring, especially after the combat with Di last night. I heard his footsteps trailing behind me, though.

"It will always be him, no mortal love for you could trump her desire to be complete." He paused behind me. *Why was he trying to get such a rise out of me?* It must drive him crazy the way I shield so much of myself from him. He needed to upset me to get a read on me. I didn't muffle my laughter as I continued on my way.

I spoke with my back to him. "I'm on to you, old man. You'll have to find new tricks, or at least a new way, to fire me up."

"We both know that isn't difficult to do, Lucas. Yessica was always your sensible side." I took a deep breath. Just hearing her name slip off his lips so casually made my skin tingle with rage. He had no idea what our relationship was like.

"Maybe the loss of Carissa has numbed your senses some, Rand. Is that why you can't perform? How long has it been since she was murdered? About three centuries now? Yeah that must take a toll on one's abilities."

Rand was in front of me now. "Don't presume what you do not understand, Lucas Healey. But by all means underestimate me, it will make it all that much sweeter when I am able to expose you." He licked his lips.

"Now who's getting a rise out of who?" I stepped past him. This time he didn't follow.

"Until we meet again." He whispered the words and then he was gone.

I'd never cared much for Rand, even before he developed a distaste for me—pardon my pun. I was always too private for his games, though Yessica found him fascinating. As much as I disliked the man — I had to be honest with myself: he was absolutely right when he said Yessica had been my sensible side. She was the reasonable side to almost anyone around her—she could talk down a running bull.

It was her way. Which in turn made it my way, when she was alive. Now I was the running bull and few could get out of my path, cage me up or talk me down. No one except for Olly.

OPHELIA

I rubbed my eyes and I could feel someone in the room. I knew it had to be Winston. It was starting to feel like that movie *Groundhog Day*.

Today felt a little different though. I could sense Winston's eagerness. I'd barely gotten even a whiff of a room's emotional climate in a while, but this was now twice in twenty-four hours. *Could Lucas' camouflage be wearing off? Maybe he was letting me pick up on more around me, maybe he considered me safe among his allies. Or what if my sense was getting stronger somehow?*

"Good morning Winston." I opened my eyes as I said it. He almost looked disappointed that he didn't get to sneak up on me.

"Good morning Miss Ophelia." Yes, definitely disappointed. "Master Elias says that Di is prepared to escort you on a walk today as soon as you are ready."

I smiled at Winston and he was out the door and I ate in silence then changed, just in time for Di to sashay into my room.

She was such a paradox: appearing like a petite, sixteen-year-old girl, but gifted in love and scary as hell. She was gone before the gate was fully raised. By the time I was outside she was skipping around in circles. "Which way?" she asked.

I was eager to do a little more rigorous hiking than a simple stroll. I knew Di was able, but was she willing?

"Can we explore along the cliff face?" I asked and pointed in the direction I had in mind.

She giggled. "I'm okay with that, but I better ask Elias." She playfully shook her finger at me. "Testing the boundaries, silly girl. Give me a moment." Then she was gone.

I did a full sweep of the countryside and when I turned back around Di was two inches from my face. She smelled so sweet. "Elias says no scaling, but I can take you along a path to a vista point that he believes will satiate your wild side."

"That's what he said, my wild side?"

"Yep. Now follow me." She skipped ahead of me.

My wild side? Did he think I *liked* to be reckless? That couldn't be further from the truth, but I did like to hike. I did an internal *humph,* then got over it. *Who cares what he thought?*

"Do you always skip everywhere?" I asked, struggling to keep up.

"Skip?" Di looked at me inquisitively. "Oh, I frolic because it slackens my pace, so mortals can keep up with me."

I quickly sped up. I didn't mean to keep love waiting. It really was a marvelous day. Not a cloud in the sky. It was clear spring was over here, wherever here was, but it must not get too hot since most of the small foliage was still green.

"We are going to go that way." Di pointed to a clear path along the rocks. I looked behind me briefly. I thought I saw something move out of the corner of my eye, but Di didn't bother to turn around. "Just a sentinel."

I assumed as much. They had to be all around but keeping a watchful distance. *No matter,* I thought. *Out of sight, out of mind.*

We hit the path. There were long strands of grasses and small shrubs sneaking up between the rock crevices. "Is this a path used for perimeter checks?" I asked.

"Yes."

"So, we are going to see the fourth side of the castle and the valley?"

"Yes." She stopped and turned around. "That is what you wanted, is it not?"

"Oh yes. I was just asking." She turned back around and continued. *Less is more obviously,* I chided myself. *Only ask the most pertinent questions.*

It did turn out to be quite a hike, and I was winded as we navigated to the vista point, hoping I hadn't bitten off more than I could chew. It would be embarrassing to have to throw in the towel. I was no wimp, but we'd been trudging nonstop in the sun for at least an hour, and I hadn't brought any water. I was relieved and astounded by the view, when we stopped. I could see the entire valley, and the fortress impressively towered over the landscape.

"Wow." I said breathlessly. "It's magnificent."

Di just shrugged. I guess she'd seen better. What could I expect from a few-thousand-year-old goddess?

"Would you like to sit?"

I looked around I didn't see an obvious place to do so. "I think I'm okay."

"Don't be silly. May I?" Before I could answer she'd hoisted me up like a toddler onto her hip and was placing me on a large rock face twenty feet up. The view was even more spectacular there. She looked delighted with herself, kicking her feet as she sat next to me.

We sat there for a long time, an occasional bird soaring above us. I studied the castle, then the valley. Di never said a word. I was about ready to go when I noticed something moving in front of the fortress, at the cliff face. I tried to get it into focus, straining my eyes to make it out. "Di, do you see something moving in front of the castle? There at the cliff." I pointed.

"That is the castle moving."

I looked at her, stunned. "The castle *moving?*"

"Yes, the castle moving." Obviously, I was going to have to ask more specific questions.

"Castles don't move." I stated.

"Well, no it doesn't get up and move." *Phew,* I wasn't crazy, I thought. *She must be referring to some weird translation of move.* Di continued. "The East Wing of the castle is constantly transforming. You were the one who used the word moving. I thought that was an odd word to use, but I do not always understand the exact translation of current slang."

"What do you mean transforming? I stay in the East Wing, I've never noticed it *transforming*." I stressed that last word.

"Well you should be more observant." *Well there you have it, I was just not paying attention.* It was clear if I wanted answers I was probably not going to get them from Di.

Then I remembered the way the bricks shifted in front of Lucas and I when he had taken me to the antiquities room, to answer my questions a couple days earlier. I shuddered when I thought of the terrible odor I smelled walking down that hall.

"I do remember seeing an entry way manifest in the bricks."

"As I said," She replied. "Are you ready to go?"

Return hikes always seem easier, I thought, happy at that. I hadn't been able to see it very well from our rock perch, but it looked like the castle had been expanding, wavelike. I was eager to learn more. I considered asking Lucas, sure he could explain it to me. But my mind kept going back to Elias, from what I could gather it was his home.

"Thank you Di," I offered when the fortress was in sight. She was still a few feet in front of me, but I didn't know when she would run off.

"Of course." Her little voice chimed in response, then sure enough, she was gone.

"How was your walk?" Elias fell in behind me. I jumped.

"It was good. Thank you for keeping an eye on me. I'm sure your sentries were everywhere, though all I ever saw was a blur of a figure."

He smiled and my stomach flipped. "Everyone in this castle understands that your safety is of the upmost importance."

I swallowed hard. Elias' stare felt like it penetrated my every cell. "I hope it doesn't come to anyone needing to protect me."

"Of course, that is what we all hope." He shifted on his feet slightly.

"I was wondering if you could come to my room in a bit? I have some questions about the castle and since this is your home, right?" He nodded. "It seems you're the right man to ask."

"Gladly. When should I come by?"

"After I freshen up?"

"I will request that Winston make lunch for two this afternoon. I will come to your quarters in an hour. Will that do?"

I nodded. He smiled and continued walking, ahead of me. Lucas caught my stride.

"What was that about Olly? I can answer any questions you might have." He sounded troubled.

"I'm sure you're very knowledgeable in many different arenas, but I wanted to ask Elias' some things about the castle." I knew he wouldn't agree, but it didn't matter.

"I've spent many summers here, I'm sure I could help you," he pressed. Then he stopped, looking at me probingly. "Is this just a ploy to spend more time with Elias? Is there something I should know? Is this because I kissed you?"

"Hold on Lucas, let's be rational. I'm not pulling some lame excuse out of my ass. Elias is legitimately the best person to ask questions about *his* home. I'm still not ready to even think about how I feel about *us* right now, or anyone else. I know there's some weird rivalry between you and Elias, but I don't want any part of it. I barely even know him, and now I wonder how much I really know you." My last words stung. I could see it on his face. "Let me be frank. If I start to sort out how I feel about us or anyone else, you'll be the first person I talk to about it. For a million reasons, you'll be my sounding board. Do you understand?"

"Okay. I'll try to be less paranoid," he said, kissing my forehead. "You're just so important to me and I don't want to lose you."

"You're not losing me! I'm right here." I meant every word. I also knew that he wasn't going to be any less possessive.

ELIAS and I finished eating and I decided to just dive into my inquiry.

"So today on my hike with Di, I was able to see the eastern-facing wall of the castle, the side that overlooks the valley. I noticed something odd." He knew what was coming, but I was going to stick with my rehearsed inner monologue. "When I asked Di, she said that the East Wing, *this wing—I think,* transforms. How is that possible?"

"It's very old magic, most of it has been lost over the generations. My parents built this fortress over many thousands of years. It started out with this structure. The East Wing, as it stands now. The foundation to this part of the castle was built with ancient magic to keep its occupants protected. She still moves with that intention."

"*She? Intention?* I'm sorry, you're going to have to elaborate for me."

"My mother called her Hafiza. That is Arabic for protected." My fireplace seemed to exhale. The flames within grew, then subsided.

"What was that?" I asked, thinking it had never done that before. Or maybe I'd just not been paying enough attention.

"Don't worry, that was just Hafiza saying hello." Elias got up and placed his hand on the mantel.

It was silly, but I felt the need to whisper. "Should I do the same?"

He laughed. "Only if you want to, a simple hello should suffice."

"Hi Hafiza," I said as warmly as I could. I didn't know what to expect in response, but there was nothing. I was disappointed.

Elias continued. "The way I understand the old magic is this—when a conduit chooses to leave residual energy of their own in a place, it leaves a mark. The old incantations allowed an individual, Soahcoit or many beings to merge together their energy with a specific intention and thus that place forever held pieces of their gifts. The intention and the individual conduits gift determine the effect of the spell." He paused to make sure I was following him.

I nodded to let him know I was following him.

"My father had the gift of growth. He was what conduits call a giant. My mother was a healer." I noticed he said 'was'.

"Are your parents here?" I winced as I asked the question, afraid of the obvious answer.

"No, my parents are deceased." His face immediately shifted. "They were ambushed, undoubtedly by Nebas. Despite the times they had always insisted on being a refuge for our kind. I am afraid that is what led to their murders."

I started to reach for him and then thought the better of it. "I am so sorry Elias." He nodded. "How long ago? Was it here?"

"No not here, you are safe here." He assured me. "It was four years ago."

I leaned in closer, I wanted to comfort him, but I didn't trust the electricity between us. "I am so sorry." Is all I could say.

"Please do not be sorry. All I can do now is honor their memory and someday I hope to get to the bottom of their murders." He straightened up his posture immediately. "This is not why you sought out my company today, let us continue with your query." Just like that he put a smile back on his face. It was clear he was carrying the weight of the world on his shoulders, including my safety and happiness. I felt immense empathy, because I had felt that way for so many years. We were more alike than I had imagined. I also knew that look, he was ready to get down to business and unwilling to wallow in his circumstances so I might as well move on as well.

"Okay, Hafiza transforms her shape, because your father was a giant and your mother a healer, then add your parent's intention for protection. So, they placed pieces of their gifts and their intention in this place and that created some kind of spell? I think I understand the way it works. This type of magic seems like it could be useful to the cause right now. Why has it been abandoned?" I asked.

"Yes, exactly, full marks Ophelia. There are a few reasons why the old practice of covening has been disregarded."

I stopped him. "Let me just clarify, you said covening, like a witch coven? That's what a place like this is called?"

"No… covening was what it was called when conduits gather to *practice* the ancient magic. But a place with this manner of magic instilled in it is called a *haven*—there are hundreds of them around the world, some are vast, some are humble. They require an invitation for admittance. They are refuges, almost entirely undetectable unless you were invited in."

He continued. "You remember how Yanni can see conduits, like beacons on a map?" I nodded. "And we told you that a Soahcoit was easier to spot than an individual and so on? You can imagine what a spell of that magnitude would attract. It would take multiple conduits in a single location exuding a colossal amount of power. Right now, it is safer to use existing havens for refuges. The magic has been around so long that it does not draw unwanted attention, do you understand?"

"Yes, that makes sense, so the magic isn't lost, only not being used."

"That is not entirely true. There are only two written volumes of the ancient anthologies left in existence. They are called The Pierses. We know the whereabouts of one, but the other remains concealed." It was obvious that Elias was assuming Yanni and Esther had it. "They are sisters, which means their magic is bound to each other. A skilled conduit would be able to detect the transactions of the other book. For now, no one uses the ancient magic."

I wanted to see Hafiza in action. "Would it be too much to ask to see a little of Hafiza, if you have time?"

"It would be my pleasure." A huge grin spread across his face, as well as mine. It was amazing how at ease I felt with him, how whole. "Shall we?" He gestured towards the door. We stepped into the hall. It was colder than in my room. Torches were lit and lined the passage. I crossed my arms across my chest to prevent myself from shivering.

"Are you cold?" Elias asked.

"A little, aren't you?"

"We will remedy that." He began whispering something in Asagi. It sounded like poetry. Within seconds I felt a warm breeze envelop my body. "Hafiza is very good at temperature control when needed," he said rather proudly.

"I can tell. Thanks Hafiza!" We both laughed.

"I am going to escort you to my chamber," he said. "Along the way you should get a good idea of Hafiza's abilities."

"How many people stay in this part of the castle with us?"

"Only you and I. There are other rooms of course—my father's study, a large library, a couple latrines, an expansive hall that shifts into many great rooms, the antiquities room where we convened before, and two guest rooms—as well as my parents' master suite. As I said, this is the original construct of the fortress, so she is not expansive."

"Sounds like plenty of space to me, but I'm used to San Francisco, where you pay fifteen hundred dollars for a small studio."

We walked until we reached a wall. It must have been the same as the one Lucas and I'd encountered before. It began to shift and fold into itself until there was another, more cavernous passage ahead of us. I braced myself for the expected assault on my nose, but this time it didn't smell.

"Is this the same wall as before? It doesn't smell in here now."

"That is because she recognizes family, the odor is to deter strangers or unwanted callers." I guess that made sense. Odor was a very powerful deterrent. It also made sense that Lucas was an unwanted guest for Elias, given the tension between them.

The passage again opened up to expose yet an even larger hall, with gigantic pillars and ornate carvings etched into its massive archways.

"I'm afraid she is showing off." Elias looked captivating in this lighting. I stared at his face. At this angle his jaw was bold, and expressed limitless strength. His high cheekbones softened his smile. His fair hair outlined his face with youthful charm—a mature sandy blond. He had grown a short beard after we arrived at the castle and it suited him. Between the youthful charm and gruff beard he was sporting a lot of mystery and was damn sexy. Elias' eyes, as from the first time I met him, were enchanting. I wondered if this was only the case with me, or was everyone else also entranced by his stare? He glanced at me and I blushed. "She only entertains with the great hall when she wants to make an impression." Just then several large sconces ignited and lit the room. It was truly striking. *Not expansive my ass. I guess she likes me.*

The room seemed to go on for miles, literally. We walked its length, then finally came to a descending stairwell.

"Are we going down there?" It was dark. "Can she light a candle for us?"

"Pardon—are you afraid of the dark?" Elias jabbed at me. I hadn't seen this playful side of him before. I looked up to make sure he saw my eyes roll. "The dark staircase is not what you should be afraid of."

Before I could mutter another word, I felt the bricks move beneath my feet and we were falling. The floor had completely disappeared. I closed my eyes, wanting to scream, but it all happened so fast that I didn't have time to react. Next thing I knew we were on a large bed in a luxurious room. The bed had four huge, golden posts and the comforter was crimson satin. I sat up immediately.

"Is this your room?" I felt like I'd been tricked, and although I was feeling tingly all over I was also pissed.

"No of course not. It is my parents' suite. Hafiza was posturing, as I told you."

"Well then how did you know what she was going to do?"

"We have a language between us. I grew up in and out of her walls. She is a very old friend."

I looked around the room, it was stunning. Impressionist artwork covered the walls—some of Renoir's work, I was almost positive. I jumped off the bed to examine the portrait closest to me, yep it was a Renoir, a nude. The walls were dotted with delicate sconces, and on the ceiling hung a magnificent chandelier with hundreds of crystals strewn together.

"Impeccable taste."

"My mother was very moved by French Impressionist art. Most of her homes reflect that."

"I love Renoir's nude portraits too. I fell in love with them when I went to Paris some years back. I spent many hours studying them at the Musée de l'Orangerie there. Most people don't find these pieces nearly as compelling as his others."

Elias was now at my back. I could feel the warmth of his body. "She shared a similar sentiment. I think you two would have carried on very well indeed."

I could feel his breath dancing across the tiny hairs on my neck. Vibrations fluttered through my body from head to toe.

"You loved her very much?" It came out as an almost inaudible whisper.

His lips were nearly brushing my ear. "Yes." His warm, woodsy-sweet scent rushed into my nostrils and I felt faint. My knees gave way and I buckled into his arms, my senses were on fire and I was intensely feverish. He drew me back to my feet, gently grabbing my waist. He pursed his lips to the curve of my neck as my heart pounded wildly. I turned around and found myself pressed to his body. I could feel him hard against me and I was throbbing with anticipation. I was ready to rip off his clothes right then and take him to bed.

He took my face into his hands and kissed my forehead. I wanted to leap on him. But then he pulled away and I felt exposed and like a fool. *What the hell, Elias? Why tease me?*

I took a couple deep breaths to regain my composure. Elias had his back to me and I wondered if he was doing the same. The silence felt suffocating.

When I was no longer shaking I spoke. "Is this the end of the tour?" I walked around so I could see his face. His golden eyes held hunger, and anguish. I knew that he wanted more too, but something was holding him back.

"Only if that is what you wish." He paused. "Forgive me Ophelia, for my forwardness. I hope you do not feel uncomfortable now." I didn't understand everything that had just happened and since I had promised Lucas I would let him know before I made any decisions I was slightly relieved that Elias had the sense to pull away. I wasn't sure how I felt about any of this, but I was not uncomfortable. *Confused maybe.*

"I am fine. We are fine." I wanted to move past this quickly. "So Hafiza can make the floor disappear? Big whoop." I made some ridiculous gesture above my head. "Is that all she's got?"

"Be careful what you wish for." He was smiling at my stupid joke. That was good.

"Should I be scared?" I tried to sound sarcastic, but I was seriously wondering if I should be afraid. Because making the floor dissolve was pretty terrifying, if I was being honest with myself.

"I don't know, I have never challenged her. I guess we will find out shortly." He smiled. The thick lust in the air was subsiding.

Instantly the walls began to close in and Elias darted for the door. I was quick on his tail. We'd barely managed to step into the next room when the ceiling started to disintegrate. Then in one fluid movement we were sliding down a narrow passage and somehow landed on the ceiling of the great hall we had entered through before. I was considering screaming *I give up!* When the spinning stopped and we were in a much smaller room.

"You win Hafiza," I said. "You're incredible." The fireplace burst into brilliant flames, then settled into a cozy crackling. I turned to Elias. "Is this your room?'

"Yes." He said quietly. It was smaller than my own chamber. It had a writing desk with a laptop and some books scattered on it. He had a chair by the hearth, same as I did, and numerous photographs on the wall.

I scanned the pictures. Two faces stood out. I pointed to a photo. "Are these your parents?"

"Yes, Sorcey and Cane." His mother was beautiful, with deep blue eyes, long, wavy black hair and flawless bronze skin. Her smile jumped out of the photo and instantly warmed my heart. I felt like I knew her. I realized that was because Elias had her smile. Cane was strikingly handsome. He was blonde, with fairer skin, dynamic hazel eyes, high cheekbones and broad shoulders. He looked like a Viking. Elias definitely had his nose.

"I see both of them in you. They are two very attractive people." His smile widened as I spoke.

I continued scanning the photos. I saw lots of pictures of Winston, Di and Aremis. I stopped when I saw Lucas, he looked so happy. He was with a large group on a beach. The attire looked to be from the 1930s. Lucas was next to Sorcey, and on his other side was a delicate woman.

"Ah I see you found Lucas. That was his wife Yessica. She was a brilliant woman, I adored her in my youth."

She was laughing at something Lucas had said. Her head was tilted back and her face was lit up with laughter lines. She appeared to be of Asian descent, with very dark and distinct features. She was exotic.

"What happened to her?"

"No one knows for certain. She was abducted fifteen years before my parents died. Lucas had entrusted Yessica with my family for safe-keeping while he attempted to evade those he believed to be hunting them. Three weeks after he left, the small posse that had been following them caught up to me, my family and Yessica. They ambushed us outside of Hanoi. My mother fled with me and my father stayed back and fought frantically to save Yessica, but to no avail. They nearly beheaded him in the process and were able to escape with Yessica as their captive. She was still alive the last time my Father saw her. He never forgave himself for what happened. My mother found him three days later, holed up in a sewer nearby, struggling to recover from his wounds."

All I could think was poor Lucas. He lost the woman he loved and he didn't even know what happened to her. I suddenly needed to see him, I wanted to give him a hug.

I turned to Elias. "Isn't it strange that we haven't seen Lucas yet? He doesn't particularly like us together."

"Oh you have noticed that? Well you can attribute our evading him to Hafiza, because I am sure he has been combing the castle looking for us."

"I don't want him worried about me." I felt terrible. I wasn't trying to hide from him. After hearing about Yessica, it was no wonder he was so protective of me. "We should get back."

"As you wish." Elias turned to lead the way.

I looked over the mosaic of photos one last time and a particular image caught my attention. I hurried over to the picture. "Who's this?" I pointed at a bewitching blonde in the back row of a group posed for an occasion.

"I do not know, I am not acquainted with her. Often my mother listed the names of the people in each photo on the back." He pulled the photograph out of the frame as I waited, holding my breath. The woman looked like my grandmother Lilith. The image was grainy, so I couldn't be positive. "That's peculiar, there are no names on the back of this photo. Perhaps it was not my mother's." He was thinking.

"Does it say anything at all?" I was desperate for a clue.

"Only a date: June 3, 1968." Elias looked at me, attempting to follow my train of thought.

My head was swirling, trying to do math. "That would be two years after Lilith killed herself."

"Lilith who?"

"The woman in this photo looks like the only picture I have ever seen of Eleanor's mom, Lilith Platz, my grandmother. If it isn't her, it could be her sister." I saw a flicker of recognition dart across his face. "You know my grandmother? Is this Lilith?"

"I do not know if that is Lilith. I apologize. I can do some investigating to see if I can find any other images of this woman. Perhaps one with a name." He scrutinized the photo. "I see the resemblance, although I have only seen an image of her as a child."

My mouth was ajar. "You knew Lilith as a child." None of this made sense.

"No of course not, I only know what my parents told me about her and I have this photo." He walked to the furthest corner of the room. There on the wall was a small oval frame with a young fair-haired beauty, no older than ten years old. It was indisputably Lilith. "I did not know this was your grandmother." His eyes pleaded, begging me to believe him.

He took the photo off the wall and handed it to me. "It is yours." My eyes welled up with tears.

"Is she alive?" Anything was possible, right? I traced her tiny face with my finger.

"No, the last I heard, she was gone." He paused and touched my shoulder. "My parents loved her very much— she spent her summers with them before I was born. She was like the daughter my mother always wanted."

I could see a light in her eyes, nothing like in the photograph of her at the institution holding Eleanor. "What happened to her?"

"I only know rumors. They are not for the faint-hearted Ophelia."

He grabbed both my shoulders and turned me towards him, the electricity was zipping between us, but I was too distracted to care. "Are you sure you want to know?"

I nodded.

"My mother told me that during the summer that Lilith turned twenty she failed to return to the haven in Costa Rica. My parents grew concerned, she had never gone extended periods of time without communicating with them. They travelled to Krakow in Poland where they had last heard from Lilith and her family. After hunting down leads they determined that Lilith's family had been murdered and that Lilith had been kidnapped by an especially heinous Nebas named Nestor. Nestor is an incubus. For centuries, he has skirted the evil flanks of Yanni and Esther abducting, torturing and impregnating promising conduits."

I shuddered. "You mean…?" I stopped mid-sentence and put my face in my hands as I connected the dots. Elias ushered me to his bed to sit down. He held me tight and this time the pulsing felt like waves of comfort. "Continue please, I need to know." I was desperate for answers.

He took a deep breath. "Lilith had shown amazing promise. My mother said she was truly gifted. She saw imprinted memories." I looked up, beckoning explanation and he got the hint. "Imprinted memories would be similar to when you enter a room and you get a feeling alike, 'this is a bad place' or you have inexplicable joy. It is as if a memory has left a mark on the physical surrounding. Lilith could see these memories to a certain extent, as though she were watching a movie play out in front of her. If she had consummated that would indeed have been a very valuable gift, comparable to time travel." That sounded amazing. I started sobbing, sad that my poor grandmother was so gifted and so tormented.

"Was Nestor her Atoa?" I couldn't fathom this monster as my grandfather.

"No." I let out a huge exhale. "But he is most likely your grandfather." I stiffened as Elias said the words. "It is probable that he impregnated Lilith at least once. Possibly more. I am so sorry." Elias squeezed me tighter still. The tears had stopped slowly, being replaced by anger.

"Please tell me everything you know." I could tell there was more.

"My parents investigated Lilith's abduction and it eventually led them to North America. By the time they pinpointed Nestor's whereabouts he was gone and they assumed Lilith was dead. That was later confirmed when they tracked her whereabouts to an institution in Connecticut. She had escaped Nestor, but apparently the ordeal was too much for her. I am so sorry I never connected the dots."

"I shook my head, so she *was* crazy. Because some psycho mutilated her for months on end and that psycho is my grandpa. A man who is part of the Nebas." My head was spinning.

"She may not have actually gone crazy, but her gift would have looked like what humans call schizophrenia. After trauma like that she might not have been able to distinguish between reality and her gift." Elias let his hands fall to his lap. "My mother never forgave herself."

I finally looked up and it occurred to me that this was the world that Elias had been living in for his entire life. He has been in a battle and the casualties were mounting. I took his hand in mine. "Thank you."

We looked at each other for a long time in silence. Elias stood up and grabbed the other photo, the one of the woman who looked like Lilith as a grown woman. "I recognize some of the people in this photo, I will find out who this woman is." He asserted. "Are you ready to return to your chamber?"

"Yes, I am," I said. We walked back slowly, through the great hall and down a spiral staircase. I definitely could not have found my way out. Hafiza did a brilliant job of flummoxing her guests. We reached the wall that dissolved. On the other side was Lucas.

ELIAS

I watched as Lucas escorted Ophelia down the hall until they were out of sight. He was livid, but the moment he saw her he was more concerned with comforting Ophelia than he was about castigating me. The haranguing would happen later. I turned to walk to my room, I was exhausted.

I mentally thrashed myself the whole way back. It was so foolish of me to lose control like that with her. It was all I could do to contain myself this afternoon. If it had gone any further I never would have forgiven myself.

So much more is at stake than your damn hard on Elias, you have got to get it together. You cannot be that foolish again. When I had berated myself to a satisfactory pulp I let up and really let the day sink in. Our bond was getting so much stronger.

I lay down on my bed, staring up at the ceiling. I knew this would be difficult, but I really could not have anticipated how challenging it would truly be. I thought about the taste of her skin on my lips and I was immediately aroused. My heart started beating erratically, so I took long deliberate breaths. This was not like me and it was a terribly inconvenient time to let myself lose control.

The prophecy was clear, she was safe as long as she was not

consummated. Our brethren were safe as long as she was not consummated. Our union would just have to wait, until I could change her fate. Which in turn meant I needed to fortify my self-control. I reminded myself of the task my father had bestowed upon me—to orchestrate a summit, an assembly of unification.

He was certain that if we could unite the Poginuli and the remaining Soahcoit that we could band together and defeat the Nebas once and for all. Three days after they were killed I received an encrypted message leading me to the whereabouts of my father's blue prints for the summit. He had everything formulated down to the tiniest of details, all except for the location.

That was where Alistair was supposed to assist. His gift for mapping was ideal for aiding me in securing the optimal location for a large coalition of our kind to meet in secrecy and security. But everything has gone awry, leaving me with more questions than answers.

I had gotten no hints from Alistair's maps, and his laptop was another cryptic mess. I was still nowhere near deciphering his journals. I had, however, found a pattern in them—and that is what I spent most of my time picking through.

For the last year and a half I could hardly get away, and none of the native people that Alistair visited disclosed their text online, as far as I could tell. I needed to get to those places in order to get tangible answers. I had no idea how I would do that whilst minding Ophelia.

I had narrowed my own search of potential summit locations to approximately fifty different sites. I had hoped Alistair might have been able to further eliminate some of the possibilities. I required somewhere well-hidden yet large, with good strategic vantage points in case a battle did ensue. I had hoped to carry out the summit the previous fall, but everything changed the moment Ophelia and I collided in Chicago. My attention was now divided.

I rubbed my eyes. It was exhausting having no one I could trust, and the prophecy weighed on me day and night. I still found myself inundated in resentment toward my parents for bequeathing this unmanageable task to me and with-it paranoia and solitude. Then I would feel terrible for having such feelings and spend another expanse of time chastising myself for resenting them and their mission.

None of this was helping the situation. *Get it together and find a solution, that is what your father would have done.*

I opened the wall safe behind my bed and pulled out Alistair's journals, I would spend the rest of the evening charting his code so that when I did find the missing link things could move swiftly.

OPHELIA

After a few weeks and several walks, I had a good sense of my surroundings. Three walls of the fortress were snuggled up to the cliff face. On the fourth side was a rocky but fairly flat jetty of land, the only really accessible entrance to the castle. Rolling hills and shrubbery lined the valley. I imagined when the castle was built this was the perfect site for eluding invaders or hostile takeovers. Hundreds of years later it still served the same purpose.

I had developed a routine, exploring the grounds by myself every day while Elias and Lucas did their perimeter check. The two of them watched me like a hawk, so when I say I walked alone, this meant they were always fifteen feet behind me.

I stood on the cliff face, closed my eyes and lifted my face towards the sun. I loved the way it warmed my skin. I sensed a shadow slowly come across my closed eyelids and immediately knew it wasn't Lucas or Elias, because they said nothing. I swallowed hard, not sure what to do next. Before I could determine a plan of action my body was flying through the air, as if I had been propelled out of a plane.

I didn't have time for my life to flash before my eyes, my body was too disoriented to know it was going to die. I opened my eyes and as I twisted in the air I could see the sky, then the floor of the valley rising to greet me. My senses were on overload, trying to recover from the shift in gravity. It seemed like I was falling for an eternity. Just when I should have hit the ground, I was suddenly zipping through the valley floor, vaulting over massive boulders and ascending huge trees. I couldn't clearly distinguish how I was being transported. I thought I felt hands, but every time I tried to hone in on details, my mind would ache. Maybe a copious amount of adrenaline had that effect on a person.

I noticed a warmth against my thighs. *I must be hoisted over someone's shoulder.* I attempted to squirm, but the grip tightened like a vice. Yes, I was being carried. I twisted my neck to see what was coming. There was a massive tree dead ahead. When my captor tried to climb it, I kicked my legs to the left and their grip faltered for a moment. Enough to drop me to the ground. I had to have fallen from at least ten feet up.

A large shadow gently pounced onto the soil next to me. I could slightly make out a feminine figure—she was reaching down to take hold of my waist and presumably hoist me back onto her shoulder. I tried to fixate on her eyes, but I must have hit my head harder than I thought because it was throbbing and nothing would come into focus. My eyes focused on her hair: it was dark, and her figure was strong, but absolutely female. There was a noise behind us, and she shifted her attention for just a moment. But it was enough.

LUCAS

How the hell did this happen? I slipped down the tree trunk adjacent to where I'd been perched only seconds earlier. I knew these walks weren't a good idea. *Why on earth did I allow him to talk me into this?* I should have been more adamant.

I slung myself to the next tree. I was nearly to the cliff face, only moments behind her abductor, but that is all it took for her to disappear. I picked up my pace, hearing footsteps behind me. It didn't matter who it was—I was going to catch up to Ophelia.

The precipice was no more than fifteen feet ahead. Again, I picked up my pace and catapulted myself off the edge. The wind flew past my face, whipping hard and fast, and all I could think was that Olly must be terrified.

I hit the ground hard and the earth dented beneath my impact. I shoved off and was again at full speed, dodging trees and winding through obstacles on the valley floor. I thought I heard footsteps not too far in front of me by then, and I could smell Ophelia's fragrance in the air—faint but distinctly hers. There was something else as well, I couldn't put my finger on it, but it was vaguely familiar.

I was making a mental checklist in case this turned into an

extended hunting party. I needed to take in every detail. Then I heard a thud and I extended my sensory net and my camouflage and felt a figure go limp ahead of me and the smell of blood filled my nostrils.

"She is over here!" Lars' voice rang through the trees. "She might be unconscious, and she is bleeding."

OPHELIA

Suddenly, she was gone.

I was rattled and my leg felt funny. I looked down to see a huge gash in my right calf. Blood was pouring out of the wound. I didn't like blood very much, especially when it was coming from me. My head still throbbed and my stomach felt woozy, so I laid back down. Whatever had scared away Wonder Woman would just have to eat me, because I wasn't going anywhere at the moment. I heard another noise behind me and didn't move. I just lay there with my eyes closed, attempting not to vomit.

"She is over here!" I didn't know that voice, but it didn't sound menacing. "She might be unconscious, and she is bleeding."

"Get out of the way! Olly, Olly." I knew that voice, that was Lucas. "Olly, are you okay? Can you hear me?" He gently lifted my head. "Please respond, Ophelia, before you give me a damn heart attack." I nodded my head. He took a deep breath.

"Is she going to be okay?" Elias was also close, not next to me, but that was his voice. "We are going to track the intruder—tell me, is she okay?" This time his voice was firmer.

"Yes Viraclay, she will be fine." Lucas scoffed. Footsteps trailed off to my right—Elias leaving to track the invader.

I tried to pull my head up. When that didn't work I opened my eyes. Lucas was crouched down next to me, his hand over my lesion.

"Lay back down," he instructed me. "I'll carry you back to the castle in a moment—I just want to get something on this cut." My head was now coddled in his lap. I tried to see who else was with us, but it looked like we were alone. The pain at the base of my head was agonizing, it felt like I'd been hit with a baseball bat. I let my eyes roll back. Lucas started yelling something in Asagi. The shouting wasn't helping the headache. I felt someone kneel down on the other side of my leg and before I could open my eyes to see who it was, Lucas was carrying me through the forest at an incredible speed. I felt safe so I just let go and I drifted into unconsciousness.

ELIAS

"Lars, you go east. Di, take the south road and double back to the castle. Ying, track the north end and then loop west. I will meet you back here." I was running as fast as my legs would carry me. I still could smell a faint trace of the stranger in the valley.

I scaled a large oak for a view of the basin floor ahead of me. As I reached the top I saw some branches shuffling no more than a half a mile due west. I bounded to the ground and hit a full sprint. My breathing was heavy and would certainly scare away any conduit that could hear. So, I concentrated on deep quiet breaths through my nose. I caught a blur directly in front of me.

I paused for a moment to see if it stirred again. Nothing, but I heard the subtle crunch of steps on dry brush. I strained my eyes to see the minute shadows between the trees. There it was a distinct shade of purple that was not native to the natural hues of the forest.

I took a deep breath and raced in the direction of the abductor. The purple darted left and I pursued. Before I could see their next move I felt a fierce blow to the side of my head. I wobbled slightly and then spun around and caught another foot coming toward my face. I grabbed and twisted and the intruder spun around, and landed facing the other direction, then without skipping a beat was off again.

I was seeing stars, so I placed my hands on my head and refocused. It was too late though, the trespasser was gone, and I could not be certain of which direction. Ying flew down from a tree branch and startled me.

"Which way?" He was poised to go.

"I do not know. My apologies. I lost them again." He put his hand on my shoulder and then was gone, following whatever scent he could pick up. I stood there for a long moment, recapping the encounter as best I could. I should have done better. This was too close a call. Ophelia was nearly taken.

I rebuked myself the whole walk back to the castle.

OPHELIA

When I woke I was in my bed. Elias and Lucas were hovering over me, both men looked intensely relieved when I opened my eyes. I tried to speak, but my mouth was dry. I needed water. Elias read my mind and he handed me a cup. I finished the entire thing in one gulp and motioned for more. *How long had I been out?* My head was still aching, but it was manageable. After I finished the second glass I laid back down in bed. I expected one of them to start asking me questions, but they didn't. *Maybe they were just as confused as me.* I was trying to make sense of my thoughts before I spoke.

"What happened out there?" That was as far as my mind would allow me to inquire. I still felt incredibly foggy, almost stoned.

Elias spoke first. "It would appear that someone tried to abduct you."

Well no shit, Sherlock.

"I pursued them as far as I could into the forest, but we lost their trail a few miles from where we found you. How are you feeling?" Elias said.

"My head hurts, a lot." I went to sit up further in the bed and I felt a twinge in my calf. "My leg hurts too."

"You did a number there, seventeen stitches." Lucas looked down at the bandage. "I'm sorry. I should have been there to make sure this didn't happen. I'm so sorry Olly." Lucas was beside himself. I didn't like seeing him this way at all. I looked over at Elias. He looked no better, his face said it all. He was feeling the same grave guilt as Lucas.

"This was no one's fault except the person who tried to kidnap me," I said. "Do we have any idea who it was?" *I knew it wasn't Yanni.* "Was it Esther?"

"Why do you say Esther? Was it a woman?" Elias was right beside me now.

"I'm pretty sure it was female, it was so hard to tell. She was moving so quickly, and then I hit my head." Elias was staring at me, absorbed, like he could pluck the memory out of my mind. I wish he could, because I couldn't.

"I think I just need some time to better organize my thoughts. Can I have a pen and paper, and maybe some solitude?" I said the last bit with a bit of a scoff, I was being held captive in order to avoid these kinds of situations—and clearly they were unavoidable. *Someone knew I was here.*

Lucas immediately got up and within seconds was back with a piece of paper and a pen.

"I'll be back in a bit," he said. "Elias will stay here with you in case you need anything." Lucas nodded at him, and I could tell it was a silent warning: stay away from her and don't talk. *Man, these two had interesting dynamics.*

When my headache began to subside, I opened my eyes. Elias had dimmed the lighting. Moments later Lucas reentered the room.

"How are you doing, Olly?" He looked down at the mindless scribbles below my pen. "That well huh?"

"The truth is I can't remember a thing about how she looked. I keep trying to rack my brain, but the image is so foggy my head hurts when I try to make sense of it or pick up on any distinct details. It's as if someone pressed the delete button in my brain and I can't get the information from the hard drive." I didn't know anything about computers, but that analogy seemed to make perfect sense to me.

"Elias! Ophelia is on to something."

I am, what might that be? I wondered. Elias moved so quickly that I jerked when I felt his hand grasp my wrist and I felt our electricity. I instinctively pulled away.

"Who do we know that can delete and distort memories?" Lucas asked.

Elias was immediately on his phone speaking in Asagi. I turned to Lucas. "I give up, who do we know that can delete and distort memories—and does this explain my deep sense of fogginess?"

"Nandi." Lucas was aware I didn't know a single person with that name. "Nandi is a conduit from South Africa. She's about two thousand years old. Esther and Yanni murdered her Atoa thirteen years ago. I don't know of any other existing conduit with powers like Nandi's, but it makes no sense that she would want to abduct you. She's seeking revenge for her lost lover, just the same as all of the other Poginuli." I looked at him, bewildered.

He blurted out three words in Asagi that I of course could not make out. *Dammit I wish they had a Rosetta Stone for this damn language. Shouldn't I learn it?*

Elias immediately repeated the phrase and hung up the phone. Elias walked quietly to my bedside and stared at me. Lucas' eyes were closed. He was concentrating

I adjusted myself in bed. "Why come after me? Would she use me as bait? A way to draw Yanni or Esther out of hiding, to avenge her partner? The question is, why me? I am not even a conduit yet. Maybe she really wants one of you." Something flashed across Lucas' face. I had said something that struck a chord. He got up and left the room.

What did I say? I wondered.

Elias ignored Lucas' odd behavior and turned to me. "How is your leg? I noticed you wincing." *Damn Elias didn't miss a thing.*

"It's fine, a little sore."

"Can I look at it?" I was hesitant, but I nodded. He pulled down the blanket and exposed my bandaged leg, then slowly unwrapped the dressing. It was pretty nasty looking, even with the blood dried. I wanted to look away, but was curious when Elias put one hand above the wound and the other below. Soon I felt trembling all over my body. He closed his eyes and the vibrations hastened. Then I felt an odd itching and tingling in the wound. I thought I saw the gash thinning, healing right in front of me. Elias began to sweat and he drew his hands away. He quickly rewrapped the incision and threw the blanket over me, just in time for Lucas to enter the room. He didn't ask me not to mention it, but I got the hint.

I tried to not even look at my leg, afraid I would give something away, but it was now extremely itchy, like when a scab is healing and the skin gets tight. I squirmed a little and of course Lucas noticed.

"Are you okay Olly?" Lucas was shifting his gaze to me then back to Elias suspiciously. I don't know how he knew it, but he detected that something just happened.

"I'm fine. I think I need to shower, though. My excursion through the woods left pine needles in places they shouldn't be." It was true—I felt really dirty. Elias smothered a smile.

"Will you need help in there?" Lucas halfheartedly asked. Both men looked a little too eager to assist.

"No, I can take care of it myself. But before I hop in the shower, can you tell me what just happened? What epiphany did you have?"

"It's nothing, I'm not sure if it will amount to anything. Let me mull it over a little longer." I looked over at Elias. I guess if he wasn't going to insist, neither was I. Plus my leg was going to drive me crazy if I didn't scratch it soon. I maneuvered myself out of bed and motioned for them to leave me alone so I could bathe in peace—reluctantly they agreed. The moment the door shut I ripped off my bandage, then buckled to the floor, astonished. The once-gaping wound looked nearly healed. I itched vigorously around the sutures, still careful not to pull them out.

What the hell? Had Elias performed some kind of incantation that sped up the healing process? It had to be that, I'd never healed miraculously fast before. *Was that his gift?* I wondered.

~

I ENTERED my room after my shower and there was an immediate knock at the door. Elias entered.

"I am sure you are curious about what I performed on your leg. With your permission, I would like to explain, I hope we can keep this between us." I nodded.

"You know they call me Viraclay?" he asked. I nodded again and he continued. "Viraclay means miracle in Asagi. My conception and birth is legend among the conduit community because my mother never should have been able to conceive, less carry a child to term. The only time a Soahcoit couple can bear children is when they consummate, because after that they become immortal and their bodies can no longer change, so under normal circumstances a pair has a single opportunity to get pregnant." He had my attention. "Are you following me? "

"Yes absolutely, immortality means a woman would no longer ovulate, let alone go through the changes required for pregnancy."

"Correct." He looked pleased that I was not only interested, but understood. "My parents were very old, among the oldest of our people. My mother had always wanted a child. I think that is why she loved Lilith so much." He nodded at me assuredly then continued. "It has been said by many that her gift far surpassed that of any other conduit that possessed a healing art. The longer she lived the stronger her gift became."

"Then twenty-eight years ago," he continued, "she decided she was going to become pregnant. She was fascinated with in vitro fertilization and what it could mean for her ability to have a child. She was able to conceive on the first round of vitro with the help of her gifts. Her body was really just a vessel to keep me safe in the first few weeks of my embryotic development."

I was silent as he explained a virtual miracle. "My mother lay in bed for two months with her hands on her stomach, willing, healing and encouraging the speedy development of my tiny elements. My father's gifts also assisted in my growth, as we had discussed before, he was a giant. He too lay beside my mother with his hands on her belly, willing swift growth. After a couple months she could no longer carry me, I was too large for her unchanging uterus and very small for a baby, she could only hope I was far enough along to survive. She would use her extraordinary gift to assist my growth the rest of the way. Once I was out of her belly I grew three times faster than a typical baby in the womb, she held me continuously for seven more months, insuring that I developed to my full fruition." He beamed with pride and admiration for the courageous effort his parents put forth to see him mature into a healthy boy. "You are now part of a world where magic does exist. I am a testimony of that."

"That's amazing."

"It was more than amazing—it was a miracle. It also disrupted the conduit world. Many felt that she had crossed a line. Others were supportive and astonished. As I grew up, it was clear that some of their gifts had somehow transferred to me, which is unusual for conduits. Perhaps the same kind of transfer that takes place during covening rituals. We believed it was because my development was bombarded with their energy for so many months. Whatever the reason, it seemed another miracle because I am not a consummated conduit—yet I possess many superfluous gifts that most conduits do not see until they have consummated." His English accent got thicker the longer he spoke.

"What kind of gifts?"

"I am faster than most, as you had observed. I am also unusually strong and healthy. I have never been sick or broken a bone in my life. As you now know I also am able to heal."

"Why do you want to keep these things a secret?"

"My mother and father agreed that with the tumultuous times it was safer for me to not divulge any special traits. It would only make me a bigger target. It is hard to trust anyone. We do not know who is perfidious and who is not. After today it seems more likely than ever that there is a traitor in our coterie. I should not have exposed my gifts to you, because in doing so I may have put you in greater danger. But I could not stand seeing you in pain." He looked down at his hands, clearly wrestling with the potential consequences of his actions.

"Thank you for helping me, and for sharing," I said. "I know you didn't have to tell me any of this." I hoped he could see how sincerely grateful I was for his confidences. Every moment with Elias only seemed to make him less resistible. My body felt tethered to his, and I felt a constant pull in his direction.

Now I was the one looking down at my hands. I was embarrassed at how much he obviously cared about me, I didn't know why, but I felt unworthy of that type of adoration.

Just then the door swung open and Lucas charged in. He looked pissed as he b-lined toward Elias, his chest puffed out. He began yelling in Asagi. Elias gazed calmly beyond him. I wasn't sure if he was assessing an escape or an attack. I was sick of this secret conduit language.

"Excuse me!!" I stood up sharply. "If you're going to barge into my room with a quarrel on your mind, I expect you to speak in a language that I can understand. I am fucking tired of you speaking in Asagi in front of me, every time you think I shouldn't know something. This is my damn life too." Lucas paused and looked at me, measuring how seriously to take my assertion.

"You're right Olly, I apologize. May I speak with you in the hallway, Elias?" He spat out the question.

"No, I see no reason to leave this room," Elias replied. "Nor do I see any point in withholding this conversation from Ophelia, so I will speak plainly. Lucas, I did what I concluded would be best for Ophelia. Given the opportunity I would do it again. I understand that you find it difficult and straining to continuously be camouflaging her, and our bond. Clearly after today's incident we can assume that you are faltering, and incapable of hiding her adequately. My actions today were with the sole intention of keeping her safe and healthy. I apologize if it perturbs you that I was able to assist her this afternoon—after you failed her this morning." I had never heard Elias be so firm with Lucas.

I could see that both men were headed for a severe altercation. I climbed back onto my bed, certain nowhere in this castle would be safe if this turned into a brawl.

Lucas stepped back and calculated his next move. Would he tussle with words, or fists? From his expression I imagined fists were his weapon of choice.

Elias braced himself. He wasn't going to throw the first punch, but he wasn't going to back down either. I wanted to scream at them both and send them to their rooms, but my mouth was too dry. I felt like I was watching a slow-motion car crash. *Should I jump in between them?* I wasn't sure I could even get there in time.

I blinked and within that brief moment their two bodies collided ferociously. It sounded like steel buckling. I couldn't see what was happening, only a contorted mass of muscle. Before I could blink again, my room was full of conduits. Seemingly everyone in the fortress had rushed to break up the fracas. I stood motionless on my bed, mouth open and eyes fixated on Lucas and Elias.

In an instant Aremis was holding Lucas while another man held Elias. The men snarled at each other as Di stood next to me on the bed, giggling. I looked down at her tiny frame and angelic eyes. She was mimicking my posture. I looked up again and everyone in the room was smiling at me. I was poised to do god knows what, in a crouched position with the duvet cover clutched fiercely in my hands. It was hard to tell if I was getting ready to hide under it or throw it at the two men. I looked ridiculous, and one and all were having a good snicker at my expense. I was slightly embarrassed, but more relieved to feel the tension in the room subside. Even Lucas began to laugh.

I immediately stood up straight and released the duvet cover. Di leapt off the bed gracefully, like a ballerina. I then marched through the assembled crowd to the pair at the center. I looked at Lucas.

"I've had enough of your barbarism—we're all adults here, and I would like you to act like it. Furthermore, you will speak in English in my presence—otherwise you will be polite enough to exit the room!" I wanted to sound stern, since with these two I didn't know if I could be menacing.

With that I trooped into my bathroom, mostly because I had nowhere else to go.

I shut the door and took a long look in the mirror, deciding that I was no longer going to be held captive in my room. I was going to take control of my life, not just sit on the sidelines.

I didn't hear people leave or the door close but after a while I sensed a stillness, and I assumed the crowd had left.

I threw open the bathroom door and sure enough everyone was gone, except for the two combatants. They stood silently like two schoolboys in the principal's office. I ignored them both, until I was confident of what I was going to say. I was pleased that they seemed to understand the magnitude of my disappointment. I braced myself for discordance as I mounted my position.

"Please let me get all of this out before either of you interrupts me. I know that you both care about me and my safety. I'm not sure I understand the deeper cause of this dispute, but the way I see it, it doesn't matter anymore." Their eyebrows raised simultaneously. "I will not be kept sequestered anymore. I will not be left in the dark about my future. I will not be a source of discontent between the two of you because both of you think you can do a better job of protecting me. I know you have resources and skills that are better suited to defend me than I do myself—I'm not dense. But from this point on I expect us to work as a team. If you two cannot work together, or with me, I will find a way to be free of both of you. Do not tempt me, because it isn't what I want."

Lucas spoke first. "I'm so sorry you feel I've disrespected you, Olly, by keeping you in the dark. I was doing what I thought was best for everyone. I will no longer speak in Asagi in your presence."

Well that wasn't an agreement to all my terms, but it was encouraging to hear that some of what I said sunk in.

"What was this about, Lucas?" I asked, pacing.

"I don't know what kind of exchange Elias conducted with you, but as I was already straining to camouflage you, I could suddenly feel the force of the bond between you two brighten and intensify as the day went on." Lucas was flustered.

It was then that I realized locking me in this room was not just for my safety, but to keep me secluded. I looked at Lucas, shocked. I started remembering the way he was when we were roommates—

even then he'd attempted to keep me isolated. He'd been so charming and such a good friend, I went along willingly. I wanted to believe that my sequestration had been for my protection, but I wasn't sure anymore.

Lucas looked at Elias. "It's becoming more difficult to disguise her, to keep her safe. The more time she spends with you, or even other conduits, her power strengthens. I'm only trying to slow the process, buy us more time." Then he looked up at me. "And to be perfectly honest I can't stand you getting closer to her."

Okay maybe I was less uncomfortable when I didn't know the content of their conversation. Too late now—the floodgates had opened and there was no turning back.

I cleared my throat uneasily. "But I'm a grown woman and I can establish relationships with whomever I choose, for whatever reason I choose. I want to cooperate with you Lucas to make your job easier—I know that keeping us under your veil of concealment is important for all of our safety. I will not, however, tolerate any other motives on your part to keep me sequestered. So please don't disguise your intentions with the ruse of intense safety precautions. I want to trust both of you because I *want to*, but also because I have to."

Lucas nodded. "You know you can trust me Olly. You've known me for almost two years now."

How could he say that? What I knew of Lucas in San Francisco was *not* the truth. I confronted him on this. "Oh really? I'm supposed to trust a man who established himself in my home to watch me? A man who lied about going to work every day, and lied to me about where he came from. Everything you said then was a tactic to get closer to me, Lucas. I choose to trust you now because deep down I feel that you were truly doing it all to keep me safe."

Then I turned to Elias.

"You were no better. Hiring a man to infiltrate my home, and creeping around the periphery of my life? You didn't have to lie, because you were so sneaky that you were not seen. My life as I knew it was a game that both of you were playing. I don't appreciate being toyed with, no matter the objectives. From here on out we are a team.

I don't know what the underlying dilemma is between you two, and although I know some of it is about me, I feel like it runs much deeper. This animosity doesn't help an already precarious situation."

Lucas looked at Elias, and I saw a silent dialogue. For the time being, there was a truce. I guess years of being a therapist still counted for something.

"I'll replace your door immediately with one you can open," Lucas promised. "However, there will still be restrictions on the grounds. I hope you understand why you cannot frolic freely through the woods." There was sarcasm in his statement but I knew what he said was dead serious, so I nodded. He gave me one more long look before he left the room.

Elias just nodded and followed Lucas out my door—which was left ajar for the first time since I'd entered this room, weeks earlier. I felt rebellious as I peeked around the corner into the hall. A moment later Aremis showed up and began ripping the hinges from the wall. I guess immediately meant immediately.

PART III

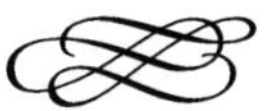

OPHELIA

It felt indescribably liberating to be able to wake up and open my bedroom door to the outside world.

From my calculations, I determined that I'd been at the castle for twenty seven days, and I was finally going to get to tour it. After seeing so many new faces in my room during the ruckus the night before, I was more eager than ever to make their acquaintance. My only restriction was that I could not go outside by myself which seemed reasonable enough. As I strode down my corridor and into the large courtyard I tried to exude confidence and a sense of belonging. Anything to mask the real feelings inside me: fear, apprehension and anxiety. I didn't know if everyone in the house was a true friend. Elias made it clear he believed there was a traitor among us and there was a good chance one of these occupants would hurt me, given the right opportunity. I needed to be on guard, but this didn't mean I had to be locked up. Besides let's be honest I was sure Lucas or Elias weren't far behind.

The archway widened into the cavernous room, and no one was in it. I was surprised. I'd been imagining that the courtyard would be bustling with people reading, chatting, coffee cups in hand. Instead it was utterly silent. Maybe everyone was locked in their rooms like I'd been, for all I knew. I wouldn't put it past Lucas to lock up the rest of the castle's residents now that I was able to roam freely.

The room was at least three stories high, lined with the same medieval stones that most of the castle was constructed with. A huge staircase curved through it, four enormous pillars loomed around the border and I counted twelve discernible arched entryways to explore. There was no visible light in any of the hallways, though. I'd be stumbling through in the dark if I explored much deeper.

I wouldn't find out unless I gave it a shot. I decided to start with the four lower passages, not including my own, since I had already got the tour of Hafiza. I didn't want to get lost, so I needed a game plan. If my wing was the East Wing then I would start with the South Wing and work my way up to the third story. I marched towards the entrance to the South passage, my heart pounding so loud I could barely hear the voice that called out to me on the other end of the courtyard. I spun around just before the darkness of the passage swallowed me.

"Miss Ophelia." It was Aremis, leaning against the wall. Although his presence looked casual it also demanded respect. He was tall with a mane of wavy brown hair. He wore nice black slacks and a long sleeved burgundy buttoned down shirt. Relief surged through me. It was nice that the first face I encountered on my expedition was a familiar one.

"Aremis! Sorry I didn't hear you." I tried to look as relaxed as he did. "How are you this morning?" I was flashing my nervous smile: big, brilliant and all a show.

"Very well my dear. And you?"

"I'm great." *I think that's true,* I told myself.

"Where might you be going?" His accent was thick, but indiscernible. "Were you looking for something in particular? I may be able to assist you."

"No, I was just going to look around."

"In the dark? I think you will find it hard to appreciate very much with no light." His voice projected so gently across the huge room. I felt like I was yelling.

"I didn't know if it would be lit, further down the hall, like mine." I gestured to the East Wing.

"Most likely not. The rest of the residents have exceptional night vision." I was feeling like I was still in the dark, literally.

"Well then, in that case, do you know where I might find a flashlight?"

Aremis began to walk towards me, his strides huge and graceful. When he was only a few feet away he stopped and studied me. It felt like he was sizing me up, as though he wasn't sure if I could handle the punch line. I stood my ground. I had to start demanding respect—so I was considered more an equal and not just a helpless little girl. I threw back my shoulders and kept his gaze.

"May I join you? My gift may be of use to you on this endeavor, if you will acquiesce to some company." That wasn't what I'd expected, I'd read him all wrong.

"Sure! So you'll guide me with your good night vision?" *I don't know how that's really going to help me,* I thought, *but it's a sweet gesture.*

He smiled and slowly opened the palm of his hand. A cluster of small dancing flames hovered above his palm. I watched as the flames grew larger, unable to take my eyes off of the small fire. It didn't move like a normal fire. It wasn't wild. It looked playful.

"I am an imposer. Do you know what that means?"

I was still entranced by the flames, but managed an almost inaudible yes. I remembered the brief explanation during the conversation in the antiquities room.

"I impose my will over fire. I do not create it, but if it is within a hundred miles I can control its force."

Without thinking I blurted out, "That must make you a very valuable weapon." I felt awful the moment I said it. Here he was trying to be my friend and I'd successfully dismantled him down into a mindless tool within two minutes of conversation. I looked up into his eyes to see if I could detect any damage. He just softly looked back at me, with no noticeable anger. I scolded myself.

"It has made me a very powerful weapon in the past, and now it makes me an even more powerful ally."

"I'm sorry Aremis, that was really rude of me. Please forgive me."

"You meant nothing by it. I understand." He smiled at me, a very warm smile. "Now that you have a light, shall we explore the grounds?"

I almost felt guilty conceding, because I was in fact using him as a tool. A torch in human form. He still seemed eager to help, so I awkwardly nodded. He extended his hand in the manner that suggested he would escort me arm in arm. I hooked my arm into his as the playful flame hovered a few feet ahead of us, skipping like a stone across the water.

"Shall we start with the South Wing as you had intended, my dear?" He nodded in that direction.

"Sure, that sounds good." We walked arm in arm into the dimly lit corridor. I looked up at him. I really hoped he wasn't the traitor. I liked him. He caught my gaze.

"Is there something on your mind?" I certainly wasn't going to tell him what I was truly thinking. So instead I asked, "How old are you?"

"I consummated when I was thirty-four, and that was five hundred years ago."

"Is your Ah-toa here in the castle?" I tried to sound out the term Lucas used.

"I lost my Natasha seventy-five years ago." He swallowed hard.

"I'm sorry for your loss." It was all I could think to say. *Boy was I batting a thousand here.* Aremis patted my hand and my shoulders relaxed a little.

"It was many years ago, but it feels like it was only yesterday. Eternity distorts time. Natasha was lovely, and I try not to shy away from speaking of her because of my wounded soul. It isn't fair to her memory. What a beautiful thing it is to connect to someone so intensely. It is a phenomenal feeling to be whole, indescribable. You must sense that when you are near Elias?"

I blushed, and hoped he couldn't see it in the dark. He looked down at me briefly, then proceeded with his own reminiscing. "Natasha could read memories—your whole life in fact."

"That is a wonderful gift."

"She was always respectful of others. It was why we were able to be waylaid. She didn't want to pry into others' heads without their permission. It should have been a wonderful defensive weapon, if I could have convinced her to use it to our advantage." He looked sad again. "She was a wonderfully stubborn woman."

"She sounds like she had integrity."

"She did. You are very wise, Miss Ophelia. Many would have seen her choice as foolishness." He stopped and looked down at me. "Thank you, for reminding me that it was her integrity, and for listening to an old man and his injuries. So many of us have lost our Atoa these days, it has become burdensome to share with each other. Everyone has their own story."

I was so deep in thought, thinking about my connection with Elias and Aremis' sad story that it scared the hell out of me to hear a man's voice behind us. I screamed like a sissy when I heard it.

"Miss Ophelia, are you okay?" Aremis asked. Before I could respond Lucas and Elias were bounding down the hall.

"Yes, I'm sorry. This gentleman snuck up on me, that's all."

"Terribly sorry Senorita," The man spoke with a thick Spanish accent. "My name is Valerian. Senior Kraus sent me to summon you for a meeting in the conference room. I did not intend to frighten you."

"You are one stealthy fellow, Valerian." I looked past him to Elias. "Show me the way gentlemen." *As I suspected Lucas and Elias were not far. Elias could have just 'summoned' me himself. I internally rolled my eyes.*

No one else spoke as Aremis led me out of the South Wing, back through the courtyard and to our left into the West Wing. It looked the same as the other passage, lots of closed doors. I felt silly for screaming now that I had an entourage following me. I glanced over my shoulder, yep all three men were still back there. I took a long look at Valerian. I had not seen him before.

He was short with mousy-blonde hair and dark eyes. His skin was an olive tone, or at least that's what I gathered in the dim light. He was handsome, but then again who wasn't in this damn castle? His skin shimmered a little more than Aremis'. He also looked exceedingly somber.

We walked the entire length of the hall until we came upon a rustic wooden door, Aremis gingerly opened it.

It was dark, but then several tiny sparks flew from Aremis' fingers and littered the room with light. The room smelled fusty. There was a large table in the middle with fifteen or so chairs, otherwise it was bare: no artwork, or even sconces. Aremis' flames danced in midair. I looked behind to see that everyone in my group had made it in, and when I turned back around a woman was sitting at the head of the table.

"Hello Ophelia Banner. My name is Nara and I believe you have met my husband Valerian." He was now by her side, what an exquisite couple. Her skin was ghostly white and she had fiery red hair that was stacked on top of her head. Her eyes were lime green—I could see them glowing from across the large room. If I had to guess from her accent and basic traits she was of Celtic descent. "Please sit," she said.

I had not seen her yesterday either. I would've remembered. She was remarkable in every facet of the word. Her figure was elegant yet demanding—you could see her muscles under the thin indigo fabric she was draped in. I walked toward the table. By the time I'd reached it everyone else had already sat down.

I glanced around at our attendees: Aremis and Elias sat side by side on my left and Lucas sat alone on my right, while Valerian stood behind his wife.

"I understand you are curious about this woman." I felt the air shift around me and smelled the fragrance of freshly cut strawberries and ginger. Then in front of me on the table appeared the photograph that I'd seen on Elias' wall.

"Yes, I think she may be my grandmother." I looked at the individuals in the picture and this time I recognized one: Nara. My pulse quickened. "Did you know her?"

"For a brief moment in time, yes." Nara looked at her husband, then back at me. "Her name is Abigail. She consummated that year with a young man named Zavier. They did not stay long in our Paksyon."

Lucas leaned in and whispered. "A Paksyon is one word for a small congregation of conduits."

I was completely deflated. I stared at Abigail's image. I had been so certain it was Lilith. "Did Abigail speak of any sisters?"

"No, I am afraid not. She did not speak much at all. She was quiet, very delicate. Zavier was the only one she would readily communicate with. She walked around with distrust. Her shoulders slouched, indicating she was protecting secrets." She again looked at her husband.

"I am not in the photo," he added, "but I was there that summer as well. I cannot say where Cane and Sorcey got the photo, considering that they were not in attendance of this covening." He looked at Elias for some kind of answer and Elias shook his head. "I fostered Zavier as if he were my own. I knew his family well. He was a good man. He fumbled about Abigail incessantly, trying to keep her sheltered. I asked him one day why he behaved in such a manner, was he not among friends? He told me a story that I have not soon forgotten."

Nara placed her hand on his and Valerian continued. "Zavier said that Abigail's family had been residing in Montreal the spring she turned nineteen. Her parents were young Soahcoit. Abigail was raised with a keen awareness of her gifts and was taught how to use them to her upmost advantage. She showed exceptional promise. Her parents were very proud, and boasted often of her abilities. Zavier would not tell me what her gifts were. One May afternoon Abigail arrived home from university to find her parents' mangled bodies in their living room. They were still alive, but only barely. Abigail lay there with their withering forms for hours, crying, expelling all the energy she had to help heal them swiftly. That night their assailant came back and further mutilated her parents while she hid in the floorboards, their blood seeping through the cracks, slowly drenching her body. For hours he persisted, never saying a word. Then he left. Abigail came out of hiding, her poor parents still clinging to life. They could scarcely mutter a syllable, but Abigail was able to discern one word from her father's mouth: run. So she did. She told Zavier she knew all along that the attacker was looking for her, though he never spoke. She no longer trusted anyone."

"Was it Yanni? The man that tortured her parents?" I was shaking with terror.

"We don't believe so—he would have most likely been able to see Abigail." Nara said.

"What if her gifts were camouflage, like Lucas'?" I looked at him, he was very focused on me.

"Perhaps, but unlikely an Unconsu could hide herself from Yanni. No, it is more likely that it was another conduit, maybe a mercenary sent from Esther, but probably not Yanni."

"What about her parents?" I asked. "Did anyone know her parents? Are they still alive?"

Valerian answered. "We don't know who her parents were exactly. As I am sure our generous host has told you, many of our people have been slaughtered. Since we are all in hiding it is difficult to keep track of who has disappeared."

"Do you know what happened to them, Abigail and Zavier?" I looked at both of them intently.

"No, Miss Banner, we do not know what happened to them. They left the Paksyon in the middle of the night that summer without saying a word, and no one has seen or heard anything from them since." Nara squeezed her husband's hand. "You must understand, this is very troublesome to my husband. He loved Zavier dearly. We both did."

"Yes of course."

"I know you had hoped for different answers, but this is what we know." She turned to Elias. "May we be excused?"

"Certainly, thank you Nara. Thank you, Valerian, for your assistance." They both stood and bowed in Elias' direction, then in mine.

"It was a pleasure to meet you." Then they were gone, leaving nothing but their sweet scent behind.

"I am truly sorry that there was not better intelligence to report Ophelia. As Lucas and I have said, it is a troublesome time to accumulate accurate information and be certain of anyone's wellbeing. We are all simply surviving." Elias said.

"Yes, I understand. Thank you for getting to the bottom of this for me. I had hoped for different news, but even dispiriting answers are better than none." I handed him back the photo. "Thank you."

"You are welcome."

I looked to Aremis, "Shall we continue our tour?"

"Let us do just that." He stood and opened the door for me. I waved to Lucas and Elias before closing the door behind us.

"What a terrible story." I was trying to erase the imagery that I'd conjured up. "I hope wherever they are, they are safe."

"That is a wonderful thing to hope, Miss Ophelia. Hope is a powerful thing. It moves mountains, trust me I have seen it."

I smiled back. I really enjoyed Aremis' company. He made me feel secure. Despite the fact that I was now acutely aware of how dangerous the world I was living in was. Between traitors and torture, compounded with my attempted abduction, I could not deny that I felt uneasy. We walked through the West Wing and found our way back to where we had been interrupted in our tour. "Tell me more about when you were human. Is that what I should call it?" We strolled slowly as we talked.

"Well I guess I was never human—we are born conduits, you know. But if you are talking about my life before consummation I will gladly share that time with you. I was born in Ireland in 1507 A.D. There was much transition and turmoil there during those times. As a boy I grew up in a clan, but by the time I was a young man these clans had virtually disbanded as King Henry VIII conquered and pillaged our land. I left Ireland for a less-volatile existence. Much of my clan had died already and my parents were in hiding. News of the disappearances had left them unsettled. I was the last to leave, mostly due to the nostalgia I felt for my native land. I met Natasha as I wandered through a small village just north of Genoa, Italy. Italy, too, was in the midst of conflict. Rome had been sacked only years earlier. Natasha had transplanted there from what is now Russia, where Ivan the Terrible had just crowned himself the first Tsar. We both dreamt of peace. Europe then was a land of upheaval and greed." There was a smile in his voice as he reminisced. "We wed three weeks after meeting and consummated that night."

"Did you know what you were? I mean that you were conduits?"

"Oh of course. How else would a Russian woman and an Irish man communicate? We both spoke Asagi, both raised by traditional families—consummated families." He said.

"Did you love Natasha? I mean was it love at first sight, or something like that?" I wondered if a pair always loved each other.

"Definitely, what wasn't to love? We are paired with our other half. To not love your Atoa would be like denying a piece of yourself. We are always coupled with love. It is part of the union."

"How did you know where to find her?"

"You don't, you have to just keep an eye out. You know when you do, though, that is for certain. But some conduits go their whole lives without meeting their Atoa." I thought about the chance meeting with Elias and how something had moved in me. Then I thought about Eleanor and how she had obviously not met her other half, and might never. Thinking of her made me sad, so I quickly moved on.

"Is Aremis your birth name?" It struck me that it didn't sound Irish. As he began to answer we veered right. Just then a shadow appeared in the distance.

"Hello Rand." Aremis identified the interloper as he stepped into the soft light of our flame.

"Aremis, my friend." The man addressed my escort, but stared at me." Miss Ophelia, it is a pleasure to formally meet you. You are more radiant then your admirers boast you to be." He took my hand in his and bowed slightly.

I blushed. "And you are?"

"Pardon my rudeness. My name is Rand Garrith."

"Nice to me meet you, Mr. Garrith."

"Oh please, call me Rand." He waved his hand in the air as if he were swatting a fly.

"Well then it's nice to meet you Rand." I was getting the impression he was a bit eccentric.

"What might you two be doing on this fine day here in the castle?" Rand's manner was bubbly with a touch of free spirit. I kind of liked him already.

"We are exploring the South Wing. What are you doing today?" Aremis seemed annoyed with this small talk.

"I was just wandering around aimlessly. The weather is gloomy outside and I had an early shift on the grounds. I am free as a bird. May I join you two in your exploration?" He clasped his hands and leaned in intently waiting for an answer.

Aremis looked at me. I didn't mind Rand's company, the more the merrier as far as I was concerned. But I couldn't tell if Aremis shared the same sentiment. I didn't want to be rude after how helpful he'd been.

"Fine by me," I offered.

"That is splendid. Do we have a destination in mind?" Aremis and I started to walk as Rand followed in short pursuit.

"Not in particular. Do you have a suggestion?" I was curious what he might choose.

"Well, has Miss Ophelia seen the library in this wing yet? It is spectacular. Vast and eclectic, almost any book you could think of. Do you like to read, Ophelia?"

"I love to read!"

"Oh yes, of course, I wouldn't send you too far afield. You are in good hands with this one. Malarin painted those hands himself." Rand gestured toward Aremis with a sweeping arm motion.

"Who is Malarin?" I leaned in and asked Aremis. "Is that your dad?"

Aremis chuckled softly. "Not exactly. Malarin—one of his many names, is the creator of all things, according to our ancestor's recollections. He is the great painter." Aremis paused. "I will tell you the story another time."

That sounded interesting, I would hold him to that. "What else is in the South Wing?"

"Well there is the small kitchen," Rand offered. "And I lodge down here, as does Aremis, Winston, and Ying. Of course, each wing has a common area, and most have one washroom. There are several closets, but they are locked. Which is quite reasonable considering that this is the Kraus residence, after all. They must be allowed some privacy. Isn't that right Aremis?"

"It seems only right." Aremis replied.

Rand decided to lead the way and stepped ahead. "Here is the common room. Not very exciting, if you ask me. I am not a fan of Renaissance décor? What about you two?" Rand looked around.

"I like some of it," I chimed in.

Rand clasped his hands in front of him. "This is just a delightful visit! I enjoy good conversation so very much. The conduits in this castle can be a rather reserved lot."

The room was wood paneled, which made the immense space much warmer than the chilly, stone hallway. The far wall had the largest fireplace I'd ever seen—it must have been eleven feet tall and at least fifteen feet wide—with a blazing fire inside.

The walls were covered with huge tapestries depicting intricate scenes of various battles, births and deaths. *Was it a family history?* I wondered. Multiple pieces of museum-quality furniture were strewn about it: sofas, chairs, ottomans. It was an impressive collection, and even more so because I knew this was only one of many common rooms.

"This is quite striking," I was impressed. Then Aremis lit the mammoth chandelier above us, and the room took an entirely new feel. It was nearly glowing. "Okay now it's breathtaking."

Both of my companions smothered a snigger. I suppose they'd seen far more astonishing things in their vast lifetimes.

THE EVENING CLOSED out harmlessly enough and although I felt at ease by the time I crawled into bed my dreams mirrored the tangled mess of fierce emotions and frightening truths haunting my mind from the day's earlier events. I had nightmares about captivity and running in tunnels for miles, trying to escape. There was nothing but darkness everywhere. I woke up in a cold sweat, my bed sheets gnarled into a huge knot. I didn't remember having such vivid dreams before my collision with Elias, but now I was frequented by them. Before the night of the car chase, they were always about *him*, but the content was different now and at times terrifying.

As I brushed my teeth I heard my door open. So, when I saw Aremis sitting on my bed I wasn't surprised.

"Are you ready Miss Ophelia?"

"Why yes I am." He put his arm out and I latched on.

"Should we continue with the South Wing?" he asked. "I believe Winston, Rand and Ying will let you see their chambers if you would like." I nodded, Yay, I was going to meet someone new.

"How was the rest of your evening?" I asked him.

"Very pleasant. I read."

I was intrigued. "What do you like to read?"

"Don't pass judgment," he said. "But I really enjoy romance novels." I thought I saw a hint of red flash across his cheeks.

I was a little shocked. Romance novels! He didn't strike me as the type.

"No judgments here. I am surprised though."

"I know," he said. "But I am a big softy." I giggled a little.

"I could see that." I squeezed his arm gently.

The little flame danced ahead of us. "Shall we call on Winston?" Aremis asked and he turned and gently knocked on a door to our left.

Winston appeared on the other side of the threshold.

"Pardon us Winston, I am giving Miss Ophelia a tour of the South Wing and I thought you wouldn't mind showing her your quarters."

"Oh, please come in." He stepped aside and we entered the chamber. It was much smaller than my room. There was no bed, only shelves of books and a small chair.

"I was just reading."

In the dark? Of Course, why not. I thought.

"It's one of my favorites, "*De civitate Dei,*" in Latin such a beautiful language."

Who the hell reads in Latin? I thought. *When was that the commonly spoken language?* Next to the book was a photograph of a petite woman.

"Who is she?" I pointed to the picture.

"That is Lucia. She is my Atoa."

"Is she here in the castle?" I winced as I asked the question, afraid of the answer.

"No… She has gone into hiding. In order to save us both, we are separated temporarily." *Oh thank goodness, but how sad too.*

I picked up the photo to further examine it. She looked younger than Winston, maybe fourteen years old. She had long, curly black hair. It was an old photo, but her beauty emanated from the worn paper. "When did you last see her?"

"Ninety-seven years, three months, twenty-eight days and nearly four hours." For the first time Winston looked melancholy. *I had done it again. Aremis wasn't kidding when he said everyone had a story.*

"I'm sorry Winston. You must miss her terribly. How do you know she's okay?" Instantly I felt horrible for asking the question. *He must already think of this scenario all the time.*

"I would know if I lost her. She is a part of me." That made sense. I let out a sorrowful sigh. Winston and Aremis appeared to connect for a moment, although I had no idea what the exchange was about. *Probably me, sticking my foot in my mouth all the time.*

Winston unexpectedly put his hand on my shoulder. It scared me and I jerked.

"It's okay." Aremis locked his reassuring eyes with mine.

"What?" I asked, getting more uncomfortable.

"Shhhh," he nodded in Winston's direction. I was feeling a little suffocated. No words were being spoken, but I knew this interchange was terribly important.

I stared at Winston and his hand settled firmly on my shoulder. "It's okay—we will protect you." He only mouthed the words, but it sounded like he was screaming them in my head. Both men looked at me and nodded in unison. I was starting to see the picture: they were trying to share something with me. Instantly my mind was flooded with questions. *Did this mean we were in imminent danger? Was the castle going to be attacked?* I swallowed hard as I imagined what I would do if the castle was set upon by Yanni. The image of him chasing the car came crashing back into my mind. I shuddered.

Winston guided me towards the furthest corner of the room. It was very dark, so Aremis sent a small flame along to accompany us. It hovered over our heads and illuminated the corner. Winston knelt down and put both his knees on a large stone three feet from one wall. Instantly a small lever appeared on the adjacent wall, He hurried over to pull it, then jumped back to the stone he'd originally knelt on, this time standing with both feet on the single square. The bricks behind him began to fold inward and collapse upon themselves until a passage emerged, just big enough for a small adult to enter.

A small piece of paper instantly appeared in my hand. The script was beautiful. I glanced at both men, and each gave me encouraging gestures once more. I read the message in silence, and took a deep breath. The secrecy was making me queasy. *Did Lucas or Elias know about this?*

Miss Ophelia,

Do not be afraid. Aremis and I are your comrades. We have been charged by Master Elias with the duty of equipping the castle with multiple secret passages to ensure your safety should the fortress come under siege by our enemies. We will share all of these clandestine halls with you, but you must keep them a secret, you can never speak of them. Master Elias was clear that neither he nor Lucas were privy to this information. All channels will lead to the river three miles from here, where Master Elias and Lucas will meet you should the castle fall. Aremis will provide you with the light you need to make your way in one piece to the outlet. Trust us, we want you to flourish and we are truly your allies. We must not converse, because we never know who is listening.

Winston

My hands shook as I stared at the note. The way I saw it, there were two significant possibilities. One, these two men were my friends and this information could save my life. The second scenario was far more sinister—they were the traitors and I was being led straight into a trap. The only certainty was that I was not safe. The veil of security was now completely in tatters.

In my head, I repeated the sequence Winston had performed. I opened my eyes to see the two men studying me with concern. They were clearly eager to assure me, but unable to say the words aloud. I still held the paper in my hands. It felt warm in my fingertips. I looked down to see it light up in flames. I instinctively let it go, and its ashes sashayed to the floor.

The narrow escape corridor was still exposed, and as I leaned in to gauge the terrain a small flame flashed through the darkness, then returned to float a few inches in front of my face. This was Aremis' way of communicating how he would light my way. I stepped back to the center of the small room and nodded. I wanted them to understand that I'd taken it all in. I still wasn't sure how I felt about it, but they didn't need to know that. They nodded in unison, then Winston pointed at a protruding brick near the entrance and gently pressed his palm on the top of it. The bricks regrouped, cleverly camouflaging the whereabouts of the door. "Thank you for sharing your room with me Winston," I said, conjuring the biggest smile I could muster. "Can we continue our tour, Aremis?"

"Indeed, Miss Ophelia, without further ado. Let us leave at once."

Winston touched my shoulder one more time before I turned and booked it for the door. In the hall Aremis assumed his position as my escort.

We continued to walk silently down the corridor. I was busy replaying the sequence in my head in the event that it could save my life. I wanted to make sure I wouldn't forget it. I thought about the traitor among us and wondered if Aremis and Winston could be trusted. Aremis squeezed my arm.

"Are you up for touring Rand's room now?" Concern spread across his face, he could tell I was feeling weighted from the interaction in Winston's room.

Worry wasn't going to change anything and I needed to know the layout of the castle more than ever so I nodded and asked. "What's Rand's gift?"

"Rand is a receiver," said Aremis. "He tastes emotions, intentions and the underlying connections between people."

"That sounds kind of similar to how my 'curse' works." I gestured my skepticism in air quotes.

"Yes, after how you described your *gifts"*, he emphasized the word, "to me yesterday evening it would seem you both share an ability to read the energetic climate of a room. I would never say this to Rand, but the way you describe absorbing the energy rather than simply tasting it would imply you may prove to be a very powerful receiver when you choose to consummate." I blushed a little, both flattered and thinking about consummating with Elias. Even though I wasn't quite sure what that entailed, I knew enough to realize that it was an intimate, lifelong commitment.

My thoughts went back to Rand's gift, and mine. "What would be the big difference?"

"Well absorption is very different then sensation. Just like touching a blouse is different than wearing a blouse. Wearing it makes it yours."

"Well in my experience, it sounds like it would be better to only sense the emotion instead of owning it."

"It is true that you may struggle with controlling your gifts, but anything that is worth having is not easy. I am an old man and I can only make assumptions, but I have watched many Unconsu consummate and I have seen many gifts develop. Yours shows great promise." Aremis winked.

I thought about this for a moment. "Aremis, do you know anyone else with gifts like mine?"

"I have not come across too many mortals that express such prominent gifts before consummation. Elias is very powerful for a mortal, but he comes from extraordinary origins."

"Do you agree with what his mother did—the measures she took to have Elias?" I hoped I wasn't overstepping. I was genuinely curious. Clearly Aremis liked Elias, but did that mean he approved?

"I don't feel it is up to me to pass judgment on Sorcey. She did what she felt was right. Her choices may very well shape the fate of all our kind, and only time will tell whether she fostered our success or our demise."

That was heavy. I hadn't realized her decision held such gravity in the conduit community. No wonder there was such dissension amongst them about her actions.

Aremis kindly changed the subject. "Let us visit our friend Rand and then finish exploring the South Wing. Ying has been looking forward to meeting you as well. You will enjoy him."

Rand greeted us as we approached his room.

"Oh come in! I am so excited to see you again Miss Ophelia." He grabbed my hand and kissed it softly.

"Thank you Rand. It's very nice to see you too."

"Aremis." Rand nodded in his direction.

"Rand."

"Welcome to my humble abode." He did a twirl in the center of the room. He wasn't kidding—it was a very small room: no bed, no chair, not even a light. Only three large, deep-purple pillows in the far corner, and a very beautiful rug on the floor. There were three small framed pieces of artwork on the wall. They looked like sketches, but the light was so dim it was hard to see.

"Do you collect art?" I squinted to get a better look at them and the flame appeared. "Thank you, Aremis."

He smiled.

"I do," Rand said. "But these are mine. These days we must pack light. We never know when we might be making a quick escape." He came up behind me. "This one is of my Carissa's left hand. My favorite hand. I loved every piece of her, but this was one of my favorite parts." I looked up at him.

"Is Carissa gone?"

"Yes. She was taken from me three hundred years ago when the last open battle was fought."

"I'm so sorry Rand."

"Naturally it is hard, but I feel her with me often. We will find each other again. She was brilliant, was she not, Aremis?" He looked for Aremis' approval.

"Of course, no one would contest that." Aremis gave Rand a reassuring nod. These men must have thought I was ridiculous to not be with Elias every moment I could, after the losses they have had to endure. I was compelled to explain myself but I thought the better of it. Rand put his hand on my shoulder and whispered in my ear.

"No one is judging." He was definitely in tune with my emotions. He must have felt my defensiveness. I took a deep breath.

Aremis interceded. "Why was her left hand your favorite?"

"I am so glad you asked that, my friend. To be fair to Ophelia I must explain that Carissa was a vixen, she bewitched. Her touch froze you in your tracks." Rand paused, perhaps for effect. The man did have a flair for the dramatic. He then continued. "When we first consummated it became very difficult to interact intimately. Physical touch was nearly impossible for the first year. But it was her left hand that she learned how to control her gift through first. So, it became my favorite part of her brilliant form." He was beaming.

"Wow that must have been hard for you guys, a year with little to no touch?"

"It was difficult at times. Luckily she didn't numb the senses. She merely rendered you motionless. There are still many pleasures one can appreciate while being still."

My cheeks flushed. This was getting a bit *too* intimate.

"Don't be embarrassed Ophelia, I am an open book."

"I gathered that." Aremis and I laughed.

"You must come look at this one, then." Rand stepped over a few feet.

"As long as it's only a picture of her right hand and not something else." We all laughed.

"It is our son's smile."

"You have a child?"

"Yes, he is a strapping young man. I hope you will meet him some day."

I studied the sketch. It was literally just an image of a smile. His mouth looked handsome. Even on paper he seemed coy with a touch of mysteriousness.

"Where is he?"

"He is hiding with his partner. I have not spoken to him in many years. You remind me of him: very smart, loving and with a wonderful sense of humor. I think you two will become splendid friends." I was incredibly touched. Rand was quickly growing on me. I liked that he was straightforward and seemingly without confines. I stepped over to the third sketch.

"What's this?"

"That was the cottage Carissa and I raised Caleb in. It was simple and perfect for a small family. We chose to raise him in what is now Innsbruck, Austria. Cold winters, lovely summers and nestled in the Alps. The cottage still stands, although it does not look the same. But I wish to go back and visit it someday. Many good memories there, and boxes and boxes of art. You would love it!" Rand put his arm over my shoulder. "Do you collect art?"

"I've collected some things over the years. I can't resist a piece that speaks to me. It's like a secret language that only you can hear." I thought fondly of my favorite painting. I'd placed it above the mantle in the living room of our apartment in San Francisco. It was a silhouette of a voluptuous woman in the nude, the curvature of her hips accented by vibrant colors. I wondered if that was one of the things Lucas had saved for me.

"Aremis are you an art connoisseur?" Rand looked genuinely curious.

"I can admire paintings, but I prefer sculpture."

"Then you *are* one of us! Isn't that wonderful? I have known this man for hundreds of years and I just learned something new about him. You are such a titillating individual. Why sculpture?"

"I prefer corporeal objects—I like to examine things from all angles. Canvas is too two-dimensional for my tastes."

"Fascinating, just fascinating." Rand was absolutely tickled. "Are we going to visit the stoic Ying?"

I interjected cheerfully. "I *am* looking forward to meeting someone new."

"Oh what, these two old men are not good enough for you?" Rand threw his arm over Aremis' shoulder too—sandwiching himself between us. "I'm just kidding Miss Ophelia, come let's go meet a new house mate."

Ying's room was further into the South Wing. Aremis gently rapped on the door and a short man answered. He had long black hair tied on top of his head in a bun. He was unsmiling and his black eyes looked menacing. I gave him my wide, nervous grin.

He stepped aside and waved us in. I was having second thoughts about seeing his chamber. He was pretty frightening. Something about the air around him sent prickles down my spine. Rand leaned down and whispered in my ear.

"Don't let the exterior fool you Ying is a very tender man." My feet felt cemented in place but he nudged me forward and I managed to stumble into the room. Ying's space was larger than the others', and the room was round. Most of the wall space was covered with ominous weapons mounted on it: countless knives, swords, daggers and other artilleries I didn't even know the names of. I did not like his room at all.

I looked up to see Ying grinning at me, and his teeth looked as sharp as his décor. I leaned closer to Aremis.

Finally, he spoke. "Greetings, I am Ying Zheng and you are Ophelia Banner." My name sounded odd on his lips. He had a faint Asian accent.

"Yes I am." I cleared my throat. He could tell I was anxious, it humored him.

"I will not hurt you."

"Of course, you won't," Rand broke in. "You only like to act like the tough guy, Ying. Stop smiling at the girl, you look terrifying." Rand stepped around the small, solid man. Ying looked like a machine—hard as a rock, and efficient, like the arsenal on his wall.

"Ying." Aremis nodded a greeting.

I let my eyes drift around the room and could envision the carnage that had been inflicted by some of the weapons. Ying watched my gaze. He was as still as a statue except for his head, which mirrored my own movements. I paused to stare at a very large staff with huge swords on either side, it must have been eight feet long. I imagined it would look ridiculous in the hands of such a slight man. The staff abruptly flew off the shelves and into the hand of its governor. I was wrong. Ying did not look ridiculous at all—he looked lethal. I stepped back.

"Easy my friend, you are going to scare our guest." Rand stepped beside me. "He is showing off Ophelia. Ying manipulates metal. He is like a large magnet and fast, boy is he fast."

"I could see that."

Ying laughed, a playful chuckle. "I will not hurt you, Ophelia Banner."

"Well that's good to know because you're doing a great job of intimidating me."

"My apologies. I saw you admiring the weapon. It is one of my favorites that I have ever made, consequently one of my favorite ones I have ever brandished." He examined it in his hand. "Would you like to hold it?"

"No I'm okay, thank you. It's so large, I'd be afraid I would poke someone's eye out." All the men laughed. *I sure knew how to work a room,* I thought. The laughter helped lessen my anxiety, considerably.

"I understand your apprehension. Perhaps I could teach you how to wield a weapon, if you would like? Preferably in a larger space, with less opportunity for casualties."

That was nice of Ying, but he still gave me the willies and I wasn't sure if I ever wanted to be alone with this particular character.

"Ying is a great warrior, he can move like lightening and manage a weapon better than anyone I have ever seen in my many years on this earth," Rand said. "If he is offering to give you a lesson you would be a very lucky student. Many would kill to have that opportunity." He clearly regarded Ying with very high esteem.

"Thank you for the offer, Ying. In that case, maybe Aremis could arrange a lesson during one of the days we're touring the castle." I wanted to make sure I wasn't alone with him. Aremis got the hint.

"Certainly. We could arrange the lesson the day we visit the fencing room."

"That would be pleasant," Ying said, again unsmiling. A grin might have sold the "pleasant" part better. Or maybe not, with those pointy pearly whites.

"Well I will have to be present," Rand said, raising his eyebrows in my direction. "Ophelia will need all the support she can get."

"You'll only come to laugh at me." I frowned at him.

"Miss Ophelia, I am appalled. I would never do such a thing." Rand clutched his chest, but his wink said it all. It made no difference to me, as long as I was not alone with Ying. The more witnesses the better.

Ying turned to Aremis. "When will that be?"

"Tomorrow. We are nearly through with the South Wing and will be moving to the West Wing."

Ying nodded. "Thank you for stopping by. It was nice to meet you Ophelia Banner." He gestured to the door. I guessed that was our hint to leave swiftly. I had no problem with that.

Once we were back in the hall, I exhaled loudly. I hadn't realized I'd been holding my breath.

"He is a good man, but a man of few words. Everything he does is purposeful and to the point." Aremis continued to face forward as he spoke.

"He was different." I admitted. "I'm sure glad I didn't run into him in this dark hall by myself." Again, my two companions laughed and I felt my shoulders fall from cradling my neck.

Finally, we visited Aremis' room, which was just as I expected it to be: filled with candles and photos of his Natasha. Natasha had pale blonde hair and a tall slender frame. Her features were classic, she could have been a runway model. Her eyes exuded empathy, even in a photograph. Romance novels littered the shelves, and unlike everyone else he had a bed. He explained that he enjoyed meditating horizontally and the floor just didn't provide the appropriate amount of comfort to let his mind thoroughly transcend. I wasn't surprised to find out that he meditated, it helped explain his calm demeanor.

When I got back to my room the fire was lit and the room was toasty warm. I was exhausted from my restless night of sleep the evening before so I showered and I jumped into bed and fell into immediate slumber.

LUCAS

I peeked into Olly's room. She was sound asleep. She looked content, I kissed her forehead. She stirred slightly and I found myself lost in memories that now seemed so distant. How different my life would be right now, I thought, if it were not for one phone call, a year and a half earlier, as I tried to heal my wounded heart in South America. I drifted off, thinking back on that time.

I LOVED *the smells down here,* I reflected. *Yessica had loved it down here too. Life was simpler, it moved slower. I need that right now.* I nestled a little deeper into my chair. The weather was sunny and clear, I could see the mountains in the distance and the litter of cactus strewn across the landscape. Cactus wasn't traditionally beautiful, but it was captivating in a landscape such as this. The Chilean wine cleansed my palate. I loved its complexity, and its powers to help me forget—even if for only a time.

I looked at the glass again. *Such a simple pleasure.* I felt my shoulders fall. *Why did I ever leave this place? I was so much more at ease here. If we hadn't left my fate may have taken a different turn, her fate may have been different.* I felt the warmth that permeates the eyes before tears well up.

I raised my glass. "To you my love, may your beauty astound the heavens." A toast like that deserved another pour. *Shit what the hell, let's drain the rest of the bottle, these glasses are large enough.*

Relaxation washed over me. I inhaled deeply. I hadn't felt like this in years.

It helped that I couldn't easily be ambushed here. It wasn't a time to leave entrances unguarded or corners unlit, no it was not a safe time at all. No one could be trusted.

I wiped the thought from my mind. I didn't need to think of the fucked up time I was living in. It was every man for himself. We had to do what we could to keep ourselves alive, and if we were lucky, save our Atoa. Not all of us were that fortunate. This was a war best waged in the shadows.

The sun was setting and another brilliant array of color painted the sky.

I felt my pocket buzz. Few living beings had my number. When I read the name illuminated on my phone I didn't want to answer. There was no love between us. It had to be a desperate situation for him to call me.

"Hello." Just hearing his voice irritated me. I said nothing.

"I need your help. I need you to protect someone very special." It was as I suspected—he was desperate.

"Please come to San Francisco as soon as you can." His voice was shrill, panicked. I hung up.

I stared at the phone, then crushed it in my hand. Anything and everything was traceable. His number was burned into my memory, should I concede to his request. I did not care for Elias, and he definitely didn't like me. I did, however, feel like I owed his father.

His father Cane was an exceptional man, his wife Sorcey was a fine woman. Together they were a paramount couple: kind, forgiving, and strong. I spent many lifetimes welcome in their homes, and Yessica adored them. Fellowship was different then, they were different then, the world was different then.

None of this ultimately had to do with Elias. Change is inevitable, this is only a season, I told myself. I cared for Cane. But should I help his son, despite our abhorrence for each other? I sat back down, not realizing I'd begun to pace on my porch. The stars were now peeking through the clouds.

He must assume I'm coming. And if I don't come, what will he do? I couldn't imagine that there was anyone else who could complete this task, or else he would have contacted one of the many other "followers" who adored him. Yes, many other conduits would leap at the chance to help their beloved Viraclay, the *prodigal* son.

He must be fraught for a powerful camouflage. There was no other explanation. *What could be that important?*

My curiosity was getting the better of me. If I didn't complete the favor, what was the worst that could happen? Elias would fail and I will be no worse off for it. Then again, I did love San Francisco.

But I had just settled in here. I reminded myself how important it was to keep a low profile, and what better place to do that than in Monte Patria? I'd be safe here, at least for a time, long enough to let the enemy find other prey to stalk. I didn't need to risk my own neck for anyone, and above all, not for Elias Kraus.

I was pacing again. *Dammit! I should have let it go to fucking voicemail.*

"Why should I run because he's beckoning?" I scoffed out loud. "Too many others come running at his call, let him find one of them with a comparable gift to mine." I stared at my glass. It was nearly empty and it wasn't talking back to me yet, so it seemed an appropriate time to open another bottle.

My feet hit heavy on the hardwood floor in the kitchen. *How dare he disturb me here. How did he even get my number?* I supposed Cane had shared that information with him. Cane must have imagined that Elias and I would become friends someday. He was sorely mistaken.

Lumbering out to the porch I realized I missed Cane, and that he must have had some kind of foresight to share this particular information with his son. I owed him this, didn't I? I would think about it until dawn, at which point I would still have plenty of time to travel north, without Elias knowing I'd wavered.

"Yes, I will give myself 'til dawn!" I shouted, then took my gaze to the stars. "If you have some input on the matter my twinkly friends, speak now or forever hold your peace."

My glass was raised to the charcoal-colored sky and the stars sparkled back. I thought, *Now if only I spoke sparkle.*

A bellowing laugh hurled its way out of the deepest chambers of my belly, and I realized I had not laughed that hard since Yessica and I were here, on this very porch.

OLLY ADJUSTED herself in bed and I was thrown back into the present. I missed Yessica more than words could ever begin to describe. At times my feelings for Ophelia felt like a betrayal to her. But Yessica was gone and I would never see her again for the entirety of my long existence.

Since I'd met Olly I had laughter again, love again, a purpose again. I couldn't imagine my life without her. It wasn't an option for me—I couldn't lose another woman that I loved. I would protect Olly vehemently, the way I should have done for Yessica.

I felt the warmth of a tear cascading down my cheek. I had not cried in many years. I wasn't sure I even could any more.

I couldn't let anything ever hurt her, she was too precious. She had already lived a lifetime full of more pain than most. In many ways, she reminded me of Yessica. They looked nothing alike. But they were both strong and stubborn to a fault. Both women gave unconditionally to everyone they met. Their kind hearts would be what got them in the most trouble.

But not this time. This time I would be there, no one would take Ophelia away from me.

OPHELIA

If I'd remembered what was on today's agenda I might not have been so eager to move the day's events along.

"Ying scares me." I looked up at Aremis pleadingly. "Do I really have to take lessons from him?"

"Do you wish to insult him?" Aremis didn't look at me when he spoke. So, I shifted my gaze forward, to the quickly approaching fencing hall. "He does not invite many into his confidences."

"Do many people want to get to know him?" The thought of anyone being eager to be in the presence of such a hard and cold-as-steel man boggled me. It was ironic that he'd seemed best characterized by the one thing he manipulated with his given powers.

"Ying may be a little rough around the edges, but he has lived many years and deserves respect, especially in the art of war." I would say he was sharper around the edges, but there was no need to correct him.

I looked down at my feet. I felt like a child being censured. "Why do I need to learn the art of war? You guys all hover over me like an infant."

Aremis stopped and looked at me fiercely. "Do not be falsely secure."

I shuddered. *Okay I need to get on my game face,* I told myself. *I obviously was not going to get out of this any time soon.*

The heavy door creaked on its hinges as Aremis opened it. In the center of the great room was Ying, his eyes closed. He didn't budge as we shuffled toward him. Something moved to my right and I saw that we had an audience. Rand was perched on top of a pillar, and Elias sat beneath him. I could feel my cheeks get warm at the sight of him, so I looked away. To my left Di crouched beside a chair, much like a lion would before it pounced on its prey. Not twelve feet from her, Lucas was leaning against an archway. I looked around searching for Winston. I heard the door shift behind us, and there he was, smiling as he scaled the wall. He got comfortable on a ledge about twenty feet off the ground. I glimpsed Nara and Valerian as well and a few more faces I had not met. *Great the whole castle was here to watch me humiliate myself.*

Aremis still held my arm, thank god because I was starting to feel sick from all the eyes upon me. Ying still had not moved, his menacing figure only steps away.

Aremis leaned down to my ear. "Enjoy this lesson and know that no one here would let anyone harm you, ever." Then he was gone.

Ying bowed and I reciprocated the gesture, because I had no idea what else to do. He looked pleased with this. He stepped back. I again mimicked his movements.

Finally, he spoke. "When facing an opponent, you must honor them with respect even if you do not care for them." His accent sounded thicker than I'd remembered. "Always keep eye contact, it shows that you are not afraid. Eye contact can mean the difference between life and death. You can learn to read your enemies intent, and therefore their next move through their eyes."

I was taking mental note of all of this, since I was sure there would be a quiz. I continued looking into Ying's eyes. They were black as coal and sunk into a depth I didn't wish to travel. I glanced to the side for relief.

"You are not holding my gaze." He asserted.

I made an excuse. "I was taking a mental note." Di giggled. I briefly looked in the direction that I'd last seen her, and before I could fully comprehend the whereabouts of my own two feet I could see them floating over my head and contorting into a position that didn't seem possible. Then I was on the ground, facing the ceiling. I wasn't hurt. He'd placed me down as lightly as a feather.

"Okay I get it, maintain eye contact." Ying reached down and picked my body up gently so that I was again standing and facing him.

"We will begin with you learning to move with intention, through the fear." I kept his stare. Even though I had no idea what his statement meant. I was pretty damn afraid, and I didn't think I could get my pinky to move with intention at the moment. "Always keep your eyes locked with mine and study them as I move. You will learn their language."

From the periphery of my right eye I could see that a large, shiny metal object had appeared in Ying's hand. Even if I was ballsy enough to break our eye contact, I was too afraid to see what it was. He showed me soon enough, as he slowly drew a massive ax across his body. It looked like it belonged in the Middle Ages at a beheading, not inches away from my face. I could feel the coolness of the blade. I wanted to cry. This maniac was apparently about to start slinging an ax at me, and I was clearly not as fast, skilled or as strong as him. What the hell were my onlookers thinking, putting me in this situation? I was pissed.

"Good. You are angry, use that. Anger is very useful when channeled wisely." *How the hell did he know I was angry?* Now I was really fuming.

"I am going to slowly maneuver my weapon around your body in motions that would mirror a battle. As I move I want you to counteract my strokes, but do not run from fear of my blade. Make intentional defensive actions—and never break my gaze." Ying stepped back again and I decided to step forward.

We were now playing a game of chess and he wasn't going to go easy on me, even if I didn't know the rules. So, I decided to make up my own and see what happened. I stuffed my fear into a hidden chamber where no one could see it, or I'd be consumed by it. Immediately I understood what he'd said by moving with intention through fear. It's hard to be intentional when you're inundated with fear.

He stepped back yet again, and again I followed in short pursuit. As my right foot planted, the ax came down and I swiftly stepped to my left, away from the heavy blow that crushed the stones beneath our feet. *He may be moving slow,* I thought, *but not without force.* I reasserted my eye contact and the ax flew in front of my face as I simultaneously stepped back. It moved gracefully in Ying's hands as it came down directly where my head had been. I stepped to the left and swallowed hard as the floor shook a little with another impact of the blade. I realized he was *trying* to make me afraid, so that I could learn to work through it.

Ying would act and I would react purposefully. No one in the crowd around us spoke, or moved. I was focused and determined to succeed.

Ying stepped towards me and I stepped back, but then the ax was gone from his grasp and he was bowing.

"Most impressive Ophelia Banner. I look forward to our next lesson." I bowed, and when I looked up he was gone. Instead Di, Winston, and the rest of my regular companions stood in his absence.

"Olly that was incredible." Lucas was gripping my shoulder. "Truly incredible."

"You showed exquisite equanimity my dear," Di was beaming at me.

"I do follow directions pretty well, especially after I'm knocked on my ass," I said, relief washing over me.

Elias finally stepped forward. "That was beyond simple obedience, you moved like a conduit. It appeared Ying was dancing with his shadow and that is…truly extraordinary."

"Even many old conduits cannot embrace the teachings of such a renowned master as completely and flawlessly as you did today in this room, as all of us looked on." Aremis looked worried as the words left his lips. I knew that meant something.

"You all are making me blush," I finally said. "Please stop before you give me a big head. I'm sure it was beginner's luck."

"Miss Ophelia, there is no beginners luck in the world of combat. Beginners lose an arm." Winston was, if nothing, but honest.

That worried me too. *Should I have done worse my first time?* But worse could have meant losing an appendage. Talk about being stuck between a rock and a hard place.

"Winston is going to go prepare you something. Would you like to freshen up?" Aremis offered me his arm.

I looked down at my blouse. I was drenched in sweat. I hadn't even noticed, but now I could smell myself and I wasn't going to be able to eat if I didn't wash the stench off me.

"Yes, for everyone's sake."

Aremis and I didn't speak as he escorted me back to my room. I was digesting my lesson, and I supposed he was too. I felt a buzz on my skin, like a residual energy. I wondered if Ying had imposed something onto me. I even seemed to move more fluidly through the halls as we crossed from one passage to the next. *And was I seeing better in the dark?* I figured it might all be in my head, after all that praise.

Rand hadn't stuck around to give me feedback, I wondered why. No sooner did I finish the thought than I heard a calamitous sound just behind us. I spun around faster than I'd ever done before, and without a thought I was in a deep crouch.

"She's special all right. Did you know she could absorb Aremis?" Rand said, he didn't wait for the answer. "We must be wary of who sees her talents my friend," Rand stepped forward and kissed me on the cheek. "You were astounding today Ophelia, simply astounding." Then he vanished.

I straightened and looked into Aremis' eyes. "Did I do something wrong? I saw the worry in your eyes earlier, and I saw it in Rand's just now."

"You moved expeditiously right then, did you notice?"

"I was jumpy."

"Right, you were." Aremis decided to drop the subject.

ELIAS

I should have requested Winston whip up something for myself. The refrigerator was full, but nothing looked appetizing, although I was famished.

I sensed her before she spoke, but I chose not to turn around until she wanted me to acknowledge her. My parents said that was the customary way to treat someone of her generation.

"Elias."

I turned to see Nara by herself just inside the kitchen entry. "Nara, always a delight to see you. To what do I owe this pleasure?"

She gestured a small bow and I returned the favor. This was her bidding consent to approach. She walked casually in front of me.

"We were watching today." Her voice was discreet.

"It would appear the whole castle was present at Ophelia's lesson in the fencing hall."

"Apparently." She looked down as though what she was going to say next might be distressing. "She absorbs. It is up to Chitchakor's strokes, but there is a possibility she is a Sulu."

"It would seem. She was very impressive in her exercises." I said it with reservation. I did not feel we could yet determine whether or not she was a creature as magnificent as a Sulu. Sulu's were literal beacons of energy or rather vortexes because they absorbed that which was around them.

"We have only seen one other of our kind with that type of ability, and she suffered a fate worse than death." Again, Nara looked at her small but lethal hands. "The resemblance is hard to ignore, Elias. Not so many should know of her talents, it is not safe."

"Valerian—he feels the same?" I knew she was right, but Ophelia also had the right to learn how to defend herself. I would have limited the audience if I had suspected what a single lesson would divulge to the other house mates and a potential traitor. Now I felt trapped, if I ceased her lessons it would confirm that she was indeed something to covet. If I attempted to limit the audience I would stir further excitement. All of this considered I had to remember what was in Ophelia's best interest.

"Valerian wants to leave Hafiza now." Nara met my eyes with a silent plea.

"Is he aware you came here to speak with me?" She shook her head, no. "You are free to leave whenever you wish, Nara. This is simply a place of refuge. I am already extremely grateful that you came when I asked for additional protection detail for Ophelia."

"I am not ready to leave. We believe in your cause Elias, in your parents' cause. We are ready to fight by your side. But Valerian is now afraid that our enemies will hear of her capabilities and come to take her—and kill us all. He is only concerned for my safety." She looked embarrassed, as though her husband's love for her was something she should be ashamed of.

"Of course, he is. Nara, there is no shame in withdrawing. And if ever you shall wish to return just as hastily, you may do so with my blessing. I do understand Valerian's unease. As he wants to protect you, I want to keep Ophelia safe above any other. But she must learn more about herself. She has been kept in the dark for too long. I cannot try to conceal her from herself now. I will find a way to censor who knows about her potential." I did not want to show it, but Nara's fears were my own.

"Thank you for hearing my case. She really is a jewel." Nara turned to leave, satisfied with her confession.

"Nara," I called out. She only halfway turned around. "You will tell me if you do decide to leave, won't you?"

Her head nodded, almost indistinguishably. Then she was gone and I had lost my appetite.

OPHELIA

There was a slight knock on my door. "Come in," I called. I was towel drying my wild hair.

"Miss Ophelia?" Aremis peered around the corner.

"Please." I gestured to the chair as I took a seat on the floor by the hearth.

"I thought you might enjoy learning a little more about your sparring mentor. I asked Ying for his permission to share his story and he conceded."

He had my full attention. This might explain Ying's powerful presence and icy demeanor. "I'd love that." I pulled my legs close to my chest.

"Are you cold?"

"A little. My hair takes forever to dry."

"I will remedy that. Besides all good stories should be told around a fire." Aremis flicked his wrist and the huge fireplace erupted with dancing flames. I felt warmth envelope me.

"Ying is of the age that I think it would be suitable to begin with... once upon a time in China there lived a wealthy merchant, Lu Buwei, with his beautiful wife Zhao Ji. The couple had just consummated and Zhao Ji was carrying child."

"They were conduits?"

"Yes. As I was saying, Zhao Ji was pregnant. During this time in our histories many conduits would station themselves in potential positions of power, and Lu Buwei was no different. He arranged for a chance encounter between his not-yet-showing wife and the prince of the Qin state. Zhao could bewitch almost any man into falling in love with her. No mortal man could resist her."

"Wait, are you trying to say what I think you are trying to say? He pimped her out?"

"What does this mean exactly, that he 'pimped her out'?"

"He sold his wife for power?" I was disgusted.

"No, he did not sell Zhao. The prince fell in love with her and he took her in as his concubine. At which point she started showing her pregnancy, and it was assumed that the child she bore was of royal blood."

"So, he did sell—or gave away—his soul mate, and his child, for power."

"No, please let me finish the story." Aremis continued. "Times were very different then. Remember Ophelia, this was in 259 B.C. and in the Chinese culture, royalty could snatch whomever's wife they chose and attain her as a concubine."

I had to wrap my head around that. Ying was incredibly old. I couldn't understand what the culture was like during his youth. I gestured for Aremis to continue.

"Zhao gave birth to a little boy in Hanan and he was given the name Ying Zheng. Although Ying was not a legitimate child, the boy was the only son the prince ever had. The prince appreciated the gift that Lu's wife had given him, an heir to his throne. He gave Lu a position as high counsel. The prince did not get to see his son grow up, otherwise he may have detected the resemblance between Ying and Lu. The prince died when Ying was only 13 years old, and Lu became the prime minister while the boy matured."

"Wow, so Lu and Zhao's plan worked perfectly."

"Yes, it did. They had much higher aspirations for Ying. China was a tumultuous place, and many warring states scavenged and scrapped over small parcels of land. The family hoped to conquer and unite them. But first Lu and Zhao had to demonstrate Ying's authority and ruthlessness. A reputation is just as important as the actions themselves.

So just after the prince died, Zhao seduced a man named Lao Ai. Eight years later Lu convinced Lao they must rebel against the king, her son Ying, now twenty-one years old, and that perhaps Lao would have a chance at the thrown."

"Does this woman, or her husband, have no shame?"

"It was her gift, to seduce men. She was a siren."

I folded my arms across my chest and Aremis continued.

"The mutiny was to occur while Ying travelled the countryside, but of course it was all a ruse. Ying came home immediately and viciously took his rage out on his conspirators. He publicly beheaded Lao and ripped Lu into five pieces—his head, arms and legs were tied to horse carriages all being led in opposite directions. The noose around his neck was pulled the slowest to make sure he could feel the tearing before the final dismantlement."

I shivered. "He killed his own father this way? Why would he do that if Lu was doing all of this for *him*?" I shook my head in disbelief. It occurred to me again that perhaps I didn't want to be near this man when he had a weapon in his hand.

"No, my dear Ophelia, Lu Buwei had his own gifts. Ying would never truly kill his father. But the rumors spread throughout China of his ferocity, and it sent shivers down the spines of the other rulers, just as it did you."

"What about his mother?"

"Ying banished her to the castle. She was publicly exiled to her chamber, never to speak to anyone for the rest of her life, ostensibly for fear that she may conspire against him once more. In reality, Ying's actions freed his parents from the constraints of hiding their youthfulness. Everyone believed that Zhao was never to make another public appearance again, and Lu was dead. The two could now have freedom in their movements throughout China. And in doing so they inflated the king of Qin's reputation until it was so large that just the thought of Ying looking in the direction of another Chinese state caused the ruler to crawl on his knees and surrender."

"So, Ying conquered the other states?"

"One by one the six other states fell. Qin had the largest and fiercest army. With the help of some natural disasters and the ever-vigilant eye of his parents—who always knew the perfect time to strike—Ying successfully united China under the Qin Dynasty."

"Holy shit. Are you saying that Ying is the first Chinese Emperor, Qin Shi Huang?" My profanity just slipped out.

"Holy shit, I guess I am," Aremis replied. We both laughed, mostly because curse words sounded especially funny coming out of his mouth. "No one can dispute that his unification did many great things for China, including the beginning of the Great Wall, the Lingqu Canal and the lack of localized authority, which allowed Ying's friends like Confucius to flourish. Nonetheless, history remembers the tragedies—and there were many."

"Confucius was Ying's friend?"

"You will find many great thinkers of this world are good friends with many great conduits, most likely because they are one themselves."

"Ying accomplished a lot and he obviously has fought many battles. If I remember my history correctly, the first emperor didn't live very long. Why did he choose to step down from the thrown so young?"

"Good question. That was not the initial intent. A family does not go to all of that trouble just to rule for only a matter of years. At the outset, the plan was to convince the Chinese people that Ying had found the elixir of immortality, so he could rule for a very long time. In the last few years of his mortal life historians would relate his obsession with the search. In many ways this is not far from the truth, Ying and his parents were in a desperate search for his Atoa and his true immortal elixir. By staging the quest for immortality, the people were more likely to believe the existence of their ageless ruler."

"Brilliant."

"It was, and he would have reigned for hundreds of years without refute. But as fate would have it, Ying met his elixir and she was a gorgeous young Indian girl. Her name was Aruna and she wished nothing of power or riches. And so, with that a new dawn had risen for Ying, and the young Emperor apparently 'died of unknown causes' only a few short years later."

"It really was a love story." It was odd to think that the icy man I had met, melting at the touch—and acceding to the wishes—of his other half. Then I remembered the earthenware soldiers he had built. "What was up with the hundreds upon hundreds of terra cotta warriors he had made?"

"Well Ying's father was naturally disappointed to see him abdicate after all the work they had put forth to see their son flourish with success. So, he had Ying make an immortal army that only he could control, if he changed his mind someday and decided that he and Aruna would once again rule over China. In each warrior is an unusual amount of mercury. Towards the end of the Emperor's mortal life he had a bizarre infatuation with mercury, they say 'that is what may have killed him'." Aremis smiled. "You know that Ying controls metal, so an army made of figures with large amounts of metal could be useful if you intended to rise from your tomb as the immortal ruler of China."

I was starting to understand the big picture. To the average person a conduit being would seem a god among men, and with that perception your opportunities would be limitless. No wonder Esther and Yanni felt this was something worth killing for. Humans had killed each other for much less.

"Are you far, far away right now?" Aremis was examining my face.

"I guess I was. Until now many things had felt abstract to me, but now they've come abruptly into focus. I now have a sense of how critical this war between the Poginuli and Nebas actually is."

Aremis nodded, looking lost in thought himself.

"Well that was not my intent, but perhaps a very significant result. It is important that you understand the gravity of the situation you are in." He put his hand on my shoulder. "I wanted you to better understand Ying. His years on this planet have hardened him. He has seen and fought in many battles for many different things, but almost all for power."

"Where is Aruna?" I hoped she was safe somewhere.

"She is in hiding." I exhaled a sigh of relief.

"Is it common for pairs to spend so much time apart? Winston is not with Lucia either."

"No, it is not common. Once you find your Atoa it is natural to never spend another moment without them. This separation has become a tactic for hiding from Yanni and his gifts. It is risky because we are stronger together and can defend ourselves better. But our strength in turn becomes our weakness, because we are more easily detectable. It is an arduous call, to leave the security of your partner. Ying knew it would be much more dangerous for Aruna here. He had to beg her to stay behind."

"I'm confused, why is it more dangerous here than anywhere else?"

"For a few reasons. The first is that so many conduits are in one place. We have not congregated like this in over a hundred years. The more energy in one place, the more detectable. "

"Why risk coming together now?"

"Why isn't it obvious dear—you." Aremis smiled. "We are here to help Elias keep you protected so that he may carry out his plans for the summit. The summit is the only way we may unite the Poginuli and Soahcoit to defeat the Nebas once and for all."

I was touched and I didn't know what to say so I deflected with the obvious question. "When is the summit?"

"I do not know. He tells us nothing for fear of the defector. It is such a huge weight to bear. One that his father dispatched to him. He was a good man, Cane."

I looked down at my hands, "So him bumping into me had to have been an unpleasant mishap. I deterred him from his mission, and now I'm here fumbling around weak and needing constant supervision."

"Now you are being ridiculous. Times are difficult, but your happenstance meeting gives him purpose. He adores you and is only relieved that he can now make sure you are safe. You are a diamond in the rough, and a true pleasure to be around for all that you encounter.

On that note, I feel that it is time for me to retire. I have much to think about, as do you."

"Thank you Aremis." I thought of something as he ambled to the door. "Is that your birth name?"

"No Miss Ophelia it is not. Aremis is French, Natasha and I spent much of our time together in France during the 16th century. Some conduits go by their birth names and others by eras or cultures they fell in love with. Take Lucas' Yessica, she was a Mongolian princess but they had spent many centuries in South America and she fell in love with her asserted name, Yessica. It suited her. Sleep well Miss Ophelia." With that he shut the door.

~

LUCAS MUST HAVE FELT his ears burning because about a glass of wine later he knocked on my door. "Come in."

"Are you sore from your lesson?" He asked.

I stretched my legs off the chair as he sat down in the adjacent seat. "No not yet." I smiled. "I am sure it will catch up with me tomorrow."

We sat there in silence for a while. I wasn't sure how to approach what I really wanted to ask him. "Lucas." I paused. He knew what that meant, it was a signal I was going to ask a question I was apprehensive about. He waited for me to continue. "Tell me about Yessica."

He stiffened. "Yessica and I?"

"During my tour of Hafiza I saw a photo of you and her on a beach. Sorcey was on one side of you, and Yessica was on the other. She was very beautiful Lucas."

"Yes, she was. That was a great day." He was pensive.

"You looked happy." I was searching his face for a sign—grief, resistance, anything.

"I was very happy, Yessica was more than I ever deserved." His voice sounded sad, but his expression was reflective. "I can assume that Elias told you what happened to her."

"Yes, he did. I feel terrible for you. Even worse, I thought you and I were best friends, but you never shared any of this with me. That's supposed to be what friends are for." I walked over and sat on his lap and put my head on his shoulder. "I'm here for you to confide in. You know I love you Lucas."

"I love you too Olly. You mean the world to me. I couldn't forgive myself if I lost you also."

"How many years were you two together?" I searched his face. "Unless you don't want to talk about this."

"It will probably be good to talk about her, I haven't spoken much about her since she died. We were together for nearly nine hundred years. She was brilliant, funny—and damn sexy." I had an unexpected twinge of jealousy. This wasn't like any relationship I'd ever had. This woman was stolen from Lucas. I knew he loved me, I knew I loved him, but whatever we had couldn't cast a shadow over this bond. The realization of that stung my heart more than I'd anticipated.

He continued. "I could go on for hours about her incredible spirit and fiery will. She made life a never-ending celebration. She loved fiercely and saw the best in everyone.

"Do you miss her terribly?" I knew the answer.

"More than words could describe. Nothing will ever change that." He looked at me. "Olly, I don't want you to think that my love for Yessica is measured next to my love for you. They are two different things. After I lost Yessica I was a shell of the man that I am with you. You make me very happy."

I nestled further into his shoulder. I would never have nine hundred years with Lucas. I would have sixty more, if I was lucky. I was starting to get a better idea of what my choices might look like: to be alone, with Elias or with Lucas? All three outcomes would be drastically different and they were decisions not to be made lightly, or anytime soon.

We sat there for a long time in silence, and at some point I fell asleep.

LUCAS

I put her in her bed gently and brushed her hair out of her face. She was as beautiful as the day I met her.

~

I HATE this charade of meeting someone and pretending like I know nothing about them. I detest facades, which is rather ironic considering my gift.

I looked down at the sheet of paper again, Clement and California St. Awww… there it was across the street, the café we arranged to meet at. She was careful on the Craigslist ad to be discreet about which streets she actually lived on in the Richmond, but after meeting with Elias last night I knew that her place was literally around the block. *Not the best choice, my dear.* Anyone answering the ad could easily follow her home.

I peered into the café window. Elias said she had wild strawberry hair. That must be her. I couldn't see her face but her tangled mane was all about her like a flaming halo. I stared for a while, trying to sense her mood, she was fidgeting in her chair. Probably safe to say she was nervous about finding the right roommate. She glanced around the café looking for a man in a green sweater and brown scarf. I knew because that was description I gave her to look for in our email correspondence. She refused to give me any details about herself, I guess it was her way of trying to be careful. I had to give her points for trying, but I would have to teach her that the meeting place when conducting a random transaction shouldn't be so close to her home base.

Assuming she believed my ruse and decided upon me as her roommate as Elias had suggested. Otherwise I wasn't going to stalk this woman for an endless amount of time. I was clear that if this didn't work, I would carry on my merry way and he would have to come up with another plan.

He was lucky I decided to even give him that much. I looked at my watch, one o'clock on the dot. Time to make a good impression, punctuality is a start. I opened the café door and she turned in her seat. I paused, glancing around, pretending to seek an unknown host. I tried not to look at her directly until she caught my attention. She waved her hand and I gazed at her face for the first time.

It was exquisite. Her cheeks were high and lavishly adorned with pale freckles. She smiled a faint but genuine grin. Just enough to reveal a small dimple in her cheek. Her hair was a surly, gnarled mess, but it added to her seeming conservative manner—alluded to another side of her. I assessed her style as classic vintage—she could have been cut out of a '50s magazine, pearls and all.

I timidly smiled back. I didn't want to seem too eager. She gestured for me to take the seat opposite her at the table. I quickly consented and we sat in a brief awkward silence, before she thrust her hand across the table and introduced herself.

"I'm Ophelia. You must be Lucas?" I shook her hand hard and nodded. "Crazy weather huh?" She looked out the window behind her chair. It was an unusually moody day in the city: cloudy, rainy, then sunshine. I swallowed hard and felt a slip in my composure. What kind of hold did this beautiful young girl already have over me?

Clearing my throat, I managed "Yeah, not your typical summer day." She turned back around and beamed a glorious smile in my direction.

"I kind of like it, reminds me that even Mother Nature has mood swings."

"That she does. I like to stay on the right side of those if at all possible."

She laughed a gentle laugh, then got down to business. "From our emails I gather you're kind of pressed for time and need a place soon? Why might that be?"

"If you're asking if I got kicked out of my last place, I didn't. I'm ending a relationship and would like to get out of the home that we shared together as soon as possible." Her shoulders softened, I could sense here empathy. "But you don't have to take my word for it," I offered. "You can call my references." I slid a piece of paper across the table with a list of five references all constructed by Elias, including an employer. She took the paper and glanced over the names.

"Were you with your girlfriend long?" I was definitely pulling her heartstrings.

"Many years, she was an impeccable woman. But according to her, it was time to leave me." There was some truth to that I supposed. In my mind, I was referring to the only relationship I'd ever had, and the loss of her was unbearable. I couldn't explain the real circumstances of her departure at the moment, so I did my best to chalk it up to a standard breakup.

"I'm so sorry." She looked sad.

"Life is a journey that's for sure." I tried to lighten the somber mood.

"Oh I apologize, I didn't mean to pry. You probably don't want to talk about such an intimate subject with a total stranger." Then she paused and rather smirked to herself. Like it was some sort of inside joke. When our eyes met again I knew she'd decided we would be a good match.

I was excited, I hadn't felt so alive in years. We chatted for two hours that day, like old friends, and she agreed to meet me at the apartment the next day. I left the coffee shop in a haze. I knew I wanted to protect her for the rest of her life. I'd do my best to keep her safe from anyone who attempted to harm her.

I wandered to the Geary bus stop and jumped on the next one that stopped. I wasn't ready to meet Elias. He was probably squirming in his hideout. I needed to enjoy what I was feeling and devise a plan. I couldn't let him see how much I wanted to help him...and her. He would know he had the upper hand. It still needed to be clear that I was doing him a favor.

OPHELIA

PRESENT DAY

I woke up enthusiastic about my next lesson. Aremis escorted me to the fencing hall. Ying was again in the center of the room.

"Good day Ophelia Banner." Ying bowed. I reciprocated. When I raised my head he was already armed. My heart flew from my chest. He swung a heavy sword diagonally in front of him. I stepped back and to the left.

"Very good, just making sure you did not forget yesterday's lesson."

My heart was pounding. *What if I had? Would I have been cut in two?*

"Today we will be doing more of the same, with the addition of two tactical blocks. Do you understand? Be on your toes or I may sever one."

I nodded. I still couldn't speak, afraid the fear may be too obvious in my voice.

The sword came down at my right, then was thrust toward my chest. I dropped to my knees and felt the blade brush against the very top of my most unruly hairs.

"I would not advise falling to the floor for any reason," Ying reprimanded. Then he was on top of me, blade to my throat. "You do not move fast enough on your feet for it to be of any advantage to you.

Now focus. You are not completely present. Fashion the fear to your benefit, use that energy." He let me up.

I took a deep breath and visualized Ying, focusing my mind's eye so even when I blinked I could feel his presence. I took in his scent. The smell of nickel and sweet plums filled my nostrils. I wanted to be able to anticipate his direction by the path of his aroma. Lastly, I sent my gift—as everyone called it—forward, doing my best to use it to ensnare his intent. I felt purpose, respect, and determination. Nowhere did I feel malice or threat, no matter because I knew the danger was still very real.

I was staring him down. I could see he saw something in me shift, and his mouth curved upward ever so slightly on either side.

He swung the sword hard to my right, but I was already behind him before he had followed through. The conduits in the room gasped. I only dimly heard the noise. I was in a trance. It was like I could see his moves a fraction of a second faster than he implemented them. I saw a shadow in front of him, telling me where the next blow would occur. I thought it might be a stroke of luck the first time, but I saw the second blow coming too, and I ducked, then moved left.

He threw strike after strike, with me managing to stay only a hair ahead of him. Ying, excited, began moving quicker, as I tried my best to hasten my reactions. Then suddenly I felt my head on the cold floor. I opened my eyes to see Elias in Ying's face. Lucas was behind him, furious.

I got to my feet. "Wait what's going on?" I was confused. I grabbed Lucas' arm. "I thought I was doing good?"

"You are doing excellent Ophelia Banner." Ying was now at my side. "I must apologize, I got overzealous and forgot that you are still Unconsu. I needed a gentle reminder to slow down."

"So why did I need to be knocked on my ass?" I heard chuckling in the dark spaces of the room. "That wasn't a very gentle reminder." I was pissed and my head hurt. I touched the back of it to make sure I wasn't bleeding. No blood, but a nice knot was already swelling.

"Sorry Olly, that was my fault," Lucas said, chagrined. I was trying to get you out of the way. You were doing exceptional, really, but I could see you weren't able to physically keep up with the accelerating speed. I may have come in a little too aggressively." He leaned over to brush off my back and as his hand moved lower I gave him a *don't you dare* look. He immediately backed off.

"Perhaps we should take an intermission? Let you recoup and put some ice on that lump? I will talk to Ying and we will continue in an hour." Elias was talking to me, but addressing everyone. Then he said much quieter, "Are you okay?"

"Yeah, I think so." I touched the back of my head again. "I'd like to continue today." I didn't want to lose whatever mojo I'd channeled. "How long had we been at it?" I asked. I'd lost total track of time.

"Three hours." Elias replied. "It is a good time for a break."

Dear god! I thought. *It felt like minutes, not hours.*

"Let Aremis show you to the kitchen, I will be behind you shortly." Elias was letting me know he'd help me heal.

"Why do you need to follow them?" Lucas sneered.

"Stop it," I said. "It's his house, he can go where he pleases." My head hurt and I needed Elias' help.

"Follow me Miss Ophelia." Aremis grasped my arm. We took a right out of the fencing hall and went through the next door down the passage. Aremis flicked his wrist and dozens of flames illuminated a large kitchen that looked like it had been transplanted from the Middle Ages, replete with old wood barrels, washtubs and a huge clay oven. Aremis instructed me to sit on a large oak island in the center of the room. He exited quickly, then returned with a small parcel.

He'd put some ice in a towel and was gently pressing it against my goose egg.

"Does that feel better?"

I winced. "Yes, I think it does." I was lying. "I'm just disappointed. I felt like I was really getting somewhere." I was frustrated, worried I wouldn't find the same groove.

"You were incredible, full marks." I jumped at Elias' voice. I hadn't heard him come in the room. "How is your head?" Elias had taken Aremis' place at my side and was holding the ice. They'd moved so fast I didn't even see the transaction.

"It's okay."

"I am sorry you got hurt. You were moving so gracefully, so swiftly that Ying forgot you were an Unconsu." Elias removed the ice pack and began touching my scalp with his fingertips. My head pulsated erratically. "How were you doing that? I have never witnessed anything like that before. Many mature conduits are not capable of such skill."

"I concur," Aremis chimed in. "I have never seen a mortal come close to matching Ying, even at his elementary level."

My face felt hot from the flattery, from Elias' touch—and probably from the bump. "I don't know, I just concentrated. I used my "gift" as you guys call it." I scoffed. "To try and see the intention of his next move."

Both men looked at each other. "I believe it is time to begin her formal training with Rand," Elias said.

Aremis nodded in agreement. Then Elias quickly replaced the ice and the pulsating decelerated.

"Is anyone going to convene with me on this particular topic?" Lucas pushed Elias out of the way and took over ice duty. "I don't think she's ready." Then he looked deep into my eyes. "I'm so sorry, Olly. You know I was just trying to protect you."

"I know."

"Did you not see her this morning? Either she will get training or she will continue to confound us all with the leaps and bounds that she makes on her own. You can't stop her development." Aremis concluded as he took his place next to Elias, it was clear they were a team. It dawned on me that I'd never seen anyone defend Lucas that way since we arrived here. I wondered why that was.

"I don't think she's ready. Furthermore, I can't shield much more. You're already stretching me too thin." Lucas was adamant.

"Stop talking about me like I don't have a say," I said as I stood. "I'm an adult and it should be up to *me* whether I want to proceed with any development." I was feeling a lot better. Elias must have worked his magic again. "I thought we agreed you guys would stop treating me like a child and let me make my own decisions. Better yet, agreement or not, this is how it is going to go. I will train with Ying twice a week, with Rand twice a week, and the rest of the time I will spend learning my way around the castle with Aremis, or wandering the grounds with Di. Does anyone have a problem with that?" I made it a point to look all three men in the eye.

"Bravo, Miss Ophelia." Rand was in the doorway. "I for one am ecstatic about your decision. I am delighted to spend more time with you." He was now holding my hand and kissing the back of it.

Lucas put his hands on my shoulders. "Can we talk about this some more later?"

"I think I was clear," I stated, shoving his hands off. "Aremis will you please escort me back to the hall? I'd like to continue with today's lesson if Ying is up for it."

"Certainly."

ELIAS

We all looked on as Ophelia was escorted out of the room by Aremis, then Rand began to circle Lucas.

"What is your aversion to me helping refine Miss Ophelia's gift? What are you so afraid of?"

Rand was prodding the bull yet again. I did not believe it was necessary but it certainly was not my place to intervene.

"I'm not afraid of anything. I think she's going to get overwhelmed with all this conditioning."

"Have you not been the one insisting that she is a strong and capable woman?" Rand had his back to Lucas.

"She *is* strong, but even the most resilient people need a break. She doesn't always know what she can handle." Lucas sounded almost desperate. It made me a little sad because although I was sure his objections had ulterior motives, I knew how much he cared for Ophelia and wanted what was best for her. An empathy I was positive he never felt for me.

"She feels as though she can handle it," I said. "If she bows under the pressure we will bring it to a halt. You must know I would never encourage her to do anything beyond her betterment?"

Lucas did not look at me. "You don't know her the way I do."

He was right, but my connection went far further than he could imagine. *Nonsense. He knew exactly how deep it ran, he has just opted not to acknowledge it.* "We will not let her fatigue," I promised. Rand nodded in agreement.

"She shows exceptional promise. As a mortal, she already has shown capabilities far beyond any Unconsu I have ever seen before. We can nurture her gift, so she can protect herself." Rand was speaking to both of us now. He was right, Ophelia was remarkable. To think she was not even aware that she was a conduit until a matter of weeks ago. If Lucas did not armor her so much, she might be even further developed.

Rand felt the same. "For me to help her, you will have to back off a little with the screen you have her enveloped in. I can barely get a read on her, you have her so well sealed off."

Lucas was fuming. "I won't do that. I'm protecting her. She doesn't need to learn to take care of herself—I'll keep her safe!"

"You may not always be around," I said. He turned his piercing gaze to me, but I continued. "We do not know when they will strike or if anyone will be there to guard her. She needs to be ready to defend herself with any faculties she may possess. It will help her feel better too, can you not see that?"

"I will be there to protect her," Lucas stated, then started to leave. "I'm not pulling my camouflage back."

"It's not up to you," Rand said. "She has already decided. If you refuse I will have to tell her why we are stunted, and she will ask you herself. You know this." He was right and Lucas knew it. Lucas left the kitchen before anything else could be said.

Rand looked to me." Why do you think he smothers her with his gift?"

"Partially for her protection, I am certain. But he is also hoarding her, keeping her from me."

"Perhaps, but I think it is more than that. He keeps her at a distance from not only us, but from himself. Our darling Ophelia is going to be a brilliant reader. She almost siphons information from people, whether they want to divulge it or not. He is scared of her."

"Scared of her knowing the truth?"

Rand nodded. "That man carries many secrets. There are things in the darkest crevices of his mind that I cannot come close to uncovering—things only Dalininkas could know. I can only taste his emotions when I get a rise out of him. But someone like Ophelia who he already keeps close—he wouldn't be able to shut her out. Not without driving her away, and he would rather die than do that."

"What do you presume he is hiding?"

"I don't know my friend, but Ophelia may be able to enlighten us some day. I for one would like to go watch her continue with her practice." Then he was gone and I was left alone with my thoughts.

I knew Lucas had something to do with my parents' death. I wondered if that was the secret he guarded so dearly. *Or was it worse?* I had no idea what he was really capable of. I hoped that my worst fears were not to be realized.

OPHELIA

"Please sit." Rand said as he lit a candle. "Don't be nervous."

"Is it that obvious?" I was fiddling with my thumbnail and chewing the inside of my mouth.

"Do you know why I was chosen to teach you?" I nodded my head. Rand continued nonetheless. "We have very similar gifts, at least as far as we can tell about yours so far. I can taste people's emotions, intentions and bonds." That sounded funny. *What do emotions taste like?* I wondered. "I know it sounds a little odd. I can't read someone's mind, but I can palatably taste their emotions. It took me a while to distinguish what each emotion or intention manifested as. But I have it down very well now, I assure you."

"Do the emotions overcome you?" I remembered what Aremis said about absorption versus observing or in this case tasting the emotion, so I thought I knew the answer.

"Oh no. They are literally like flavors in the air. I can choose to partake or not. But they are always there, and everyone gives off their own vintage. Some are stronger than others and if a room of people is captivated by fear or joy, I find it much harder to not sample the mood." Sitting on the edge of his seat, he then turned the conversation to me. "Tell me about your gifts Ophelia."

"I'm still adjusting to the idea that they *are* gifts." I shrugged. "It's been more of a curse for the majority of my life. Anyways…I'm not sure where to start. It's been a while since I've been really immersed in them. Lucas has kept me shielded from the onslaught. It's been a relief, to be honest." I felt like one of my patients.

"I see. Well, may I speak plainly?" Rand scooted even closer.

"Of course." *Did he know how to speak any other way?*

"I am sure in the human world your gift was a hindrance to deal with, but for our purposes, you may want to ask Lucas to give you a little leeway. I think you will find conduits won't be as overwhelming. And to make the most of our time here, we really need you uninhibited."

I nodded. "That makes sense. Do you really think he's hovering that much?"

"It is not my place to make a judgment there. I can only say that in order to help you understand and work with your gifts, we need full access to them."

"I'll talk to him." I took a deep breath. I couldn't imagine that conversation going over well. I didn't want him to think I was unappreciative for all that he'd done for me. He really had made the last year or so bearable. I had, however, suspected he had been smothering me, not just protecting me with his camouflage, this confirmed it.

Rand brought me back to the present. "Don't worry about it yet. Describe to me what you remember about your gift."

"Well, before Lucas came into my life I was just starting to get a better feel for what might be taking place. It's as if two things happen simultaneously: people are compelled to share their innermost thoughts and emotions with me, and at the same time I absorb whatever it is that they are feeling." I wasn't sure if that was making any sense.

"Interesting, you feel that you *absorb* their emotions? Can you elaborate on that for me?"

"I'm not sure what else to say, really. If someone was mad, I would feel anger stirring inside me. I didn't even have to be talking to that person if the feeling was strong enough. I could take in the emotional climate of the room. The more the emotion resonated with me, the more it affected my own mood." I paused, not sure what else to say. It felt like it had been a lifetime ago.

"Continue."

"As far as everyone's *need* to dump their emotional trash on me, it was just that. From the time I was a child adults— complete strangers, friends, family —would tell me secrets or inappropriate information. I could see the relief in their eyes when they were through. It was like I absorbed the weight of their knowledge. It's been like that all of my life. I didn't need to read minds, because I always knew more than I wanted to anyway."

"Fascinating. Then you would take this absorbed information and subsequently feel anger or anxiety?"

"For a time. Then it seemed to process and dissipate, I guess. It depended on the subject matter. Some things just stuck with me because they were awful to hear about."

"Certainly, but you would say that was not their feelings anymore, but your own?"

"Yeah I suppose."

"This is very curious. I am excited to see what we discover as we work together."

"Why?"

"Absorption is a unique talent. It usually indicates some pretty powerful implications." Rand looked lost in thought. "This is all very good food for thought. I am formulating a game plan. Anything else that you can think of to describe how you felt or how those people around you acted?"

"No. As I said it's been a relief to not feel swept away by others' emotions over the last several months. I really try to block out the bad memories." I almost added that I thought I was picking up on more emotions here in the castle. I remembered how I felt after Ying's lesson, like he imprinted something on me. I'd also had a couple instances where I seemed to be absorbing emotions again. But I changed my mind. I wasn't sure any of that was true, it had been so inconsistent. Plus, I still didn't know who was listening and what their intentions were.

I stared at Rand's face. I could tell he picked up on my hesitation, but he didn't ask any further questions.

"I understand." Rand put his hand on mine. "We will help you protect yourself from unwanted, what did you call it, emotional garbage. Trust me my dear, you have amazing talents and we want you to relish in them, not feel bogged down." He smiled at me assuredly.

"That would be nice. What will we do today?"

"Today I'd like to test your absorbency while Lucas' shield is encompassing you. Okay?"

"Sounds interesting. How will we do that?"

"I am going to project a feeling at varying levels from my person. You tell me what you pick up on, and to what degree. Please take note of any colors, shapes or images that accompany what you feel. Does that make sense?"

"Why colors and stuff?"

"Well, for example, my gift presents itself as flavors. Think of me as a food critic of emotions. Someone bestows upon me a medley of emotion and intention, and I have to decipher those things. My palate has been refined, because it is through my sense of taste that I decode the pastiche. Here, I will show you."

He moved his chair so he was better facing me. "This may be a little more difficult with you right now since you are very heavily guarded, so please project your feelings as openly as you can." He grabbed my hands. "I am going to say a name, and you will just think and feel the first things that come to mind. "I will simply say what I read."

"Okay." I was nervous. It sounded very intimate, and I wasn't intimate with many people. I squirmed in my seat and took a big breath.

"Winston." He chuckled a little, as I explored my feelings. "You are intrigued, cautious. You believe him to be odd and have an ill sense of humor. Upon which I agree totally. You are not sure how much to trust him— there is fear underlying—but generally speaking, you like him."

"That sounds pretty accurate." I was relieved he didn't say his own name first thing. Rand was smirking to himself. I pulled my hands back, realizing I didn't entirely understand how this worked, and when it stopped and started.

"It's okay to be relieved, I am not trying to get you into any trouble. Would you like to try some others?"

"Sure." I said hesitantly.

He clasped my hands again. "Aremis."

Rand closed his eyes and didn't speak for a few moments. I tried to stay focused on Aremis and not get distracted by his pause.

"You like him very much. You are apprehensive with everyone in the castle but least of all him. He feels like a father figure to you. You feel bad for his loss. You empathize with him and enjoy his company immensely. He is your friend. Desperation, I sense a hint of desperation because you yearn to trust him completely."

I hated the word *desperate,* it sounded so futile.

"Desperation can be a good tool," Rand noted. "Do not disregard it as complete folly. Oh, I am sorry." He shrugged his shoulders as if to say oopsie. "Oh, but I do wish to ask you about Elias, Lucas and myself. May I?"

"No! Absolutely not!" I yanked my hands away. He was grinning. I could only assume by just mentioning their names he caught quite a bit. "I'm not ready to sort those feelings out in my own head, much less in yours."

"I completely understand. Another time then."

"I have some questions."

Rand leaned back in his chair, looked pleased as punch and very casual. "Fire away my dearest Ophelia."

"Do you always need to be touching someone to read them?"

"No, usually I can get a very good taste from quite a distance."

"Than why did you insist on holding my hands?" I felt duped into exposing more then I wanted to.

"Well everyone tastes a little different. The basics are the same, but the details take honing in. Of course, it doesn't take long to figure out the subtleties from one individual to the next, but it is easiest when in complete contact. Plus, as I said, you are heavily armed. Lucas has you fastened tighter than a fifteenth-century chastity belt. I needed a little help."

I narrowed my eyes. There was something crafty about him.

"Ophelia, I am here to help you succeed. I must get to know you as best as I can in order to see that you rise to your full potential. Surely you can understand that." His hands were dramatically clutching his chest.

I moved on. "Okay so you demonstrated your powers. How do we go about testing mine, before I ask Lucas to loosen the reins?"

"Excellent question, way to stay on course." I rolled my eyes. "I am now going to project feelings at you." He picked up a pen and journal. "Would you like to write down what you see, or shall I take notes for you? I don't want to impose."

"I'll do it," I said, taking the thick, leather bound book. It was beautifully made, and the paper inside shimmered slightly. "This is beautiful."

"I am glad you like it." He looked delighted. "Now, I am not going to tell you what emotion I am projecting. I will simply continue the projection until you feel that you have collected all the data you can. I want you to write every detail, no matter how insignificant it may seem. Are you ready?"

I nodded.

"Just breathe and relax. Look at me and try not to get lost in foreign thought."

"Seems easy enough. Let's do this."

Rand sat up, completely intent on me. I started to feel my face get warm, my hands sweaty and my chest clammy. I couldn't nail down the feeling yet, but my stomach was bubbling with anxiety.

He put his hand on my knee. I felt a jolt of complete humiliation. Bingo! I moved from under his touch. "Write. Write it all down," he reminded me. I started frantically scribbling down everything I was feeling: a tingling sensation that hit the back of my ears, the intense urge to run, to cry, and more. I couldn't get it all down fast enough.

Finally, I put the pen in the bind of the book and sat back, sweat spilling down the back of my neck. I used the journal to fan myself. "Okay I'm done," I said, relieved.

"What do you think I was extrapolating?" he asked.

"It was obvious, you were humiliated. Although I couldn't tell by your outward demeanor." I took another deep breath.

Rand peered at me. "Superlative."

I raised my eyebrows. I was a sweaty disgusting mess and he thought that was amazing. His power was way less intrusive on him. I looked and felt like I had just fell off a stage on Broadway opening night.

"Tell me dear Ophelia, what did you see, feel, taste, smell? I need to know any and all of it." He was sitting with his hands on his chin like a captivated child during story time.

I tossed him the journal. "Read it yourself." What was the use in hiding anything at this point? Whatever he didn't pick up from my bodily reactions I was sure were mirrored back to him in my horror.

"Fascinating," he said as he read. "You genuinely absorb the emotion. It consumes you. And I would assume that if you can identify with it, your own emotions well up. This is a profound reaction, especially for someone under so much protection." He shook his head. "You confound me child. You will be a very gifted conduit." He laughed and slapped his knee. "My god, you are already an amazing Unconsu."

"Thanks, I guess. I still think a gift that didn't knock me on my ass would be far more useful than one that 'consumed' me, as you so accurately described it."

"All in due time. That is what we will teach you: how to put up boundaries without hindering your abilities. You will see, you will learn to love your talents, my dearest Ophelia."

I sure hope so. That mini-session wore me out. I felt more overwhelmed then I had in years. *Then again,* I thought, *maybe I'm so out of practice that this is going to be how it is for a while. I'll have to get used to dealing with emotional hurricanes again.* I frowned.

"Cheer up dear. Are you okay?" Rand looked jubilant. I wished I could absorb some of that.

"I know this is going to sound silly, but that little exercise just took it out of me. I'm not sure I can do another one today. I don't mean to be a sissy."

Rand put his hand up. "Now stop right there, I am not calling you a sissy at all, nor do I pretend to comprehend what this experience is like for you. We can pick up another day. But if I may..." He gestured for my hand. I hesitantly gave it to him.

Immediately I felt tremendously better. Balminess and contentment filled my chest. I was gleeful, butterflies fluttered in my belly. My skin felt like sunrays were setting it aglow. I tasted a hint of milk chocolate on my tongue. *That was odd, I had never 'tasted' anything before.*

"We can't have you leaving here on a bad note, not for your first lesson."

"Thank you." No one had ever intentionally left me with resonating happiness before. I was euphoric. It was different then feeling someone else's happiness, or even my own. This felt like an offering, something I could keep for myself. As we sat there beaming at each other there was a rap at the door. It was Aremis.

"Splendid timing my friend." Rand chirped. "I believe our Ophelia is ready for alternative company."

~

"Is everything okay?" I looked up at him. He had not said much since we left Rand's quarters.

"Oh yes, everything is fine Miss Ophelia. I apologize I am a little lost in my thoughts today. "He smiled at me. "I have something to show you. We are in the West Wing, are we not? Today we are going to better examine the fencing hall."

"Okay." I followed in his steps. I wasn't aware that there was more to see in the hall, though I hadn't seen much besides Ying while I was in there. We promptly arrived at the massive door.

"Here we are," he said as he pushed it open. Take a good look around, Miss Ophelia It is quite magnificent." He threw his hands up toward the ceiling, and for the first time I noticed the detailed mural above. There were gruesome demons fighting alongside beautiful angels. There was blood everywhere, yet the artwork somehow manifested a peace amid the chaos. I noticed the gold-plated carvings that littered the walls all the way down to the enormous ornate sconces. There were several Roman pillars encircling the center floor. I walked under and around each one, and when I got to the eighth Aremis was on the other side. His finger was to his lips.

He pointed to a small in discrepancy in the marble on the pillar. His finger slid over it three times, each time from top to bottom, and the tile on the floor between the two of us moved. The tiles had to be three square feet in diameter, and looked heavy. He then followed the same discrepancy in the pillar, this time moving from left to right, and the tile moved again, this time further to the left. Aremis grabbed my palm and placed it over the spot. The tile disappeared completely, opening up a passage. He raised his hand and silently counted to three. The tile reappeared as if nothing had happened.

He scanned my face for recognition, and I nodded. "Truly brilliant architecture," he said dramatically. "Sometimes I think it a shame that all we use this space for is battle sequencing, wouldn't you agree Miss Ophelia?"

"Yes, it's a very nice room. I hadn't noticed. Thank you so much for insisting that I get more familiar." With that, Aremis gestured I take his arm.

He leaned over and whispered in my ear. "Did you get enough time to admire it, or shall we stay longer?"

"I'm good, thank you," I said, busy replaying the sequence in my head. I felt confident I had it memorized.

We walked slowly down the hall and my mind drifted back to the difficult conversation I was going to need to have with Lucas about retracting his shield. I let out a huge sigh.

"Are you okay Miss Ophelia, that was a heavy sigh." I looked up at Aremis, not sure where to begin.

"I am going to have to have a conversation with Lucas." Aremis looked at me inquisitively but before he could ask about what, another familiar voice spoke up.

"Talk to me about what, Olly?" His hand was around my waist and he was practically whispering in my ear. Aremis pulled away immediately, he was clearly uncomfortable, which in turn made me uncomfortable. I stepped back so I could see Lucas' face.

"I need you to withdraw your safety net," I blurted, looking him in the eyes. "I need to be able to train with my gifts unfiltered. I know you can understand that." I didn't expect for that to come out so plainly. Aremis had stopped walking and was a few paces behind us. Lucas was clearly caught off guard and agitated. I stood my ground literally and Lucas stared at me his jaw tight.

"When exactly am I supposed to jeopardize your safety?" he snorted. "Just during these lessons, or all the time now?" His posture was defensive. I reached for his arm to calm him, but when I touched him all I felt was enmity, so I pulled away. Apparently my gifts were already starting to retune themselves. I had never felt a specific vibe off of Lucas. Aside from the one and only time he'd raised his veil, when he first showed me his true conduit self. He saw my recoil and quickly eased his stance. "I'll back off during your lessons with Rand, but that's all."

"That's all I ask—for now." He understood what I was implying, and it infuriated him.

"You're not safe if I'm not guarding you, Olly. You're just a beacon waiting to be discovered. I will not have you in danger, even by your request. It is not an option." I reached for him again and this time didn't retreat despite his aggression.

"I appreciate you protecting me, Lucas, you know that. You have no idea the gift of peace that you've given me over the last year and a half. I know you've been my guardian angel. I love you for that, and for many other reasons." I smiled at him. "But I need this. I want to be able to utilize any powers I have to help protect myself, in case you're not around."

"I'll always be around," he insisted.

"I know you'll do your best, but as we both know things happen. Remember the night that we barely escaped Yanni back at the apartment? Please Lucas, for my own peace of mind." I was still holding his arm and I moved my hand to hold his. "You've always been my biggest cheerleader. Don't let me down now."

His mood lightened. "I'll do my best. One step at a time." I threw my arms around his neck, it was a compromise and for the time being good enough. I gave Aremis a thumbs up down the hall. Then I felt Lucas' pant pocket buzz.

"Excuse me Olly, I need to take this." He kissed me on the forehead and was gone.

LUCAS

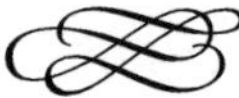

We had had another perimeter breach last night, the first since Olly's abduction. She didn't need to know that her abductor was still circling the castle. I had called Astor last night and he apparently just found the time to get back to me.

"Where is she?" I was curt, no need for fluff.

"Why are you calling me? You should know better Lucas. Your inquiries are not welcome here." He wasn't going to help me without a fight. Perhaps he would for the right price.

"It's important. Otherwise, as you can imagine, I would never bother to contact you." There was silence on the other end. "For Christ's sake man, it's for your beloved Viraclay."

He laughed. "You never were a good liar, Lucas, and we both know you would rather die than help Elias. Are you in trouble? Did you finally bite off more than you can chew? Thank Daininkas for this stroke."

"No not at all, and believe it or not, this *is* just as much for Viraclay as it is for me." I wasn't lying. "She's meddling in things she shouldn't be. Do you know what she's up to?"

"If Nandi is fucking with your plans, then I am all for it."

"It's so much bigger than that. Is this about me? Is she trying to get back at me?" My voice was becoming shrill. I needed to do a better job of masking my frustration.

"I am astounded that you think I will help you at all. Nandi is my friend, and if she has found a way to get under your thick skin then I applaud her." I could hear the smile in his voice. "You don't have any friends here. You can burn in hell Lucas. Don't ever call me again."

He hung up and I just stared at the phone. He knew something, I was sure of it. I'd find another way to get some answers. I still had a couple aces up my sleeve.

OPHELIA

What was Eleanor doing here? How did she find me? Shit, I hope she wasn't followed here.

"Mom, how did you get here? Did Lucas bring you?" Eleanor turned and looked at me, and I noticed the shackles around her wrists. "Mom?" She just looked at me with no expression on her face. Eleanor looked empty.

I had to get to her. I leapt forward only to be abruptly stopped. I looked down. I was chained to the floor, as she was. I felt the cold harsh rub of metal on my own raw wrists and ankles. There were red abrasions where I'd clearly fought my containment. I scanned my memory for answers. What had happened? I must have been unconscious for quite some time.

"Mother! How did we get here?" I yelled. She just stared. "Eleanor? Answer me!"

My brain was giving up nothing, all my memories were evading me. The castle must have been attacked. I hoped Lucas and Elias were all right. I knelt down. The floor was damp, the texture was clay-like. I saw something move out of the corner of my eye.

It was another woman, restrained in the far crook of the room.

The light was dimmer there and I could barely make out her figure or who she was.

"Hello! My name is Ophelia. How did you get here?" She didn't move. "Please. I need your help. I can't remember how I got here."

The woman moved slightly and I could see she was naked. *That must be why she was hiding in the darkest part of the room.* She shifted again and her long, blonde hair spilled down her back. It was dirty, and matted in spots, but still beautiful.

I again addressed the stranger. "The other woman over there is my mother, Eleanor." I looked back, Eleanor was still unmoving. "I want to help us get out of here. But first, please, help me remember how we got here."

The woman looked at me from over her shoulder, trying to shelter her bare body as best she could. Her eyes were terrified and piercing. I could tell she recognized something in me, she moved swiftly and was now facing me fully.

"Ophelia, you know how we got here." The woman in front of me was my grandmother Lilith. Her body was covered in bruises and lesions. I turned to Eleanor. She was now naked as well. Similar wounds littered her body. My mother stared at me horrified, her sharp eyes looked pained.

I looked down and saw that I was now nude, the same lacerations shrouded my skin. I couldn't breathe. *Where was I? How long had this been happening?* I started to feel my chest tighten. I looked back up to see Lilith, but she was gone. Her shackles were on the floor where her huddled figure had been.

Eleanor was gone too. "Mom!! Lilith!!" I curled into a tight ball, trying to cover my body as best I could.

No one answered, but I could hear a loud bellow of laughter echoing from some far-off place. I pulled my legs in tighter. The laughter grew louder and reverberated off the walls, shaking the ground beneath me.

I closed my eyes tight but a glow began penetrating through my lids.

Then a man's voice whispered in my ear. "Stand up my child." I started to cry. His voice was menacing and commanded attention. I closed my eyes tightly. "Ophelia, you asked the question, and as your father I intend to answer it."

A violent scream pierced my ears as I felt his hand brush my shoulder, venturing for the chains that bound me. The screaming persisted and I opened my eyes to see where it was coming from.

I sat up in bed, Lucas was holding me tightly in his arms. I realized the screams were coming from me. I was shaking wildly, I pulled away from him to check for my clothing. He swept the hair from my wet face.

"It was just a dream. You're okay," He whispered. I threw myself back into his chest and he rocked me softly. "You're okay." I let his arms encase my body. I don't know how long we sat there. It felt like an eternity. I needed the foul taste of that dream to leave my subconscious before I would even consider going back to sleep. I was too afraid I would just fall back into it, right where I left off.

I HAD SLEPT terrible for the third night in a row and was ready for a new day and a new start. Rand was waiting and I was eager so I followed him silently to his chamber. He didn't speak until we were both seated.

"I would like to try some blind tests. How do you feel about that?"

"What do you mean by 'blind tests'?"

"I would like to blindfold you and turn off the lights, then experiment with how well your senses work to formulate the emotions of each person in the room. It should be harmless. I am still gauging your abilities, and this will help."

"In that case yes, why not?"

"Perfect." Immediately Rand covered my eyes with a thick velvet cloth. "Is that too tight?" he asked kindly.

"No that's comfortable, thank you." I shimmied further into the chair, then heard footsteps shuffling on the other end of the room. "Are you going to tell me when to start?"

"Yes, give me a moment to formulate my plan." That sounded a little diabolical.

"Why do I feel like you are tricking me into something Rand?" *I'm giving him thirty seconds before I am taking off this blindfold and giving up on this drill,* I told myself.

"No need for threats—I am ready. Throw your feelers out there, tell me what you see or feel?"

I pressed my eyes together tight and tried to cast my sixth sense beyond my own skin. I envisioned it like a net, throwing it out there and seeing what I caught. It didn't take more than a second to pick up a signal.

"I feel admiration, love and compassion. A little bit of fear I think, maybe it's insecurity. No, I think its fear for sure. I see a faint image of a person in the far corner of the room. They are standing there, almost glowing a soft golden hew." I tried to outline the figure further, but I couldn't make out anything else, nothing distinguishing. "Wait, Rand that isn't you, is it? What are you up to here?" I was peeved.

"Nothing, my dearest Ophelia it is a simple test of your ability to read others besides myself. I fashioned the help of your favorite people in the castle. We are just working together as friends."

"Well are you going to tell me who they are?"

"After we complete the exercise. I don't want you to have any hints, you understand dear?" I heard a hint of a smile in his voice. "Okay, let us try our next volunteer. When you're ready my dear girl."

I cleared my head. I immediately felt a bombardment of emotion from across the room. "I feel love, a deep love, lust and passion. I feel a sense of nurture, protection. I see a clearer image, the person is glowing a dim red. Wait there is a second image, equally as defined, but it's very angry, envious and extremely jealous." Then everything disappeared. I heard a door slam. "What the hell is going on?" I shouted. "I'm taking this off now. Turn on the lights, Rand."

As I pulled off the cloth I heard several feet scuffle for the door. It closed behind the last person just as the torches were lit.

"What was that about?!" I was annoyed.

"It went awry. You were only supposed to read one person at a time. Lucas apparently was having a hard time selectively shielding people." Rand smiled a mischievous smile and I knew I wasn't getting the whole story.

I sat back in the chair. "So that was Lucas who I saw so angry? That must make the other person Elias. Am I right?"

"Yes, you are. Good deductive reasoning. I am floored by your progress. I am afraid that we may be done for the day, however. I don't think that Lucas is going to be eager to unveil your protective veil for the moment. Poor guy is feeling a little vulnerable I think. He isn't used to having his guard down." Rand was shaking his head as if he disapproved.

"Maybe I should go talk to him then." I was concerned.

"That is a perfect idea. Perhaps he would be willing to work one-on-one with you, probably less intimidating to be exposed to the woman he loves." Rand was at my side now, ushering me out the door. "Let me know what kind of read you get from him. I personally have never been able to get a good taste at any depth with our friend Lucas."

"Why do I feel like you are eager to get rid of me, are there other motives behind this?"

"Don't be silly my dear girl. I want you to console your friend and continue with your practice. We need his cooperation in order to continue our progress." With that he gently pushed me into the hallway and shut his door.

I wandered back slowly. For all I knew Lucas was blowing off steam outside. When I reached the courtyard, there was no one in sight so I continued to my room. *What a strange day,* I thought. I was frustrated with how it had developed. I turned the corner and saw my bedroom door ajar.

Lucas was crouched by the fire. I came up behind him and nudged him gently. "I hear you didn't appreciate the training exercises."

He shrugged me off and continued stoking the fire. "Are you mad at me?" I sat down on the ground next to him.

"No, I'm just tired of always being the bad guy. I miss when it was just you and me. Don't you?" He looked at me with the saddest eyes and I realized how exhausted he must be, always guarding me from the next villain or onslaught of emotion.

"Oh do I ever miss those days! But we're here now, and I've found it only makes me sad to look back on things I can't change. Maybe you should pull back from constantly shielding me, Lucas. That has to be taxing for you. If you would let me train more, maybe I could protect myself and take some of the load off."

"Protecting you is only one piece of the puzzle and I enjoy doing that." He put his arm over my shoulders and pulled me closer. "Why are you so hell bent on refining the very tools that you have hated your entire life? Weren't you happy the way we were before, me protecting you so you could be comfortable in your own skin, without effort?"

"Don't get me wrong Lucas, I appreciate all that you've done for me. But you know me—I like to be able to take care of myself. And it's empowering that for the first time in my life I feel hope. Hope that I may be able to not only control my emotional state, but use my curse to help myself, and maybe others." I looked at him long and hard. "Don't you want that for me?"

He was silent. We both stared at the flames. Then he grabbed my hand. I saw his camouflage lower, his whole body radiant.

"I want you to be happy." I could feel the sincerity in his words. This must have been the reason for him unveiling himself in that moment. I could see and feel the truth in his words. "I'm scared to leave you unprotected, I could not forgive myself if anything happened to you."

I knew he was being truthful, but there was a glimpse of something—fear—that I didn't expect. He was afraid of being exposed to my gifts. He wanted to protect me, but he also considered this boundary between us a self-preservation maneuver on his part. Why would Lucas need to protect himself from me? I didn't want him to notice that I felt something that he was clearly trying to hide, otherwise he would definitely never take down his guard.

"I understand. We'll get through this, but you also have to trust me." His shimmering presence disappeared and we were back to two sheltered beings. He obviously was not ready to trust me yet.

"I trust you." That was all he said and I didn't pursue the subject. I needed to think about what I'd discovered before I approached him about it. I knew for now he'd let me continue my lessons, and that was what was important.

~

SINCE LUCAS HAD LEFT on a perimeter check and since my lesson with Rand was cut short I asked if I could practice with Ying.

I stood in the center of the fencing room. Ying positioned himself against the wall this time.

"Today we are going to teach you how to defend from a vulnerable position, such as the ground." Ying spoke so quietly I almost couldn't hear him.

"Wait—you said not to ever maneuver myself so that I would be on the ground."

"Absolutely never drop to the ground on purpose. But should you find yourself at a disadvantage where your opponent has brought you to your knees, or even on your back, you must know how to regain the upper hand." He looked at me for comprehension. I nodded. He bowed and I knew it was time to begin. *Ready or not here he comes.*

I bowed in return and he pounced. Before I could fully concentrate on the task at hand I was on my back and Ying was wielding a sword. It was long and menacing, over half the size of its commander. I locked eyes with him and felt myself slip into the familiar rhythm I had the last couple sessions.

I saw his intentions, so I rolled to the left as the sword hit heavy on the floor to my right. He smiled a wicked smile then struck again just right of my ear. I didn't move. He was trying to mystify me with fear. His intentions gave him away and I rolled left again and came onto my knees. He swung for my head and I ducked, managing to pull out my right leg from under me, ready to boost myself up onto my feet.

He was behind me now and I had to concentrate harder to feel his next move. Then the strangest thing happened as I felt Lucas' veil rise. I saw brilliantly colored shadows all glittering in an odd sequence, illuminating Ying at my back. It was as if he was standing right in front of me. The sword he carried was an animated shade of grey. I felt his energy pulsating within the metal in his hand. I saw how it was all one synchronized object—his energy was the energy of the sword, and the sword was a fluid part of his being. The vibrations were now reflected in my own person and I could feel I was absorbing some piece of Ying, his intentions, and his ability to manipulate metal. All of this happened in a moment and then it was gone.

He swung to my left. I jumped from my knees and sprang to my right, hurtling over the sword. I faced him once more and he looked astonished but unyielding. He again moved forward and the veil lifted a second time. His next move played out as clear as day in my mind, and I moved before he could implement his assault. His gaze didn't falter but I saw—or maybe I felt—he was bewildered. I wasn't sure.

I was still on my feet, so I backed up, waiting to countermove him again, but this time he moved at lightning speed. The veil was still lifted and I sensed he was onto my game, so he was going to move instinctually instead of with intention. I was aware that this was much more dangerous for me. A Ying unleashed and only working on instinct could be terrifyingly vicious. I swallowed hard and concentrated my gift on his sword. He couldn't hide that from me. I was feeling the unity between all three of us: myself, Ying and his weapon.

I turned three times to my left while he pursued relentlessly, striking at my torso and just missing as I moved. On the third turn I stopped. I had not interpreted the next move properly. The sword came down and I was directly in its trajectory.

I heard someone yell as I put my hands up, and when it should have split me in two I saw the sword was no longer in Ying's grasp but instead hovering just above my hands in midair. I felt the veil reinstate itself and the sword fell in what felt like slow motion, but it never hit the floor. Then Elias was by my side and Ying was gone.

"Where's Ying?"

Elias ignored my question. "Are you okay?" He was examining my body.

"Yeah I'm fine." I looked around. "Where's Ying? He didn't hurt me."

"Ophelia," Elias' face was stern. "Do you know what just happened?"

I looked around again, no one was left in the hall. "What do you mean?"

"You stopped Ying from managing his sword."

I stared at him for a second, not sure what he meant. "No, that was Ying, he obviously saw he was about to cut me in two and decided to stop mid-blow. I should have seen it coming, but he changed his strategy and I couldn't stay on top of his next move."

Elias was now staring at me with the same bewildered look that Ying had. "Ophelia, the things you are saying, the fact that you manipulated Ying's sword, these are not normal abilities for an unconsummated conduit. I never should have let the household watch you during these lessons. I am so sorry." He sounded horrified.

I realized someone very important was missing from this conversation. "Where's Lucas? He let me out from under his shield, that was why I could see Ying's intention more clearly." I was almost panicked. Did this mean he was hurt? The shield faltered again.

"He is working the perimeter. I will have someone track him down immediately." Elias' eyes softened. "Ophelia..." he paused. "Never mind." He grabbed my shoulder and escorted me towards the door. His touch felt like nothing I'd experienced with him before, it felt warm and like an extension of my own arm. I couldn't pull away from him, it would have been like severing a limb. I just let it wash over me as I moved in a daze next to him. This was his effect on me when it was unfiltered through Lucas' camouflage.

Before we entered the hall he pushed me against the adjacent wall and pressed his body to mine. My head started to swim, when his mouth touched mine and gently parted my lips. Suddenly the whole world aligned into distinct focus, while our bodies were blurred lines. That sporadic pulsating, I had felt was now a karmic rhythm and I felt complete. Then the shield appeared and our link was severed and I felt a huge void.

Elias whispered in my ear. “Forgive me.” My knees gave and I closed my eyes. When I opened them Elias was gone. Aremis stepped in the hall and brought me back to reality and my room, then quickly flitted away. I lay on my bed, staring at the fire wondering what had happened.

ELIAS

No one was saying anything, they all just stared past each other. I looked at Nara to my left and Rand to my right, but neither of them moved a muscle or gave me any insight as too their thoughts.

I stood up and immediately all eyes were on me. "I called you all here because each of you witnessed what happened in the fencing hall today." The group stayed, unmoved. "I am only requesting that any information about what you saw never leave the confines of this castle. I do not need to tell you what is at stake if someone were to attain that information and pass it along through the wrong channels."

"What did happen in there, Ying?" Nara's voice was pointed and accusatory.

"I cannot say. It was out of my hands." He was solemn, almost ashamed.

"Then describe it for us. I know what I saw, but words do not do it justice. Surely you can enlighten us." Nara said.

"My dear Nara, I think we are getting ahead of ourselves, certainly this is counteractive to Elias' wishes." Rand nodded at me. "It would be best for Miss Banner if we explored this mystery no further."

"I think Rand is right..." I went to continue but was interrupted by Di.

"Elias, we should know if Ophelia is a Sulu. We are all in danger if that is the case."

Aremis piped up. "She is something extraordinary, but to say she is any more of a draw than you or I is improbable. I have spent many days with her and she has shown great promise, but certainly she cannot be any more of a Sulu then a group of Consu." He was firm.

"What she demonstrated today cannot be controlled, the unknown is dangerous right now." Valerian stood and was pacing.

"Why do we need to control her? She is just learning her gifts bestowed upon her from Malarin, she clearly needs training so that it is familiar." Winston sounded sincere.

Rand jumped back in. "Ladies and gentlemen, she is an Unconsu exploring her abilities. We owe her the freedom to do so. Besides have we all not seen talent such as this before? I know I have in my centuries on this planet." Rand was trying to generalize the situation, but I was plagued with many of the same worries. Would this exploration alert our enemies?

"Yes Rand, we have seen talents similar to Ophelia's," Valerian answered heatedly. "And last time it was the inciting incident to this war and many others. You will have us just sit by and let the chaos begin again?"

"Valerian, my friend, calm down." Aremis spoke slowly and intentionally. "We do not yet know what Ophelia will manifest into. As Elias said, as long as her gifts do not leave this castle, our enemy has no better reason to hunt her any more than the rest of us."

"That is babble and you know it!" Di was now standing too. "Her attachment to Viraclay leaves her exposed already."

"Everyone needs to calm down," I said. "We need to help nurture Ophelia's gifts so she can keep them under control. With Lucas' shield she will be safe. None of this is cause to spur panic. I just need your word that this information will never leave this room." I was not asking, I was telling.

"Where was Lucas' shield today?" Ying spoke up.

"I do not know, he was running the perimeter. Ophelia was not supposed to have a lesson today, perhaps he got lost." I suspected he stormed off after the episode in Rand's quarters.

"Why do you trust him?" Di questioned. "We all know what he has done, but I am not sure we all know what he is really capable of."

"I have to trust him, because Ophelia does. Besides I do not know a greater shield, do you?"

No one said a word. A second later Lucas shot through the conference room door.

"What the hell is going on here?" He was agitated.

I ignored his question and proceeded. "We are all in agreement that this information never leaves this room. If you have any further concerns you can meet with me privately."

One by one I got a nod from my compatriots as they swiftly left the room. Even Valerian conceded after a noticeable hesitation. Rand was the last one to leave.

"Viraclay, all will be well." He put his hand on my shoulder and then he too was gone.

"What happened? Is Ophelia okay?" Lucas was anxious now, but I was not going to make this easy on him, not after the fiasco today.

"She is okay, however, everyone in the castle aside from the few out on patrol with you today now knows her abilities." I was trying not to get to angry. "Where were you?"

"What do you mean 'her abilities'? What the hell are you talking about?"

"Where were you?" I repeated.

He took a long moment before answering me.

"I caught wind of Nandi's scent this morning and I followed it as far as I could, but I lost it."

"How far? Far enough to misplace your shield?" I could see the realization in his eyes as he deduced what I must have meant.

"What happened? What lesson did she have today, her lesson with Rand was over before I left? I thought she was touring the castle with Aremis."

"She requested to spend the afternoon with Ying."

He threw me up against the wall. "What the hell were you thinking letting her do a lesson without my supervision?" I stood there under his grip, content not to say a word until he got his filthy hands off of me.

He let go and I brushed off and sat down. "You never said you would be going on a wild goose chase. I sent Lars to find you. He searched all day and could not track you down until a few minutes ago when you re-entered the boundary. You also never said that your shield was faulty when you were distracted." I saw him wince.

"Faulty? My camouflage is not faulty, I may have had moments, no —tiny windows—of lapsed guard, but I was trying to get to the bottom of Nandi's attempted abduction of Olly. What happened in her lesson?"

I stood up and walked toward the door, I had expected him to try and stop me but he did not. "Let's just say it was abundantly clear today how smothered you have been keeping our lovely Ophelia, and now the whole castle knows." Then I shut the door and let him stew in his own questions and failure.

I took long, deliberate breaths as I walked to my room. It was getting increasingly harder to keep my distance from her, but I had to stay diligent. Getting closer to her only increased the potential for us being exposed to our enemies. Every time I lost control I put her in further danger.

I hit the wall with my fist and Hafiza shook slightly with disapproval. "I am sorry Hafiza. You do not deserve that." I felt like I was losing control. First by being so foolish and continuing to let the other occupants watch her lessons with Ying. After the first happening I convinced myself that by barring their participation I would incite further intrigue and draw more attention. To be utterly honest I assumed if I banned it, they would just find other means of observing and I would risk losing loyalties for the sake of spectacle. I could not have fathomed how quickly her gifts would escalate. I see now how wrong I truly was. Then when Lucas' shield was down today I could not contain my lust for her, for our connection. I found myself grateful that Lucas kept her at such a distance from me, for her protection.

The prophecy was clear: she would not be in true danger until she consummated. I needed to weave her another fate before we could truly be together.

LUCAS

I watched Olly and Aremis move slowly around the second story of the North Wing. After yesterday's fuck-up, I wasn't letting her out of my sight if I could help it. I watched her body language with him, it was casual and comfortable. She really liked him. I guess I understood why, he was a respectable man. I wasn't sure what his motives were though, befriending her this way. I couldn't trust him entirely. I didn't trust anyone in this castle.

They turned a corner and lingered in the game room for far too long. I got closer to try to hear what he was saying to her, but I heard nothing. I closed my eyes to sense where both of them were within my shield. Very close to one another, huddled in the furthest corner. I heard metal move. *What on earth was he showing her, and without a single word? Was he attempting to abduct her or lead her out of the castle?*

I entered the room, but they both had moved. They were now sitting by the fire.

"Lucas, what are you doing in this wing?" Aremis was nonchalant, but Ophelia was fidgety.

"Just thought I would see how the tour was going, the North Wing has a ton of stairs. Making sure my Olly isn't too beat up." I sat on the armrest of her chair. She beamed at me, her nervous smile. This made me uneasy. She had been fraternizing with Aremis for weeks now. If he was up to no good she was already in the thick of it. I needed to speak to Elias. He must know what's going on, and if he didn't I would be paying Aremis a visit as well.

"I'm holding up just fine thank you. You should have a little more faith in me." She tried to sound annoyed, but I knew that tone. She was feeling disconcerted about something.

"Oh, I know what you're capable of sugar. I've hiked up Castle Crags with your ass." I nudged her gently. She gave me a sheepish grin and nudged me back. That was an incredible day, excellent weather. We'd already been camping just outside of Dunsmuir in Nor Cal for three days when we finally tackled the legendary hike, amongst six-thousand-feet tall granite spires. It was one of my favorite trips.

The three of us sat quietly for a few moments before I broke the ice and excused myself. But I was going to keep those two in earshot for the rest of the day. As I left the room I realized this was the first day I wasn't busy running some errand for Viraclay during the time that Olly was engaging with Aremis. I hadn't thought much about it, but now I wondered if that wasn't because they were keeping me out of the way.

I waved one more time at Ophelia and then found a suitable vantage point to follow them for the remainder of the tour. They were in no hurry to leave the game room. I leaned against the cold stone wall, waiting. The conversation was light, until the mood shifted.

"Aremis." Ophelia paused. Whenever she did that I knew she was getting ready to ask a loaded question.

"Miss Ophelia." Either he didn't know this about her, or Aremis wasn't afraid of questions.

"Why do conduits come in pairs?" Her voice was low and cautious. She couldn't have known I was listening. Aremis may have, but she wouldn't.

"Certainly, my dear. I think it is time I tell you that story I promised. It's a fable that my father told me in order to elucidate our kind." I heard Ophelia settle into her seat. I was nervous as hell. *What was he going to say?* I couldn't barge in there again, they'd know I was following them.

I should have taken the initiative earlier to talk to her about this, I chastised myself. *Shit!* What was done is done. Now I just had to listen and provide damage control after the fact.

"I was six when my father decided I was old enough to better understand my heritage. We sat at a fire similar to this one." He paused for an extended moment. "I will do my best to repeat the story just as he did. I hope you find as much wisdom in it as I still do when I recall it."

"Once upon a time, a very, very, very long time ago many different beings inhabited the earth. These creatures were kind-hearted and benevolent. They were created by a master painter, the first creator of life. He has many names, Chitchakor, Malarin, Dalininkas, but they are all simply an epithet for the creator of all things, the painter. The painter created this world and his creatures with vibrant blues—sensational purples, golden yellows and flashy reds. It all worked in harmony together: the air, the sun, the clouds the earth, the fire and every beloved creature were all one long, vivid paint stroke. The paint went on and on and formed the mountains and the seas. And since everything was from the same palette everything and everyone enjoyed the sun and the moon at the same time, the stars and the birds all flowed on the same endless sky." Aremis sounded like he was reading poetry.

I recollected hearing this fable once, but I couldn't remember who had told me. It may have been Cane.

"The painter was pleased with his work and decided to take a reprieve. He left the brush and his palette beside the easel and walked to the stream to get some water. While he was gone one of the frolicsome creatures named Fih got curious and began playing with the colors of the sun and the rabbit in the meadow and the flowers by the bank, and before he knew it the colors had all blended to a dull gray. Fih thought it was beautiful, because it was his creation. So, he began to dance across the canvas, turning everything he touched to gray. At first the rest of the creatures didn't understand how the change had happened, they couldn't understand how the vivacious colors had merged to create such a dismal shade. They were frightened that they would never see the same colors again." Aremis paused, but Ophelia said nothing, so he continued.

"When the painter returned he was surprised to find his canvas transformed to a gray landscape. But he thought to himself, 'This is not so bad, this is what happens when all the colors come together and we are all one constant shade, the world should not see any difference between one object, creature or thing to the next, because they were all created by me, all move and come alive with my spirit. So, the painter took his brush, stirred all the colors on his palette and created the same gray Fih had. He painted swirling lines of gray energy throughout his beings: the swirling energy of giving and receiving. He painted the eternal cycle of chi—the life force—connecting and fulfilling each creature he created. Then he stepped back and was happy with his work so he decided to eat his lunch."

"While the painter was away Fih decided to blend some more of the colors. He blended the seas and the clouds and the stones and the insects until the color he fashioned was a deep charcoal black. Then he began to paint lines. These lines separated him from the plants he saw and the shells he did not like. He painted a box around his favorite spot, so only he could appreciate the beauty of it. And when the painter returned he saw many boxes, many black lines strewn across his beautiful blended masterpiece. The painter was angry. At first, he thought he would wash the canvas clean and begin again. He walked toward the River Tins, prepared to start anew. He watched his creatures obliviously drawing lines and making boundaries, deciding what pieces they wanted to keep of the world they had been privileged to celebrate life in.

Then he saw Fih perform the worst defilement of all: he drew a line separating his fellow being into two. The energies were no longer spiraling in a magnificent unison, and the painter cried." Aremis paused again. Ophelia must have been captivated, because she said nothing.

"When the tear landed on his spoiled masterpiece he saw the lines blur and caught a glimpse of the vision he had once had, returned to his mind's eye. He decided that not all was lost. He placed the canvas back on the easel and began making his own lines. Separating the hues of grey into blacks and whites. He divided all his creatures from one another, he divided the earth from the skipping wind, the sun from the moon and the stars from the skies. After he completed those lines he looked at his creatures, his children and he divided them too. He divided them into one black and one white being, two beings that used to be as one and grey. The white beings wandered around at night when the sun was hidden and reflected their energy to the stars. The black beings wandered around during the day while the sun was bright, and received the energy of the day."

"Imposers and receivers." Olly whispered.

"The creatures were devastated, destined to live the rest of their existence torn in two, their energies no longer swirling inside of them, only a constant flow of receiving or imposing energy without a way to replace and fulfill themselves. Eventually the energy would dissipate and die, and so would the black or white creature exhausted by a lifetime of unreplenished reserves.

But the painter left hope. At dusk when the sun and the moon waved hello or goodbye the creatures could seek their other half. The time was brief and many failed to find their counterpart, but for those that did, they found themselves a warm shade of melded grey once more. With the lines removed the creatures could once again eternally spiral their energy, reconnect and blur the lines once more between earth, fire, beings and water. New powers arose when the grey creature emerged. Separate beings became one, stronger than ever. And they continued to grow forever."

Ophelia was holding her breath and finally let out a huge sigh.

"The painter hung the painting above his mantel. He no longer paints lines or blends colors. Instead he watches the creatures, his children, blend their own stories, find their other halves with the hope that his children will eventually find their way back to variant shades of grey, when lines are no longer drawn."

Neither of them said anything for a long while. I was waiting to hear something, anything from Ophelia. What had she taken away from that story? What was she thinking? *Give me something Ophelia!*

Finally, she spoke. "I think I understand the idea behind the receiver of energy. A receiver can take in someone else's energy like Rand or like me. I absorb people's feelings. But why are you considered an imposer?" If that was her biggest question then I felt good about the way this was going.

"I impose my will on the energy around me, as the beings in the story who reflected their energy to the stars. I can reflect the energy of fire, if you will. I don't receive or absorb the energy of the fire, I manipulate by reflecting its energy and imposing my own. Does that make sense?" Aremis was infinitely patient. No wonder she liked him so much.

"So that would also make Winston an imposer. An imposer of heat." She paused. "Lucas is an Imposer." It was a statement. My ears drew unconsciously closer.

"He is an imposer, he reflects an image of camouflage." Well done, Aremis.

"If I'm a receiver and Lucas is an imposer, does that mean we can consummate?" *Shit! This was the exact question I wanted to be the one to answer.* I was shaking, waiting to hear how he would broach the question.

"No that isn't exactly how it works… he is an imposer and it would seem you are indeed developing receiving skills. And yes, you two could have sex and children, but you would not consummate or change, and he would stay as he is—already a fully consummated conduit." *Well he answered the question, I might have phrased it differently. Who the hell was I kidding I would have danced around the question until my feet fell off.* Ophelia stood up and was pacing, I could hear her feet gently drumming on the floor.

"Aremis." She paused. This wasn't going to be good for me. I could feel it in my bones.

"Miss Ophelia."

"I am destined to be with Elias, aren't I?" She was holding her breath again.

"What do you think?" Aremis said softly.

"I know I am, I can feel it. You must think I'm terrible. Here he is so close to me and I deny being with him." Her voice had that anxious pitch that she got when she felt overwhelmed. "I know you don't understand this, but I love Lucas. He's been my best friend since the day we met. He's the only person I have ever really trusted. And I love being with him. I know this whole thing is killing him and me..." *Breathe Ophelia, breathe.*

"... but I'm also unbelievably drawn to Elias. He moves pieces of me that I never imagined existed. It's a daily struggle to fight the feelings I have for Elias and hold onto the love I have for Lucas. And all the while they fight over me. Sometimes I think I might break in two. And you know what else? I don't get Elias. One minute he looks like he wants to consume me and the next he's avoiding eye contact. At least I know where I stand with Lucas." She had broken the damn and it was going to spill out until she felt better. She had done this with me a few times before. She continued, though I wasn't sure how much more I could take.

"If Elias is my other half, how come he hasn't swept me away? If Lucas knows this, why won't he back off? To top it all off, where do I get a choice in all of this? Why don't I get to pick who I want to be with for eternity? What if I can't trust Elias the way I trust Lucas? I feel like I can, but so much is happening and I'm so confused. Am I going to wake up and this is all a dream? I went from taking care of myself and everyone around me for my entire life, to now having hardly any say." I felt my shield around her crumple into a chair.

"Aremis, why can't I have time to sort through all of this?" She paused. "I'm so sorry. You don't have Natasha anymore and here I am whining about two men. I know it's pathetic."

Aremis waited a long while before he answered, probably afraid she wasn't finished. When he finally spoke his voice was calm and commanding. "Miss Ophelia, I cannot fully comprehend your predicament. As we have discussed I always knew what I was and that I was meant for one person. I can say without a shadow of a doubt that you are not terrible, pathetic or whiny. You have been propelled into a war between gods and have just begun to feel comfortable in your own skin. I commend you every day, for working at becoming that much stronger. The real choice you were never given was when you were a child and born to two conduits who could not share with you your heritage. Since then you have been surviving. When you are ready to let go of just surviving, you will begin thriving." I felt his figure move toward her chair and place his hand on her shoulder. "Miss Ophelia, have patience. When you realize that you are safe to just be you, the true you, then and only then you will understand that it isn't about choice. There are no lines, there is only energy swirling and moving in shades of grey."

I had heard enough.

OPHELIA

"May I come in Miss Ophelia?"

"By all means, Winston."

His smile widened and he blushingly looked down at the breakfast he'd brought. That particular expression made him look twelve years old.

"You know, I cook too Winston," I said as I grabbed my fork. I nodded as I spoke to reassure him I was telling the truth.

"Really Miss Ophelia? Do you cook French cuisine, German, Italian?"

"I cook a mean lasagna."

"I love lasagna. If you will give me your recipe, Miss Ophelia, I can prepare it for you."

I shuddered slightly as I thought of the last time I'd made it, our last night in San Francisco. "Well I wouldn't mind getting back in the kitchen. I know you conduits don't need food, but you enjoy it, right? What if I cooked for you this time?"

Winston nodded enthusiastically.

"Would you like to be my sous-chef? I could whip up something for the castle-folk tonight if you could get the ingredients."

"I will amass them personally." Winston said.

"Sounds like a plan. I will just need you to show me around the kitchen?" He excitedly pulled the tray off my lap just as I was taking another bite. "But can we wait until I am done eating?"

He looked down, embarrassed by his eagerness. I laughed.

"When you are ready to see the kitchen, I will be here to show you." I looked at Winston, I was pretty sure that meant he was going to be right there, exactly where he was standing until I gave the go-ahead. I felt like I was the kid sleeping in Christmas morning while everyone else was ready to open their gifts. So, I grabbed the tray and set it aside.

"Let's go."

"Are you sure? I didn't mean to rush you."

"I know you didn't, Winston. Let's go." I said.

Winston was moving so fast, I was jogging trying to keep up. We entered the courtyard and headed into the South Wing. I couldn't see a thing, there was no light without Aremis.

Just as I began to panic, I felt a hand grasp mine. "Where are we going?" Lucas playfully whispered.

"To the kitchen." I responded just as quietly. Then we turned right and into a modern kitchen, which included electricity. The room illuminated.

An enormous stainless steel fridge occupied half of the far wall. There were three sinks, tons of wide counters, and loads of pots and pans hanging decoratively from kitchen racks. A huge china hutch resided in the corner, with enough place settings to feed a classy army. It was a far cry from the primitive kitchen near the fencing hall.

"Wow. This kitchen is impressive."

I was formulating a cooking strategy when I noticed a crucial piece of equipment was missing. "Where's the oven?"

"I am the only heating necessary for cooking today." Winston smiled. *Oh of course.*

Lucas was holding back a smirk.

Then the kitchen door opened and Elias stepped in. The feel of the room instantly shifted from jovial to tense. I felt squeamish—and like the massive kitchen wasn't big enough for the four of us.

"Hey Elias." I raised my hand in his direction. This was the first time I had seen him since the kiss in the fencing hall and my stomach flipped and flopped and my abdomen ignited with tingles.

"Master Elias, Miss Ophelia is going to cook for all of us this evening," Winston said, grinning again. "With my assistance, of course."

"Lovely, what is on the menu?" He slowly made his way to my side. Lucas wasn't smiling anymore.

"I'm going to make lasagna. Do you like pasta?"

"I do. Do we have all of the ingredients you will need?" Elias asked.

"I haven't checked yet."

"Miss Ophelia was just going to give me her list." Winston looked at me intently.

"Pen and paper?" Before I got the rest of the sentence out Winston was handing me both items. I leaned over the counter to write down my grocery list. When I finished he whipped it out of my hand and within seconds had ransacked the fridge and pantry. Before I could blink again he was checking off all that was already available in the kitchen.

"All we need is lasagna noodles for twenty," He said matter-of-factly. "I will be back shortly."

"There is a market only fifty miles away. He should be able to run there and back in a very short amount of time." Elias deduced.

"How long will it take him to get there?" I asked.

"Only a matter of minutes." Lucas answered.

I nodded. I couldn't imagine that kind of speed. The two men continued to stare at me. I was usually okay with silence, but I was feeling extremely uncomfortable.

Elias must have sensed my distress. "If you will excuse me. I look forward to sampling your lasagna later this evening Ophelia." He smiled at me and my forehead tingled. Then Elias casually left the kitchen.

Lucas watched me watch Elias leave the room and then spoke up. "I know you will be busy doing prep. I will get out of the way. Let me know if you need anything, okay?" He brushed my hair out of my face.

"Although you may want to brush those teeth and get out of your pajamas." He winked at me and I remembered I literally crawled out of bed and into the kitchen.

Embarrassed, I patted the top of my head. Yep, it was a mess. "Okay lead me back to my room so I can become presentable."

LUCAS

"Viraclay!" I saw him turn the corner. He was waiting there when I made my way down the hall. He didn't say anything. I positioned myself in front of him. "We need to talk."

He nodded.

"I've been thinking, about Olly and what is best for her." His expression softened. "This tug of war we're playing with her is taking its toll. I can see it." I also heard her have a mental breakdown with Aremis the day before, but he didn't need to know that.

"I agree." His tone was sincere.

"Let's call a truce for a while. Let her wrap her head around this new world she's been thrown into. And when she's found her footing —and only then—will I again make it clear to her that I'm ready for something more than friendship." I hated every word that left my mouth. But I was the aggressor, and if I backed off, he would too. I didn't exactly understand why he wasn't chomping at the bit to consummate her, but he had been more than fair. "If we can both let her make up her own mind, and perhaps listen to her own heart without the fear of hurting either of us, then she will feel much better."

"I could not agree more." I heard the relief in his voice. *Was this what he'd been hoping for?* I felt my pride face plant into my gut and there was a deep aching in the pit of my stomach. I needed to remember this was what was best for Olly. And I had to be honest, the bigger thing to do would have been to simply back off myself. Viraclay would have followed suit on his own. But I needed a level playing field, he already had the advantage of destiny on his side. I had to know he wasn't going to swoop in and just take her from me.

I reached my hand forward and we shook on it. "I will back off, and so will you, until she is ready. Until then, I will tolerate the situation and not make advances."

He was still holding my hand firmly. "Agreed."

My stomach was still twisting. I felt like I had rolled over and let her go. But I could never do that, not until she asked me to. We both turned around. It was over, for now.

~

I WAS DRESSED FOR DINNER, and considering asking Ophelia if she needed any help. As I turned the corner to the industrial-sized kitchen I heard faint voices in Asagi, which meant that Ophelia was not present.

I paused in the hall, out of sight, to capture what was left of the conversation.

"Have you shown her all of the passages?" It was definitely Winston's voice.

"Yes." Aremis answered.

"After the last defense lesson I am afraid we cannot wait much longer. They most certainly will be alerted." Winston sounded convinced, and Aremis didn't respond. "Do you think she trusts you? She has not said a word to Master Elias, or he would have questioned me about it."

"She trusts me. That poor girl, I think she just wants a father. She never had a real one growing up." Aremis had definite pity in his voice.

"You are far friendlier, and a much more convincing comrade than myself. I suppose that is why your charge was to make friends with her." Winston chortled.

"You have always been an odd one, my friend." Aremis joked.

I waited to see if they would say more, but there was silence. Maybe they knew someone was listening. I turned to go. *What the hell were they talking about? Do I go to Elias with this information, or warn Ophelia that her friend Aremis is not what he seems?* I didn't want to ruin her evening after all of her hard work making dinner for all of us. But I planned to talk to Elias later that night and would definitely clear the air with Olly in the morning.

OPHELIA

I was pretty proud of what Winston and I had cooked up in the kitchen. He insisted I shower and relax a little before dinner. I really appreciated the down time in my room. Now it was time to get ready I put on one of my favorite dresses, one of those that Lucas had picked out for me. It was violet blue, with white polka dots and lace around the collar. I even did my hair. A little mouse and a gentle blow dry and it almost looked tamed. It felt like an occasion that deserved a little extra primping.

After I gave myself the once-over and decided I approved, I hurried to the kitchen. There were only forty-five minutes before the castle residents would be piling into the dining room. I had given Winston specific instructions for the final composition, but it made me nervous to not be doing it myself. The aroma in the air indicated he had done a great job. The familiar scents of warmed basil, tomato and cheese tickled my nostrils and made my mouth water. I was getting excited.

Winston was lounging in the far corner of the kitchen, three huge pans of lasagna several feet away from him, simmering away, cheese oozing over the sides. He looked pleased with himself. The kitchen was spotless and clearly dinner was ready.

I was smiling at him, excited to share this moment with my friend.

"Smells wonderful, Miss Ophelia."

"I think we have you to thank for that. I didn't prepare this feast all on my own." I noticed Winston was dressed for the occasion as well, with nice slacks and a very handsome bow tie that matched his neatly pressed teal-colored shirt.

"Aremis and Di are arranging the dining room."

"Well that's kind of them."

"They are using the fine china. Everyone in the castle is delighted with our supper plans." He nodded reassuringly. "They will not be disappointed."

The excitement now melted into anxiety and landed in the pit of my stomach. I was not nearly as confident as Winston. How could I possibly satisfy hundreds-of-years-old taste buds? Surely they had sampled all the delicious cuisine the world had to offer. I placed my hand on my belly, attempting to lull the upheaval. I gave Winston a nervous smile.

"It will be nice to sit in Hafiza's formal dining room. Master Elias' family has not hosted an event here in over seventy-five years." My stomach felt worse. Could Winston not pick up on my uneasiness?

"Are you sure we made enough food?"

"Plenty. Shall we head to the dining room? I can heat as we go." *Oh of course he could.* I guess it was better to get there early rather than make a theatrical entrance when everyone was seated.

"Okay. Let's go. Should I carry one? Where are the oven mitts?"

"Oh no, I can handle them." Sure enough he did just that, carrying two huge pans on a tray in one hand, and the rest in his other hand. I ran to open the kitchen door just so I didn't feel useless. Winston walked gracefully down the hall as I traipsed behind.

As we passed through the dissolving wall of bricks and down a passage I didn't recognize from my tour with Elias, we entered a huge chamber. I think it was the great hall we had run through. It looked similar, but something felt different. It was majestic. In the center of the room was a large wood-and-cast iron table that could easily sit fifty people, I did not remember seeing it here before. There would be only seventeen of us this evening.

Di was fluttering about, placing ornate table settings in the center of the long dining table. On either side of each setting was a gorgeous crystal glass that shimmered slightly in the light. Since we were only having one course, there was a single fork and knife placed on the lace napkin folded delicately on top of each dish. Detailed red vines skipped along the edges of the snowy white china plates.

Large silver sconces littered the table, each with twelve slender ivory candles, placed perfectly. I looked over to see Aremis smiling at me. Then he waved his hand and the entire room lit up—every candle was illuminated, including the ones high above us in the chandeliers. It was amazingly warm and inviting. I was in awe. I felt like I had stepped back in time to join King Arthur and his knights for a feast.

Di was wearing a breathtaking champagne colored gown, so fluid and flawless she looked like an angel. Aremis wore a chocolate brown pressed dress suit from what looked like the 1700s. He looked very dapper.

He was instantly at my side. "You look lovely Miss Ophelia."

"Thank you, you look very handsome yourself." His long hair was pulled into a soft ponytail, and it reminded me of a character from an old-time photograph. He bowed slightly, a silent 'thank you' of sorts.

"The food smells wonderful." Di stood to my right side. She took my hand like a daughter would. "I chose your seat already, I hope that suits you?"

"Perfect. Now I won't have to awkwardly choose who I should sit next to." I smiled at her as she led me to the center of the table. There was a small sheet of paper on my lace napkin. The script was striking. My name never looked better. I checked out the names of my dinner companions. On either side would sit my two chivalrous suitors. *Sneaky Di.* I hoped this didn't mean the whole night I would be bombarded by testosterone.

"Please be seated, everyone will be arriving soon and you have done far more than your share for tonight's merrymaking." Aremis announced as he pulled my chair out and slid me right into my place.

Immediately everyone was flickering about at a pace I could not lucidly see, but I could hear and feel the air moving around me. I closed my eyes and took some deep breaths. I was ready for a glass of wine. My nerves were heightened to a pitch that was deafening. I didn't want to let anyone down. I slowly lifted my eyelids and miraculously a delicious glass of Cabernet had appeared. *Thank god!* To my right Winston sat only a few chairs down, his glass also full.

A cool hand grazed the top of my shoulders. Rand was taking his seat not too far to my left. He wore a deep blue suit, modern and seamless.

"Good evening Miss Ophelia. You look stunning, and the food smells splendid." Rand winked at me as he too poured himself some wine.

"Thank you. I couldn't have done it without Winston. He's an incredible help in the kitchen." Rand lifted his glass to Winston and nodded.

A familiar fragrance filled my nostrils as Lucas leaned in and kissed me on the cheek. It smelled like home.

"You look radiant," he purred. I looked over to see him in a violet-purple dress shirt. The top two buttons were undone and I had to tear my eyes away from the copper skin that was showing. His eyes were glowing. The blue rings within mimicking the magnificence of a bright blue sky. Purple was definitely his color.

"You look pretty sharp yourself. You showered I see." I teased.

"Yes, as a matter of fact I did. Turns out people find you much more appealing when you don't reek. I never could have imagined." He smiled the coy smile I loved, and for a moment I forgot we weren't back in our little apartment in San Francisco. He scooted the chair closer as he situated himself in front of his plate. I didn't even hear the rest of our company enter the dining hall and seat themselves. It wasn't until Di giggled that I remembered we weren't alone.

The hall was full except for Elias' chair. It really was an occasion. Everyone was dressed so elegantly and talking animatedly amongst themselves. Each individual's apparel hinted at the derivation of their lives on this earth. It was a medley of colors and lace, bow ties and coats. I was flattered that my cooking had inspired such an affair.

ELIAS

"Alright Hafiza. I need you to be extra vigilant tonight until we have finished dinner." I placed my hand on the wall in my room.

I was ready for the supper, but I could not leave the perimeter unguarded while we all dined together. My parents had a boundary invocation that I first needed to implement. Between the added border security from Hafiza, Lucas' shield and the admittance rite—changed for the fifth time since we had begun our residence on the grounds—it would require an intimate defector to get through our security.

I raised the large gate and stepped out onto the earth. It was a pleasant night—you could see the billions of stars in the sky above, and the breeze was cool and soft. My mother had only shown me the incantation once before she died, but I was certain I remembered it.

I picked up a handful of dirt and stepped in the pattern of a square three times. Then I repeated the words she had said in Asagi many years before. I felt the breeze pick up and I again repeated my steps three times. Then I let go of the dirt and watched it dance in the wind to the west.

Instantly I felt Hafiza's buffer fall over our borders. That would do for the evening. I would retract it in the morning. I immediately felt better.

I thought that I should give Ophelia this chance to celebrate before we uprooted everything again. I did not know how she was going to take the news that we were going to disband and leave the castle. After her lesson the other day I knew I did not have a choice. It was time to move to a new location, just Lucas, Ophelia and I. I had already made the arrangements.

"Let her have a wonderful evening." I said aloud as I stepped back inside and lifted the gate.

OPHELIA

I raised my glass to Ying: he was wearing a brilliant black silk suit. Next to him sat Nara and her husband Valerian, they both had on the same shade of emerald green, a truly handsome couple.

The wine was going down far too easy. Lucas poured me another glass. As I set my crystal down another familiar perfume filled my senses. Elias was here. He appeared on my right with a huge bouquet of red tulips, my favorite.

"You look ravishing. These are for the hostess. On behalf of the entire castle we thank you for honoring us with your efforts in the kitchen." The table erupted into applause and the flowers instantly appeared in a vase directly in front of me. Once again I was entranced by Elias' eyes. He was wearing a burgundy-red shirt that made his skin luster and his caramel-gold eyes gleam. He kissed my hand as he took his seat.

I shook my head as I heard someone say my name. Winston was standing with his glass of wine in hand.

"Thank you to Miss Ophelia for taking the time to prepare this meal. She is a pleasure to work with." Winston raised his glass higher. "Now without further ado let us partake in the decadence!"

With that, all of our plates were immediately overflowing with warm saucy pasta. I wasn't sure which conduit had the capability to serve food without raising a pinky, but it was clear someone within our midst was quite the host or hostess themselves. Everyone looked ecstatic, so I picked up my fork and dug in.

The evening was amazing! The conversation was fun and lighthearted. I met all the conduits that I had not yet been acquainted with in the castle. Everyone had more than one helping of lasagna, and couldn't stop raving about how much they enjoyed it. *Maybe I'll cook more often, I thought.*

I don't know how much wine was consumed, but I was feeling very gluttonous as the dinner carried on. For the first time in weeks, I was completely relaxed. Sitting between Lucas and Elias was ultimately very pleasurable too. Both men took turns conversing with me but I didn't feel like I was engaged in a mental skirmish. *Thank you boys.*

Aremis sat across from me at the table and we laughed as we imagined how much trouble I would have gotten into in the last few weeks had I tried to stumble around the fortress by myself in the dark. Everyone was engaged in seemingly light and witty banter. The climate in the room was pure joy. I could feel it in every atom of my body.

"What do you think Lucas? My best lasagna yet?"

"Best yet!" He paused. "It kind of feels like home, right?" I just nodded. I felt my eyes well with tears. *I must be getting drunk, I only get this emotional when wine is involved.* Lucas grabbed my shoulder and pulled me in closer. "We'll get back there again someday Olly, I promise." Then his face turned to stone and the dining hall fell silent.

"What?" I asked playfully.

"Shhhhh." Lucas put his hand over my mouth. My heart began to race out of control. My eyes searched the faces of the dinner guests that only moments ago were exuberant, celebrating life and fellowship. Now no one was moving. All were staring at me.

I could see Elias out of the corner of my eye, he was almost in a crouch, hovering over me. They were all listening for something, searching the night for a menacing noise. Then I thought I heard something. *Or was it that my mind was playing a horrible trick on me?* It sounded like buzzing, a faint but steady buzz.

The room shattered into a dozen whispers, everyone speaking in Asagi. I was pulled out of my chair now and flung over Lucas' shoulder. Elias was behind us along with someone else. I couldn't make out the voice.

"What's going on?" I whispered frantically.

"They have found us." Elias said it so quickly I almost convinced myself I'd heard him wrong. We stopped and I was on my feet.

"Are they in the castle?"

Lucas put his hand on my mouth again and whispered "Close." I was disoriented and not sure anymore what wing we were in. It was so dark. My mind was racing with various scenarios. I realized I might have to take one of the escape routes Aremis had shown me. I'd have to decide fast. But I didn't know where I was, and I still wasn't sure who the traitor was. *Maybe I wouldn't get separated from Lucas and Elias,* I thought. *Even better, maybe the enemy wouldn't get in.* Just then the stones beneath my feet began to tremble, and seconds later a thunderous cracking echoed through the halls.

I was once again thrown over Lucas' shoulder and we were racing through the corridor. Elias was screaming something at him, and the third party—who I'd determined to be Ying—was mumbling to himself. The cracking reverberated off the walls again and Lucas threw me to the ground. I fumbled around, feeling in the dark for something familiar. Nothing. Only cold stones. I couldn't hear voices or smell my companions. Then I heard screaming and yelling in a far corner of the fortress. I crawled around until I found the ninety-degree angle of the wall. I wobbled to my feet and dusted off my knees. They were stinging with scrapes, and I felt warm blood dripping down my elbow.

LUCAS

I hope I didn't hurt her when I put her down. I couldn't gauge how rough her landing was. My head was humming with different scenarios, various strategies, and the plans I had already put in motion should the fortress fail. I had to get Olly out of there, but for the time being she was safest alone. All of us surrounding her would be an indicator for the enemy.

I turned and ran up the stairs to my chamber. I needed to grab a few things and burn a few others. I'd already counted ten foreign conduits within the castle walls, I couldn't tell how many more were waiting in the shadows. My camouflage was not going to help the group right now, so I retracted it to covering just me and Olly.

I opened the door and saw that my room was still untouched. I stuffed the paperwork I needed in my pants pocket, and threw the other stuff in the hearth and lit it on fire. No sooner did I complete my mission than I heard the heavy footsteps of a conduit I knew well. I stepped into the dark passageway.

"Lucas, you are still as fetching as ever." Her voice was raspy, just as I had remembered.

"Vivienne I'm very surprised. Why on earth would you be here with Yanni and Esther?" I didn't need to hide the shock in my voice.

"Luey, you should know better than anyone that some people pay better than others." She was smiling and her teeth were already beginning to elongate into the shape of things that haunted children's nightmares.

"Enough chitchat I guess." I leaped at her just as her figure began to convulse and morph into her favorite barbaric creature, the manticore. Her body contorted and a huge scorpion tail with poisonous spines erected along the length of it. Her torso turned a fiery, furry red and her smile widened to show three rows of razor-sharp fangs.

Her tail whipped around and darted for my jugular.

"Luey." She now had a lisp from the excess of teeth. "Stay still and I will make your death swift."

"Fuck you Vivienne."

"Have it your way, lover. You know if that's an offer, we can play first and finish this up later." She let her face morph back to the picturesque features that usually occupied her crown: mesmerizing blue eyes framed by auburn tendrils, a petite and symmetric nose, strong cheekbones and a pearly white smile bordered by plump pink lips.

"I think I'll pass. I'm not really into bestiality, Sugar Lips." I blew her a kiss and her face turned instantly back to terrifying. A fierce growl erupted from her mouth as she dove at me.

OPHELIA

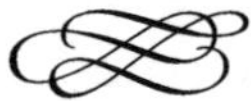

I could feel someone very close. *Was I still in Hafiza? What wing was I in?* I tried to retrace my steps in my head. I didn't have time for this, they were closing in.

Ying. Think of my lessons with Ying, I told myself. I closed my eyelids tight, I needed to concentrate. It was too dark for me to see exactly where my attacker was coming from.

I could sense someone, no more than seven feet behind me. They smelled like brass and sour milk, a bizarre combination, and they were waiting for me to move. So I didn't. I would take a defensive stand as Ying had taught me to do. I felt Lucas' shield lift and immediately saw the figure just down the hall. I opened my eyes and a female image filled my sight.

It felt like an eternity of standing there. *Did she know I knew she was there?* I couldn't be sure of anything. Then I heard a soft voice. She spoke in Asagi. When I said nothing she must have concluded I didn't understand her.

She changed her tactic. "It is a standoff," She said, her accent sounding Russian, or at least Slavic. Then the shield was back, smothering any extra senses I had. *Dammit Lucas.*

I glanced behind me. There was no sense in running. I couldn't outrun a consummated conduit. She approached as I turned and was now no more than a foot away. I stood my ground.

"Are we?" I practically whispered. It was all I could conjure up. The shield lifted again and I could see her face: it was attractive, young and bold. Her hair was platinum blonde, her skin glowed with a faint pale light. She was slightly shorter than me, with a tiny frame. I was relieved she didn't have the build of a two-hundred-fifty-pound line-backer. But if I had learned anything over the past few weeks, fierce gifts often came in small packages.

"What is your name?" She purred.

"Is that necessary? You're going to kill me anyway aren't you?"

"It may depend on your name." She conjured a tormenting smile. "I would like to report those I kill to my masters. Some are more valuable than others."

"Well, I'm sorry to disappoint you, but I'm not in a sharing mood."

"No matter, I will just bring them your head." With that she lunged forward and I maneuvered left. I needed a weapon, and fast. I slid alongside the cold, stone wall. I couldn't see her anymore. The shield was turning on and off like a strobe light. She was laughing hysterically.

"You are quick for an Unconsu. Someone here must have trained you."

She liked the chase, she wanted to hunt me. She could smell my fear and reveled in it. I swallowed it and used it to sense her next move. This bitch wasn't going to kill me without a fight.

"An Unconsu?" I played dumb, thinking I might attempt a distraction—keep her talking so I could better gauge her whereabouts in the passage.

"You poor thing. They are keeping you ignorant? What a neglected little pet." She was walking very leisurely in my direction. "In other words, you are still a pathetic little mortal."

I found something along the stones. I grabbed it with both hands. It was metal, and long. As I gripped it tightly I felt her pounce in front of me. I blindly swung and hit something very hard. Then the blinders were off again and I could see where I had struck her head. She growled, deep and guttural. She leapt towards me again. I noticed that the angrier she was, the clearer her image was to me. I turned and faced her, repeating Ying's words in my head. *Do not run. Stand and demand respect form your opponent.*

She flew directly onto the staff I had in my hands, and I was hurled backwards by her force. My weapon was gone. I had impaled her. She wasn't making a noise, her shape crumpled on the ground twenty feet ahead of me, radiating pain and rage. I wondered if I should run.

"Alright, now you have frustrated me," she threatened. She was still on the ground, and I started backing up slowly. "Where are you going?" she demanded.

I said nothing. Everything in me was screaming *Run!* But that was the old Ophelia. I was going to stand my ground. Then I felt the passage vibrate. She was glowing again, but not the same as before. This time her skin was neon green and sparks fluttered all around her.

"You won't get far!" She cackled.

"I'm not going anywhere."

"Well then you are a fool and you will die."

She dragged her fingernails along the wall and they generated flashes. I could see her face all too clearly now, and I didn't like it one bit. I stood there bracing myself for an impact as the surface below me began to shake. My knees gave and I stumbled to the ground. She had quickly cleared the divide between us.

The ground shook again, and this time I knew the floor was going to give beneath me. If my attacker sensed the immediate shift in my perspective, she didn't care. She continued her pursuit, and as she reached for my neck I felt my stomach drop. I was in midair.

She was still tossing her body in the air, trying to get hold of me. I threw my arm up in defense, and her lightening-bright skin burned me. I screamed from the pain. Then I was back on my feet and in Hafiza's dining hall. It still smelled like lasagna and wine. Elias was there too. He dusted off my knees and gave me a once-over to assess the damage. He grabbed my hand tightly.

"Ophelia. Run! Find a way out, now!" He wasn't yelling, but his words were sharp. I deliberated quickly. *He must be referring to the secret passages that Aremis and Winston had shown me over the last few weeks, right? That must mean that I can trust them.*

I took off down the dark hall. I only looked back for a moment, just in time to see the lightening woman darting towards Elias.

ELIAS

"Run Ophelia, Run." Her whiny voice was sarcastic. "Really Viraclay? Where will she run too?"

"My apologies, have we met?" We were circling each other, both crouched forward, ready to spring.

"Of course. I knew your parents." She raised an eyebrow looking for recognition. "I held you as a baby." She mimicked the little "goochy goo" gesture that you would use to entertain a child.

"Sorry, you must not leave much of an impression." I shrugged my shoulders, emphasizing my dismissal of her presence. She looked slightly shaken.

"Well, in that case maybe you will remember me when I kill your pet." She flew down the hall toward Ophelia. I sprang at her and caught her left foot, but immediately my hand began to burn as though I was holding the hot end of an iron, and I was forced to release her. She toppled forward but continued her quest down the hall, out of my reach before I got to my feet. She was fast. There was no way I was going to catch up with her.

I paused, and she turned around and crowed.

My next words were nearly silent. I did not want her to have an ounce of warning. "Hafiza, protect our family."

Instantly the castle walls collapsed on top of her delicate feminine figure. I heard her scream in horror. The stones continued to fall and roll into each other. I saw a faint blue glow under the rubble, but the heap churned again and the light disappeared. It would not kill her, but it would slow her down.

OPHELIA

My hand was still burning.

I was turned around. The secret passages were no use to me if I had no idea where I was. A crush of thoughts flashed through my mind. *Was Aremis okay? Why did Lucas throw me, and where did he go? Was Elias going to be okay?* I couldn't let the thoughts consume me, though. I had to get out of there.

I systematically moved down the hall. Hafiza had changed again, and I couldn't be sure of the way to the courtyard. My knees were shaky and the cobblestones underfoot were exceptionally irregular. I was pretty sure I'd never been that way before, which was bad news for my escape plan. I heard a battle cry in the distance behind me. *Should I be going towards the noises, or away?*

As I careened forward, I hit my right shoulder along the wall and I fell to the floor. My ankle had been twisted by an exceptionally large crevice in the floor. My foot was throbbing. I let my body go limp. *Shit! What the hell am I doing?*

Hopelessness swept over me. I had no clue where I was, I couldn't see a thing, and for all I knew I could be walking straight into a trap. I was probably not going to make it out of here alive, especially all alone. My breathing grew shallow as I tried to swallow that thought.

Then I gathered my reserves. *Stop whining Ophelia and think past the fear, as Ying taught you. Concentrate, as Rand trained you, and remember what Aremis said: When you are ready to stop fighting what you are and just be, then it would all come together.*

"Hafiza," I whispered. "I need your help. I need to get to the courtyard. Please help me." A breeze wafted around me and I stiffened, because on the air was the distinct scent of an unfamiliar conduit.

I was not the only one in this hall. I sat up slowly, trying to move cautiously, unsure which angle the attack would come from. I threw out any senses I had, and waited.

I wiggled my feet out of my shoes and closed my eyes, trying to hear something—anything. Lucas' shield was down again.

I still couldn't tell where the individual was, but I could definitely track their intent. They were looking for something absorbedly, probably me. Their thoughts were not laced with viciousness though. They were on a mission. I heard the sound of sniffing. Whoever they were, they were getting closer. I got to my feet. I rolled my shoulders back and braced myself, I was ready for another fight. I had to make a choice and quick: right or left? I put my hands on the wall behind me, and instantly knew where the stalker was: they were on the other side of the wall, and they now knew exactly where I was too. I stepped back and studied the barrier between us.

Then out of nowhere a flicker of flame appeared in front of me. *Aremis, had found me!* I looked to see which way I should go. My pause was just enough for my hunter to barrel through the stone wall in front of me. The flame moved a foot to the left, only seconds before the wall came crashing down. I instinctively followed. Aremis had saved my life. I would have been crushed. I stared down at my predator, but I couldn't make out who it was. They seemed to be morphing into an animal. Fur was flying, limbs were contorted in unnatural forms, and snarls were escaping a clenched jaw. I froze.

Suddenly Rand flew out of the hole in the wall and pushed me out of the creature's way.

"Run, Ophelia, run!!"

~

I TURNED and chased after the flame leaping in front of me. I was limping but taking off my shoes made it easier to charge ahead. There was an eerie silence behind me. It was worse than hearing screaming. I made a left at the end of the hall and then heard yelling in the direction I was heading. For a second I wondered again if this was a trap. But I had no choice. I would be blind without Aremis, a sitting duck. I stretched my senses to see what I could pick up. To my dismay I was guarded again.

The flame sailed up a staircase. At the top, the doorway opened onto a walkway above the main courtyard "Thank you Hafiza." I exhaled the words. I knew she, along with Aremis, had gotten me here.

I looked down to see Lucas, Aremis and Winston cornered by five masked intruders. I wanted to shout to them, but something inside of me told me that was the last thing I should do. I watched in horror as they descended onto my friends, onto my Lucas.

Then something caught my eye to my right—it was Di. She was diving from the third story above the courtyard. Her body was shaped like a missile, and with one fatal swoop she tore through the five trespassers, ripping one of them in two.

I screamed. I didn't even know where the noise came from, but it caught everyone's attention. Lucas looked up and repeated the now-familiar refrain: "Run, Olly!!" He pounced on the person in front of him and a horrific tearing noise followed as I picked up my feet and ran away as fast as I could. At least I finally knew where I was. On the second floor between the East and South Wings. I had an idea of how to get to Winston's chamber from here. I practically slid down a back staircase. I couldn't hear anyone behind me, but that didn't mean much.

LUCAS

I watched her move out of sight, then redirected my focus on the coward in front of me. He was in a mask.

"What's the deal with the get-up asshole? Too scared to face me like a man?" I taunted. He said nothing. I reckoned that if he was trying to conceal his identity, then he would not be using his powers to defend himself. I cloaked him with my shield anyway. It would make him foggier than he expected.

He noticed the transition. His eyes widened slightly, then he lunged for my throat. I stepped to the side and narrowly missed the assault. Di was on my other side, fearlessly battling two masked enemies. In my periphery, I saw that Aremis was heading for where we'd last seen Ophelia. I stared too long though, because when I turned around I was greeted with a cracking fist to my jaw. My camouflage faltered. It was difficult to maintain my shield and concentrate on battle. It was flickering in and out, and with every blow it got weaker. *Dammit!*

"Now you've pissed me off," I said as I leapt onto his torso, tackling him to the floor. He wiggled under my weight, but it was futile. I reached for the mask and tore it off. It would be satisfying to know the name of the conduit I was going to tear apart.

The instant the mask was off, I realized I had fucked up. I should have looked at his face after I beheaded him.

"Oh fuck." The words slipped out of my mouth as a nasty smile swept across the familiar face of Royce, a royal pain in my ass and a grimly dangerous opponent. He was still under my weight, but for only a second more because he quickly widened his mouth and aimed to spit at me. One drop of his acid-like saliva and I would be blinded.

I smothered him with more of my camouflage and got to my feet. As did he.

"What Lucas, afraid of my cooties?" Royce snickered.

"Did your mother ever teach you manners? Spitting is rude Royce." We were circling each other, waiting to pounce.

"Didn't your parents ever teach you not to hover?" he jabbed. "To be around you is just stifling." He pulled at his collar as if it would help him breathe easier.

The duel ensued. We were both fully committed to causing as much damage as physically possible. Blow after blow, strike after strike, stunning each other with force.

I repeatedly dodged his venomous attacks, until he finally nailed my arm. The acid spread like wildfire from my elbow all the way up to my shoulder. I cried out in pain.

"Enough fucking around," I growled, fumbling for his wrist, the only thing in arm's reach. I twisted it hard, and the familiar sound of ripping conduit flesh filled the room, a sound not unlike contorting metal. His hand snapped off on my second rotation. "Tit for tat asshole," I boasted.

"I never liked you much Lucas," he hissed through his barred teeth. He came at me again. I threw aside his useless hand and hurled myself onto his shoulders, this time wrapping my grip around his horrid little neck. I stepped off his shoulders, gripping his neck with all my strength, and cast it over my knee. It hit with such force that his head snapped clean off, and the nasty smile on his face was finally gone. His body lay twitching next to his head. I knew if I let him lay there undisturbed, eventually humpty dumpty would put himself back together again, but not this time, asshole. I looked around for a lit torch, but didn't see one.

"Lucas!" Elias threw one from across the courtyard, and I swiftly set the pathetic mass on fire.

Di was still fending off her two assailants, and Winston was in no better shape. Normally I didn't care for either of them very much, but now we were all fighting for the same cause. Before I could assist them, though, Nara and Valerian came shooting out of the South Wing like a pair of hawks and descended onto the four remaining enemies. Ying appeared with a small arsenal on his person, and just like that the four traitors were dismantled and up in flames.

I took a deep breath and turned around. I knew there would be more than the ten I'd initially counted, but now I saw a wave of Nebas flooding through the entrance. Aremis still hadn't returned from the passage. I needed to make sure Ophelia was safe before the onslaught.

OPHELIA

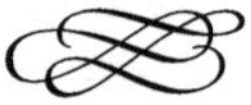

I landed on the bottom step in a lunge. I leaned forward to sprint again, my ankle began throbbing and it gave me pause, then my back leg was pulled out from under me. I landed face up, my tailbone aching from the impact. A dark figure hovered over me and I couldn't see again, *Where did Aremis go?*

The person was talking to someone in Asagi, her voice was gentle and seductive.

I concentrated on the woman's energy and I was sure I knew exactly who these two were.

"Ophelia?" The female whispered my name.

Should I respond? I wondered. *Was it a question, and if so did I want to answer?*

"Are you Ophelia?" Apparently, it was a question.

"Yes." I could barely get the word out. My mouth was so dry.

"Do you know who I am?"

"No." That was a lie, I knew exactly who she was.

"My name is Esther and I am the one who is going to kill you." She stepped on my twisted ankle.

I closed my eyes and let my body relax under her weight. It was futile to fight. Her intentions were rolling over me like a thick San

Francisco fog—slow, steady and unstoppable. I opened my eyes to show my resolve. As I did the room illuminated and I could see the face of the woman whose aim was my death. She was majestic. Her black hair swept down to her ankles, her olive skin shimmered, and her eyes were deep and fierce like black holes. She smiled a brilliant smile, then looked up to greet the small flame in front of her. The man next to her was gone. I wiggled under her foot.

"Aremis, my beloved. Do you miss Natasha? I know I do." She laughed and the flame ignited into a ball of fire. The distraction was enough that she released my ankle and I scrambled to my feet. Esther was cackling as the ball hurled at her head. She retreated up the staircase.

"Run little Ophelia. Run. I will be right behind you." The words echoed off the walls as I hurried down the hall. Aremis' fireball was only going to briefly deter her from pursuing me.

I heard a door open just behind me, but I was almost to Winston's room. I had to make my legs move faster. Suddenly the air beside me was disturbed, and I was stopped by a hand on my chest.

"Take this! You will make it, my dear. You are dearly loved." Rand handed me a small leather pouch. "Now run, as fast as you can."

He moved aside and I heard another door open. Then Rand laughed boisterously.

"Oh Yanni, I have missed your disgusting stench. You smell better than ever, my friend, please take a minute. Let us catch up." A battle call ripped through the air and again that horrible tearing noise, reverberated off the walls.

ELIAS

I saw the enemy army storming the castle as I threw the torch to Lucas and headed to my chamber. I had to make sure I was not being followed before I went back for my bag. As far as I could tell, I had lost my last tail when I reached the courtyard. They would be swarming all of the grounds in a matter of minutes.

"Hafiza, evasion," I instructed. She moved and throbbed when she heard my words. She would buy me a little more time. I darted down the hall and threw open the door to my room. I quickly plugged in the code on my wall safe, and grabbed the emergency bag I had been storing since we arrived. I double-checked the contents: three new passports, a prepaid cell phone and a hundred thousand dollars in cash, plus my personal laptop. Everything was there. Then I stuffed the rest of Alistair's belongings in the bottom.

I tossed the bag over my shoulder and left for Ophelia's room. I had something I needed to get for her in the event that the castle was completely destroyed—which was seeming more and more likely.

An intense jolt of pain surged through my gut as I imagined Hafiza as nothing more than rubble. I had to move through it. I would mourn her loss later.

"Thank you, Hafiza. Until we meet again." She rumbled under my feet, and I was instantly in Ophelia's room. I grabbed what I needed and entered the courtyard.

There I saw Ying, Nara and Valerian in the thick of a large mob of invaders. Winston, Di, Lars and Renata were also surrounded, but were holding their own. Lucas was doing his best, but it appeared he was the one that needed the most assistance. I took a deep breath, secured my bag and barreled through to his side. There were still friends unaccounted for. I had to assume that Ophelia was safe with Aremis. *Where were they, though? And where on earth was Rand?*

I backed up to Lucas, and Ying pitched me a large sword. It was light and moved effortlessly in my hands. Lucas was wielding a huge maul. Guns did far less damage to our kind than the blunt-force trauma in hand-to-hand combat. We circled and swung. We had a slight advantage against those who were attempting to remain cloaked, it meant they would not expose their gifts.

I charged, and directly ahead of me I saw a familiar face. His henchmen stepped aside as he slinked up to Lucas and me. Lucas recognized Akiva as well, and shielded us both immediately.

"What an unlikely alliance," Akiva began. His voice was nonchalant as he moved around us, clearing a circle. "Viraclay I have not seen you since you were a young pup. And Lucas, what can I say. A day has not gone by where I have not thought of your disgusting face. But how Malarin's fortunate has fell upon me— that I stumble on the two of you together? Chitchakor has my favor." He looked up and raised his hands in the air. "Thank Dalinkas."

"Akiva, I think you are incorrect. This is an unfortunate happenstance for you, meeting us on the battlefield. A misfortune indeed." I looked at Lucas as I finished speaking, confirming we were on the same page. Show no fear and no mercy.

"Really?" He snorted with disdain.

"Yes. Today we are going to kill you," Lucas said as he made the first move, carefully maintaining his shield over both of us. As he lurched forward Akiva smiled, then rapidly moved just out of Lucas' reach. I saw his hand form a fist, then Lucas' foot made a terrible crunching sound. He fell to the floor for a moment, but was able to rebound quickly. The distraction gave me a second to swing my sword hard against Akiva's right shoulder. The blow left his right arm dangling against his side. He looked at it and laughed, then gestured with his left hand and I found myself whirling in the air. My face planted hard on the floor, and I was certain I'd broken my jaw.

When I looked up Lucas was perched on top of Akiva's mangled shoulder, ready to give the detaching blow with his maul. He managed to strike milliseconds before he too was flying in the air.

Di and Lars simultaneously flew over the crowd of onlookers, gracefully flipping and striking blows on the heads of the masked assailants. Di landed effortlessly in front of Akiva and bewitched him long enough for Lars to strike him in the back with a spear. He buckled for a second, which incited the crowd to no longer just look on. They tackled Lars as Di whipped through their bodies, tearing and ripping as she twirled angelically between them. Torsos littered the floor in her wake.

Akiva was recovering swiftly. He waved his left hand again and all of our allies were flung against the far wall of the courtyard. We all rose to our feet, Nara on my right and Winston on my left. The enemy stood taunting us from the opposite end of the cavernous room.

"I am tired of this game, it is time to end this charade. Farewell. May the Tins wash your canvas clean." Akiva looked around at the others on his side. His arm was already beginning to reattach as he held it to the gaping wound in his shoulder. Winston grabbed my wrist and looked at Lucas sharply. Again, I felt the heavy shield come down. Winston then looked forward in deep concentration, and immediately the opponents were writhing in their own skin. All twenty or so that were still standing, including Akiva, were boiling in their own bodies.

Ying took the opportunity to hurl every metal object he could find in the room at the mass of thrashing bodies, impaling several of them and beheading at least two. We forged across the gap, and while they were still in shock Di dove once more across the crowd, ripping through their ancient flesh like a jackhammer.

Akiva held Winston in his gaze as he pulled an axe out of his left thigh. Just as he was ready to strike, Aremis skidded into the hall and sent a flurry of flames into the air, systematically bombing the enemy with fireballs. I ran to his side, Lucas right behind me.

"Where is she?" I demanded. Aremis met my eyes and I was certain she was safe. I turned just in time to see Esther charred and stumbling out of the dark passage.

"Aremis!!" She screamed, and for a moment the entire battle paused. "Aremis—that was not nice."

He turned to greet her. "If you had stood still you would already be out of your misery. Now I have to start all over." He backed up and Winston and Ying took his flanks.

"I will finally know how terribly painful it was for your precious Natasha to be burned alive by your own hand. I will be sure to be descriptive, so you can spend the rest of your existence reliving the night you killed your wife."

"*You* killed my wife." I could see Aremis shaking –the firebombs had stopped. "Know this, when you die tonight. It will be much slower and far more painful." Lucas and I stepped behind Ying, ready to strike.

"Oh Aremis, you always were a softy." Esther stared longingly at her foe with wanting, desiring his power. "But Natasha, she was a bleeding heart. What a fool to not use her assets. She may still be alive if she wasn't such an idiot."

Aremis' chest heaved with anger. His eyes were fixated on Esther, unyielding and menacing. "You witch! You have no right to talk about my Natasha. You are a murdering coward who hides behind other peoples' powers to commit atrocities. Every ounce of you is pure cowardice." His words could not possibly communicate how much he loathed Esther, or how deeply he was scarred by the loss of his Natasha.

Before any more could be said, Di and Valerian chorused in a tremendous battle call as they tore a leg and an arm from the torso of Akiva.

Then in my periphery I saw the image of a man bullet from the second floor. I turned to see Yanni behind me. "Hello Viraclay." He whacked the side of my face with the broken jaw, and my knees buckled.

The courtyard was a flurry of bodies. Ying began wrestling with Yanni, and it appeared he had the upper hand. Aremis was closing in on Esther, carrying a huge ball of fire. Lucas was fending off someone else behind me. Esther's body went up in flames, she cackled loudly as though she was being tickled.

I got to my feet. Ying had Yanni pinned to the wall, and was maneuvering his hands around his neck. But then Vivienne launched herself on top of Aremis and went for his jugular. Her huge fangs were poised to bite when the scorched figure of Esther casually walked up and placed her hand on Aremis' head.

"Retreat!" I screamed, sprinting toward the nearest exit. I knew Esther now had possession of Aremis' body and the destruction she would cause was unimaginable.

"Viraclay," I heard her sinister voice trailing behind me as I ran. "I will find her."

OPHELIA

The little flame stopped –we were there. I entered Winston's room and locked the door behind me. I just had to remember the sequence. I felt the pressure mounting and my heart racing. I could picture Winston walking me through the succession of steps to open the secret passage. I mimicked them precisely, and the covert door opened. I almost threw up with relief.

LUCAS

My fucking arm still hurt like hell from the acid, and my foot wasn't healing right. I knew I'd have to rebreak it when this was all over. I could hear the carnage behind me echoing off the walls of the courtyard. I needed to find Olly.

"Where are we going?" I shouted at Elias' back.

"Right now, we are doubling back to see if there is anything we can do for Aremis, or anyone else for that matter."

"What? Where's Ophelia?" I was infuriated and terrified that she might already be dead.

"Aremis confirmed she is safe."

"That's it? Where is she, then?" We were on the second story of the North Wing, and someone else was there with us. Elias was apparently going to ignore my question.

Ying came out of the shadows, his right side obliterated by flame.

"Ying, are there any survivors?" Elias was at his side, both of his hands assessing the damage.

"I do not know. We have to get to him, to touch him. So that she cannot control his power." Ying's voice was hoarse. He seemed to be getting better with Elias' touch, though. "Follow me."

He moved toward the second-floor balcony. We could see the

courtyard and its occupants. Aremis was alone in the middle of the room, while the rest of the walls were lined with the few remaining Nebas, no more than eight. Yanni and Esther were assessing their own damage. I sent my feelers out to see who else I could find under my shield. I couldn't get a clear read anywhere, but one thing was for sure: none of our allies were still in the courtyard. If they were, they were not alive.

I concealed our whereabouts. I tried to find Olly in the castle, but she was not presenting herself anywhere on the grounds—maybe she had gotten out safely. I knew the best thing was for her to be separate from us, but I was scared that she was dead. She was still a mortal, after all.

"Come out, come out, wherever you are." Esther's voice chimed through the halls. "I know you are still here Viraclay."

Ying crouched down and I noticed his side was nearly healed. "I am going to ascend down to Aremis. I need a diversion."

"Is that the best course of action?" Elias was leery. I couldn't blame him. Aremis had killed his own Natasha the last time he was under Esther's manipulation. He was as lethal of a weapon as you could have.

"I must try," Ying retorted.

"I will distract them for you. I can give you mere seconds," Elias whispered.

I wondered what Elias had in mind. "I can shield you," I offered. It was the least I could do.

"Very well," Ying said. "I am going to move to the South Wing, look for my signal." Then he was gone.

"What are you going to do? They'll suspect a trap." I looked at Viraclay intently.

"I am aware... I just need to give Ying a few seconds."

"This is stupid," I said, worried that if Elias died I might never know where to find Ophelia It made me invested in this fucking plan, despite my better judgment. Maybe he knew that.

"I am going to inquire where Ophelia is," Elias explained. "It should give them pause for a moment, and perhaps she will direct her aim at me. Lift your guard when I tell you." Then he stood and walked toward the balcony. I saw a flicker of something from across the way as Elias whispered, "Now."

I lifted my shield and he walked into clear view of Esther and her minions.

"Viraclay. There you are my dear," she hissed.

"Where are you holding Ophelia?" Elias demanded. For a brief moment, I saw a subtle bewildered look flash across all of their shitty little faces, just long enough for Ying to launch himself off the south balcony.

Esther saw him, though. She knew if he reached Aremis, he could release him from her torment. She manifested a giant firebomb and hurled it toward Aremis himself. I saw a flicker of recognition just before Ying landed on him: she had released the fiery imposer so he could see his own death. In an instant, Aremis threw Ying off, then went up in flames.

We immediately took off running again. "Where are we going?" I asked.

"To the river." Elias' voice cracked as a tear streamed down his face.

OPHELIA

I followed the light into the tunnel. It was moist and cold. The earth was muddy under my bare feet. I had to crouch to keep from hitting my head. I couldn't quite run, so I jogged as fast as the passage would allow. I watched my feet, hoping I didn't step on a snake or rat. I had no idea what was down here.

It felt like I was in the tube forever, and my mind started to wander again. *Where was Elias? Did Lucas make it? What if this was a trap?* I was beginning to feel claustrophobic and panicked, continuously putting my feelers out to see if anyone had entered the tunnel with me. Lucas' shield had disappeared. *If I died here,* I thought, *no one would even know where to find me.*

Then it went dark. I stopped. *What had happened?* I whispered, "Aremis."

Of course, there was no response. Tears filled my eyes as darkness and fear flooded my whole being. I was afraid everyone in the castle was dead. I was afraid that I would reach the end of the tunnel and it would be a setup, or worse, a dead end: my dead end. I started to hyperventilate, my breaths coming in gasping sobs. I lay down flat on the ground. I had to get it together. I checked for Lucas' shield. It still wasn't there.

If Aremis had wanted to kill me, then why wait until I was here alone in the dark? I supposed that the traitor would have wanted to remain in hiding until all of my friends were no longer a threat. Could someone have followed me down here? I thought I was alone. I checked my senses again. Still no sign of anyone else.

My ignorance was starting to suffocate me. *Where are Elias and Lucas? Why did they leave me alone to begin with? What was that half-animal beast thing that tracked me down in the hall? Was Rand okay? He couldn't be the traitor. He'd saved my life twice.* I squeezed the little leather pouch in my hand. *Why did Esther need to kill me?*

I felt my body buzzing, thinking I was suffering from some sort of shock. *I can get myself out of this,* I told myself. *I've already narrowly escaped several run-ins with death. Stop fucking whining, Olly!*

I sat up and shook my head. I resolved right then and there, on that muddy ground in the dark, that this would be the last time I let myself be consumed by fear. Never again would I let circumstances take away my sense and determination. I got to my feet and repeated *never again* in my head several times, and instead of fear, absolution took over my body.

I was free. Free from fear. My thoughts came into focus and I remembered something that Aremis had said to me: *Can't you feel Elias?* I decided that maybe I could sense him if I concentrated hard enough. Maybe he was looking for me. I needed to let my mind slow down, send out a net. Without Lucas' shield I could feel again. I sat unmoving in the dark, not entirely sure what I was even waiting for, just waiting.

Finally, in the silence of the passage I thought I heard a voice. It was Elias. It was so quiet I could only hear it if I stilled my mind completely.

"Ophelia." It was not in the tunnel. It was definitely in my mind. I heard it again. I stood up, and as I did my head brushed against the low ceiling. He was alive. And as long as that was true, I had to get to the end of the tunnel to see who else had survived the ambush. Hope filled my chest. I put the small satchel that Rand gave me in my bra, and began crawling through the passage.

I crawled for what felt like forever. My knees slid in the mud as it caked on layer after layer. My fingernail beds were pressured by the earth filling under them. My dress, the one I'd been so excited to wear to dinner, kept catching under my knees and I would face plant, but I kept going.

At long last the tunnel started to incline, and my excitement welled up. It could only mean one thing: I was ascending to the surface. I didn't care anymore whether it was a trap—I just wanted out. I dug my toes in to get leverage, and the air began to clear ever so slightly. There was a draft ahead, then twenty feet from the end I saw moonlight.

A shadow passed by the exit but I didn't even flinch. I was going to see the moon one more time before I died. My life would not end in this hole.

Another shadow moved, and in seconds I was in Lucas' arms. We were on the river embankment, and he was examining my body intently for wounds. I doubt he could see a thing through the mud.

"Are you okay?" he asked, stricken. "Are you hurt?" His forehead was pressed against mine as he held my head in his hands.

"I'm fine...only self-inflicted wounds, I think, and a lot of dirt."

He started to chuckle. "Thank God."

I saw the other shadow to my right. I turned to see Elias pacing.

"I'm so glad you are safe, I was questioning every ounce of my being for allowing you to venture here alone. But I saw no other way." He came to my side and held my hand as it tingled that familiar buzz. "Please forgive me Ophelia. I knew the two of us together would be too easily detectable for Yanni. Please forgive me."

I stared at him, dazed.

LUCAS

Now that she was safe and out of the tunnel I focused all my energy on encompassing her with my camouflage. I also made sure no one could detect Elias or myself—we were completely off the radar.

She was caked in mud, but she looked to be uninjured. I had no idea how she'd made it out of there alive. I didn't think any of us would. I knew she was strong, but I'd underestimated her abilities.

"What happened? How did they find us?" Her throat sounded dry. Elias quickly brought her river water cupped in his hands. She drank it, then sat herself up and out of my arms. I reluctantly let go.

"Lucas, what happened?" she repeated.

"I can only assume I'd spread my gift too thin, and that our large gathering must have popped up on Yanni's radar." I was afraid that I had to admit my guilt.

Elias glared at me, but then Olly suggested, "Isn't it more likely that it was the traitor?"

"Yes, I am sure it was the traitor," Elias said, locking his gaze on me.

"Well, do we know who it was?" Olly sounded desperate for a second.

"No, I'm afraid we do not." She immediately deflated as I spoke.

"Where's everyone else?" The words no sooner left her mouth than an explosion ignited the sky, and a gust of heat spewed from the tunnel she'd just escaped. Any longer in there and she probably would have been incinerated or died of smoke inhalation.

Elias started walking. "We need to move now, Ophelia. I promise we will answer all of your queries later. I stored a boat about a mile down the river." She stood, aware of the urgency of the situation.

I put my arms out. "May I?" She silently jumped into them. I could tell something had changed in her.

We ran along the river after Elias. The moon was bright and the breeze carried wafts of smoke. Ophelia said nothing. I didn't know what to make of it. But I didn't want to upset her, so I didn't speak either.

We reached the jet boat a few minutes later, and started north on the river. Elias didn't let me in on his plans, and I didn't care to ask. I knew whatever he'd put in place it would be safe enough for the night. We could discuss our next move in the morning, after Ophelia—all of us—got some rest.

I was curious about the bag Elias was lugging around. But I clearly couldn't waltz up and ask him about it. Time would disclose its contents, or I would take a look myself when he wasn't paying attention.

I studied Olly, sitting at the front of the boat, lost in thought. *What was going through her mind?*

It was a longer boat ride than I expected, nearly two hours. We finally arrived at a small tarmac with a single plane resting at the other end. It wasn't the jet we used before, but it would get us a good distance away in whatever direction Elias intended. *Was he a pilot or was he expecting me to fly?* I wondered, glancing around as I pulled Olly to shore. There were no nearby buildings or identifying markers.

"I had this built when we arrived," Elias explained. "The jet was too conspicuous, so I made other plans. It is just a landing strip and that Cessna 172S." He threw me some keys from the front pocket of his bag. "Am I correct in assuming you prefer this model aircraft? Are you prepared to pilot? This is our destination." He handed me a sheet of paper with coordinates scribbled on it. I looked at him with what I thought was curiosity, but what he interpreted as hesitation. "I can fly if you wish," he offered.

"I got it." We loaded in and it started right up. I encased our craft with my camouflage, just in case someone had caught our scent. The runway was the perfect length. In seconds we were up in the air. Ophelia didn't even ask for a sedative, she just looked on, still silent. I was starting to worry about her mental state.

"Ophelia, I have something to ease the flight," Elias said, holding a pill in one hand and a cup of water in another. She hesitated.

"No, thank you." Yes, something had definitely shifted.

I relaxed a bit as I settled into my seat. We'd be in the clear for a while. The coordinates Elias gave me were a good distance away, we'd be in the air for a minimum of six hours. Plenty of time to think.

PART IV

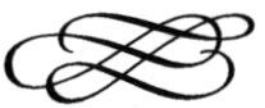

OPHELIA

I was still caked in mud when I woke up on a very comfortable bed in a well-lit room. *Thank god, a window,* I thought sleepily.

"I wanted to bath you, but Elias thought you'd kill me." I looked up to see Lucas' silhouette at the end of my bed.

"He was right." I rubbed my eyes. "Maybe he does like you, since he saved you from certain death." I smiled.

Lucas was carrying a tray with a carafe of coffee and a bagel with lox and cream cheese.

"It's no Winston meal, but it'll give you some nourishment, and some caffeine." I sat up as he nudged closer and put the coffee on the nightstand. I went to reach for the plate, then thought the better of it when dirt flakes fluttered off my hands.

"It looks great, but would probably taste better after I showered."

Lucas smiled. "Yeah, you're probably right. You look like you rolled in a pigsty." He leaned in playfully and gave me a sniff. "You don't smell much better."

I playfully punched his shoulder. "Bathroom?" He pointed to a door on the other side of the nightstand. "Alright, I'm going to shower, then I'll partake in breakfast in bed." I stood up and felt the mud crackle everywhere, then looked back at the sheets. "Maybe I'll eat in the living room."

"Deal. See you in a few." He kissed my dirty forehead and left the room.

The bathroom was nice, but not nearly as large as my last one. The thought of my old chamber made me take pause. I was going to take it a moment at a time. I still didn't know all the damage or who survived. No need to work myself up until I had answers, if there were any.

I peeled off my now-ruined dress and the small leather pouch from Rand tumbled onto the floor. I'd forgotten about it. It was crusty with mud as well, so I gently peeled it open. Thick, fragrant leaves with a crimson hue lay crumpled inside. *I wonder what these are for?*

I retied it and placed it on the counter, unsure if I was going to share it with the boys. Whatever they were, they had a special purpose, and I wanted to figure it out first. Something was telling me to keep it to myself until the right opportunity presented itself.

I kept glancing at it while I was in the shower, hoping Rand was safe somewhere. *Who knows,* I thought. *Maybe he'll be seated in the living room when I go out there?*

My mind drifted to Aremis, by far my closest friend in the castle. He'd directed me to safety, without him I probably would be dead. How would I ever thank him? Would I ever get a chance to?

The shower took me longer than I thought. I found mud in places that I didn't even know existed. My curly hair was so encrusted, I had to wash it four times—and even then, I didn't think I got it all. I patted myself dry and reentered my room, wondering if I'd even have clothes to change into. Sure enough, there were clean sheets on the bed and a comfortable pair of pants and tank top as well. Flip-flops were neatly set by the door. I dressed quickly.

I put the small package from Rand in the top drawer of the nightstand.

I paused as I reached for the knob. *Would it be locked? What was I going to find on the other side?* Whatever happened, I decided, it was time to face facts and find a way to move forward. I took a deep breath and turned the handle.

ELIAS

She was managing it all extremely well. Lucas had just finished with the worst part, the only casualty we knew for certain, Aremis. Still she did not crack. Only a single tear spilled down her cheek. She sat in silence for a long time. Neither Lucas nor I wanted to disturb her until she was ready. We had already agreed that she would be in control of the rhythm of the discussion.

So we sat there, Lucas holding her hand. Both of us staring at her. Something was different, the siege changed her. She looked stronger, harder and more comfortable all at the same time. I had expected her to walk away damaged, scared and perhaps even bitterly angry. But none of that was evident.

"Can I have a journal?" She looked up.

"Of course." Lucas answered.

"I'm sure you're both wondering why I'm not crying. I am sad, very sad. I desperately want to know that Rand, Ying, Di and Winston are okay, and of course everyone else in the castle as well. But in that tunnel, I realized this is a war and I have to embrace it. I can either be bulldozed by it, or I can properly honor my friends."

A second tear fell, and she continued. "Aremis told me a story I don't want to forget. I think that's the best way to honor his memory, by remembering his wisdom. Rand would want me to keep working on my gifts, and Ying would ask me to do the same. Winston, well, he would definitely want me to eat." We all chortled a little.

"Yes he would." I moved a plate in front of her and she smiled.

"Will we ever hear from the survivors again? Will we ever know?" Her voice was forlorn.

"Yes, I believe we will," I said, and I meant it. "It is likely we will have some answers sooner than we expected." *As soon as I can secure the summit,* I thought.

"No one saw Rand?" She looked at both of us intently.

"Not since dinner," Lucas responded. I nodded. I was abruptly aware of the lack of tension in the room. Certainly he and I had come to a truce before the fall of the castle, but this was more than that. I did not think it would last, but it was a blessing for Ophelia, and I was certain that she was attuned to it as well.

"The important thing is that you are safe," I said, showing my own relief. "We knew there was a possibility that we would be discovered at Hafiza eventually. Everyone in that castle was prepared to do whatever it took to get you out of there unharmed. They succeeded." I could not tell what she was thinking, but she nodded.

We sat in silence for a while again, until she asked, "So where are we now?"

"We are in a small villa outside of Serpa Portugal. This is one of the temporary safe houses I have installed. We will not be here long, though. Just long enough to get our agenda in order."

"What would that be, and where?" She said amicably.

I looked at Lucas. We had not discussed it yet, and I was not certain how much I intended to fill him in on. I wanted to visit the last five villages Alistair had been to before he was murdered. I was definitely not going to disclose this information, but I had not devised exactly how I would rationalize the transplanting to several remote locations. Furthermore I had not had time to arrange safe houses there yet. So I was honest. "Lucas and I have not discussed that yet."

"Why do we need to move? Are we not safe here?" She looked eagerly between the two of us.

"I think we are perfectly safe for the moment," Lucas said gently, "but until we figure out exactly what happened at the castle and how they found us, we should keep moving." He was right. No matter how I convinced him where we needed to go next, one thing was for sure: we were not staying put anymore.

OPHELIA

Elias left after breakfast and arrived back at the villa in the late afternoon, with groceries, a journal, several new pairs of pants and shirts, shoes—and thankfully a bra.

Elias threw me an overnight bag. "This is for you to carry whatever you wish to keep. Disregard whatever you do not care for—I will take no offense should you leave something behind."

"It all looks great, thank you." I wasn't lying. His choices didn't look half bad. They weren't glamorous, but it wasn't the time to impress.

"How was your day?" Elias sounded a little tired. I wondered how all this was affecting him. I couldn't get a read on anything.

"The villa is remarkable. The view on the veranda is breathtaking. I wish I could see more of Serpa." I knew that was impossible this time around, but maybe someday when we weren't on the run, being hunted like animals in the middle of a war. That seemed a long way off.

"Someday, definitely someday." He looked longingly at me. "Are you hungry? I am going to prepare a traditional Portuguese dish, arroz de pato."

"Yes, what is that?"

"It's a dish concocted with rice and duck essentially." He stepped closer and gave me a gentle hug, my body buzzed and hummed but at a very minimal level. "You should go have some wine on the terrace and let me fuss about dinner." He squeezed me one more time, and when he pulled away I saw that Lucas had entered the room with wine in hand. He didn't rush to separate our assembly, as he usually did. I was relieved to see the clash between them was, at least temporarily, at a stalemate.

"Join me?" Lucas walked outside with me and we sat facing the west. "How are you doing Olly?"

"Surprisingly okay. I'm sad and it's a whirlwind. I'm not sure the gravity of it has really sunk in. I know you expected me to be a wreck, but I promised myself something in that tunnel and I intend to keep that promise. Aremis told me I needed to stop trying to control everything. He felt I was holding on too tightly to what I thought my future was going to be. Since we left San Francisco, so much has been out of my hands and I've fought it tooth and nail. But by not succumbing to what I thought things should be, but what they *are*, everything changed. I could never control anything in my world before this. Why should I fight to do so now? Besides, this fate is far more real than anything I ever could have dreamt up."

Lucas stared at me for a long time. "I'm glad you're feeling so grounded. And of course, I know that grief comes in waves. You know you can cry or lean on me, whatever you need. It doesn't make you weak."

He didn't understand what I was saying. I thought about explaining it to him further, but it struck me that perhaps Lucas was afraid of this shift. He had always been my rock, my guardian. If I didn't need that anymore, what was he to me? He was scared. I didn't need to exacerbate that.

So I just acknowledged his gesture. "I know. Thank you. And how about you and Elias? I don't want to rock the boat, but you two seem to be getting along well." I smiled.

"Yeah, I guess he's been less obnoxious lately," he said with a grin. He then stood up and poured himself more wine. "We came to an agreement, and honestly right now in the midst of fighting everyone else, I don't have time to fight him."

"That makes sense." I adjusted myself in my seat, and when I looked up Lucas was inches from my face.

"Don't forget—I love you Olly." He breathed.

"I know… I love you too." He put his finger on my mouth.

"The thought of losing you the other night has put some things into perspective. You escaped on your own, you're brilliant and courageous, and a woman who can make her own choices. I know all of this is crazy and mind-blowing, and then you have us… and Elias. I don't want to pressure you anymore. I don't want to add to your stress. I know that you will follow your heart." He kissed my nose. A part of me knew that he would never stop fighting for my affections. I also came to realize that with his shield around me I would never be able to know how I truly felt about Elias—and Lucas knew that too. But for now, a truce worked.

"Thank you for trusting me," I said.

Elias stepped out onto the deck with a tray of delicious-smelling food. Lucas disappeared and reappeared with a full spread of plates and utensils. The patio table was set and we had a somewhat-normal evening drinking wine, eating and sharing our favorite stories about our castle mates. It felt good, like a memorial of sorts.

LUCAS

I stood rooted at the sink, thinking about the evening and Olly.

I still wanted to loathe Viraclay, but I couldn't find the energy to do it. I thought back to two days earlier, while the castle was being attacked.

"WHY ARE we going to the river?" I sprinted beside Elias as we prepared to propel down the cliff face and onto the valley floor. "How do you know Ophelia will be there?"

"Because I prepared precautionary measures to ensure her escape from the castle." Elias was short of breath. I had to admit, he had stamina for an Unconsu.

"What kind of measures?" My foot was starting to throb and my arm was still sizzling and oozing from Royce's acid. I was not at my personal best.

"Aremis and Winston constructed several secret channels in the castle for her to securely flee. I do not even know the whereabouts of them. Winston fabricated the one that you and I just used to escape the castle. Her escape routes exclusively lead to the river bank." Well he was efficient. He most likely saved her life.

I sped up as the scent of the river hit my nose. I tried to find her in my security net, but she was nowhere within my range. I hadn't been able to locate her with my shield for so long, it felt like I was missing a piece of myself.

I had Elias and myself very well guarded, and hoped it was enough to keep anyone from following us, from leading them to her. We arrived at the river and looked around. No sign of her.

"Do you know where she'll end up?" I asked, wincing. I wasn't healing as fast as I normally would, there was something more in the acid, some further venom.

"I do not know the exact location, however, it is the vicinity. It will be an exhausting trek for her, assuming she is running." He came over to examine me. "You do not look good."

"Thanks, I'll be fine." I sneered. I *didn't* feel good. Elias looked almost as good as new, come to think of it. That wasn't at all normal after the way he'd been tossed around. He should at least be moving slow. *What the hell was going on here?*

"May I?" he asked. "It will upset Ophelia to see you hurt." He was right about that.

He placed his hands on my arm. It stung immediately, then itched terribly. But within seconds the wound was completely healed. He'd been holding out on me. This explained Ying and Ophelia's miraculous recoveries. *That fucker has his mother's gift of healing.* He had already healed himself.

He knelt down beside my foot. "Do you want to break it, or should I?"

There was no way I was letting him get the pleasure of breaking my bones, even if was to ultimately help me. "I'll do the breaking." I grabbed my foot and crushed every bone. It hurt like hell. "Fix it fast."

He laid his hands on my foot and I felt all the tiny bones shifting and realigning back into place. Then it was back to normal, as if Akiva had never pulverized it.

"Thanks." I watched Viraclay as he got to his feet and paced by the riverbank. That was the third time tonight that he'd helped me, maybe even saved my life. I know he hated me, and he was convinced I was the one who'd ambushed his parents. I bet he also suspected I was the traitor. Could this all be to keep her happy? Because in that case he was a better man than me. I knew that. I could return the favor by not being such an asshole. I'd consider it.

"She is over here!" He ran down the bank. I didn't hear or see anything.

He moved some branches and revealed a large hole.

"We should go in after her?" I leaned down and still couldn't see her, but I was able to sense her down there, crawling toward the opening. She was still a ways off. "It's her, I'm going in."

"She is almost out, let her do it herself." I looked at him, bewildered, but gave him the benefit of the doubt. Maybe he knew something I didn't.

She crawled out a moment later covered in mud, and I quickly enveloped her with my arms.

HE KNEW OF HER SHIFT, her desire to take care of herself. Their bond was so much greater when I wasn't masking it. Someday she would ask me to lift my gift, and I would have to concede. I took a deep breath. But that wasn't today and I wasn't going to let go of my place in her heart until she forced me to.

"I'm going to go for a run. Make sure there is nothing unusual around the perimeter." I said to Elias, Ophelia was still on the deck. Then I was out the door, alone and surrounded by the warm night air. It felt good.

OPHELIA

"Where are we?" Lucas looked my way and motioned for me to be quiet. I could hardly see a thing. "Where's Elias?"

"Ophelia be quiet or they will hear us," he snapped. *Who was they?* We were in a muddy tunnel. This all felt far too familiar, like déjà vu.

Then the surface got slicker and I slipped, then slid down a long shaft, but I couldn't scream. I landed alone in a huge cave. "Lucas?" I whispered, but he said nothing. There was a small flame on the other end –the largest part of the cave. "Aremis?"

Still no one answered me. I walked toward the flame and it skipped away. I started to run toward the tiny light, but as soon as I would get close enough to really see anything around me it would jump away. It finally stopped at a large rock. I knew instinctively to push it aside.

It opened up to a larger cavern with high ceilings and huge stalactites hanging from every surface. The small flame flew up. I watched after it, and when it reached the top it grew into a massive fireball.

With its light, I could see that I was no longer in a cave, but a large room, and the stalactites were no longer large erected pillars, but people—conduits I knew.

Aremis was in the middle, and Lucas and Elias were at his flanks. Behind them stood Winston, Ying, Di, Nara and Valerian. Even the other conduits from the castle that I'd briefly met were there. Rand was the furthest away, almost out of sight. I tried to speak, but couldn't get words to leave my mouth.

The fireball grew larger above them. I wanted to yell that we needed to leave, but I couldn't. Then I felt an icy hand touch my shoulder. A familiar soft, sultry voice whispered in my ear. "Kill them, kill them all." I tried to move, to see the person who commanded the voice, but I was frozen.

The fireball began to dive toward my friends, and my eyes watched in terror as it descended onto everyone I loved.

The voice began to laugh and the massive bomb hit the floor, encompassing everyone in it. Their faces expressed their agony, but their bodies didn't budge. I felt tears streaming down my cheeks, but it was as though they were on the inside of my skin.

The laugh grew louder, and as my friends' bodies slowly turned to heaps of ash I felt a rage like I'd never experienced before. I still couldn't move, but two animated figures were moving toward me from the belly of the fire.

Esther stood in front of me, and to her left was a familiar face that I'd never put a name to. It was the young man from outside the bookstore. The one that chased me, that made me feel as though he'd violated my soul with one look.

They walked closer still.

"Good work my pet." Esther purred in my ear.

"I knew I saw exactly who you were the day we met. A killer," the young man hissed in my other ear.

Then I was erect in my bed, sweat and tears mixed in a wet mess on my face. Apparently if I thought I was doing fine consciously, my unconscious mind felt a little different. Elias burst through the door. I would have expected Lucas, but either way I was relieved. He came to the side of my bed.

"Are you okay?" He wiped my face with his T-shirt, which he'd managed to get off without me noticing, until I was all too aware of how close I was to his half-naked body. My face got warm.

"I'm fine. It was just a nightmare." Thank goodness. My heart was still pounding. I reached for his hand. I wanted an anchor and he was the closest one. A familiar wave washed over me and I was instantly more relaxed. Our connection buzzed in my palm.

He sat down next to me on the bed. "Have you always been so tormented by nightmares?"

"Yes... and no. I always had nightmares, but they were different than they are now. These nightmares are more vivid, and contain monsters I never could've imagined before I knew about this world."

"I am sorry that you are suffering from them now." He squeezed my hand. "I do not know if this is the right time, but I have something for you. Give me a moment to get it."

He slipped out of the room, but was back immediately. He handed me an object wrapped in a beautiful scarf. I unwrapped it to find the picture of my grandmother as a child that he'd given me while we were staying in the castle. I stared at the framed photograph, speechless. The photo meant the world to me when he gave it to me the first time, but to think that he'd saved this, of all things, while his childhood home went up in flames. It was overwhelming.

Without thinking I kissed him on the lips. They felt smooth and soft, like velvet, and tasted like the first perfect sip of hot chocolate on a winter's day, exactly the way I remembered them in the fencing hall. I could smell his rich breath, sprinkled with accents of vanilla and rose. My head went woozy and heat swirled down into my abdomen. Then he pulled away.

"Is it safe to say you appreciate the gesture," he said, embarrassed. "You are welcome. I hope you sleep better for the second half of the night." Then he left.

Kissing Elias was like nothing else in the world, just as before it was intoxicating and fulfilling, like we were one being. It wasn't as deep a connection as I knew it could be without the shield but it was the comfort I needed in that moment.

I looked at the image of Lilith and stroked her face. I closed my eyes, and a thought occurred to me that I'd almost lost in the heat of the moment.

The young man from Barnes & Noble: I knew who he was. I shoved my blankets off and hurried out the door, still holding the picture. Both men were in the living room, neither looking very pleased. They stepped back as I entered.

I held up the photo. "Do you have a photo of Yanni?"

They both looked at me like I was crazy.

"A photo, an image, a drawing, anything?" I blurted out.

"A picture, no," Lucas said. "But I could sketch him for you. Dare I ask why?" He grabbed a piece of paper from the home printer, and a pen, while he looked at me wearily.

"I'm not sure yet. I've never actually seen him, even though he's come after me twice. He was too far away in San Francisco, and he was behind me when Rand fended him off in the castle." I was talking fast. But I couldn't talk faster than the speed that Lucas' hand traced over the sheet of paper, slowly divulging the face of our stalker. I gasped when the image reaffirmed my thoughts.

"That's the man who chased me in Chicago! I thought he was just a homeless guy. He said he knew who I was, and asked if *I* knew who I was. It really had me rattled then. And now..." I shook my head in disbelief. I should be dead.

"Wait Ophelia." Lucas grabbed my shoulders. "You're telling me that you've met Yanni—this man—before?" He pointed at the portrait. I nodded.

"Yes. The day I ran into Elias in the alley." Both men stared at me, their mouths agape.

ELIAS

I had not slept much the night before. I was trying to figure out our next move, how I would complete my quest for answers about Alistair and still keep it from Lucas. Then Ophelia kissed me and presented me with a flurry of emotions and thoughts. The last thing I wanted to do was push her away, but I could think of no other way to keep our location secret at the moment. Would she understand and forgive me later?

Finally, Ophelia's revelation about Yanni. That meant he had been watching her for a while... or had we lost him in Chicago? *Did he really know what she was capable of, or that she was my Atoa?* If he did, why did he not kill her right there?

I walked out to the terrace where Lucas and Ophelia sat eating lunch. He had hardly let her out of his sight since she had kissed me, but he was not acting as volatile as he had been before.

I grabbed the sandwich Ophelia had made for me and retired to my room to complete the accommodations I had started the night before. We would begin in South America. I had already arranged the first flight—to Central America to evade any tails—then we would swap jets and continue our journey. I would simply convey to Lucas he was on a need-to-know basis, and that until we had reason to think my methods of evasion were inadequate, he would follow my direction.

He would appreciate the time with Ophelia while I was busy with my investigation. This way she would also preoccupy him enough to keep him out of my hair. If I suspected he was getting too curious about my plans, I would desist until it was safe once more. Admittedly I still needed him to keep a watchful eye on her while I worked on the summit.

I sat down for dinner with them that evening. Ophelia was more radiant then I had ever seen her. Every day she appeared to come more into her own. It was captivating.

"So when do we leave?" She asked casually.

"Tomorrow afternoon. A car will arrive at three to escort us to a nearby city with a small private hanger. From there we will take a jet to Panama City." Lucas looked at me with intrigue, but I did not elaborate.

We finished our meal, and Ophelia insisted that it was her turn to do dishes.

"I am going to attend to perimeter detail," I said. "I will be back to enjoy a glass of wine on the veranda shortly."

Ophelia smiled and waved me on with a hand full of suds. "I'll have it ready for you," she said, then continued her conversation with Lucas. They were arguing over where the best place in San Francisco was for Ethiopian food.

I heard their voices trail away as I started at a run out the door.

It felt good to stretch my legs after sitting and staring at a computer all day long. I let myself fall into a meditative state as I jogged. Perhaps that is why it took me a moment to realize I was not alone in the dark. I paused when I heard the footsteps for a second time.

My company was twenty feet to my left, a close enough distance that I thought I could catch them. I turned and hit my stride full throttle. I saw a shadow move and I lurched for it, but bounced off the side of a tree. I hesitated just long enough to see a note tacked to the bark. I pulled it off and read the message.

I folded the sheet of paper and put it in my pocket, then ran as fast as I could back to the house. I found them outside with three glasses of wine and Ophelia reading a book. I was out of breath.

Ophelia looked alarmed when she saw me, as did Lucas.

OPHELIA

"She has contacted us," Elias heaved, possibly one of the only times I'd seen him winded.

I looked at Lucas, questioning. "I give up, who?" I said, continuing to peruse my book, waiting for him to fill me in.

"Aurora." He had Lucas' attention so I put my book down.

"Who is Aurora and what did she say?" I leaned forward in my chair.

"The Oracle contacted you?" Lucas sounded astonished. *The Oracle. Now he had my attention too.* "I haven't heard of any sightings of her since she disappeared. How do you know it's her, Elias?"

"Because I received a note similar to this one when I was thirteen and I spoke with her for the first time." Elias was looking at me. Lucas was looking floored.

Then I remembered the conversation that we three had in the antiquities room. It felt like a lifetime ago. "Aurora was the talented conduit that Apollo kept captive for several hundred years because of her gifts?"

Elias nodded then read the note aloud.

It is pertinent that I meet Ophelia Banner tomorrow morning. My car will pick you up at 11 am.

"How can you be sure that this is from her, couldn't it be a trap?" I asked. "How did she know we were here?" I was skeptical. And it was unsettling seeing my name in unknown penmanship.

"It is her. She has the gift of foresight, which is how she knew where we were." Elias started toward the patio door. "You should get a good night's sleep, Ophelia. Lucas, can you maintain the perimeter for the rest of the night? We all need to pack and be prepared to leave, in the event there is a sudden change of plans in the morning."

Then he was gone and I was looking just as baffled as Lucas.

"This is a big deal isn't it?" I asked Lucas.

"If Elias is correct, yeah this is a huge deal."

"In a bad way?" I was worried, this was another curveball. I thought I'd been handling everything so well, but to see both of them so alarmed was nerve-racking.

"I don't know, Ophelia, really I don't." Lucas stood, downed his own wine as well as Elias' neglected glass, then he too headed for the door. He turned the knob to leave, and then doubled back and kissed my cheek. "It'll be okay, Olly, I promise."

WE HEARD a gentle rap at the door.

"Are you nervous?" Lucas grabbed my bag from my shoulder.

"I feel like I should be, because of the way you two are behaving." I reached for my bag and pulled it back. I wasn't being stubborn—I had my secret package from Rand inside, and I was being slightly paranoid. I wanted to keep it with me. "I can carry my bag, thank you though."

"Are you mad at me?" Lucas looked concerned. Exceptionally concerned. It struck me that he was really worried about what we were going to find out at this meeting.

"No, of course not. I just felt the need to carry my own bag. Are *you* okay?" I knew he wouldn't tell me if he wasn't okay, one because he was so private, and two because he was probably afraid of scaring me.

"Yeah, I'm just really baffled. There aren't many things I haven't experienced in the centuries I've lived on this planet, but this will be a first for me. You get used to just knowing what to expect." Wow! That was real vulnerability on Lucas' part—not in his nature.

I put my hand on his shoulder. It felt odd to be comforting him for a change. "Welcome to my world." I smiled. "Trust me, we'll be alright."

He laughed, finding it ridiculous to experience such a weird role reversal. "You're right, of course you are." He gently nudged my shoulder. "Now get in the car before they leave without us."

The car ride was very quiet, but Lucas looked more at ease. Elias didn't look afraid, but rather stoic. He was preparing for something, but it wasn't anxiety that plagued him.

"You will have to unshield us during the reading, Lucas." The look of alarm was back on Lucas' face.

"What do you mean? That doesn't seem like a good idea at all. Absolutely not."

"You have no choice. Aurora will disarm you if she must. But you need not worry—she has her own protection she administers, and no offense intended, but it is exceedingly affective. How do you reason she has stayed hidden for so long?" Elias had a point. Thousands of years of hide-and-go-seek, and she was still evading her captors.

"I still don't like it. I won't subject myself to that."

"That is entirely up to you of course." Elias turned to me. "How do you feel about it, Ophelia?"

"Well the woman came out of hiding to meet me. It would be rude to not acquiesce to her request." I didn't really understand what I was signing up for. If it was as simple as a palm reading, then these two wouldn't be so worked up. But I wasn't going to cut and run, not after what we'd gone through. I was taking it all on from here on out.

Elias smiled and Lucas grimaced—I'd never seen him so uneasy. We drove for a few more minutes, then came to a huge, almost-vacant shopping mall. I expected we would be meeting in a discreet location, far from the general populace. The car stopped.

I hadn't caught a look at our driver on the way over, since they sat behind a deeply tinted pane of glass. They now opened the car door.

It was hard to distinguish if it was a boy or girl. Long black hair framed the individual's face. The hue of their skin was a soft green, and their hands were noticeably too large for their limbs. The person was short—shorter than me—and very slender. I caught a quick glimpse of their face. It was long, with high cheekbones and an oversized mouth that held long fangs instead of teeth. I turned away when the mouth turned up into a smile. Whatever it was, it was terrifying.

When I turned around again the car was gone, and Lucas was brooding behind us. I stepped back and took his hand. "We are going to be fine."

He just nodded. His expression confirmed he was walking the plank.

Since the building was mostly empty, it was easy to deduct which suite we were supposed to enter. Elias did so first. I quickly noted the plainness of my surroundings. There was no art, not a thing on the walls, only plain white paint. Nothing could identify this room from any other in a thousand other office buildings anywhere in the world. The chairs were like every other office chair: uncomfortable, black and easily transportable.

"Not much in the way of décor, huh?" I was trying to lighten the mood.

"Aurora never stays in any one place for very long," Elias answered. *Tough crowd today,* I mused.

Elias continued. "Her entire existence is devoured by fear, so she makes minimal connections, especially with her own kind. It is our kind that she fears the most. I do not think Aurora realizes that by fearing captivity she had imprisoned herself."

"Can't she hear us?" I was more than a little taken aback by Elias' brazenness, especially about a woman he clearly respected.

"It always helps to be candid in the presence of a psychic." He had a point. "I believe my mother was her closest confidant, and when she was murdered the last of Aurora's humanity died with her."

Lucas still had not said a word. He looked as if he was sitting on a bed of needles. I went and sat beside him.

"So you've seen the Oracle before? Since she was close to your mother?" I was holding Lucas' hand, but my eyes were on Elias.

"I have seen her three times." Lucas' eyes were now also on Elias.

"Three times" Lucas confirmed, astonished.

"Yes."

"So what happens next? Is she going to appear in the room?" I said it half joking, but honestly he could have said yes and I would have believed him. Especially after the look of her driver.

No sooner did the words leave my mouth than a small bell of a voice echoed down the hall. "Ophelia please come in."

Lucas stood with me, both of us peering down the corridor. There was a single open door. I turned to him. "Remove your shield. I'm going to be fine."

He held me close and whispered. "I love you, remember that. No matter what." It sounded like a goodbye.

I pulled away, and as I did, so did his barricade. I saw fear emitting off him like steam after a hot shower. All I could do was reassure him.

"I love you too. I'll be fine." But his fear didn't subside, and when I turned to Elias I heard Lucas leave the suite.

"Be honest." He smiled at me without an ounce of apprehension or worry. "Be yourself." Elias oozed with admiration, love and tenderness for me. I felt a pull to just stay here with him. I had to compel my feet to move down the hall. I made it into the room and shut the door.

ELIAS

I stood there for what felt like an eternity, staring at the door. Struggling to hear anything and everything I could, striving to decipher and dissect the meaning of any small noise.

I wondered if Lucas could hear what was being said. His senses were more advanced than my own. I momentarily took my attention away from the door to survey the room. He still had not returned. He was acting especially peculiar about these happenings.

I mused over this sudden reappearance of Aurora. I had not heard from her in several years. I thought about our last meeting. Everything I said about her to Ophelia was true—something had hardened in her, something deep in her being. She appeared to have lost the thing that permitted people to love and connect.

The door opened at the end of the hall, and immediately Lucas was beside me, intently waiting for Ophelia to exit. Instead the gentle voice called for me. I could see the disappointment in his shoulders as they slumped forward.

I took purposeful steps down the corridor, entered the room, and shut the door. Ophelia was sitting across from Aurora, at the table in the far corner. Neither of the women looked up at me.

They could be sisters. Aurora had long, wavy copper-red hair, only slightly darker then Ophelia's. Their lips were both full, and always a vibrant shade of pink. Their fair skin was illuminated with scattered freckles. From my angle, even their body types looked similar: slightly framed, with curves in the appropriate places. I figured Aurora must have been about Ophelia's age when she consummated, no older than thirty years of age. In silent unison the two women rose from their chairs and faced me. Then Aurora turned to Ophelia.

"Ophelia, I cannot begin to articulate what a pleasure it is to finally meet you. I will always be here for guidance should you need it." The Oracle then made a small bowing gesture. Ophelia grabbed her by both shoulders and drew her in for a hug. I smiled. I could see how awkward the moment was for Aurora.

"Thank you Aurora." Ophelia was beaming as she walked across the room.

I watched as Ophelia closed the door. I turned to face Aurora.

"Elias." She gestured for me to sit. I chose to continue standing.

I stared at her. She knew what my questions would be. Even if she could not see them coming with her exhaustive visions, she knew what they would be because I always asked the same ones.

"Has the prophecy changed?"

"My child, you exasperate yourself by trying to change her destiny, and in turn your own. It has been this way since you were a youth. You are a miracle, therefore you believe that they still exist, constantly searching for hope. Your mother was this way. Indeed, she changed her destiny and the fate of our kind. We should be so lucky that you would do the same."

"You are taunting me with evasion."

"Elias, her destiny is the same. Your destiny is the same. The fate of our kind continues to parallel with your future, and in turn we all are rushing to our own demise. I only came here today to confirm it."

It has always been the same, ever since my mother took me to my first reading. I was not giving up, I was determined to save her. Since the strands of fate had interlaced her death with the annihilation of our kind, it was impossible to unravel the two outcomes. If I saved her, I saved us all.

"Can you see the traitor?"

"They escape my vision even now. I cannot see who they are, where they are, or how they may strike. I am sorry my dear Elias, I have no better rejoinders for you." Aurora looked down at her clasped hands, and then fiercely into my eyes. "You have done your best. You could do nothing to save your parents, as you can do nothing to save Ophelia. This battle is a futile one. I say this out of love."

"I *will* save her," I said, heading toward the door. I did not know how I was going to do it, but in my heart I saw no other option except her survival. I glanced over my shoulder. "I will see you at the summit."

Aurora said nothing, there was nothing else to say. I would proceed as planned, keep Ophelia safe, find the defector and prepare for the summit.

I walked down the hall, toward my companions.

On the right was a man that I despised. He desired nothing less than to take the woman I love. I could not trust him. I was certain he was hiding deviant secrets.

On the left was the woman I loved, caught in the crosshairs of inevitable defeat, resulting in the loss of her brilliant life and the extermination of our kind.

I took a deep breath. They both looked to me for direction.

"We will be in Chile by tomorrow," I said without hesitation. "Grab your bags. The car is waiting."

They followed me as I walked out the door. I glanced over my shoulder to see Aurora standing at the end of the hall. She was wrong and I would die proving it.

GLOSSARY

Conduit- A semi-immortal being that expresses extraordinary powers when consummated with their other half or pair. Upon consummation conduits no longer age. Conduits are always coupled as a receiver and an imposer.

Receiver- A conduit that receives or absorbs another object or being's energy.

Imposer- A conduit that can impose their will or energy onto another being or object.

Unconsu- A conduit that is still mortal and has not been consummated.

Consu- A consummated conduit.

Swali- A human that has some conduit heritage or a demi-god.

Soahcoit- A consummated conduit pair.

Atoa- A conduits other half or partner.

Pai Ona- The 'good' conduits, those fighting to unite and end the war.

Poginuli- A broken conduit, an individual conduit whose partner has been slain.

Nebas- Evil or 'bad' conduits who most likely align with Esther and Yanni either in secret or openly.

Covening- The act of conduits gathering to perform the ancient magic.

Paksyon- A small congregation of conduits, who are usually participating in covening.

Haven- A place of ancient magic, often a safe house.

The Pierses- Sister books that contain ancient magic spells.

The Rittles- Weapons forged with magical poisons that inflict severe injury.

Chitchakor, Malarin, Dalininkas- The master painter and creator of all life in the world

The River Tins- The magical river where your colors can be cleaned according to the creation myth of the conduits.

Sulu- A beacon of energy, often in the form of a group of conduits. In rare occasions an individual conduit that creates an energy vortex.

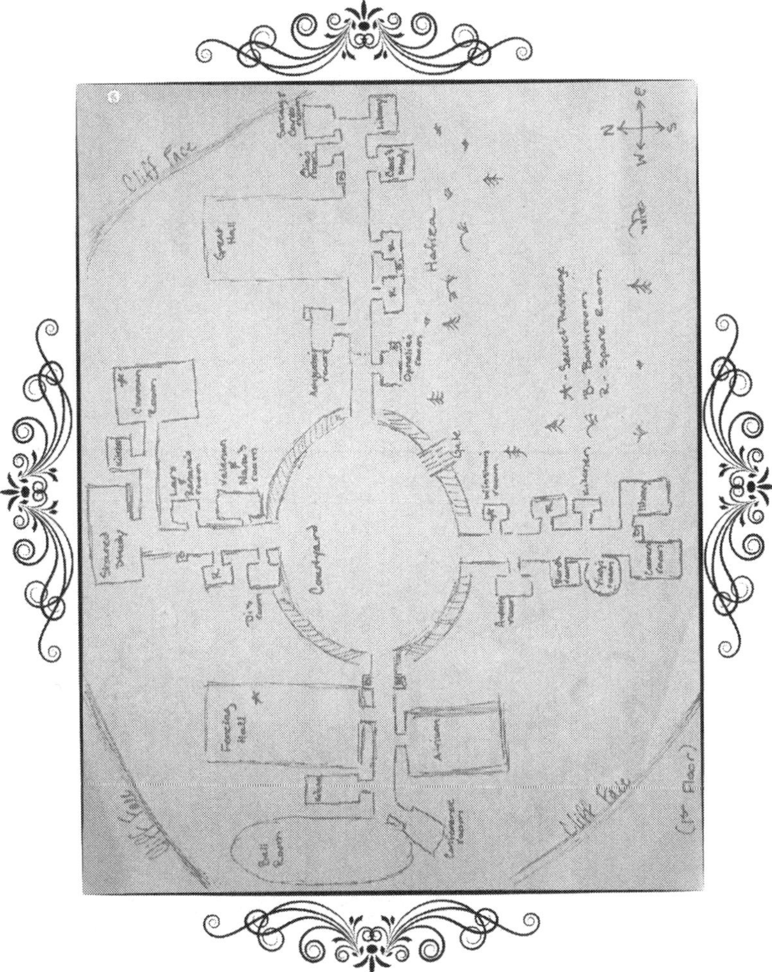
Cliff Face
Cliff Face
Cliff Face
Ball Room
Fencing Hall
Conference Room
Shared Study
Common Room
Courtyard
Great Hall
Gate
Ophelia's Room
Kitchen
★ - Secret Passage
B - Bathroom
R - Spare Room
N
W
E
S
(1st Floor)

Cliff Face
Billiards
Courtyard
Fencing Hall
Atrium
Ball Room
Art Gallery
Cliff Face
Cliff Face
(2nd Floor)

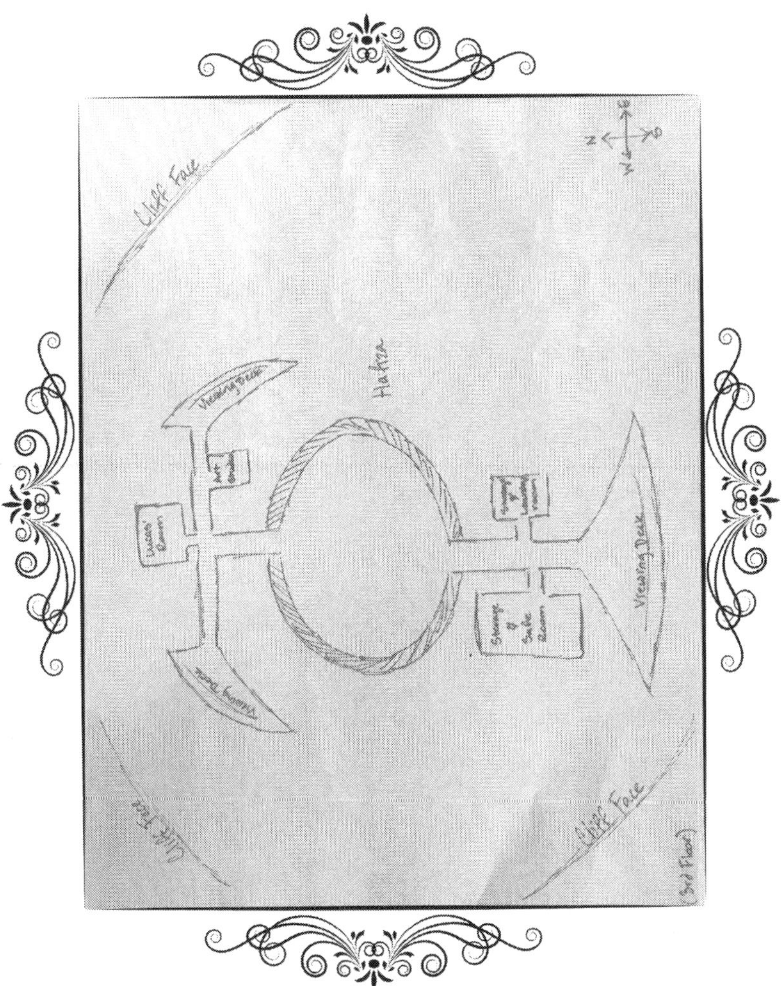
Cliff Face
Viewing Deck
Viewing Deck
Cliff Face
3rd Floor

A NOTE TO READERS

I want to say thank you so much for taking the time to read my first novel *FOUND*. This has been a dream of mine for many years. I am so excited to take you on this journey through The Conduit Chronicles.

If you would like to get the latest publishing news for the next book in the series *FORSAKEN* please visit my website and make sure you click FOLLOW.

Turn the page for an excerpt from the second installment.

https://ashleyhohenstein.com

FORSAKEN

SNEAK PEAK

"Trolls?" I scoffed, "As in the big angry barbarians that live under bridges and demand payment?"

"Yes. Fucking trolls." Lucas replied without a hint of sarcasm, maybe a touch of dread in his voice. "Trolls are portals and just like in fairytales they demand a price for safe passage."

I stood there my mouth agape. I looked to Elias, expecting to see a nod of assurance. But his face was ghostly white and he seemed just as skeptical.

"Lucas I have never heard of these trolls you speak of, not from my parents nor from any other conduit I consort with." Elias shook his head in disbelief.

"Of course you wouldn't have, most conduits stopped using their services after the last open battle three hundred years ago. Some Pai Ona felt that the trolls were favoring the Nebas and rumors spread." Lucas waived his hand in the air nonchalantly. "You know how that goes and business has declined for the trolls."

Elias stepped in front of Lucas. "If that is indeed the case then why on earth would we utilize their services?" Elias' voice was slightly elevated.

Lucas moved around him. "Because I know a *guy* and we are in a bind." I was struggling to keep up with their pace, the two of them were walking faster than usual.

"What do you mean you know a guy?" Elias stopped and crossed his arms, I was grateful for the opportunity to catch up. "Enlighten me before we proceed."

Lucas paused and waited a moment before he turned around, probably trying to regain his composure. He didn't like being questioned— especially not by Elias.

"Six hundred years ago when troll channels were still widely in use, Yessica and I stumbled upon a troll being mugged by a Powrie. Yessica hurtled herself between the two beasts before I had a chance to figure out a plan or better yet convince her to stay out of it." He turned to me to explain the next part. "Yessica was a receiver of light —she is called a lantern. She could absorb it and essential blind you with massive amounts, light radiated off her skin." He seemed to say the last bit to himself. "She was my sun." He quickly shook off the reverie and continued. "Trolls don't care for light and Powries even less so, so the Powrie ran off and the injured troll laid their bleeding to death. Yessica demanded we escort the troll to Sorcey and Cane's home in Greenland to be healed by your mother." He gestured at Elias.

"What is a Powrie?" I asked.

Elias answered. "They are headhunters, assassins. Dispatched by all forms of evil to murder for hire. Lucas and Yessica interrupted a hit."

"Sorcey worked her magic and the troll was good as new. She has been eager to help me whenever she can since." Lucas started walking again. "Her name is Fetzle and she would never cross me."

"When was the last time you spoke to Fetzle? What kind of magic does she use? How do you know it will not set off any alarms with Yanni?" Elias assaulted Lucas with questions.

"Look Viraclay, the way I see it, we don't have much of a choice here. We are currently being hunted by Vivienne and Nandi, the jet is gone and Olly can't travel as fast as we can on foot." He gave Elias a once over like he was sizing him up, not sure he could run fast enough either. "I last saw Fetzle two years ago when I travelled up to San Francisco. She clearly didn't trigger anything then because it was an entire year and a half before we were detected." Lucas spun around sharply. "And I don't know what kind of magic she uses, it's troll magic and these portals crisscross all over the world and have since the beginning of time. So, I doubt the magic will set off any alarms. Satisfied?" He threw up his arms and turned on his heels and continued walking.

Elias didn't say anything for a while and I didn't know what to say so I kept my mouth shut.

"Very well, how do we take passage?" Elias sounded slightly defeated.

"We are almost there." Lucas pulled a coin out of his pocket and began flipping it in the air. "This medallion is like a transit pass. I can call on Fetzle whenever I like, with the right conditions."

"What might those be?" I asked.

"Exposed tree roots." He pointed at the horizon of trees just ahead. "We should find something in there, don't you think?" I nodded and quickened my pace to try and meet Lucas'. Elias had positioned himself just behind me. I was sure it wasn't because he couldn't keep up with Lucas but more likely to make sure no one came up from behind me. The edge of the forest fast approached and my heart beat quickened. It was clear Lucas thought we were in good hands but a troll sounded scary. *What on earth was portal travel going to be like?*

Not to mention I could feel the uncertainty radiating from Elias like heat off a wood stove in December.

We got to the wall of trees and Lucas navigated about ten feet into the forest. He knelt down and brushed away some leaves exposing several large roots. He placed the coin on the flattest root surface he could find and started reciting something in Asagi. The roots began to tremble and bulge. The tree shook violently and Elias grabbed my arm pulling me back from the convulsing arbor. Lucas continued to recite the three words while concentrating with his eyes closed.

The tree was shaking so violently now that the ground was vibrating. Then it stopped and a loud high pitched voice trilled from inside the belly of the trunk. Lucas jumped back and positioned himself in front one me so that I was flanked by both men. I was alarmed. *Was something wrong?*

Lucas replied to the voice in words I didn't understand except for the word Fetzle. The tree shook again with shrill laughter and a huge figure manifested in the shadow of the tree. The figure stepped into the light and continued to grow.

The thing was enormous both in girth and in height. The individual legs were the size of the tree trunk it had just materialized from. The skin was clear white, almost translucent but it looked like she had been rolling around in the mud because there was dirt all over her body. I wouldn't have known it was a female if Lucas had not told us in advance. She had no hair and no genitals, her torso was slim and muscular. My eyes followed her form all the way up to her face. Her eyes were huge. More than half her face was consumed by her eyeballs. I caught her stare and saw they were teal blue, piercing and inquiring. Her giant right arm that dragged on the ground slowly drew up and pointed a titanic finger at me. I noted she only had one finger and what looked like a thumb.

Then her petite voice chirped something and Lucas responded with a laugh.

I nudged him, "What did she say?" He laughed louder.

Fetzle leaned down and got one of her eyes real close to my face, clearly examining me. "Saydwhothisshe? Thissmelldingfunny?" It all came out as one weird word. Then she took a deep inhale through her mouth. She was close enough for me to notice she didn't have a nose or nostrils. *Was she smelling me through her mouth?* I heard Elias chuckle behind me.

"Did she just say I smell funny?" I nudged Lucas again.

Fetzle's face got closer to mine, took another whiff, then her giant finger pushed me aside and she peered into Elias' face.

"Whatsyou?" Again she inhaled, now clearly getting a solid whiff of Elias without my stench in the way.

"Hello Fetzle, my name is Elias Kraus. I believe you met my parents Cane and Sorcey." Before he could get the last syllable out she had him on her shoulder twirling in circles and jumping up and down yelling something neither in English or Asagi. Elias looked like he might get sick.

Lucas interceded. "Fetzle." She paused. "You might want to be gentle with him, he is Unconsu." She immediately stopped parading about— but didn't put Elias down.

"ApologeezSorcayCanechildren." She patted Elias' head with her thumb. He looked uncomfortable. A giggle escaped my mouth. Then, all of us erupted with laughter. After a moment the chorus died down. "FetzlemelovingmySorceyCane." She shrugged her shoulders. Elias leaned in and she took another big whiff of his scent. "YousmellingSorcay."

It was clear she was reminiscing her friends. "Thank you Fetzle, would it be too much to ask that I might be put back down onto the forest floor. I am getting rather ill up here with all of the commotion." Even in this dark wooded area, I could tell that Elias looked a little green. A flash of disappointment swept across the trolls face and then she conceded to put Elias down.

"Again thank you." Elias nodded as his feet stabilized on solid ground. Fetzle smiled and her lips rolled up exposing four rows of needle pointed teeth, that had been previously hidden in her mouth. Chills ran down my spine. I didn't know what she used those teeth for but I was sure it wasn't for a vegetarian diet. No one needed choppers like that for a fresh salad.

"Fetzle, we need your help." Lucas wasted no more time getting to the point of this little reunion. "We need to get far from here and quickly. What are the portals like today? Can we travel safely?"

Fetzle looked past him and set her gaze on me again. "Whosethisshe?" She repeated.

"Sorry, my name is Ophelia Banner. I am friends with Elias and Lucas." Fetzle looked at the two men wearily and then back at me.

"Frendzbethis? Smeldingfunnylikessoursandsweetsnotsso-goodthisbe." She was now addressing Lucas is Asagi. Elias looked alarmed and pulled me closer.

I whispered, “What is she saying? Did I offend her? Do I really smell that bad?” I lifted up my arm and tried to find out for myself.

“No you do not smell funny, you smell amazing. Trolls read auras, your aura is questionable to her.” He said hushed.

“I think that is even more offensive.” I said.

Elias stepped forward and positioned me behind him. He was attempting to shield me in case something went awry. He interjected into the discussion Lucas and Fetzle were having. Whatever Elias said seemed to diffuse the situation. Fetzle took one more enormous breath, closing her eyes as she inhaled.

“AwesnowsIseesitsthismaybesnotsobads.” She leaned in, “Hellos-OpheliasBannersthisisFetzle.”

I smiled my huge nervous smile and tried to remember to breath.

“Notssogoodsdaytotravelmanytravelersmanyslimeybeingstoday.” She said with a sigh. “Yousandthiscouldsstayinmeshuttletodaysthen-travelswhenclean.”

Elias looked at Lucas despairingly. It was clear he wasn’t sure if that was a good idea. But they also couldn’t have a conversation about that in front of Fetzle—afraid they would offend her. They were trying to communicate with their eyes. Truth be told I had no idea if this was a good or bad idea. The only one of us who had even the slightest clue as what to expect would be Lucas. I for one trusted him. Elias apparently didn’t. After a long stare down Lucas had clearly won.

“Fetzle, we would be honored to stay in your shuttle.”

ACKNOWLEDGEMENTS

I would like to thank all of my family and friends who have cheered me on throughout this process. A special thanks to my early readers who had to endure unedited wordy drafts. You ladies know who you are.

A huge thanks to my editors at Verve Editorial.

I also want to show my appreciation for the team that help put my rocking cover together. The original art was designed and created by Walt Barker. Digital editing was completed by Jennifer Pearce. Final work up and design was finalized by Amy Pinkston.

A massive shout out to my Arbonne family! My Arbonne journey catapulted me into becoming a fearless pursuer of my dreams and for that I am eternally grateful!

Lastly, I have a special acknowledgment for my furry friend and companion Franky. He has since passed, but I was so grateful for the hours he spent curled up next to me while I wrote.

ABOUT THE AUTHOR

Ashley Hohenstein lives in Northern California with her husband and daughter.

If you would like to get the latest publishing news for the next book in the series *FORSAKEN* please visit my website and make sure you click FOLLOW.

https://ashleyhohenstein.com

Made in the USA
San Bernardino, CA
31 January 2018